Madison Smartt Bell

DEVIL'S DREAM

Madison Smartt Bell is the author of fourteen previous works of fiction, including *Soldier's Joy* and *Anything Goes*. He was born in Nashville, Tennessee, and grew up collecting bullets on the same fields where many of Forrest's battles were fought. He now lives in Baltimore, where he has taught at Goucher College since 1984.

ALSO BY MADISON SMARTT BELL

The Washington Square Ensemble

Waiting for the End of the World

Straight Cut

Zero db

The Year of Silence

Soldier's Joy

Barking Man

Doctor Sleep

Save Me, Joe Louis

All Souls' Rising

Ten Indians

Narrative Design:
A Writer's Guide to Structure

Master of the Crossroads

Anything Goes

The Stone That the Builder Refused

Lavoisier in the Year One:
The Birth of a New Science in an Age of Revolution

Toussaint Louverture: A Biography

Charm City: A Walk Through Baltimore

DEVIL'S DREAM

DEVIL'S DREAM

Madison Smartt Bell

Vintage Books
A Division of Random House, Inc.
New York

FIRST VINTAGE BOOKS EDITION, NOVEMBER 2010

This book was completed with support from a Harold and Mildred Strauss Living fund awarded by the American Academy of Arts and Letters.

Portions of this book originally appeared in slightly different form in *Blackbird, Boulevard, Five Points, The Idaho Review, JMWW, Story Quarterly,* and *The Texas Review.* A portion also originally appeared in slightly different form in *Gathering: Writers of Williamson County,* edited by Currie Alexander Powers and Kathy Hardy Rhodes (Sepulpa, OK: CPO Publishing, 2009).

The Library of Congress has cataloged the Pantheon edition as follows:
Bell, Madison Smartt.
Devil's dream / Madison Smartt Bell.
p. cm.
1. Southern States—History—Civil War, 1861–1865—Fiction. I. Title.
PS3552.E517D48 2009
813'.54—dc22 2009009534

Vintage ISBN: 978-0-307-27991-0

Book design by Robert C. Olsson

www.vintagebooks.com

Printed in the United States of America
10 9 8 7 6 5 4 3 2 1

In memory of Andrew Lytle,
with thanks to Dan Frank and Sonny Mehta,
for believing it was a good idea,
and thanks to Jack Kershaw,
for telling me a story

Soldiers do not fight any better because of a good cause or a bad one.

—George Garrett, *Double Vision*

The separation between past, present, and future is only an illusion, although a convincing one.

—Albert Einstein, letter to Michele Besso

DEVIL'S DREAM

CHAPTER ONE

July 1861

HE PASSED THE NIGHT in a canebrake a little way south of the Ohio River, still in earshot of the river's sluggish flow. Amid the cane he found a raised flat shelf of limestone, harder than sleeping on the ground would have been, but apt to give him some relief from ticks and chiggers or so he hoped. Before he lay down he splashed a little water on the four directions at the edges of the oblong stone—not too much water, for there was a moon, and he didn't want to leave the cover of the cane to fill his canteen from the water's edge.

When he stretched out, the walls of his empty stomach shrunk together, contracting like wet leather as it dried and cracked. Shadows of the slender cane leaves danced over the moonscape of the stone, and the pocks in the surface griped his back and shoulders, or his hip and elbow if he tried to settle on his side, so that he thought he would not sleep, most likely. He heard the crying of a screech owl and watched a bat wing flick across the curved edge of the moon— his eyes as hard and parched as the moon itself—but then the ancestors were sitting round him in a circle, one plucking slowly on a gut spun and strung across a gourd and another clicking time with two hollow bones against each other. The faces of the Old Ones were hidden from him in shadow, but what came toward him was the face of a white man, hard-favored with his dark eyes bored deep, dark caverns carved away under his high cheekbones and just above the bristly black of the beard that hid his mouth. This white man had the air of a slave-catcher, he thought, and he didn't like the penetration of his look, and yet when the big pale hand spread across his forehead it was a gentle, almost a healing touch.

So he woke up shivering, with no coverlet, only his loose-yoked linsey shirt and nankeen britches. Surprised at his movement, a copperhead poured itself over the edge of the stone and slipped away, rustling the bed of dry cane leaves. The reddish brown braid of it was out of sight before he thought to draw his knife. A bright burst of saliva stung the inside of his mouth. That snake had been big around as his arm . . .

He poured water, pissed off the edge of the rock, took a sip from the canteen, and with the long knife back in the twist of cloth that served him as a belt he stepped down and moved toward the edge of the canebrake, watching closely for the copperhead or his brothers and setting his bare feet down carefully to avoid cane stobs buried in the leaves. He'd had a better kit when he left Louisiana—a pack with a spare shirt and pants and a little money rolled up in it, a hat and socks and a pair of stout shoes. All gone somehow along the way. He'd stowed away on a steamboat headed up the Mississippi River, then made the trip across to Louisville, hanging between two boxcars in the dark. In Louisville things had gone against him and he had come away in a great hurry, following the bends of the river but none too closely—maybe as far as Brandenburg, he thought.

At the edge of the woods he found a cluster of new white mushrooms and ate them raw. There were shoots of poke sallet too, which ought to be boiled to drain their poison. They might have been small and new enough to be safe, but he wouldn't risk it. Yesterday he had happened into blackberry brambles and found a few, still reddish, underripe and sour on his tongue and afterward in his stomach. He was still considering the poke weed when a plump rustle in the leaves behind him made him turn, and there was a young blue jay, downed from his nest—a windfall the Old Ones must have laid before him. With one movement he'd wrung off its head and was catching the first warm jet of blood in the back of his throat. That alone was enough to strengthen him. He still had flint and steel in his pocket but he was wary of smoke from a cook fire, however small. He carried the bird back to the limestone shelf to pluck it, and then ate it raw, all but the viscera and the feet, chewing the little bones and the skull of it most thoroughly.

Encouraged, he walked westward, till he struck a deer trail which he then began to follow. The trail meandered roughly along the same course as the river, now and then coming in sight of it, through a gap in the trees. There were vast clearings with corn just beginning to tassel, south of his way, in the direction of Brandenburg. In the end he might gain the Mississippi again, but that would be days, on his bare feet. And there were soldiers beginning to move in these parts, both the gray and the blue. When war became general he could make his own way, but this circling suspicion was hard for him to navigate.

He began to know that he was being watched, by nothing human though, he thought. He stopped moving, hand on the grip of his knife, and looked, barely breathing, only his eyeballs moving. A doe, a big one, between the river and the trail. Melting brown eyes turned on him through a cluster of black oak and maple leaves and the pale slender leaves of the cane. When he dropped his hip to free the knife she was up and away, the white tail flashing.

He didn't run after her. No man can run down a deer. A panther maybe, or a wolf, or two wolves working in concert. He might have brought her down with a pistol but his pistol was lost in Louisville along with his boots. He cut a six-foot length of stout green cane and split one end of it and set the grip of his knife in the notch. With this rough blade-chucker in his right hand he went the way the doe had gone, following sign. She had not run far, and sometimes he could hear her light hooves crunching dry leaves of the ground cover. He heard the silence when she stopped and twice he made out the line of her shoulder and her head turned back, long ears revolving as she looked at him, but he never had a clear throw, with the under-growth—not until she broke across the open road. Then he lunged forward, using every ounce of his breath and his heartbeat to whittle a few yards off of her lead as he whipped the green cane forward. The knife released as he'd meant for it to and buried its blade behind her left shoulder.

The doe ran on, smoothly at first, but then there came a hitch, one leg stuttering in her gait. When she slowed and turned back to nuzzle the hilt of the knife her forward leg gave way and she fell down.

He caught his breath. Horsemen were coming up the road from the direction of Brandenburg, clop-clop-clop at a steady trot on the corduroy. He had time to disappear in the brush but still they might well ride him down and he would have lost his knife too, and his kill—he would not be driven off his kill as easily as that. Huffing and covering his heart with his palm, he walked to the fallen doe and crouched, looking in her liquid eyes as the light went out of them. He drew the knife free and when the blood came he thanked her for letting her life pour into his. He pulled her head back then and turned it to bring the big vein up thick beneath the wedge of white fur, and cut it carefully so she could bleed dry into the ditch beside the road.

The horsemen had reined up by then. Five riders in long linen dusters, one black among them, leading a pack mule behind his horse. The one who seemed to be their captain had a short carbine in a scabbard by his right knee and a saber and two pistols in his belt. He wore a hat with a broad brim curled up on one side in the style of a cavalry officer, and he was the same gaunt-faced, hollow-eyed rail-thin specter from the dream he'd had on the limestone shelf the night before. A slave-catcher maybe, he'd thought when he woke alone on the stone, and he recalled the copperhead that had poured itself away from him at his first movement, and he reminded himself he was no slave.

"I be go to Hell," the captain said, his voice harsh as a crow's. "In all my days I never seen sech a trick as that. Son, kin I git ye to tell me yore name?"

"Henri." I'm not your son, he thought, and I'm not anybody's slave.

"*Onn wi?*" The white captain squinted and screwed up his mouth. "You shore don't talk like folks around this way."

The other white men laughed; the black who held the mule was silent, studying the split logs of the roadway.

"Ain't no kind of name for a natural man. Ornery. I cain't hardly wrap my lips around it."

"Henry," Henri said.

"Well then, Henry, would ye pass me up that air cane ye got so I kin git a look?"

The captain prised open the notch in the cane with his calloused thumb. He opened his duster and plucked a foot-long Bowie knife from inside his waistband and let it into the grip of the green shaft, then, turning his horse a little away from the other, tried the flex of the thrower and grinned.

"I be go to Hell and *burn!*" he said. "Ye got some enterprise about ye, Henry. I'm bound to grant ye that." He loosened his knife and tucked it away, then handed the cane back down to Henri. The horse he was riding was white and with the curly brim of his hat and his confident seat this captain reminded Henri of pictures of Saint Jacques Majeur he had seen a long time ago before he ever came into this country.

"Henry," the captain said, taking a deeper bite of the name. "Kin ye ride a mule?"

Henri looked at the mule and the black man holding it. "I can," he said.

"Then you best gut that doe and load her up and ride along with us a ways. We're gitten up a company to fight for the Confederacy. Do you know what that is?"

"I know Kentucky isn't in it and I know you're in Kentucky."

The captain laughed. "Ye're a right knowledgeable feller. We're bound for Louisville—ye best ride along."

By then Henri had opened the doe's white belly and scooped her entrails into the ditch. A few greenbottle flies were gathering. He cleaned his knife on a tuft of grass and stood.

"I just now came from Louisville."

The captain looked him up and down—bare head to bare feet. "Did ye now," he said. "Ain't brought much away with ye, hanh?" He snorted. "Hit don't matter none. This time ye'll be riding with me."

Henri crouched to lift the carcass of the doe and slung over the mule's withers. The mule shied at the first movement, tossing his black maul-shaped head, but quieted once the load had settled. Henri vaulted up behind. The black man tossed him the lead rope and he leaned across the still warm body of the doe and into the mule's neck to fasten the loose end to the hackamore for a make-shift bridle.

"Henry," said the captain. "You must be hongry to run down a deer and kill it with a knife thataway."

Henri, straight astride the mule's back now, lifted the lead-rope reins an inch and nodded. The blue jay fledgling had about worn off—there'd not been much meat on those brittle bones.

"Ginral Jerry." The captain turned to the old black man beside him. "Issue this man a hoecake please."

Ginral Jerry as he was called reached into a saddlebag and tossed Henri a flat disc of cold cornbread. He raised his left hand just soon enough to catch it as it spun across his shoulder.

"Thank you," he said. But the white captain had turned and was riding ahead, and the one he'd called Ginral Jerry paid him no mind either.

Henri broke off a piece of the cornbread between his side teeth and let it soften in his mouth a minute till he could chew it. The cake was hard as the stone he'd slept on the night before but he could taste a hint of bacon grease in it once he began to wear it down. He squeezed the mule's sides with his knees to encourage him to match the horse's trot. Three men rode abreast ahead of him, two in the rear. All five had as good of horses as any he had ever seen. He'd not get away from them along the riverside, though if ever they came into real mountains the mule might give him some advantage there. It was a good mule too, strong and sure-footed and a rarity being broke to carry fresh-killed meat. He didn't think he wanted to get away but it was always good to have an idea in his mind how he might accomplish it.

It was beginning to get hot, and he could smell the sweat of men and of horses and the raw blood smell of the doe under the sun. He worked the last dry crumbs of cornbread down his throat. They had ridden no more than a mile when one of the white riders turned toward his captain and said, "That's some kind of a foreigner you just now took up."

The captain didn't answer. Clop-clop went the hooves of the horses on the corduroy road. A minute passed and the same rider spoke again.

"He ain't just only a foreigner but a nigger to boot."

The captain didn't bother to turn his head. Henri looked at the back of that white rider's head, a greasy lock of brown hair spilling from under the hat and the red tip of a boil rising between the tendons of his neck. If I were you I'd let it go, he thought, just before the brown-haired rider spoke for the third time.

"Do you not see that man's a nigger?"

"Well don't let it worry ye, Monty." Forrest said, and spat into the roadway. "That man's a volunteer."

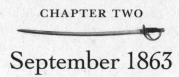

CHAPTER TWO

September 1863

W HEN HENRI WOKE he felt the eyes of the General on him, though it was yet too dark to see them or anything else, but he felt that Forrest had not closed his eyes all night. For three days they'd been fighting around Chickamauga Creek and yesterday the Federals finally broke and ran away as far as Chattanooga. Forrest was still in an evil temper because his superior, Braxton Bragg, had given no order to pursue. *The time to whup somebody,* Forrest said, *is when they runnen,* and how he hated to miss that chance.

Eight days before, at Tunnel Hill, Forrest had taken a bullet in the back at the end of a long fight with Federal infantry under Crittenden. The wound still made it difficult for him to lie down at his ease, but what irked him even more was that the sawbones Cowan had persuaded him to rally himself with a dram of whiskey when he was first hurt and it was a great point of pride with Forrest that he never ever took a drink.

And twenty-four thousand men between both armies killed for nothing. A battle that nobody won. *Unless ye calculate the Yankees won it because they kilt a couple thousand more than they lost.* And yet the Yankees had been driven from the field.

It was too early even for the birds. Away to the west a lone screech owl chittered loopily in a high branch of a dead tree. Henri couldn't see the owl but he had marked the tree in his mind before he lay down. He could just begin to see the black sky fracturing along the edges of the leaves of the oak under which they sheltered.

"Henry," said Forrest, just above a whisper.

"I'm here."

"Saddle up."

When the light had just begun to turn blue they were riding four hundred strong down the Lafayette–Rossville Road. Henri rode half a length back of Forrest's right shoulder, his usual position, the place he liked best. There was not enough light yet to see it but he knew Forrest was biting his lips under his beard to master the pain of the wound in his back. By the time the birds did begin to sing, he had warmed to the saddle and loosened his jaws. At cockcrow they came upon a troop of Federal cavalry just outside of the village of Rossville.

"Well, boys," Forrest said, grinning now and happy. "What say we give'm a dare?"

Now the light was cool gray and the mist just rising from low rolling pastures either side of the road. As they spurred up, the high wild skirling of the Rebel yell rose all around and above them, eerie as the shrieking of the predawn owl. Henri could not get his lips or throat or larynx to make that sound, any more than the men he rode with could ever manage to pronounce his name. He would only let his jaws drop open so that the screaming would meet no obstacle as it ran through him; it came from outside, certainly, but at the same time seemed to inhabit his whole body. Whenever he felt that cry ring in him, his blood turned cold and his eyes turned clear and fear was driven from his body and flew out ahead of him to stoop down on the enemy. That he stretched out along his horse's neck during the charge was no more than a practical consideration. Forrest however stood straight up in his stirrups screaming his fury from the bottom of his gullet and ready to catch the bullets in his teeth and spit them back where they came from if anyone had the nerve to stand and fire.

In fact the Federal horsemen did get off a ragged volley or two before they turned to run. They had those new Spencer repeaters. Henri heard the whistle of a ball passing through the space his head had occupied before he'd leaned forward into the charge, and then he saw another pass through the muscular neck of Forrest's horse a hand's reach away, on his right just ahead. A fountain of blood leapt up after it.

That horse would collapse on its next stride, Henri saw, and he knew that Forrest would not be pleased at this turn of events, since only two days before he had lost another good horse in the same situation—an excellent mount which had been a gift to him from the citizens of Rome, Georgia, in gratitude for his having captured a division of Federal raiders just before they could reach and pillage that town.

"*Shitsonofabitchsuckingspawnofthehornedevilsbilenassholeinhell!*" Forrest exclaimed. "Goddamme to the eternal fires of *Belial* if I give up another horse before I bury the Yankee sonofabitch that shot him!" He leaned over and plugged the wound with the ball of his right index finger. The blood geyser stopped and the horse galloped on as if unaware of the injury.

Henri sat up straight, astounded. The Federals were no longer firing; their horse tails were receding to the point where the road met the horizon. Forrest, finger properly inside his horse's pulse, continued the pursuit until a fissure opened in the world of space and time and Forrest's horse left the ground altogether to jump through it. The door was still there, a rent in the world's fabric, with the rest of Forrest's cavalry refusing the jump and passing to one side or the other of the tall narrow ogive as if they hadn't even seen it. The passage had the look of a mirror now, like a high pier glass in a rich man's hall. When Henri rode to it he could not see anything beyond it, not Forrest or his warhorse or the fleeing Federals, but no more did the ogive reflect himself or his own horse—it only showed white cottony clouds hurrying across the lightening sky. He caught his breath and swallowed hard—then he whipped up his horse and went through on the trail of his general.

BUT HE DIDN'T SEE FORREST or his wounded horse on the other side—instead he was riding alone through mist on a surface of fog on which the hooves of his own horse made no sound. He must have passed over to the place where the Old Ones abided. But everyone know that the Old Ones were dead.

He sawed his horse to a rough halt and clutched at his skull, which seemed intact. His horse was hot between his legs and was breathing hard, as it had the right to.

And now he noticed he was back on solid ground: a bare knoll with one hollow tree on it like the screech owl's tree from the night before, but different too—the rent in the trunk held the same swirling mist as the mirrored passway he had come through to be here. Ginral Jerry was hunkered over a small greenwood fire, cooking fatback in an old iron skillet.

Henri hobbled his horse and walked around to the other side of the tree and looked down between the roots. There indeed was Forrest well out ahead of the rest of his troop and riding down hard on the outskirts of Rossville, closing on the last Federal horseman ahead of him. His right hand was taken up with stopping the wound in the neck of his horse but his left arm was free to lash out with his saber and split the coat of the Yankee horseman from the collar to the tail. The Yankee shrieked his terror and slammed his heels to the sides of his horse, but Forrest only laughed the more wildly and chopped the heavy blade down again, now opening a red gash alongside the bare knobs of the other man's backbone, and this time the Yankee screamed like a girl.

"That hoss ain't gwineter hold up forever," Ginral Jerry said, turning meat with a chip of greenwood. "No matter what he do."

CHAPTER THREE

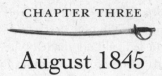

August 1845

A s soon as he had come to the riverbank Forrest understood that Ned would never get that buggy free, the way he was going about it. Ned was a sensible nigger, smart with a horse, but he couldn't both push from behind and drive from the box at the same time, and the ladies in the buggy were not helping any. They rocked on the leather cushions whenever Ned heaved and the horse thrashed in the shafts, and the silk orbs of their parasols (one blue, one green) bobbed with the wasted motion.

On the far bank, two young gentlemen in their Sunday best sat their horses in the shade of a stand of water maples, waving now and then to encourage the ladies, waiting for the Sons of Ham to sort out the problem—those whose lot it was to labor in the muck. Rodham and Burke—Forrest knew them by sight, from Hernando and Memphis. He glanced at them once as he tied his horse to a low-hanging branch of a live oak and waded out into the stream.

"Well, Neddy, hit don't look like ye're gitten nowhar."

"Nawsuh, I ain't." Ned flashed his teeth and ducked his head. He had a fine set of teeth, though up in his forties. A stout nigger for his age, though the job was too much for him. He was up to his waist in the slough. To Forrest, who stood nearly six foot two, it was no more than thigh deep.

"Let's study a better way to set about it," he told Ned. By then he had come to the buggy's left door, and he held up both his hands to the passenger there.

"Ma'am, if ye don't mind."

The elder lady peered out through the shivering white fringe of her parasol. "What is it that you mean to do?"

"I mean to carry ye over to yonder bank." He pointed with his long arm. "Then I'll tote Miss Montgomery over thar after ye. Then we'll git yore buggy loose and ye can git back on yore way."

On the far bank a jay was chattering. Forrest turned his head toward the sound and saw the blue and white wing flash out of the maple leaves. Had the lady still not made up her mind?

"Ma'am," he said. "Ye best fold up that brolly."

She seemed to be mostly made of whipstitch and whalebone and weighed no more than a shock of hay. He held her chest-high, to be sure that her skirts would not trail in the wet. He climbed the far bank and set her down, supporting her shoulders till she was sure of her balance.

"Thank you," she said. "I hardly know what we would have done . . ."

Forrest looked again at the two mounted dandies. Rodham made as if to touch his hat brim, but didn't, quite. He had on kid gloves. Both of them wore knee-high calfskin boots which doubtless they didn't mean to spoil in the mud.

He waded back toward the buggy where Mary Ann Montgomery was waiting. He had seen her a time or two on the streets of Memphis, where she went to buy her clothes, and the second time he had turned right around and watched her out of sight. After that he had learned that she was second of four children and that her mother was a widow who had lived for three years in the new Mississippi town of Horn Lake, where her brother had been appointed pastor of the church. He knew that Mary Ann had been to a finishing school in Nashville and lately had come home to stay with her mother. He knew it was not very likely that they would ever be introduced.

She folded her parasol and stretched out her arms to him with a smile. "Off to the races, are we?" she said. Her voice was weightless and gay. As he caught her up she settled her arms around his neck and kept on smiling up at him. Her hair was light and fine as corn silk. Though she was slender, there was more heft to her than to her mother. When he felt her haunch slip against his belly, soft and warm through the cloth of her dress and his shirt, there was such a surge of hot blood up his thighs that he wondered if maybe she felt it too. Her eyes had fluttered halfway shut and there was a pretty flush on her cheek and her red lips were slightly parted. He was near enough to know her breath was sweet.

When two fighting blue jays swooped out of the maples, he saw that he had stopped, stock-still, midstream. He came to himself and carried her the rest of the way and climbed the bank and set her down. She held on to his hand in both of hers as she thanked him, then let it go. He felt the damp air move between his loosened fingers.

It was then he realized he did not at all care to leave her in the company of Rodham and Burke.

"If you ain't the sorriest shitsucken sonsabitches God ever let live," he told them. "Setten on yore fine horses with yore fangers up yore fat asses that way. The sight of the pair of ye makes me want to puke."

Rodham colored a little and raised one gloved hand. "I resent that."

"You're welcome to. I wish ye would."

Rodham moved his hand toward the inside of his coat.

"Think twice," Forrest said. "I'd hate to waste a bullet on ye."

"You dare to speak that way to my face?"

"If ye ever had any face ye done lost it," Forrest said. "If ye don't want a good horse-whuppen, with a roll in that slough to finish it off, git yore sorry asses out of my sight."

Rodham dropped his hand and glanced at Burke. Both men had now turned pale. Without a word they wheeled their horses and trotted off down the road to Horn Lake. Forrest turned to face the ladies. Mrs. Montgomery seemed to have stopped a titter by placing her fingers across her lips, though by her expression she was not truly amused. Mary Ann was looking at him with the kind of fascination one might feel for a wild animal in a traveling show. Forrest could think of nothing to say. He coughed and turned to watch the retreat of the pair he'd driven off.

When they were out of sight, Forrest waded back out to the buggy. "All right now, Neddy," he said. "Ye look to be about wore out. Take the horse's head and leave me put a shoulder to the wheel."

Lightened, the buggy came out easily enough. Ned led it up the bank and Forrest followed. He handed Mary Ann Montgomery up into her seat. Ned helped her mother and climbed to the box.

"I'll just cross over and git my horse," Forrest said to the general company. "I'll not be far behind, in case ye should run acrost any more trouble."

"Your courtesy will not be forgotten," Mrs. Montgomery said.

"I'm right glad to hear that." Forrest took off his hat. "My name is Nathan Bedford Forrest, ma'am. I ask your permission to call on Miss Montgomery."

"Why—" Mrs. Montgomery let out an audible titter this time. She put her hand to her mouth and then took it away. "I certainly see no way to refuse you." Her gloved finger pointed. "Mind, Mister Forrest, in my house no one takes the name of the Lord in vain."

"Yes, ma'am," Forrest said. "I'll do my best to fix that in my mind."

Mrs. Montgomery was no longer looking at him and he didn't mean to turn his eyes to Mary Ann again until tomorrow. Ned saluted him from the box, then lifted the reins. Forrest touched the black driver lightly on the forearm, then crossed the river one more time to retrieve his horse.

HORN LAKE WAS a little more than halfway to Memphis from Hernando where Forrest lived, and had mostly been settled by gentlefolk in quest of a pastoral retreat from the big town over the Tennessee border. It wasn't very big yet though, so it didn't take him long to find the Montgomery house. Out front was a cast iron nigger holding out a brass ring, but a couple of good-looking saddle horses were already hitched there, so Forrest tied up to a corner fence post. As a matter of fact he recognized both horses. He was just reminding himself that he didn't give a green goddamn that his boots were scuffed and his coat a mite short for him when a voice hailed him from the porch.

"Well, Mister Forrest," Rodham said, with the hind of a smirk. "If you've come to call on Ned, you'll most likely find him around back in the stable."

Forrest's courting nerves evaporated. He took one quick look at Mary Ann to see how well she was amused by her caller's wit and was pleased to see she had not even smiled.

"Why no," he said. "I come to put yore head on a stick." Burke was there too, seated on the joggling board on the other side of her, fondling a mandolin in his lap. The two of them wore short light-colored jackets and shirts with ruffles over the bosom where young blades of their stripe liked to conceal their dirks and derringers. Forrest grinned at them as he came up the steps.

"I thought I got ye tolt yestiddy, the G—" He stopped.

"At a loss for words?" Rodham smiled.

Forrest looked up at the porch ceiling, where a big daddy-long-legs walked. Mrs. Montgomery was nowhere in view, but still.

"Tolt ye the very d—jest the ugly sight of ye makes me want to puke. And ye ain't got no better sense than to turn up here today."

Rodham got up, reaching into his breast ruffle. Forrest caught him with one hand below the elbow, the other above, wheeled around and threw him out into the yard. He moved toward Burke, who thought it better to bypass the steps and vault over the porch rail. Rodham had rolled to a stop at the yard fence. He got up cradling his right arm in his left, the whites of his eyes showing, and dust in his brown hair.

"Tolt ye once, tolt ye twicet," Forrest said. "Now put yore tails between yore legs and *run*."

"We'll see you later," Burke muttered, with as much menace as he could muster with ten yards and a waist-high fence between them.

"I shore will look forward to it." Forrest picked up the mandolin from the porch floor and walked out in the yard. Burke was helping Rodham, who still nursed his right arm, clamber on to his horse. When he was done Forrest handed him the instrument.

"If ye ain't left no other propitty here, I reckon ye won't have no call to come back."

Burke took the mandolin without a word and mounted. Forrest turned his back on them. Mary Ann had picked up a book and hidden most of her face behind it. The front door was open now and her uncle, the Reverend Cowan, stood in the frame.

"You make yourself free in a house not your own," he said.

"Well sir," said Forrest. "If ye was to see varmints usen round my porch I spect ye'd run'm off or shoot'm."

"I don't know if I can satisfy your expectation."

"Sir," Forrest said. "I mean Reverend. I ain't no flower pot I know. My speech is rough and my manners is plain. I don't own no frock coat nor yet a silk hat. But if I was to need them things I would git'm somehow. I come up hard and I come a long way. But I ain't halfway yet to whar I'm a-goen."

"I congratulate your fortitude," Reverend Cowan said.

Forrest took a breath. "I don't lie nor cheat nor steal. I do what I intend and I keep to my word. I don't chaw nor smoke and I don't use whiskey." He paused and looked down the length of the porch. Mary Ann had laid down her book and was stroking a cat that had climbed into her lap.

"I tried whiskey oncet to know what hit was," Forrest said. "I ain't tetched it since, and I won't never agin."

"You don't mean to tell me you don't cuss."

"I cain't tell ye that," Forrest said. "I'll say I'm not proud of it. Hit's a vice I hope to master."

"With the Lord's help."

"I ain't never asked no help from nobody."

Reverend Cowan sighed. "But my niece Mary Ann is a good Christian girl."

"I know it," Forrest said. "That's jest why I want her."

"Dear Lord," said the Reverend. "How am I to answer that?"

"Ye might give your consent," Forrest told him.

"You're in a powerful hurry," said the Reverend.

"They say life is short. We ain't promised tomorrow."

"It's short for some," Cowan said, with raised eyebrows. "You have the name of a violent man."

"I'll ast ye to jedge fair if I deserve that name," Forrest said. "I never once started a fight in my life."

"You don't have to tell me you've finished a few," Cowan said. "And men's lives into the bargain."

"If you mean that business over to Hernando last spring—Reverend, them Matlocks didn't leave me no choice. They was out to murder my Uncle John and I wouldn't stand by and not try and stop it. They was four against one and I had not but two balls to my pistol. They'd of kilt me too if a neighbor hadn't of thrown me a knife."

"I see," said the Reverend. "I'm sorry for your uncle's death. Untimely." He offered his hand and Forrest took it.

"I thought I heard you were left-handed," Cowan said.

"I can manage a knife with my left hand. Ginerlly I shake with my right. I'm able with either."

"I don't doubt you are," said the Reverend. He let go Forrest's hand and pressed his fingertips to his eyelids. "Well. I don't see how I can stand in the way of your conversing with my niece, so long as she's willing." He turned. "Mary Ann, you have a caller, if you care to receive him."

"Mister Forrest is welcome." Mary Ann stood up and the cat slipped down to the floor. Reverend Cowan shaded his eyes with his palm.

"I believe I'll go indoors a spell," he said. "Behave yourselves, young people."

Forrest heard his boot heels booming on the boards of the porch as he walked toward her. She fluttered her fingers in his palm, then pointed to the joggling board—a fifteen-foot plank pegged between two square posts that bowed it up like a spring.

"I believe I'll jest set on this chair," Forrest said. "I don't much trust a seat that moves, unless it would be on back of a horse."

Mary Ann laughed and bounced herself once on the board, as if to show him how it worked. He watched the movement ripple through her body and thought of the merry scene he'd interrupted: the three of them laughing on the wiggling plank. The movement made them all rub up against each other. He had prepared what he meant to say, but no idle pleasantries to precede it.

The window behind Mary Ann was open, and through it he heard Mrs. Montgomery's thin voice declare that she had a headache. A chair creaked as the preacher settled into it, and presently he commenced to read from some book of moral philosophy, in a low dull voice like the drone of a fly.

The cat floated up onto Mary Ann's lap—a big ginger cat with rings on its tail.

"You've driven off my gentlemen friends," she said, "and left me with nothing but poor Pussy."

"I don't much feel sorry for that cat whar he's at," Forrest said, surprised at the ease with which he said it. Mary Ann smiled, but absently.

"You know," she said, looking somewhere past him, "till yesterday I couldn't tell which one I liked better. William plays and sings so sweetly. But it's Teddy who knows how to make me laugh."

"How about today?"

When she tossed her head her yellow hair shook out. "Today? I don't know that I like either one of them, so much."

"Miss Montgomery," Forrest said, leaning forward in the ladderback chair where he sat. "If ye was to go with either of them, they'll leave ye mired in some slough like whar ye was at yestiddy. Come go along with me and yore wagon will roll down the center of the high road with all my strength behind it."

Mary Ann caught his eye for a moment. "I don't know that I take your meaning."

"I think that ye do."

She dropped her eyes. Inside the room behind her, the burr of the Reverend's reading stopped for a moment and then resumed.

"I'll tell ye a story," Forrest said. "I mean it ain't no story, hit's the truth." He hadn't planned this part, but it came out more easily. "When I was a boy we lived out to Tippah. It was wilderness then, and no neighbor nigh. My mother rode ten miles, one day, for a basket of chicks to start us a flock. It was coming on dark when she got near to home, and a painter came onto her trail." He paused. "I don't know if ye've heard a painter scream."

"It chills the blood," she said. "Go on. I'm listening."

"The painter is a witchy critter," Forrest said. "Hit smells the blood inside the feathers. Hit hears a heartbeat from a long ways off. My Aunt Fannie begged my mother to throw that basket down behind her so the painter might stop. She wouldn't do it. Right when she rode in the yard the painter sprung up onto her back. Hit torn off her dress and left stripes on her back like she had been whupped."

"That's a terrible story."

"I don't know that it is. My mother was right satisfied with what she done. She brought them chicks safe inside the house."

Through the open window behind Mary Ann, silence came streaming out like smoke.

"Miss Montgomery," Forrest said. "What would you do? Hang on to them chicks or throw'm down?"

"I can't answer that. How could I?" She looked at him and held the look. Her eyes were a deep liquid green. "I couldn't know, unless I was there. I couldn't know till I'd already done it."

"You have beautiful eyes."

"What did you say?"

"I mean they're honest. That's what I said."

"Your eyes are black." Mary Ann shivered. "They go right through me."

"I could answer that question."

"I'm sure that you could." She stood up and the cat dropped out of her lap and poured itself over the rim of the porch like water.

"You know your mind better than I know mine," she said. "I hope you'll come again tomorrow."

FORREST SLEPT POORLY and woke before dawn. He split wood for an hour, then bathed, and cut himself shaving, and staunched the cut with a spiderweb. It was still far too early to set out for Horn Lake, so he went to Hernando and, after some casting about here and there, succeeded to obtain a marriage license. At eleven o'clock he hitched his horse to the brass ring the cast iron nigger offered him in front of the Montgomery house.

Today no other callers had preceded him. As a matter of fact the porch was empty. He stood before the front door, hesitating to knock, but before too long the door swung inward. Mrs. Montgomery greeted him, courteously, deferentially even, but without real warmth. There was a little pinch in the skin between her eyebrows, as if maybe she really did have a headache. As she showed him into the parlor, Forrest thought he saw the silhouette of Reverend Cowan, coming in the back door at the end of the hall.

"Good morning, Mister Forrest," Mary Ann said, offering him the white dove of her hand. "You seem to be an early riser."

Forrest didn't know what to make of that. There was not an hour left in the morning. "I was up fore day," he finally told her, squeezing his hat brim, turning his head this way and that and blinking like an owl. They shut up the parlor to keep out the heat: the windows were open just an inch from the sash and the room was curtained to such a darkness that he could barely make out the shapes of the furniture at first. Mary Ann, who wore a light cotton dress and kept her face pale with her parasol, stood out of the gloom like a revenant.

He set down his hat on a fragile-looking little table his eyes had adjusted just enough to discern, and touched the fold of the marriage license inside his coat pocket. The feel of it reassured him less than he'd hoped. The front door squeaked, then the porch floorboards, and he heard a rustling as Mrs. Montgomery and her brother settled themselves out there, between the windows.

"Come and sit down," Mary Ann was saying. Forrest squinted at one chair and another—none struck him as stout enough to bear a grown man's weight. But she was patting a cushion on the little horsehair love seat, where she had taken the other place. There was a reed of huskiness in her airy voice which he wasn't sure had been there yesterday.

"Did ye not tell me ye meant to answer my question?" he said, remaining where he was.

She raised her chin to him. "Which question was that?"

"I'm a patient man," said Forrest. "I try to be patient. Ye oughtn't to trifle with me, though."

"I don't mean to trifle," she said. "You asked me two questions that I recall, but there was just one you asked outright."

She beckoned him again, he didn't come.

"I'll be your wife, if that's what you want."

"That was the question," Forrest said. "Yes."

From the porch came a murmur and a slither of muslin, as if perhaps Mrs. Montgomery had fainted. Forrest turned his head just a hair toward the sound, but it seemed as if the Reverend were ministering, and Mary Ann didn't seem much concerned.

"Come to me now," she said, and when he had done so, she took his head in both her cool hands and looked at him closely, then stretched up to kiss him quickly on the cheekbone, lingering just long enough that he felt the startling rasp of her tongue's tip along the fine edge of the cut his razor had left there that morning. When she drew back he wanted to follow but she stopped him with a light palm on his chest.

"Tell me," she said. "What happened to the panther?"

Forrest smiled broadly in the dim. "I'll give ye his hide for a wedding present if ye want. I'm sorry to say a good deal of the har has fell out."

"I thought so," she said, and drew him to her. The outside curve of her breast fit naturally into the palm of one hand, as the other slid over the round of her hip to the small of her back. The kiss seemed to open her whole being to him.

"Oh," she gasped, coming out of it at last, one hand pressed to her high-buttoned throat. "Oh my God. Well I never."

Forrest was struck by a horrible thought. "Have ye let one of them rascals tetch ye?" he blurted.

"Hush, Bedford," she said, folding herself into his side, and covering his mouth with her fingers. "Nobody ever touched me like that."

CHAPTER FOUR

IT CAME ABOUT after some battle or other—Shiloh, Fort Pillow, Franklin (or no, it wouldn't have been Franklin)—that Henri found Willie and Matthew fighting. Or they found him, brawling out of the undergrowth to swarm each other on the bare packed ground before the hollow tree. It was just dawn, the white mist rising, and all around the graybacks lay, some few snoring, most just barely breathing, exhausted from the work of war. None would rouse to intervene. Those two were fighting to hurt each other, knuckles and elbow, sharp knees and mean kicks aimed to the groin. Both were banged up and a little bloody, from each other's efforts as much as from yesterday's fighting; Henri knew that neither had been gravely wounded the day before.

"Eh!" he said, and rolled up from his scrap of blanket. "Stop that."

The two ignored him, panting, circling each other, looking for a way to close. Willie was bigger of the two, long and rawboned, though gaunt from scant rations, but Matthew was older, cannier, and probably more dangerous. He slipped and struck and coiled and sprang, like a bobcat or a snake. On happy days he could do a back flip standing, and all the men would laugh and cheer, and Matthew smiled bright with all his white teeth, but this morning his jaw was hard set and even his eyes had turned yellow with rage.

Henri took a step and stood between them. Willie let down, just a little, when he did that. But Matthew whipped from behind Henri, throwing a quick one-two that caught Willie hard on the breastbone and the eye socket, the second punch twisting to cut around the eye.

The first blow had clipped Henri in the back of his ribs as it went through. He stepped aside. Willie gave his head a hard shake and dropped it and ran at Matthew with his head low and his hands high.

"Bon, si c'est comme ça," Henri said, raising his shirt tail to touch the bump that had risen on his rib cage, *"Allez-y."*

A handful of other soldiers of the camp were getting up to the watch the fun. One bet on Willie, another on Matthew, all merely for sport as no one had a crying dime to pay real stakes. Henri was inclined for Matthew, but Willie had a plan. He charged in hard and lumbering like a bull, took a punch on the fleshy part of his nose and didn't let it slow him. He threw his whole weight on the other like a sack of corn, and brought the both of them to the ground. Wrassling, stomp and gouge in the dirt, gave Willie's greater weight and longer limbs the advantage. He seemed to pin Matthew, just for a moment, and certainly slammed the back of his head against the hardpack.

"You give?" he said. "Say calf rope!" His voice was muffled by his bloody nose. Matthew stuck a stiffened finger into his throat and weaseled free, landing a swift kick in Willie's midsection as Willie struggled up, then catching him with an open hand across the cheek when Willie came upright. Matthew danced back, out of range. A demon was in him, Henri saw—it unnerved him more than a little. Some of the graybacks had begun to clap, on a pounding rhythm, to move the fighters harder.

Henri whipped in and caught Matthew on the forearm. *"Mathieu,"* he hissed, distracting him with the queer pronunciation. "Come back."

Matthew's arm throbbed against his palm like a strummed brace wire. His hand and the arm it grasped were much the same shade: coffee with a swirl of cream. As quick as that Matthew broke the grip and twisted away and turned his yellow-burning eyes on Henri.

"Why are you fighting *me*?" he said bitterly. "Why *me*?"

If I had a hundred men like you, Henri thought. Or twenty-five or even ten. In New Orleans or Charleston or Louisville . . . Harpers Ferry. Though Matthew was a boy yet. He'd soon be twenty, Henri guessed, and if Matthew had really been a slave the boy in him would have long since been extinguished.

Matthew turned his burning eyes on Willie again. In an instant they were rolling on the ground once more. The back of Matthew's shirt tore loose in Willie's clutch.

"Goddamn yore eyes git up from thar." General Forrest had come out of nowhere, himself in a towering battle rage. Henri moved out of the line of his approach. No man wanted to meet that head-on.

"Don't ye know hit's still yet Yankees to fight? They ain't no shortage of'm neither. And you pair of fools a-wasten yore strength on each other. Git up out of that and look at me."

Willie stood, his hands dropping to his hips, and looked at the region of Forrest's belt buckle, snuffling and swallowing the blood that kept drizzling from his left nostril over his upper lip. Matthew rotated his eyes onto Forrest like muzzles of a pair of cannon.

"My own blood son a-wasten hisself in sech foolishness," Forrest snapped. "And you, Matthew, my boy. Hadn't ye got no better sense than that? Look at yoreself the both of ye. Look each other in the eye."

Both boys obeyed him then. The yellow fire faded from Matthew's stare. Henri saw that both pairs of eyes were the same—black, hard and shiny like obsidian.

Willie was first to drop the gaze. He broke away and stalked off into the brush around the clearing. Matthew turned to Forrest then, his open hands held up.

"If I'm yours," he said, "why won't you own me?"

Forrest's own rage had drained out of him now. He looked around the clearing. The men of his escort, white and black, were doing their best to seem as if they'd never had the least interest in this fight or even known it was happening. Some cleaned their guns, or searched for dry socks, or rummaged in their kits for rations. Ginral Jerry struck flint and steel over a frayed heap of deadfall sticks, then crouched down to blow on the spark. The sun had come up somewhere now, sending green-gold dappling through the brush. When Forrest spoke, his words seemed to come out of the same sad bitterness as Matthew's.

"I own the lot of ye," he said. "Cain't ye see that?"

He looked all around to be sure no one would answer. Now even Matthew's head hung low. Then Forrest turned and strode away, in the direction of the horses.

Ginral Jerry was molding cakes with cornmeal and cold water. They didn't even have any salt left now. But when the first hoecake hit the hot iron, the sizzle and smell clenched up Henri's stomach, and he felt that ache at the back of his jaws.

He looked away from his hunger, anywhere. Matthew, head lowered, wandered out of his view. On a low springing branch of a pin oak sapling, two goldfinches shone bright in a sunbeam. In the hollow of the tree, the stub of a white candle obscurely burned.

CHAPTER FIVE

April 1854

THE CHICKENS WERE JUST going to roost when the man named Herndon left the Adams Street stockade, unsatisfied with the half-dozen slaves Forrest had paraded for him around the brick walk in the center of the cabins. Forrest showed him politely to the gate in the high board fence, and chained the gate to its post when Herndon had gone out, rattling the iron to prove it sure.

"I'll wager he'll be back tomorrow," he said to his brother John, who leaned on his cane by the back door of the brick house that closed off the fourth side of the stockade. John only nodded and smiled at his feet.

"Put'm up, then, Jerry," Forrest said, and the black man moved forward, motioning the slaves toward the cabins with the short stick he held in his right hand. A speckled banty hen flew up to a post of the stockade and perched there, bobbing her head between her shoulders, rustling her wings. As the line of slaves passed the pump, the slave Benjamin broke away and kicked a chamber pot from the row of them that Aunt Sarah had set on the brick rim of the cistern to dry. The chamber pot flew into the red iron of the pump and shattered. In the next instant Forrest had picked up another and smashed it over Benjamin's head. Stunned, the slave rocked on his heels like a tree in the wind. Forrest wheeled on Jerry.

"What air ye looken at? Put'm up now like I done tolt ye."

He turned to face Benjamin, a fine stout buck, near his own height. Like the others he had stripped to the waist to parade before the customer. His bare chest pumped; the sinking sun glanced off a point of the nine-foot stockade and caught the sheen of sweat where his breath moved. A trickle of blood ran down from a cut above his left ear.

"Well now, Ben." Forrest lifted the shard of crockery that hung from its looped grip in his left hand and glanced at it with an air of surprise. Then he squinted back into the eyes of the tall slave. "Ye done cost me might near a dollar on them two pots." He watched as Benjamin's eyes came clear.

"Whup me then." The slave looked past him, to the post that stood a few paces from the house door—a whitewashed six-by-six beam about chest high, with a rope end trailing from a hole drilled near the top.

"Ye been whupped plenty," Forrest said, and stepped to the side; he raised his right forefinger toward the old welts the lash had carved across Benjamin's back, but stopped short of touching them. By the back door, John shifted his cane to his left hand and swung back his coat with his right, freeing the grip of the pistol in his waistband—yet Benjamin was worth close on a thousand dollars, far too valuable to shoot.

"I don't see as whuppen has done ye no good," Forrest said. "Jest make ye more ornery is what I suspect. I ain't got a mind to whup ye no more. Jest aimed to call ye back to yore senses."

Benjamin's heavy shoulders let down. "Yassuh," he said. "I hear what you say."

"Let that be the end of it." Forrest turned and tossed the potsherd into a corner of the fence. "Aunt Sarah? Would you please come and wash this boy's head?"

John shifted his weight with a wince, letting his coat flap cover the pistol. As the old woman hurried toward the cistern, Forrest pumped water into his own cupped hands and dashed it into his face. With his fingers he raked back his hair and smoothed down his beard. The flutter of a curtain in the window of the brick house caught his eye and he frowned briefly at the movement. Aunt Sarah had taken Benjamin by the hand and was clucking as she led him to the pump. Forrest lowered his head and went inside.

The children swarmed him as he entered the parlor, pulling at the square tails of his jacket.

"Kin we go and watch the sun go down on the river?" Willie

cried. "Kin we?" His sister, Fanny, crowded up behind him, dark eyes round and excited. Mrs. Montgomery turned away from the window where she had been working and pulled a handful of pins from her mouth.

"That's 'can,' not 'kin.' 'May we.' Say 'May we,' William."

Willie looked from his grandmother back to Forrest. He opened his mouth but nothing came out. He jumped up and down a couple of times, bare heels slamming on the board floor.

"Git on, then," Forrest told him, running a hand across his hair. He lifted Fanny to his hip and turned backward, spinning her; the child arched her back over his elbow, shrieking with pleasure, her dark hair flying. Forrest set her down, and steadied her. "Keep a close eye on yore sister," he told William. "See ye both git home afore dark."

The children ran out. Mary Ann, flushed from her work, got down from a stool by the left rear window, tucking up a loose strand of hair behind her ear. She followed the children as far as the parlor door, and called out to the servant girl to bring coffee. Mrs. Montgomery lifted a swatch of flowered calico from the right rear window and let it drop back into place.

"What do you think of our curtains, Mister Forrest?" she said.

Forrest's mind still ticked with her schoolmarm corrections. *Kin. Can. May we?* He flexed his fingers. "They shet out the light," he said briefly.

"It is the fence around your slave pens that shuts out the light," she said sharply. "My object is rather to shut out the view."

And yet nonetheless she drew back the curtain. The slave Benjamin sat on the edge of the cistern, chin propped on his folded hands, while the old black woman dabbed a wet rag at the cut and swelling across his temple. Mrs. Montgomery sniffed and let the calico fall.

"I had hoped, when you removed to Memphis, you would not keep my daughter above another Negro barracoon."

Forrest's fingernails bit into his palms. "Ma'am, you can hope in one hand and—"

"Bedford!" Mary Ann cut him off.

"Well, and she oughtent to put my blood up thataway!" Forrest stalked out, swinging the door hard behind him, but he turned and caught it on the butt of his palm before it struck the jamb. The force of his glare lingered with Mary Ann for a moment after his footsteps had receded toward the street.

"Now he'll go and get drunk," her mother said.

"You know very well he'll do no such thing," Mary Ann said. "You know better."

"Of course," said Mrs. Montgomery. *"I tried whiskey oncet to know what it was. I ain't tetched it since, and I won't never agin."*

Mary Ann turned white along her cheekbones. "Sarcasm doesn't become you, Mama."

"I suppose it doesn't." Again, Mrs. Montgomery drew back the new curtain. Beside the lever arm of the pump, Aunt Sarah was poulticing Benjamin's cut, leaning in close to peer with her watery old eyes from under the crisp blue line of her head cloth. She leaned one hand on Benjamin's shoulder, for support, or possibly to comfort him. The red line of the sunset light drew away from them across the packed dirt of the yard.

Mrs. Montgomery moved away from the window and lowered herself onto the edge of a slick horsehair love seat. "I'm sorry I provoked him," she said, looking down at the hooked rug between her feet.

"Let it pass, shall we?" said Mary Ann.

"But slave-trading, really!" her mother blurted. "He might have done well enough with the horses and mules."

"The whole country runs on slavery, Mother. Even the cloth from the Yankee mills. Slaves picked the cotton for the curtain we hang to shut out the sight of them."

"Well!" said Mrs. Montgomery, working her fingers in her lap. "I'm sure you got those opinions from him."

"It's right that I should," Mary Ann told her. "He is my husband."

Mrs. Montgomery sighed and shifted slightly on the edge of the seat. The girl came in with the coffee tray and set it down, just a little shakily, on the table before the love seat. Her dress was rather too snug at the hips and bosom for Mrs. Montgomery's taste, and a warm scent seemed to pour out of her dark velvet skin, overpowering the coffee. The girl straightened, paused for a second, then moved toward the door, hips switching and her long hands swimming around them lazily like fish.

"Catharine."

At Mary Ann's voice the girl stopped, resting one hand on the door frame. There was something almost impertinent in the way she looked at her mistress, Mrs. Montgomery thought, or perhaps it was only that everything irked her because she was quarreling so pointlessly with Mary Ann.

"Do tell Master John we'll have supper at seven."

"Yessum," the girl said, and took her sinuous way out.

"There's a sassy wench," Mrs. Montgomery did not forbear to say. "I can't say I much like the eye on her."

"You don't find much to your liking this evening."

"Oh child," Mrs. Montgomery said, melting suddenly. "You do put me to shame." She clutched her daughter's hand and pulled her down to sit beside her. "Of course it's right that you should know your duty to your husband. And he *is* a good man—even I know it."

Mary Ann kissed her cheek, then disengaged to pour the coffee. With a sudden clatter the children ran in.

"You're back soon," their grandmother said.

"Pa sent us," Willie told them.

"You saw your Pa on the riverside?" said Mary Ann. "Did he go into Mason's?"

"We didn't see," said Willie. Fanny pressed against her grandmother's knee and gazed up at her wistfully. Mrs. Montgomery plucked a lump of sugar from the bowl and popped it into the little girl's mouth.

"Mama!" Mary Ann reproved her.

Mrs. Montgomery bridled and looked away. "And Mister Forrest?"

Mary Ann shook her head, just slightly. "I don't think we'll wait supper."

MARY ANN SLEPT COLD, knees curled to her breast. When she woke the first time the bed was still hollow. At her second waking there was a small fierce warmth attached to her back like a limpet— Fanny had wormed her way into the bed and wrapped her arms around her mother from behind. Mary Ann worked herself free and shifted the sleeping child onto her lap and stroked her smoothly back to sleep, then carried her to her mother's room and put her into the bed. Mrs. Montgomery stirred, though without entirely waking, and gathered the child to her. Cautiously, Mary Ann backed out.

She stood for a moment in the passage, listening to the sighs of the sleeping house, before returning to the room she shared with her absent husband. It was two hours yet before dawn, but she dressed for the day, and went down the stairs with her street shoes in her hands. John Forrest sat in a straight chair in the parlor, now leaning forward, now back. A teacup on the table near held sweet-smelling dregs of a laudanum brew. A bullet in his spine from the Mexican War had left him crippled and he could not get comfortable to sleep stretched out. Indeed he slept little in any posture. For most of any night he waked and watched.

When Mary Ann caught his eye, he shook his head. She perched on the edge of the love seat and began buttoning up her shoes.

"I'll go along with you," John said.

"I'd be glad if you did," she said. "Maybe you can rouse Jerry too."

John nodded, climbed his cane hand over hand to reach his feet and took a second walking stick from beside the door as he went out. By the time Mary Ann had wrapped a shawl over her shoulders and opened the front door, the two men were waiting for her below the stoop.

They went slowly, John laboring along with his two sticks poking up like the hind legs of a grasshopper. Jerry shuffled and stooped and sucked at the stem of an unlit cob pipe. Once Mary Ann tripped over a ridge of dried mud from a wagon rut and Jerry ran a hand under her elbow to steady her.

"Watch yo step, Mistis."

"Thank you, Jerry." With a turn of her waist she slipped free of his hand and stepped forward, slim and straight under the dome of brilliant stars that arched over the town to the Mississippi, where the crescent moon pricked into a cloud bank like a fishhook sinking into fluff mud.

They went north along the river, going carefully over the rickety plank walk above the mud, toward the lamplight and grumbling of Mason's.

"I'll go in and see," John said.

"Thank you, Brother," said Mary Ann. John passed her one of his sticks and ran his free hand over his waistband before he pulled open the door and went in. Mary Ann stood aside from the wedge of light that spilled out, and soon someone had shut the door, muting the burr of urgent voices and the rattle of the dice. Jerry studied the cloud bank rising on the west side of Mud Island.

"Mi' rain dis mornen," he suggested.

"It might do that," said Mary Ann.

John limped out, his head tucked low. "Sister, he ain't in there."

"Did you look well?"

"I looked all over, but you know I'd seen him if he'd been there, first thing when I crossed the sill."

Mary Ann nodded and turned away. There was God's plenty of gamblers and gambling dens in Memphis, shifting up and down the riverside like the packs of rats that also infested the docks, defying all efforts to exterminate them or drive them permanently away. The three of them worked their way south on Front Street, with John stepping into a second, a third gambling room, while Mary Ann and Jerry waited in the shadows by the door. At the fourth, just around the corner from the Gayoso Hotel, he was slow to return.

"Sister, he's there but I can't budge him," John said when he finally did come back out. "He's on a winning streak, at least."

"That's no matter," Mary Ann said. "He'll play till he loses the lot of it. Whatever he's won and whatever he's got."

John took his second stick from her and rocked back on the pair of them, looking across at the lightening sky above the river. "It'll soon be day."

"You know that won't stop him," Mary Ann said. "It won't stop a one of them." She waited, then looked sharply at John. "Did you tell him that I'm here?"

"In a manner of speaking," John said. "He ain't able to hear it, the state that he's in."

He paused. Mary Ann was looking intently at the stain of light under the door in front of her.

"Might send Jerry after him," John said, and forced a short barking laugh. "Jerry's got a way with a mule."

Jerry hummed and chuckled, but didn't move. Mary Ann only

clucked her tongue. "I won't send him in there alone," she said. "They're apt to mistreat him." Her pale hand darted for the handle of the door.

"Well, *you* can't go in there—" John was saying, but he was too slow. Using both sticks, he struggled in after her, into the thick funk of liquor and smoke. Jerry stuck the pipe in his pocket, snatched his hat off his head and followed. Someone had risen to block Mary Ann's path.

"Miss, you cain't—"

"Don't you dare put that hand on me." Flaring her nostrils, she drew herself up.

The man fell away from her. "That's Forrest's wife."

"Run the nigger out, at least!" someone called, with a curse, and another man said, "That's Forrest's nigger."

Forrest sat at a table with his back to the door, his head sunk between shoulders so stiff they seemed to tremble, lank hair running sweat into his collar. It was close in the dark room, but not so hot as all that. At his left hand was a heap of silver dollars, and a neater stack of gold eagles high enough the sight of it made her breath come short. Under his right hand was a pistol.

She moved counterclockwise around the table till she had come within his field of vision, but he did not seem to see her. The red holes of his eyes tilted toward the spot on the table where the dice rattled between a pair of nail-bitten hands that scooped and shook and rolled them again, all to a low monotonous chant—she did not even want to make out the words of it. She had seen him so before, though seldom—when he was in his most terrible rage. Or not quite so. As a child she had once seen a fire eating away the core of a house till all its timbers were red coal and ash in the shape of a house with none of its substance, and maybe what she was seeing now was more like that.

"Mister Forrest," she said. "It's time to come home."

The dice spun on the table, were smothered by a greasy cuff, raised and rolled another time. She called again and still he did not hear her.

"John," she said. "Pick up the money."

The other gamblers' faces were hidden, shaded away under the

brims of slouch hats, plug hats—only Forrest was bareheaded, his
hair flaming out like the mane of a lion. John nodded to Jerry, who
began scooping the coins off the table edge into a bag so long and
narrow it probably had once been a sock. At that Forrest coiled and
clutched up his pistol, but John dropped one of his sticks to cover
the gun hand.

"Goddammit, Bedford. You'll not shoot your own blood over a
dirty pair of dice."

Mary Ann completed her circuit of the table and set her hand on
Forrest's other shoulder, a calming touch she meant it to be, but
now he turned his red rage on her, flinching and twitching this way
and that like a blind man stung by invisible bees. The man across the
table had palmed the dice and scraped back his chair, beginning—
"Lookahere, lady, you got no right"—but another man snatched at
his sleeve to quiet him. Forrest might well remember an insult to his
wife when he came to himself and if he did he would make them pay.

"Come away, Mister Forrest," she said. "Your children want you."

Still he did not seem to see her, though he'd stopped writhing in
his seat.

"Fanny wants you," she said slowly.

Something collapsed in Forrest's face as he turned in the direction of her voice. "Whar is she? Whar's little Fan?"

"Come along with me," Mary Ann said. "I'll take you to her."

John managed to get the pistol away from Forrest as he rose,
knocking over the chair he'd been sitting in; he tucked it into his
own belt. Forrest's hat had fallen under the table; Mary Ann
crouched down to retrieve it. The pack of onlookers parted before
them. Outside, the dawn was turning blue.

"Go on home," Mary Ann said to John and Jerry once they were
clear. "I'll walk him cool."

Jerry raised the sock of money mutely.

"Just set that on my chest of drawers, if you would," she said. "I'll
see to it when I come back in."

She guided Forrest north along the riverside. A yellow dog came
down past them, trotting over the planks, tail tucked and head riding low. Forrest was still white and shaking, though he smelled no
worse than hot and sweaty; they'd left the reek of tobacco and

whiskey behind them in the gambling den. With a shudder he turned toward her.

"Whar's Fan? You said—"

"Hush. Fan's all right. She's with her grandmother."

Forrest's eyes came partway into focus; she thought a glimmer of last night's quarrel might have returned to him.

"What day is it," he asked.

"My Lord!" said Mary Ann. "It's only Tuesday. But it can't be that you don't know. Keep on with this and you'll ruin us all."

"I was winning." He held her shoulders and leaned fiercely toward her. "I was winning, I know I was."

"That money has gone home ahead of you," she told him. "I mean to set it by. For Fanny's wedding and to give our Will a start when the time comes. Don't you see, there's no amount of money worth you losing yourself like you do! Every man has a weakness, and this thing is yours. You must know you can't master it and just keep away."

He let go her shoulders and lowered his eyes. "Let me have a minute."

She watched him scramble down the bank to the water's edge, where he crouched on his heels and gathered water in his hands to throw back all over his face and his head, not caring how he wet his clothes. For a minute or more he stayed hunkered down, his head turned toward the south point of Mud Island. Kingfishers skimmed the surface of the brown, slow-moving water. Of a sudden the sun cleared the buildings of the town with a great scattering of light, and the cloud bank west of the river was edged with copper and gold.

His eyes were clear when he came back toward her, combing his hair back with his fingers. Downriver, a white steamboat was chuffing toward the piers. A cloud of small birds gathered behind the paddle wheel.

"Pretty," she said, pointing over his shoulder. He turned and they watched the boat together till it was securely docked. She handed him his hat and he put it on his head and when he had fixed the angle of it, he slipped an arm around her waist. She let him walk with her that way.

"And what is your weakness, Missus Forrest?"

"You," she said, feeling a warmth in her face as they moved shoulder to shoulder, hip to hip. "I don't mind to allow it, my weakness is you."

FOR TWO WEEKS RUNNING, Forrest woke in the night with a weight on his mind . . . something he couldn't get a sound hold on. The full moon lowered through the window; he could not return to sleep. Shadows of wisteria vine danced over the rag quilt, shifting with the slight rise and fall of Mary Ann's sleeping bosom. Forrest slipped silently out of the bed. In the hallway he stood for a moment, holding his trousers in one hand and listening for the light breath of his daughter.

Downstairs, John Forrest slept sitting up with one arm hooked over the post of his chair. A little oil lamp had burned itself out on the table at his right hand. Moon from a fanlight washed over him, pale as milk.

A good night for a coon hunt, surely, to listen to dogs running under the moon. But that was a country occupation, and here they were in town. A drinking man would take such a restlessness somewhere to be drenched in drink. Forrest might have gone to gamble, except that Mary Ann had named it to him as a weakness, and he would brook no weakness in himself. The thought that he was bound to play again one day oppressed him.

He let himself into the slave stockade through the house door. Stone doorstep cool beneath the curve of his bare feet. The iron pump cast a long spectral shadow across the yard.

Sensing the same wakefulness in one of the stalls, he padded toward the set of iron bars, cast all of a piece and bolted into a square hole of the door. The moon was behind him, and his shadow must have fallen into the interior. Benjamin charged the door from the inside, with such dire purpose that Forrest had to steel himself not to skip back. The whole door jumped in its hinges when the big man struck it with his palms.

For a second, they were nose-to-nose, with those few stripes of iron between them. Then Benjamin blew a gust of air through his nostrils, turned and went back to his stool. He lowered over something on his knees, ignoring Forrest. By damn, but this one was hardheaded! A whisper of wood came away from a chunk of cedar he held braced in one of his hands. In the other, a sliver of blade caught a gleam of the moon. What was he shaping? Something round—a bedpost knob, or a darning egg.

Forrest turned away from the door. Aunt Sarah stood by the iron pump now, her matchstick figure upright and still. Forrest crossed the yard toward her and sat down on the edge of the cistern.

A tin cup hung from a horn of the faucet. Aunt Sarah pumped it full of water, took one sip and passed the cup to Forrest, who drank about half and returned it to her. Aunt Sarah took another swallow and dashed what remained into the yard. She hung the cup back in its place. Forrest sensed her light weight settling on the step above him. The shadow of her kerchiefed head fell over his bare shoulders.

"You aim to tell me what he's doen with a knife?" he said.

"It settles him some to whittle," Aunt Sarah said.

Forrest snorted, much as Ben had done. "Don't seem to settle him enough," he said. "Somebody's apt to find that twixt their ribs, afore we're through."

Silence obtained. In a tree somewhere beyond the palings, a mockingbird whistled the first notes of a popular air, then gave it up.

"I shore could use a carpenter, don't ye know," Forrest said. "But I do believe he's too peevish to work."

Moonlight pooled around them in the yard. A little gray mouse stepped over the sill of Aunt Sarah's cabin and looked at them for a moment and then went back inside.

"He ain't naturally mean like that," Aunt Sarah said.

Forrest waited. The water stain on the dirt of the yard was fading as it dried.

"Don't know what turned his heart bad, do you?"

Forrest's chuckle was inaudible, even to himself. "No, Auntie, I don't know," he said. "But I reckon I must be fixen to find out."

THE SACK OF COINS from his last gambling spree was hid beneath a fireplace tile. It wasn't that they didn't use the bank, but this gold was special, something apart, and Mary Ann had planted it there like a charm.

"I need a piece of money," Forrest told her, looking toward the fireplace from where he sat at the table with his bacon, biscuit and coffee. If you pressed on the right top corner of the tile it would rock up on the other side and you could slip a knife blade into the crack and lift the whole thing out. Mary Ann might think he didn't know that but he did. He couldn't have said why he needed the money to come out of that hidey-hole, when he could have got it somewhere else and not said anything about it. She asked him only with her glance.

"I need to buy a black gal," Forrest said.

"You what?" Mary Ann had stood up sharply, tall as she could draw herself.

"Wait a minute," Forrest said. "Not for me."

She stared at him, both eyebrows high. I must want her to know, he thought. What I'm doen, and why.

Mary Ann took her fists off her hips. She opened her hands and looked at her palms, then back at him.

"All right," she said. "I'm listening."

HE WENT ALONE on a fast saddle horse, because he didn't know just where he was going or how long it might take to get there. All he had to look for the girl with was her first name and an anecdote. Turned out she had been sold twice, first to a broker and then to a place called Coldwater Plantation, a couple of miles north of Hernando. He knew the owner, a little bit, but that didn't help much—he still had to pay extra since the girl was expecting, and since he couldn't hide the fact that he wanted her special and wouldn't nobody else do.

He didn't name his reasons while they were dickering over the price—the other man would have thought he was crazy if he had. Hell, maybe he *was* crazy. If he went around doing this kind of thing for every wild nigger, he would be out of business in no time. He had to borrow a wagon to carry her home, since she was too far along to ride, and that cost him some extra too. He had to drive the wagon himself, with his saddle horse coming along behind on a lead rope, for that wasn't a horse you could ask to draw a wagon.

His man ran from the horse to the troublesome Ben. A man you couldn't ask to set in a cage or drag a chain . . . He shook his head, like a horsefly was after him, to chase that thought away.

The girl sat on the box next to him, bowed-up and silent, staring down at the ruts in the road below the wagon tree. She was short and heavyset, hair so tight on top of her head she nigh about couldn't close her mouth.

"Nancy," he said. He could feel the effort it took her not to even glance his way. By damn they make a lovely couple, he thought, hoping Ben might prove a good enough carpenter to make this whole expedition worthwhile. He didn't even bother to worry if the idea might not turn out, because Aunt Sarah was usually right about things like that and if she wasn't this time, well . . .

"Benjamin," Forrest said. "Ben. That's why—"

The girl seemed to fist up even tighter; now she was biting her lower lip.

"What's the matter with you?" he burst out. "Why would I name him to you except—"

"For meanness," Nancy said.

"Simmer down, would ye?" said Forrest. "I ain't that kind of mean."

When he did get her back to Ben, he thought, she'd find him with that half-healed wound where Forrest had busted the pot upside his head, but he hadn't done that for any kind of meanness, but just only because he had to, that's all. He hadn't thought about it before he did it, and there was no use thinking about it now. Maybe he should have stuck to trading in mules. There'd never be the same money in it, but it was rare to end up feeling like a mule owned you as much as you owned the goddamn mule.

A man and his wife came along in a buggy and Forrest raised his hat to them. He couldn't call their names right off but they were people Mary Ann's mother knew from Horn Lake. They weren't too far from Memphis now and he would be mighty glad to get off of this wagon and get shet of this surly gal.

"Yore man ain't no use at all without you with him," he announced. "That's why I'm carryen you back to him, and that's all they is to it. Ain't no meanness come into it, not that I can see. World's hard sometimes. I didn't make it."

He shut up and looked at the road ahead, looked at the mule's tail switching greenbottle flies. Nancy still didn't say anything, but he could feel the knot of her temper coming undone. In a little while she raised up her head and began to look at the scenery.

THEY ROLLED BACK onto Adams Street in the cool of the day. Jerry drew upon both gates of the stockade so the wagon could come in. He looked at the wagon curiously as it went past.

"Mm-hm, that's right," Forrest said. "You git to drive this wagon back to Coldwater."

"Wheh Coldwater at?" Jerry said.

"Down to Desoto County," Forrest said. "Don't fool with me. You know where hit's at."

Jerry smiled sideways. "Reckon I'll git theah."

A good many of the other slaves in the pens were out and about, drawing water to wash themselves down. Some sat in their doorways to eat the evening ration of grits and gravy. Ben's door was shut.

"He still in that sull?" Forrest said.

Jerry shrugged. "He off his feed." He was looking up at Nancy, who still sat on the box, not looking at him or anyone else in the yard. Presently he offered a bony hand to help her down.

"Glad to see you back," Aunt Sarah said. "He won't eat nuthen since you left."

"Who'd a'thought he'd miss me that much?"

Aunt Sarah ducked her head to hide a quick grin. Forrest walked up to Benjamin's door, peered in. The big man sat slumped on his stool in the corner. There were a couple of small whittled objects in the dust by his shoe, but Forrest couldn't see them plain in the dim light. He wondered what became of the bed knob or whatever it was. If Ben had made something useful maybe somebody was using it now.

Forrest had been gone about thirty-six hours, and if Ben had really taken no nourishment in that time he'd have a right to be feeling low.

"Ben," he said. "Benjamin."

The man moved his head but didn't look up. Forrest turned away from the door, his eye drawn by a movement at the second-story house window, above the posts of the stockade. The wisteria was just barely in leaf, just beginning to put out the tight purple cones that would soon open into blossom, and through the vine he could see Mary Ann, pulling back the white curtain to look down at him with a curious interest. Or maybe she was looking at the back of Nancy's head. The girl had got down from the wagon and stood like a dark little shrub rooted in the hard dirt of the yard.

Forrest thought he saw Fan pull herself up to peep over the windowsill, but her dark eyes were there for only a second. He turned back to Ben's stall, unlatched the door and pulled it open a crack. Enough of the fading light spilled in for him to see the little carvings on the ground by the legs of the stool: a stump-tail bobcat and some kind of fice dog. Small as they were they both looked like they'd bite you.

"Ben," he said. "I got somethen for ye."

"Don't want any damn thing you got."

Forrest sighed. "Well never mind whar hit come from, then. Fer I'm right shore hit's somethen ye want."

He pulled the door wide and stepped out from between the man and the woman. Nancy made some kind of low sound, took half a step forward and paused as if leaning over the edge of something. Forrest waited a long moment, watching, till Ben got up shakily from his stool and came toward her, holding out both his hands.

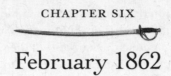

CHAPTER SIX

February 1862

THE WEATHER TURNED BITTER overnight and in the morning the sparse trees around the camp between the Fort Henry road and the river were glazed over with ice that gleamed like crystal. The sun was pale and distant and by midday its light was near blotted out by the rain of iron that the four Federal gunboats were hurling into Fort Donelson from the Cumberland. All who remained in Forrest's camp had taken such cover as they could find, save Major Kelley, the Methodist preacher, who sat placidly by his open tent flap, reading his Bible with all apparent absorption.

Sergeant Major Strange nudged Henri and pointed; the two of them went crouching toward Kelley's tent. Once Henri's feet almost shot out from under him on the sheet of ice that covered the ground. There had been heavy rain before the freeze. Kelley read on, with no sign he was aware of their approach or of anything else in his surroundings.

"I don't see how you can hold your mind to a book with all this racket going on," Strange began.

Kelley raised his head, holding his place in the text with one finger, cupping his other hand behind his ear. As Strange opened his mouth to go on there was a nasty whistle and a rush of wind. A rag of iron crashed down to splinter the ice pack just past his boot toes. Strange went skipping backward over a fallen log and dropped out of sight behind it.

"Ah," Kelley said deliberately. "Henri." He was one of the few men among Forrest's Rangers to give the name its proper French pronunciation. Others called him Henry, or more rarely Hank. Forrest, when he was feeling humorous, addressed Henri as Ornery.

"You wonder why I sit here reading?" Kelley asked, and Henri nodded, though in truth he wondered just as much why he himself kept standing there.

"As you know, the cavalry is not called to this engagement, it being chiefly a matter for artillery," Kelley said. "The enemy compels us to study war, but he may *not* compel us to depart from our civilized practice and lapse into the ways of savagery. Thus I improve an hour which otherwise might be lost to idleness. *Commit thy works unto the* Lord, *and thy thoughts shall be established.*" He smiled, sighting down the finger that held his place. "Proverbs, sixteen-three. But as for yourself, Henri, you are still more exposed than I. Have you no thought for your own safety?"

I was killed at Chickamauga, Henri thought to say, but it occurred to him that Chickamauga hadn't happened yet, and another tumbling shell was blotting out the sun. He skittered backward from under its shrieking shadow, and fell over the fallen log himself, discommoding not only Sergeant Major Strange but also Ginral Jerry, who had taken shelter with them there. Below, the fort's single 128-pounder coughed and roared, and the gunboats answered. A horse let out a screaming whinny, then fell silent.

Henri risked a peep above the log. The last chunk of shrapnel had sheared away the tent pole on which Kelley had been leaning (for the camp stool where he sat had no back to it). The minister stood up, arms akimbo, Bible pinned beneath an elbow, peering irritably at the mess of collapsed canvas. Weak sunlight glinted from his spectacles. A birdlike twittering emerged from between his lips.

"What the hell is that chatter?" Strange inquired.

"He cussen in Chinese, thas all," Jerry explained. He had rolled onto his back and lay relaxed with one knee up and his hands laced behind his head; a straw or a splinter moved in the corner of his mouth as he talked.

"*Chinese?*" Strange propped up on an elbow, looking at Jerry, but Jerry was gazing further off, at a quartet of rag-winged buzzards turning in the cold wind above the fort.

"Chinese," Strange said again. His tone shifted from outraged disbelief to a sort of resignation. Jerry rolled one eye toward him.

"He been a preacher ovah theah. In China," Jerry said. Again Henri raised his head above the log. With a sigh, Kelley settled himself on the canvas triangle of his stool and bent his attention back onto the Bible. Henri snuggled into the cold gray wood. Another hail of shrapnel pelted down and Jerry rolled tighter against the log, which Henri himself embraced still more closely.

Then something changed in the pattern of the cannonade down by the riverside, as if a voice had left the choir, a bullfrog been gigged out of the pond. An exploding shell bloomed over Fort Donelson, and in its orange aureole the broad bearded face of Kelley appeared, hovering over the fallen log.

"Come on, boys, let's get out of this mess," he said, glancing over his shoulder as he slipped the Bible into his coat pocket. "There's too much commotion to read anymore. And the colonel went down there an hour ago—I want to see what's going on."

Jerry only smiled and stayed where he was, curling closer to the log. Henri and Strange got up and followed Kelley. They found their horses in a grove of pin oaks in back of their camp. With Kelley leading they threaded their way through a peppering of hastily dug rifle pits to the right of the trenches which Buckner's men occupied, waiting for a landward assault from the Federals. The outer works of the fort were three miles long and the Confederates on the ground were too few to man them as they were meant to be manned. Henri rode with his shoulders hunched against the swelling noise of the cannon, following Kelley down a gulley that fed into Hickman Creek, which gave them and their horses some cover from the shells. At the mouth where the creek flowed into the Cumberland, Forrest stood beside his trembling horse, soothing it by stroking the withers as he stared at the four Federal ironclads closing in on the inner redoubt on top of the bluff to his right. Fort Donelson's 128-pounder had gone silent—only four smaller cannon remained.

"Hello, Parson," he said, turning the whites of his eyes on them. "Ye'd best git to prayen now that ye're here—ain't nothen but Godamighty can save that fort."

THEY DIDN'T STAY LONG to pray or to watch, but the fort did survive, by the hardest, despite the loss of its one long gun. At closer range the smaller pieces cut up the ironclads handily and set them adrift away downriver. But Grant's reinforcements were still closing in overland.

That night it snowed, and at first light, diffused by a hovering fog from the river, the Confederates led by General Pillow attacked the Federals below the little town of Dover, downriver from the fort, hoping to open a line of retreat along the road to Nashville. Henri rode between Kelley and Strange, shaking from the cold he could not get used to, following Forrest as the cavalry rode in advance of Pillow's left. They made their first charge through a fog so thick they could not see the Federals till they were in hand's reach. An hour later the sun was blazing back from the strips of snow that had not been stained crimson and Forrest was raving mad because he could not get permission to charge the retreating Federals again and run them clean off the battlefield. With his breath steaming from the chill, every curse he uttered was haloed in smoke.

He led his cavalry to the right, sweeping outside the entrenchments manned by General Buckner's troops, and cheered himself up a little by capturing a Federal battery of six guns, killing most of the men and horses that served it. Moving further to the right, he came upon General Pillow under fire of another battery at the head of a ravine.

"If you must charge something," Pillow said, "Charge *that*." Forrest said nothing, but put his head down, directing his riders with a sweep of his arm. Henri swung in after him, outdistancing Kelley and Strange—but that was his horse's idea, not his. The ravine was steep and choked with buck bushes, a few pinkish berries clinging to the scrub. Horseshoes shivered the ice and slipped on the frozen mud beneath it. At the head of the ravine the cannon thundered and Forrest's men screamed back at them. In the general uproar Henri couldn't even hear what sound was pouring out of his own raw open throat and he didn't know if he was screaming in anger or fear. To his right Captain May of the Rangers toppled, dragging his mount to a halt with his dead body trailing from one stirrup, and just behind that, Jeffrey Forrest's horse reared up and fell over backward on the steep grade, rolling over the rider. Forrest looked back for half a second, just long enough to see his youngest brother sit up coughing painfully but anyway still breathing. Two minié balls tore through the sleeves of his coat, and Henri saw more bullets striking the forequarters of his horse, like fat raindrops plopping into a pond, but Forrest, impossibly, did not stop, and so none of those still in the saddle behind him stopped either. In the next moment they had ridden right over the cannon and the Federals who weren't killed were running away.

"By God we done it!" Forrest yelled, turning back to Henri, who was the first man behind him now. His black beard jutted, his face was on fire with pleasure. "Come on boys, let's go find'm!"

As he dug in his spurs, his horse went down on its front knees, spurting little fountains of blood from seven bullet holes. Forrest slipped down and held the animal's head. He didn't know which of the blood leaks to stop. Henri watched him watch the horse's eyes go dim, and for a second it looked as if Forrest would weep, but then Ginral Jerry came tearing out of the sour smoke of the captured battery, with another horse all saddled and bridled and ready go, and Forrest was astride again, beckoning Henri to follow him—there didn't seem to be anyone else with them just now.

There came a long deep droning sound like wind over the mouth of a long bottle, and a hole opened up into the next world where the Old Ones sat cross-legged smoking their pipes and playing their strange music, then out of the hole a tapered artillery shell came majestically sailing; it entered Forrest's fresh horse just behind the crook of Forrest's own knee, and then the horse exploded.

Henri lay facedown, embracing the frozen dirt. He had stopped feeling the cold during the first charge that morning, eight hours before. But now he felt frozen all the way through and the only warm spot in the entire world was his horse's nostrils nuzzling the back of his neck, wanting to know that he was all right, wanting him to get on again. But the last place Henri wanted to be was on a horse right now.

"Git up if ye don't want me to kick ye." Forrest's long shadow stretched over him; Forrest shaking his head. "Git up now, Henry, if ye ain't dead."

Reluctantly Henri sat up. He let Forrest help him to his feet.

"Goddammit!" Forrest said, his beard's point shaking. Henri felt his sorrow transmuted to rage. "That's two good horses in less'n five minutes—by damn, them Yankees need to pay—"

Down the slope, General Pillow was calling for his men to retreat to their breastworks.

"The devil!" Forrest hollered. "Goddammit to the eternal fires of Hell, *cain't ye see we got'm on the run?* There's three good hours of daylight left, we ought to be killen Yankees with that!"

Henri leaned against his horse's shoulder, stooping enough to shelter his head from whatever projectile might yet come hurtling out of the next world in his direction. Forrest's face had turned that hot-iron color. He kicked shale loose from the frozen ground.

"Goddamn if I aim to go back to any goddamn breastworks," he said.

AT DUSK they gathered around a campfire Ginral Jerry had built in the lee of a snowbank, which did something, though not exactly enough, to cut the bitter rising wind. Forrest sat on a tripod camp stool, his long arms wrapped around his knees, reflected firelight flickering from the deep hollow of his eyes. Though he was in his shirtsleeves he didn't seem to feel the cold. Is he even human? Henri thought.

Kelley sat across the fire from Forrest, quietly contemplating him. No one spoke except for Jerry, who was counting out loud slowly.

"Thirteen, fo'teen . . . Cunnel Forrest, you done leff me a *whole lotta* menden to do . . . Fifteen bullet holes in dis here coat . . . doan even know as I got enough thread . . ." Jerry spread the coat so that the firelight shone through minié ball tears, to Henri it looked for a second as if the coat was studded with glowing jewels, or more like a dozen-odd lightning bugs had lit among its folds.

"I got a mind to ax Ole Miss to he'p with dis job a work," Jerry grumbled.

"Miz Forrest has gone back to Memphis," Forrest said.

"May God keep her safe there," Kelley added.

Forrest looked at him thoughtfully, then turned to Jerry with a smile on at least one side of his mouth. "Don't know as she's so far off yet she caint hear ye callen her 'Ole Miss,' " he said. Then he stood up, as Jerry mimed a cower at the thought of Ole Miss's wrath. Forrest's gangling shadow lay back a long way from the fire. "Hand me over that coat," he said, reaching for it. "Ye can sew on it some more later, I reckon. Right now I got to go down to Dover and *parley* with them ginrals." Shrugging into the coat, he turned from the fire and spat into the snow.

"Too many cooks spoil the broth," Kelley said.

"That they do." Forrest looked into the shadows beyond the ring of firelight. "Brother Bill?"

"Brother Bedford." William Forrest stepped into the fire's glow. He was as tall as his brother, and favored him considerably, except that his hair and beard had gone to an early gray, while Bedford Forrest's were still hard black.

"How's Jeff a-maken it?"

"He'll live," Bill Forrest said. "Got a sore bruisen but it aint a-goen to kill him."

"Would ye take a couple of the boys and go scout out the Nashville road? I'd admire to know what's out thar, if anything is."

Bill Forrest nodded to his brother, and turned toward the trees where the horses were hitched. Henri stood up. "I'll go," he said. The fire only got one side of him warm anyway, while the other side was frozen numb.

"Too many cooks," Kelley repeated ruefully, thumbing the edges of his beard. Starnes, sitting to his left, poked a wet stick into the fire. There were three Confederate general officers on the ground at Fort Donelson—Pillow, Floyd, and Buckner—and so far their cooperation had been less than perfectly harmonious.

"You know?" Kelley said to the fire, "The first time I saw him run at the Federals that way I thought there was a good chance he was out of his mind. When he did it today I saw he was right. This army ought to be halfway to Nashville by now."

"Don't you know it," Starnes said.

"Fifteen bullet holes," Jerry muttered from the depths of a blanket he'd furled over his head. "You'd think Cunnel be satisfied he still alive. But you know he ain't."

"I got a bad feeling," Starnes said, and then they all were quiet.

No sooner had Bill Forrest and Henri found their horses than the mulatto boy Matthew came out to join their scout. Since the weather had turned cold most of the men had been sleeping in pairs to improve their chances of not freezing to death. Matthew had been sharing Henri's shebang—distinguished by a rubber ground cloth scavenged from the Federals, as well as the square of canvas stretched over a low branch to shed the rain and snow. Henri felt a certain sympathy for the boy, though usually he was sullen. Matthew was supposed to be a teamster, it appeared, but he didn't seem to be very thick with the other wagoneering slaves, except when somebody needed a harness fixed, for Matthew was handy with that work, and had been trained to it, back in Memphis, it appeared. He had a good pistol, but nó sword, and a horse strong enough to keep up with the cavalry, though as a rule he rode toward the rear.

Under chill starlight they rode over the jaggedly torn and trampled snow, trotting their horses outside the Confederate trench lines. They followed the curve of the works to the southeast and once they had crossed the Fort Henry road they halted to look out over the field where the Federals under McClernand had been camped the night before. Tonight a good number of fires were burning brightly in that area.

"What do you think?" Bill Forrest said.

"We were all over there this afternoon, before dark," Henri said. "Seeing to the wounded and picking up guns and cartridges. There was no enemy left there then, none sound enough to get away."

"Ain't none thar now neither," Bill Forrest said. "That's the wind blowen up the fires from this mornen, effen ye ast me."

South of Dover they found the Nashville road flooded from a slough off the Cumberland. A wide expanse of water lay eerily still under the starlight. Bill Forrest rode out into the water, while Henri and Matthew watched him from the bank. Ripples swirled around his horse's legs. When the bottom of his stirrup touched the water, he reined up and looked over his shoulder.

"Hell yes we can git acrost this," he said. "And I expect we will."

FORREST WAS in such a state when they returned to camp that he seemed hardly to listen to their report. "We got ginrals don't know when they're a-winnen—and we got three of'm too!" he complained. "They got the idee the Federals all have come back right to whar they were yestiddy—when we just got through runnen'm out of there today. Brother Bill, did ye see anything such as that?"

"No," Bill Forrest said.

"I'll wager ye didn't," Forrest said. "How much water is it down there anyhow?"

"Some," Bill said. "Might git yore feet wet."

"Might git yore feet wet," Forrest repeated. "Them three ginrals got a doctor a-tellen'm the whole army'll die if it gits they feet wet. Doctor Cowan?" He called to the surgeon who sat on a stone beside the fire. "Is this army all bound to catch pneumonia and die if they was to oncet get their feet wet?"

"Some might catch cold," Doctor Cowan said.

"Some might catch cold," said Forrest. "Now that is such a godawful risk I druther have my sorry ass drug off to a Federal prison not to run it. How about you?"

"Not necessarily," Doctor Cowan said.

"Well jest you try tellen that to them three ginrals down there," Forrest said. "They're a-setten up in that there Dover Inn a-studyen jest *how* to set about surrenderen nigh fifteen thousand men to an army they just got done whuppen. So they won't get their *goddamn* feet wet! Jesus Christ nailed on the cross wept tears of burning blood!"

Kelley, sitting by the fire, uncrossed his legs and crossed them again the other way.

"Brother," Bill Forrest folded his arms across his deep chest. "What do we aim to do?"

"Boots and saddles," Forrest snapped. "We're a-goen to Nashville and we're goen right now."

YET WHEN THEY CAME near the floodplain below Dover, Forrest was taken by a spirit of caution. Earlier that night Buckner's scouts had brought in a report of Federal troops moving in, under cover of darkness, along the Nashville road.

"Come on, boys," Forrest said to Henri and Jeffrey, who had limbered up enough to ride. "Let's run out ahead and have us a look-see."

The chilly stars of Orion glittered above a field of empty snow. Henri let his head roll back, gazed up at the hunter's jeweled sword belt. The stars where he came from were different from these.

Forrest guided them under cover of a straggle of thorn trees on the slope. When he reached the last of them he raised a hand for the party to halt, still hidden in the bristly shadow of the trees. Henri's breath clicked off when he saw a line of infantry still on the crest of the next snow-covered rise. For a long slow time no one moved or made a sound and even the horses' breath steamed out in silence.

Then Forrest let out a sour chuckle and nudged his horse from the shelter of the thorns. He pushed his mount into an even canter, turning parallel to the enemy line. Henri and Jeffrey exchanged a quick glance and went after him. At closer range the immobile rank of enemy troops was revealed by the weak starlight to be a picket fence.

MOST EVERY RIDER carried a foot soldier behind when they crossed the slough, for a good number of Buckner's infantry had chosen to take their chances with Forrest on the escape. First-dawn light was pale on the water as the horses waded through. On the far shore Henri's passenger thanked him as he slipped down, and Henri overtook Forrest, who was talking, though he rode alone. Maybe he was encouraging his horse, or praying. But Forrest never prayed.

". . . bilepukenlilyliversnakebellysonsaJehosophat," Forrest was chanting as Henri drew alongside him. "If they think I raised up all these men and armed'm and fed'm and brung'm up here to surrender the lot of 'm to a *goddamn picket fence,* well they got another think comen, them fleascratchenscumlickeneggsuckensonsa—"

Strange rode up on Forrest's other side. "That's kind of a rough way to talk about your superior officers, don't you think?"

"Superior to what?" Forrest said.

CHAPTER SEVEN

November 1857

T HERE WAS A PLENTY of white and dark meat both on the Thanksgiving table, for Forrest had surprised a flock of turkeys drifting across a pasture on his Coahoma County plantation, at dawn a few days before the holiday. In fact he knew they scratched there almost every morning, and there were nigh on two dozen of them too. He'd roused Willie at first light, and they crept up on the turkeys under cover of a fringe of trees that curtained the field. Kneeling by a stump at the pasture's edge, he'd helped the boy steady the long rifle and take aim on the eye-bead in the wattled head of a big gobbler. When he squeezed the trigger the turkey dropped. Willie couldn't help himself from jumping up with a shout, but still, Forrest bagged four more birds before the flock had scattered into the woods.

He brought the turkeys back to Memphis in his leather saddle-bags, and hung them by their feet a day or two in the crisp fall weather. In the yard, sitting on the edge of the cistern, Aunt Sarah plucked the birds one by one while Catharine's toddlers chased the feathers and caught them all into two bags: down for pillows, wing feathers for pens. Catharine mixed cornbread with onion broth to make stuffing, while Aunt Sarah took charge of roasting the birds— and it was she who brought the first turkey on its platter to the table, never mind the weight, while Catharine had charge of a dish of sweet potatoes following behind. Both black women stood back from the table, in case anything more should be wanted straight away, as the oohs and ahs went up—they had a big crowd, this time. Forrest's mother was there and his twin sister, Fanny, and three of his older brothers too, though Jesse and Jeffrey had dodged the occasion and gone deer-hunting across the river in Arkansas. On Mary Ann's side: the Reverend Cowan her uncle, her mother of course, and her first cousin, J. B. Cowan, who with his surgeon's skill was carving the birds—a task at which Forrest tended to feel clumsy.

Reverend Cowan asked the blessing and after the chorus of *amen,* bowls of greens and rice and taters and relish began to go round, along with a platter of sliced white bread. At a whisper from Aunt Sarah, Catharine padded into the kitchen and returned with a cream-colored gravy boat. She held it, standing to the left and a little behind Forrest's chair, waiting for the plates to be served. She had worked herself warm in the kitchen, and he was aware of the heat radiating from her skin, and the hot sheen on her face and her open throat and her glossy forearms, though he did not turn his head to look.

"Mister Forrest, white meat or dark?" From the opposite end of the table, Doctor Cowan saluted him with the carving knife.

"I like the dark," Forrest said, with a lip-licking smile. Surreptitiously he ran his thumb inside his waistband to assure there was room for the meal coming his way.

"*Yes,*" Mrs. Montgomery said, with an untoward sharpness. "We *know* that you do." With that she turned her pursed lips and pointedly raised chin toward Mary Ann.

The gravy boat sloshed a bit as Catharine set it down on the table, turned her back, and started for the kitchen. Mary Ann's large eyes were picked out with blue flame. He could read the thought that flared in her gaze: *How dearly I'd love to whip that slut till her hips stop switching.*

His sister said something to Doctor Cowan, who batted the conversational shuttlecock toward William Forrest—soon enough the talk had resumed; there was a reasonable semblance of a festive conversation, though Mrs. Montgomery kept her silence, pecking at her plate like a croupy hen, and Mary Ann, though she spoke pleasantly enough if addressed, did not even pretend to touch her food.

Forrest made himself clean his plate, forced himself to down a small second helping even, though the meat was like chewing fibers of a pine board now, and the surfeit lay like a stone below the topmost button of his trousers. Presently the children were excused and ran out laughing. A quarter-hour on, the ladies retired to the parlor. Forrest followed Doctor Cowan to the porch. As they went out, a red-bone hound came yawning and stretching from under the table and loped around the house to the back door of the kitchen where the chances of scraps might be more favorable.

Reverend Cowan went for a post-prandial stroll with two of Forrest's able-bodied brothers. John Forrest laid his cane against the wall and slumped, with lidded eyes, into one of the several freshly caned rockers. Doctor Cowan bit the tip of a cigar and spat the remnant over the porch rail. He lit up and sat down, gently rocking. Forrest settled into the chair next to him. The aroma of the cigar seemed not so unpleasant, and for once in his life he almost wished he had acquired the habit of tobacco.

Of all the relatives in Mary Ann's train, Forrest liked J. B. Cowan best. The doctor was certainly aware of the obus that his aunt had detonated in the dining room, but he did nothing except blow lazy smoke rings and talk on soothingly dull subjects such as the price of cotton and tobacco and the shifting of land values in North Mississippi and West Tennessee.

From the kitchen came a smash of splintering crockery, and the younger woman's voice shrilled. Aunt Sarah's lower tones came in behind the first frustrated shriek, soon had covered it and smoothed it all away. By now it had grown dark outdoors. Forrest heard a splash as someone tossed a basin of water out the back kitchen door, and a dog yelped for getting a wet tail.

"It's a mite chilly." Doctor Cowan got up and stilled his rocker with a hand on its top post. "I believe I'll go in."

"Good night, Cousin," Forrest murmured.

In the corner of the porch, John Forrest was not quite snoring, lost in a laudanum haze. The cold Forrest felt in his own bones had little to do with the weather. Though he did not see his twin sister now as often as he used to, he knew she would come a few minutes before she laid her strong square hand on his right shoulder, and he knew what she was going to say.

"Brother," Fanny Forrest said. "You have got yourself in a right ugly fix."

He reached across his chest and caught her right hand in his left. "Don't I know it," he muttered.

"Nothen to do but meet it head-on." Fanny said. "Yore wife will be expecten you to make it right."

"Some things are jest wrong all over." Forrest looked up; her eyes were deep-set and dark as his own.

"Is that a fact?" she said. "I expect you know more about that than I do." She gave his hand a parting squeeze and let it go.

"I'M NOT ASLEEP," Mary Ann's voice said, as soon as he had crossed the threshold.

Forrest maneuvered the bedroom door shut behind him. Of course he'd known it futile to hope she would be. The whole dark room seemed to hold its breath. He listened to the slow pump of his heart. Though his wife was a lady, it was not unknown for her to fly out at him if provoked. She'd shout until her hair came loose and red patches flared beneath her cheekbones. But not tonight. The house was packed full as a straw tick, with even adults sleeping three to a bed, children rumpled together like puppies in a sack. No more than he, Mary Ann didn't want all her kin and his to know their trouble. The cutting would be quietly done. Almost in silence.

"You asked me once about those chicks." Her voice was husky in the dark.

Chicks? What chicks? Forrest's mind scrambled. He stood with the door an inch from his back, and he still had his boots on. It came to him that she must be harking back to one of the first conversations they'd ever had, long before the least shadow of trouble fell between them. His heart raised up a little at that.

"I've decided," Mary Ann said. "I'll hang on to my chicks come hell or high water. Be damned to the panther or the Devil himself."

"And you a good Christian woman to talk that way." Forrest had the faintest hope the quarrel could be turned to banter.

"You better not think I'll stop at talk." A match sizzled, flared up, and Forrest's eyes contracted. On the far side of the bed from him, Mary Ann was lighting a lamp.

He sat down in the chair beside the door and began working off his left boot with the wooden bootjack. "What do you want me to do?" he said.

Her look was a blue bolt between his eyes. "Tell me the truth about those high-yaller brats she's whelped in the yard."

Forrest swallowed. "Her chirren and our'n are brothers and sisters. Well, you ast me." He peeled off his stocking and draped it over the top of the empty left boot. "I mean the least'n. Not Thomas. The one she come here with."

"Well, that is surely a comfort. *Thomas* is not one of your *bastards*. And what about the one she's toting in her belly?"

Forrest felt his face beginning to color. The bootjack hung slack in his right hand. "I won't lie to ye about that one neither."

"No," she said. "You don't lie." She lowered her voice to a slashing whisper. "You deceive, but you don't lie. You go down there to the pens at night and shoot your seed into her black belly like a boarhog rutting on a sow. And you think I don't know about it! So my own mother has to throw it in my face at the family table?"

"That was her doen," Forrest said. "Not mine."

"It was your doing made it possible," Mary Ann snapped. "And well you know it too."

Forrest peered down at his one bare foot, which seemed very ugly to him.

"What do you expect me to do?"

Mary Ann stood on the far side of the cannon ball four-poster from him, fingers trailing in the tangled sheet. Bearing two children had thickened her only a little. He could see the outline of her breasts against the thin cotton of her gown. "There's some things I expected you *wouldn't* do," she told him.

"Well," he said miserably. "I cain't go back and fix that now."

"No," she said. "You can't. But you can get that—get her out of my house, and her spawn with her."

Forrest raised his head. "You want me to sell her down the river?"

Mary Ann's eyes bored into him, then lowered. "No. I suppose I don't want that."

She looked him more calmly now, across the field of crumpled linen. Forrest didn't much believe in God but what if God had a face like hers? Ashamed for him. Sorry for him. Not about to move toward him.

"Do you think it is wrong to use someone and sell her away afterwards?" Mary Ann said.

"Think twice if you want to throw that up to me," Forrest stood up, feeling his one bare foot cold on the floor, unbalanced from the booted one. He put one hand on the cannon ball at the top of the bedpost nearest him. Benjamin had carved it—had built them a whole new bedstead. "You use people yoreself and then have me sell them. Yore precious Momma too. All right, I don't mean nothen against yore Momma, but they ain't no truth in the way folks think about that round here. Find me some other fine lady who looks down her nose at the man sold her the maid that laces her corset and brushes her hair. Washes the pee stains outen her drawers. Who you think picked cotton for them sheets you sleep in, that gown you got on? And Yankees ain't no better, no matter what they think. They're in it right up to the neck with the rest of us. It ain't only they brought most of the niggers over here in the first place. Why, they got white chirren worken in them mills up there, no better'n slaves and mebbe worse when they ain't got no master charged to feed'm. And some no bigger nor stouter than—"

Forrest broke off. Mary Ann bit her lip and looked away, toward the heavy blinds suffocating the room. The shade of Fan, dead for three years, drifted in through a crack and passed out through the wall. Caught now like a fly in amber, she could neither grow nor change. Bedford had covered his face with his hands.

"You see," she said slowly. "There's something you can't bear."

He slowly nodded his masked head, and his fingers tightened against his face.

"I can't bear this other thing," she told him. "I won't bear it."

Forrest lowered his hands to his waist. He had not wept. His eyes were a little red, but dry, and there were white vertical stripes where his fingers had pressed, from his eye sockets to the first springing of his beard.

"You want for me to set her free?"

"Would you throw away that much money? Unless it was over a gaming table?"

"It ain't that simple." Forrest began to walk around the foot of the bed toward his wife. "I set people free a time or two. Look at them now. They still ain't free."

"Don't touch me," Mary Ann told him.

"Look at me then." Forrest held her eyes. "You don't have to be a slave to think like one. You have to set yore own-self free."

She turned from him and blew out the lamp. Forrest retreated, limping on one bare foot and one booted one, in the direction of the door.

"Where do you think you're going?" she said out of the sudden dark. "You made this bed. Now lie in it."

CHAPTER EIGHT

December 1861

THAT FIRST CAMP CHRISTMAS in Kentucky, Forrest was in a genial mood, for his wife had come up from Memphis to join him for the holiday, and he and their boy were all quartered together in a big warm tent with a partition and an iron stove and a plank floor. Better yet, there were floored and heated tents for all the men in his command. December 23 they'd shot some wild geese and come back to camp with a couple of dozen to hang and tenderize for a Christmas feast. There was a keg of brandy too, though Forrest didn't touch a drop of it. He was flushed and expansive anyway, maybe from horseracing just before dinner, when he'd won some money on son Willie's ride.

A pair of fiddlers had been found, and they rosined their bows for the country dances. Forrest handed his wife a little jealously around the square —a few ladies had turned up from the Hopkinsville area but not enough to make even couples. The bugler Gaus played fanfares to mark the figures, though more than a little off-key from the strings. When the fiddles struck up "Devil's Dream," the breathless dancers took their seats, leaving Forrest dancing a hornpipe alone to the quickening tune, capering and clicking his heels and somehow finding wind all the time to pronounce a long brag of how he and his Rangers would whup the Yankees and drive them home; counting off their heroic virtues one by one. When the tune had ended, Forrest fell into his chair (there was still a loaded plate before him), but he wasn't quite done yet with the roster—

"Old Ornery here," Forrest stabbed the air between him and Henri with his fork, "ye'd not think hit to see him now, but when I first come across him he was a-walken barefoot . . . and now ye couldn't dream of a finer-looken sojer." Henri only smiled and thumbed the nap of his butternut lapel and flexed his toes inside the fat leather of his new high-topped boots and toasted his captain with an inch of brandy in his enameled tin cup. The eyes of the company flicked across him briefly, then returned to Forrest, lately promoted to colonel and happily holding forth—he'd bought most of them uniforms out of his own pocket, the same as he'd paid for the five hundred revolvers, Colt Navy sixes all shiny and new and one of them snug now in Henri's waistband, the grip of it denting into his belly as it swelled out with hot goose. He and couple of the others who'd met him that day with Forrest on the Brandenburg road had toted the pistols under their dusters (Forrest issued Henri a good linen duster straight away) from the warehouse to a Lexington livery stable where they were packed in old potato sacks, a few taters on top of each load for show . . . By the time they left Louisville, there was word that a couple of companies of Union Home Guard meant to waylay them on the road south. But by then Forrest had strengthened his hand with ninety-some recruits under the name of Boone's Rangers. He passed every man a pair of pistols and rode to the town of Nolin with a huge Confederate flag flying back over his column. At the Nolin station enough of the people turned out to watch that Forrest's number looked three times what it really was to passengers whipping through on a southbound train—who carried word of a large, fierce and well-equipped Rebel army to every whistle-stop on the way to Nashville. Forrest carried his guns and men back to Tennessee without seeing a ghost of the Union Home Guard . . .

By December 28 the goose had worn off enough that Henri's pistols rode more comfortably in his belt. Forrest had parted from Mary Ann at Hopkinsville, and he and his men were riding up the road to Sacramento, following a report of five hundred Federal cavalry in those parts. The people in the little town of Rumsey came out in a state of high excitement to see them pass, children and dogs racing at the heels of the horses for a quarter-mile, and a young woman came riding out on a horse almost as fine as Forrest's own. All the men took off their hats as she overtook them (she was an able rider too) and as she passed Henri a blue ribbon slipped loose from her strawberry hair. Private Terry, riding a length behind Forrest, caught it with a shout. But the girl had eyes for the commander only. She rode beside him, loose hair shimmering in reddish streaks on the wind. Forrest bowed to her from the saddle, and for a moment their two horses seemed to waltz.

Then Captain Bill Forrest came pelting back along the road with word that the Federal rear guard was just around the bend ahead, and someone, maybe Captain Starnes, called out, "Will somebody send that wild filly home before she gets herself killed out here?" But the girl was gone; she'd jumped her sleek gelding over a rail fence and was cantering away across a field of corn stubble. Terry, staring after her, flourished her blue-ribbon favor in his fist, but the girl did not look back, and Forrest had forgotten her altogether, was hissing orders for Starnes and Kelley to leave the road on either side to flank the Federals, now forming to advance. Forrest himself drew out his saber with his right hand and stood up in the stirrups as he yelled for a charge on the Federal center.

Henri rode in his wake, closing his left hand over the reins, drawing a Navy Colt with his right. His horse was good but not the best in the vanguard. Private Terry and Captain Merriweather were well out in front of him, neck and neck with Forrest practically, when Henri saw the back of Merriweather's head come off just in time to duck and to miss it splashing into his own face. Merriweather crashed down dead in the road and his horse shied off into a thicket of blackberry bramble. Henri, still leaning low, got off a shot between his horse's ears, aiming as best he could at a clutch of brass buttons and a patch of blue, not seeing the effect. Forrest's saber had somehow traveled from his right hand to his left and was running through the Federal Captain Bacon as Forrest shot another man off to his right with a six-shooter. Bacon had barely time to fall dead from his horse before Forrest barreled into the Federal Captain Davis, a second too late to stop him killing Private Terry with his saber (Terry had ridden between the two at a moment when Forrest's head was turned the other way), too close and too quick to bring his blade to bear; Forrest struck Davis with all his weight and the weight of his horse, flinging the Federal Captain hard to the ground and riding through him till his mount tripped over another fallen Federal horse and fell, sending Forrest flying twenty feet forward over its head. Henri swept by, carried by his own momentum, firing his revolver into another melee surrounding Starnes; Forrest had already rolled to his feet, or had landed on his feet like a cat, and Starnes hurled his empty revolver at the back of a fleeing Federal—they were all on the run now.

Henri pulled up his horse and turned. Forrest stood in the roadway, saber sheathed somehow, training his pistol on Captain Davis, who clutched his broken shoulder with one hand as the other weakly signaled his submission. Forrest's face had turned the color of hot iron and the two little scars above his right eyebrow glowed like two red chinks in a stove, but his eyes burned liquid yellow. "A wild Indian!" Kelley yelled, bursting from a thicket left of the road. "No, a panther. My God, do we even know this man?"

"Name of the Lord, Chaplain," Starnes said cheerfully, dismounting to recover the pistol he had thrown. But Henri was thinking of something else he had seen. Forrest, still aiming his pistol firmly with one hand, had crouched by the still warm corpse of Private Terry and touched the boy briefly with the other, on the wrist just below the fist still gripping the blue scrap of ribbon, and when he did so his face was pale and tranquil as a dreamer's. Henri didn't know when it had time to happen but he knew that it had.

"I'm no chaplain," Kelley was saying. "A chaplain is a useless thing in war. I'll fight when the fight's on and preach when it ain't." He watched Forrest carefully as his burning eyes cooled and he lowered his pistol, finally accepting Davis's surrender.

CHAPTER NINE

GINRAL JERRY HUNKERED over a greenwood fire, turning hot grease in his iron skillet, tilting the crackling fat to the rim so the aroma drifted toward Forrest where he lay on a pallet of green boughs, resting from the wound he'd taken that last day of Shiloh. It was rather strange that he lay on his back since it was there the bullet had struck him, low and dangerously near to the spine. On the packed ground beside was a bare saber and on the other side a Navy six. His hands were folded over his breastbone and his cheeks sunken, skin waxy and pale, though Henri knew he was not dead. His nostrils flared slightly at the odor of the sack sausage Jerry was slicing into the sizzling grease, but his eyes stayed shut, shifting in dream beneath the lids.

Ginral Jerry worked cornmeal mush in a tin cup. Matthew sat on his heels beside him, balancing a bowl of pastel-colored birds' eggs he had been climbing trees to forage. Henri heard rustling in the brush, over the brow of the hill behind the hollow tree, and he got up to investigate, covering the six-shooter in his belt with the palm of his hand. Montgomery Little and Nath Boone were climbing toward him, one holding back a snag of blackberry bramble for the other to pass. Henri was a little surprised to see them there since Little didn't die till Thompson Station in 1863 and Boone, in fact, survived the war.

"My my," Boone said, "Don't that just smell good." And Little: "Y'all mighty handy at foraging."

Ginral Jerry showed them the whites of his eyes and said nothing, setting small white hoecakes into the grease. Henri looked the other way. Boone was all right but he was a little wary of Little, who'd been the one to point out to Forrest that Henry wasn't exactly a white man, back when their paths first crossed that morning on the Brandenburg road. His *Y'all* meant *you people* meant *you niggers* maybe.

"How's the Old Man?" Boone's shadow fell across Forrest's pallet.

"He resten," Ginral Jerry said. "He ain't got no appetite."

"A shame," said Little. "When for once there's something to feed him."

Ginral Jerry's eyes showed a little white. He pushed hoecake and sausage to the walls of the skillet. Matthew leaned forward and broke the tiny birds' eggs one by one into the hot black ring of bare metal. They bubbled up quickly and were done almost at once.

Ginral Jerry served a portion onto a clean shake of wood and ran it under Forrest's nose. When the commander didn't stir, he set it down on Forrest's chest, above his folded fingertips. Then he passed food around to the others.

"One?" said Little, looking at his miniature fried egg.

"One," Ginral Jerry replied.

"They ain't very big."

"They ain't very many of'm neither," Jerry told him.

Little subsided. "Lord we ask you to bless this food. And to preserve our lives for your service." He glanced toward the Roman, who whispered in Latin, eyes half-shut, clicking beads around the circle with his thumb.

They ate.

Forrest's portion rose up and down on his chest with his slow breath. Little watched the regular movement. Henri felt that the white man was not sated and that his hungry attention would soon shift to him.

He opened the cylinder on his pistol and shook the cartridges out in his hand. Idly he spun the cylinder with his thumb, peering as if he meant to clean it. At the end of one tube of oiled metal he saw a vignette of Forrest, raising the head of his dead brother who'd just been shot, and in another he assiduously turned a grindstone against the edge of a long blade. Here was Henri himself, diving out an upstairs window of a Louisville tavern, and there he was again, running barefoot and breathless after a young doe.

"Well, Hank," Little said. "I've oftentimes wondered."

Henri sighed. He reloaded his pistol, snapped it shut, and tossed the chip of wood from which he'd eaten onto the fire.

"What exactly were you up to that day we found you on the road?"

Nath Boone, squinting a little, picked at his teeth with a wisp of straw.

"You had the look of . . . a runaway. Maybe?" Little said. "But you seem like an educated man."

"Run away from where," Henri said. "I was born free. The same as yourself. Well, not exactly. I'm not from this country."

"I can tell that much from the way you talk," Little said. "But why would a free nigger want to run South?"

"You don't know where I was coming from, do you," Henri said. "The world is round, if you haven't heard that. And it's bigger than you seem to think."

Little opened his hands palm up on his knees. The fingers were long and slender, though calloused. "I'm just asking is all," he said.

Henri got up and walked widdershins around the bare top of the knoll. The blackberry patch had vanished in fog. Through an aureole of the mist, a long way off and a long way down, he saw Forrest riding, riding, one hand holding a six-gun high and the other reached forward to stop the wound in the throat of his horse. When he passed behind the hollow tree he looked down again and saw the weary remnants of the Army of Tennessee marching over winter-hardened ground toward the trench south of Franklin where six thousand of them were to die. The air was full of the reedy music of Old Ones.

Henri walked back into the circle of men. "I came to raise a revolution," he said. "Kill the white men and set the black men free."

Little's mouth had opened, round and dark. "A nigger rebellion."

"A revolution, I said."

"And kill the white people?"

"That's what I said."

"Then why in the hell are you fighting with us?"

"Who knows?" Henri said. "But I get to kill white people almost every day."

Little looked over at Forrest where he breathed softly on his bed of green limbs. "What about him?"

"I don't know about him," Henri said. "He's hard to kill."

"And me?" Little was on his feet suddenly, as if something had stung him. "You think I'm easy?"

Easier than you want to be, Henri thought, but he didn't say it. He felt sad for Little, who would soon be dead, and regretted having upset him. An Old One was blowing a flute in his ear, drilled out of one of Little's own rib bones, and Little couldn't even hear it.

Jerry was scraping his skillet with a bundle of twigs. "Y'all white folks done et," he said. "Now you mise well go on about yo bidness."

Little opened his mouth again. Nath Boone flicked his straw away and stood up. "Come on, Monty," he said. "Don't devil these people. There's trouble enough."

"All right, then," Little said. He looked at Jerry. "We thank y'all for sharing your food."

The two white men walked away from the hilltop. Two paces off the brow of the knoll the mist had swallowed them completely. Henri stood still, feeling his hands swing from his wrists like a pair of cannon balls hanging from chain. Matthew, sitting back on his heels again, was staring at him openly. Ginral Jerry was looking anywhere else. Forrest's breath was just barely audible, a faint hiss like a bellows sustaining a coal.

CHAPTER TEN

May 1861

AT SUNRISE Forrest stepped down from the squared-off log that served as a back step for his house in Coahoma County and strode out toward the cotton fields. It was already warm and he wore no jacket, just linsey breeches and a pullover shirt with the lace hanging loose at the throat. He beat a straw hat against his thigh as he walked.

When he came out of the grove of oaks that shaded his house he was walking down a double row of cabins in the quarters. There were twelve of them, sound buildings all, the gaps between the logs chinked tight and the plank doors and shutters properly white-washed. Benjamin had built them, one by one as they were needed, drafting help as he required it from among the middle-sized boys in the quarters. There was one of those boys might make a pretty fair carpenter himself before he was through. Benjamin had steadied up right well since Nancy had been returned to him, and they'd got three more children besides the one she'd been carrying when Forrest went to buy her back from Coldwater.

Women worked in their dooryards, cleaning skillets or cracking corn for the next meal. A shirttail baby with her hair braided into tight little nubs ran ahead of him, chasing after a cackling hen. That would be Ben and Nancy's least one, near as he could tell from looking at the back of her cornrowed head. Well now, what was her name?

At the end of the quarters lane, Forrest paused where Ben had raised a wooden gateway. There wasn't any fence or gate to go with it so it was just for show—one of Ben's own notions. The posts were set wide enough to pass a wagon with no trouble and the crossbar would be nigh on eight feet high. Forrest squinted up, raising the straw hat to one side of his face to shade his eyes from the climbing sun. Since he'd last come this way a week or so back, Ben had carved the joins of post and lintel so that two hands clasped each other at each corner. He would have needed a ladder to do that.

Morning glory vines were climbing each post from the ground. If they had been planted there a-purpose, Forrest couldn't say. The vines looked fragile and they had a long way to go before they'd reach the joined hands on the high crossbar. Ben's own cabin was considerably ornamented with such whittling, and so were quite a few of the others—he probably earned himself a little something in doing such work on the side. The big house here, still being finished, might have had such decoration, except that Mary Ann thought it uncivilized—said that it gave her the willies, in fact.

The men had gone out ahead of him, but not by much. He could hear the cadence of a song from the cotton fields hidden behind the next low rise, accented to the point where hoes chunked into the dirt in unison, pausing there and beginning again.

The banty hen had been chased clean out of the quarters, and now broke one way, toward the creek, while Ben and Nancy's little girl ran the other, picking up speed as she dashed into the open shed by the creek bank, built in the shade of two big water maples, where Ben sat planing white poplar boards for cabinets in the big house. He stood up quickly and caught her to his bare chest. The girl squirmed, looked back at Forrest and then away, pulled at the pendant Ben wore on a string around his neck: a half-hickory nut he'd whittled just a little bit, to improve its natural resemblance to a barn owl.

"Be still, now," Ben told her. "What got into you?" He looked at Forrest with the hint of a half-smile. "She act like she think you the booger-man."

"Hattie," Forrest said. The name had come to him when she turned her little round face his way. She stared at him a moment, then wildly shook her head.

Benjamin set her on the ground and gave her a tap on the bottom. "Get on back to yo momma then," he said. "Effen you don't want to act like folks."

Hattie dodged around Forrest's left leg and bolted back toward the quarters. He glanced after her for a second, watched the pale dusty soles of her feet flying up. When he turned back, Ben was just straightening. The zigzag scar came out of the close-cropped hair above his temple and down by his ear like a lightning bolt.

"Reckon she don't see too many big ole bushy black beards round here," Ben said. "Cep'n when you comes to see us."

A couple of the middle-sized boys had stopped pulling their crosscut saw when Forrest arrived at the shed, but now, when he glanced at them, they went back to it. The one with the best feel for the work was coming twelve probably; he had a pair of big soft ears, shaped like handles of a jug. Forrest ran his over the board Benjamin had been planing. Smooth grain and more than two hands wide.

"Doen a fine job with this lumber," he said.

"Mmm-hmm."

"Might need to put this job off a while though," Forrest said. "Why don't you walk over to the field with me a minute."

Ben's eye's flicked over him, quick a snake's tongue, then went out to the horizon.

"No, I ain't senden ye to chop no cotton," Forrest said. "Not even studyen that. Hit's a piece of news and the men need to hear it, that's all."

He turned and stepped out from under the shed roof. Ben pulled on a shirt and followed him along the curving, rutted path toward the first cotton field. They were about halfway to the rise that concealed the field hands when Forrest heard the saw teeth stop pulling through the wood. He glanced over his shoulder and saw the two half-grown boys trailing after them at what they must consider a safe distance. Well, let'm come on then.

"What news," Ben said.

Forrest tried to catch his eye. "What d'ye hear?"

"Trouble aplenty," Ben said after a pause. "Even white folks can get some now."

He looked at Ben hard; Ben was facing him head-on but somehow their eyes still just didn't meet. By damn that was a sassy remark . . . but it was true too, and Forrest thought he'd as well let it go. No telling what kind of wild tales might be going round the quarters and if he didn't want a smart answer he'd have done better not to have asked.

"Let's git on," he said shortly, pulling down his hat brim. Ben followed him to the top of the rise.

Thirty-some slaves were thinning cotton, fanned out over the long black furrows. The plants had come a good four inches high. Forrest turned left and walked along the outside of the split rail fence to a point where he could see down to the pocket by the tree line and the creek, where another handful of slaves was working. He cupped his hands and hallooed to them, and while he waited for them to come he stooped and broke a clod of the black earth with his fingers.

"Mmm-hmm," Ben said again, at his back.

A blue-veined earthworm slipped over his thumb and burrowed back in the loosened dirt. Rich land it was. He had bought most of it three years ago. He'd take a thousand bales off it this year, if not for the war. In spite of the war, if they all pulled together.

Slaves had straightened from the work and were shading their eyes to look at him. But they seemed uncertain if they should come. The day in the field had barely got started. Forrest turned, looked over his shoulder. A big iron bell stood on a post left of another gateway Ben had raised—this one with a good stout gate in it. He flipped up his shirttail and drew a pistol. Bracing right hand over left wrist, he took aim quickly and pressed the trigger. When the bell sounded the slaves dropped their tools and came running.

Forrest put his hands on his hips and stretched out his spine till two vertebrae popped. He had an odd premonition that a day might come when he would regret the waste of that frivolous shot. The sound of the bell was bringing women and children out of the quarters too, and Forrest hadn't really counted on that. But grown gals not nursing babies were in the field anyway, and the rest were coming quick, and would get there soon.

When they'd all gathered round he took off his hat.

"Hit's a war comen shore enough," he announced. "I know y'all bound to been hearen that talk. Well now I mean to tell ye the truth on it. The Yankees are fixen to come down from the North. They aim to kill all they can and take what we got."

He looked from one black face to another. Some looked worried, others unreadable. Men's eyes shaded by fraying straw brims. Women's heads bound in plain or checked cloth. He told off their names under his breath, his lips just barely moving. But for a couple, he could call their names true. They all seemed to sway from the ground, like rushes.

"The war's agin slavery, that's what they claim. If the Yankees whup it, they'll set ye all free. That's right. You heard me right. They ain't studied on what's to be done with ye after that but they aim to set the lot of y'all free."

At that there was a swell among the slaves and they turned to one another and murmured. He let that happen for close on a minute, then raised up his palm and they fell still.

"I've jined up already to fight for the South," he told them. "Y'all most of ye've known me fer quite some time. Have ye ever seen me to take a whuppen?"

Nawsuh, we ain't. Don't spec we will.

"Well then. If the South whups it, we'll still have slavery in this country. And that's the side I'm fighten fer. I'll tell ye that straight out and no doubt about it. I don't mean to have nobody waltz in from somewhar's else and start in a-tellen me what to do and not do—"

Forrest could feel the blood beating hard in his temples now. He stopped a minute, fanned himself with the hat.

"Now here's what I come down to say to ye. War ain't just a-comen, it's done already started. I aim to fight for the side I jest said. That's all they is to it. But any man among ye wants to fight alongside of me—when the war once gits over with, I will set that man free."

In the silence that followed he could hear a late-rising rooster crowing back behind him in the quarters. He thought he could hear water trickling in the creek a quarter-mile away.

"What about the women," Zebulon said.

"Huh." Forrest put his hat back on. He actually hadn't thought about the women. "Now that's a right reasonable question. Here's what I say. If ye want to carry a gal free with ye, be shore ye step over the broom with her afore ye go to the fight. And not more'n one to a customer, mind."

At that there was a little laughter and a louder rustle of whispering. Young Alma came up on her toes to say something deep into Zebulon's ear. Forrest raised his voice a little.

"Ye can't hardly lose with this proposition," he said. "The Yankees win and ye go free thataway. Fight with me and I'll set ye free."

"And effen we gets kilt?" Benjamin said.

"Then ye'll be dead." Forrest looked at him, not especially hard. Benjamin held the gaze this time, till Forrest told him, "Don't nobody live forever."

ZEBULON HAD SAVED a long section of gut from last fall's hog-killing, rescued it from the iron rim of the chitlin pot. He'd cleaned it and cut it into long thin strips and laid the strips to dry across the railing of the tiny porch that Benjamin had built onto the front of his cabin. He had softened the strips again and rolled them into slender, milky cords, then coiled them carefully to store away in a clean rag.

When he saw Ben coming through the twilight he went into the cabin and came out carrying the rag full of strings in one hand and the mostly finished banjo in the other. Alma set a chair for Ben, one of the two that they had in the cabin. There was just room for the two men on the little lean-to porch. Alma settled on a chunk of stone outside the rail and bent her head to a pair of britches she was mending.

As he stepped up, Ben took five pegs from his bib pocket and rattled them in his hand. With a smile Sap pointed to the empty chair and handed him the banjo. Ben had made it mostly himself, but all to Zebulon's directions; it was the only instrument he had ever made. He set the drum of it on his knee and held the walnut neck up vertical. He'd made the headstock into a horse's head, improving on the abstract form of fiddleheads he had seen. Little chips of white cow bone were wedged in for the eyes.

The banjo drum was a cedar hoop, with half a big gourd for a resonator. Ben had put all the parts together, impressed how Zebulon knew just how to tell him what to do. The only part Zeb had done himself was stretching the hide parchment over the hoop, soaking it soft and letting it temper up as it dried. He'd needed to get Forrest to give him a pass so he could go a dozen miles south to where there was a white man crazy enough to be raising sheep in the suffocating Mississippi heat.

Ben lowered the banjo head to the floor and, with the horse-headstock resting against his knee, began to set the cedar pegs in the holes already bored for them. Each peg was flattened at the top to accommodate the ball of a thumb. Two of the four he had to whittle a little more to get them settled right. Satisfied they'd turn and hold, he raised the banjo to his lap and pushed the fifth peg into place on the side of the neck. He tapped the skin head once, for a soft belling tone, then handed the banjo back to Zebulon.

No other note had yet been sounded, but little children began to turn up, to watch Zeb knotting on the strings. Little Hattie hung by both hands from the rail, peering in underneath it. Beside her, just tall enough to see over the rail, was Eli, Ben and Nancy's next oldest child. A few more children of the quarters were trickling over, drawn by the attention of the first two, and more came quickly, once Zeb thumbed a string and twisted the first peg to a true note.

He looked across at Benjamin as he tuned. "What you aim to do?"

"Do bout what?" Ben had taken another, bigger piece of cedar from his pocket and was whittling; you couldn't yet tell what it meant to be.

"Mist' Forrest goen to war tomorrow, what them say."

Ben looked away along the alley of the quarters, where Nancy was coming along barefoot toward Zeb's cabin, between the rows of other cabins Ben had built.

"I spec to go with him," he said.

Zeb shook his head and tuned up three more notes. With hammer strokes he sounded each against the fretless fingerboard.

"Boy, are you outen yo mind?" he said.

"What you mean to do yoself?" Ben asked him. He was watching Nancy as she sat down beside Alma on the chunk of the stone; Alma shifted over to make room for her. Nancy glanced up once at the men on the porch, then looked over the way, where a file of speckled chickens were flapping up to roost in a hackberry tree. Ben turned his piece of wood under the knife blade in his hand; the red cedar smell sprang up as he worked.

"Plant cotton. Chop cotton. Pick cotton. Pluck on the banjo eve nens and Sundays . . ." Zeb rolled an arpeggio on the four lower strings. "Live till I die."

He began tuning up the short fifth string, wincing a little as the note climbed higher. There was only one lone extra string, till he might get his hands on more gut sometime. The fifth string held and didn't pop. Zeb picked out a quick melody line, thumbing the high drone note. As he fell into frailing the chords, the women on the stone below began to hum the tune. "Follow the Drinking Gourd." The children who were already there smiled and nudged each other; more children had begun to come.

"Don't see what you want to go for," Zebulon said.

"Listen at what you playen, Zeb."

"Just playen. Ain't singen a word."

"You know you want to get free same as I do," Ben said.

At the word *free*, the grown folks who'd started drifting in the direction of the banjo all looked everywhere except at each other. Nancy and Alma hushed a minute.

"You be lucky you don't get dead," Zebulon said. He stopped playing and muted the strings with the heel of his palm. "Yankees get here, they set us free."

"You don't know they gone get here," Benjamin said, "and you don't know what gone happen effen they do."

"How you know the Old Man word be good for what he say?"

"Forrest don't tell no lies," Ben said, scraping shavings more urgently from the cedar. He was talking to Zeb, but looking over the porch rail at the back of Nancy's head. The knot in her kerchief, lying between the cords of her neck. "He got a mean mouth, and don't we all know it. Hot temper and a hard hand, I know it better'n most." Ben touched the scar that flashed out of his temple. "But I ain't never known him to lie to nobody, and neither have you."

A murmur of assent went round the group. Most of the quarters, young and old, had by now assembled, standing or squatting in a loose semicircle before Zebulon's cabin.

"Jerry goen," somebody said.

"Go on," said Zeb. "Sho Jerry goen. Jerry go everwhere the Old Man go. Jerry ain't never gone be free no way. Ain't no freedom in that man head. You give him that free paper yesterday—he won't be free today."

Having pronounced the syllable *free* four times, Zebulon pressed his lips together and started playing another tune. Alma and Nancy were rocking their heads and when the chorus came around they took up singing like they couldn't help it.

Wade . . . in the water . . .

God gone to carry the *wa-ater* . . .

Zeb broke off his playing sharply, as if the secret meanings of the song had spooked him. The women's voices disappeared. Doves called, like breath across a bottle, as they rose to the shadowed eves of the cabins.

Zeb played the opening run of "Devil's Dream."

"White folks' music," Benjamin said.

"Ain't no sech a thing." Zeb kept the tune rolling. "All music for everbody, what I say."

Sampson broke away from the group and into a quick buckdance. A girl a year younger broke away from the railing and did a little caper with him. Ben watched his oldest boy strut, thinking how Nancy had been carrying Sampson when Forrest went down to buy her back from Coldwater seven years before. It occurred to him that Forrest hadn't said he'd set a body's children free. More than likely he hadn't thought about that part. It could add up to a lot of folks, and that would run to money. But then there weren't so many men that had spoke up to go with Forrest so far, though Benjamin knew that a few more would if he himself decided to. If he was free, and Nancy was free, he could earn the money to buy his children free.

Zeb finished the tune and dampened his strings. "Bound to go, ain't you," he said to Ben.

"Man got rabbit in the foot." Nancy had her back still set firmly to Ben, so it was more like she was talking to everybody, or herself, or to nobody. "Lawd, don't I wisht he would stay here by me. Y'all know *I* ain't goen. I got chillen here. Chillen ain't goen. Marse Forrest ain't invite no gals no way." Another communal murmur went round, mostly among the women this time.

"What if I want to see the elephant?" Benjamin said softly.

"Ben," Zeb said. "They ain't got no elephant. That just a story they tells to tempt folks. Elephants is in Africa. Here they got blood, and they got death. They ain't got nothen else."

"I know that," Ben said, "But maybe I still want to see it."

Zeb moved his hand over the strings without sounding them. He peered over at the wood in Ben's lap. There was scarcely enough light to see by this time.

"What that you maken?"

"Don't know . . ." Ben was carving now entirely by touch, gazing out into the night sky, over the limbs of the hackberry tree. "Won't know till I get there and see."

"Well," Zeb said. "I reckon that's you."

CHAPTER ELEVEN

April 1862

LICK CREEK was a lovely spot—clear water running over reddish rock, and as they waited for their orders, Henri and Matthew rolled up their trouser legs and waded, their calves soon going numb in the bright cold water. Matthew seemed to have a sixth sense for which stone had a crawdad underneath (and Ginral Jerry was following on with a gunnysack, bagging all the crawdaddies Matthew could uncover). Henri was more interested in the creek stones themselves—so smoothly rounded by the long caress of water that they scarcely even hurt his feet, and some were bright and intricate as jewels, though if he raised them from the stream they soon went dull.

Matthew caught his upper arm and held him back, pointing upstream where something dark came turning through a notch between two of the reddish boulders—a stick, Henri thought, but then he started when he saw it twisted, swam of itself, undulating in the silvery threads of the stream. The snake was more than three feet long, and patterned with two tones of chocolate diamonds.

"Mista Mossakin . . ." Jerry said through a gap between his blackened teeth. He straightened, stiffly, laying a hand on the small of his back. The burlap bag trailed in the water to keep his catch alive. To the east, in the direction of Shiloh Church, was the thunder of cannon and crashing of small arms. General Johnston had launched his first attack on Grant there at dawn.

Henri moved forward, toward the next bend in the creek. Beyond the red rocks was a long oval of still water, its blue so darkened he knew it was deep. There he might swim at his full length, perhaps even dive. The water would be so cold his vitals would shrink within him when he first submerged—

Forrest was walking on the bank, stalking rather, slapping his hat against his thigh, muttering irritably under his breath, *I don't see why I cain't git no orders if they's anybody hyar as is FIT to give orders . . . them eggsuckenlowwalkenyallercurdogs. . . .*

Henri shook his head and headed to shore. He sat on a boulder, trying to dry his feet with his bare hands before putting on his socks and boots. Matthew was hopping toward the main body of their men, barefoot still, his shoes swinging round his neck by their laces. Only Jerry kept on upstream, watching for snakes and stopping for crawdads.

Forrest had drawn himself up before his company. "D'ye hear that racket over yon way?" he said, waving a pistol in his left hand toward the north, where artillery grumbled around Shiloh Church.

A few men piped up— *Shore we do*.

"*And* do you know the meaning of all the shivaree?" Forrest called.

This time silence returned and the men looked at each other.

"Them's our boys gitten shot full of holes over yonder right now whilst hyar we set watching over a goddamn crik—and this here regiment wa'nt never called for that—this here regiment ain't never been known for that—I will be *damned* I will be *goddamned* I will be *double-dog-damned* if I stop and wiggle my toes in the water when they's a good fight a-waiten on us yonder way and plenty Yankees to be kilt. Now come on boys, what do ye say!"

The yell went up and around them all like wildfire blowing over a grassland. The men got up and bounded for their horses.

"Boots and saddles." Forrest said. "Let's get after'm."

Henri rode in a pocket with Matthew, Kelley, Willie Forrest on his other side. In a few minutes they had come onto a high section of the Corinth road below Shiloh Church, with the Tennessee River just out of sight on their left. It was an inauspicious place to halt, as Federal cannon were dropping shells on the road and all the horses shied. Forrest found Cheatham, who had just been driven back hard from his attempt to charge the Federal artillery posts, one in a black-jack thicket and the other in a peach orchard on the far side of the field west of the road.

"We cain't stop hyar," Forrest said. "I cain't leave my boys under this fire. It's go back or go on. What say we get up a charge all together?"

Cheatham gripped a sore shoulder and looked around at his wounded men, slumped against wagon wheels or stretched on the torn grass below the east side of the road. "I cannot give you any such order," he said. "If you charge it will be on your own order."

Forrest looked at him. In the thicket of his beard one side of his mouth turned up and the other down. "Hit don't bother me!" he said, with a gesture of the six in his hand toward the thickets.

"Luck to you, then." Cheatham sighed. "It's a regular hornet's nest over there."

Forrest tightened the reins on his side-stepping horse and swung his arm down. His riders swept down the bowl of the field, horse hooves hacking up divots as they descended. Though the day was bright it had rained for several days before and the bottom of the field was a swamp. The Fedcrals were hauling their guns around quickly to address the new targets and some of Forrest's horses were going down to their hocks in the slough.

"Goddammit," said Forrest. "Git out of this!" His own mount uprooted itself from the mud and he cantered straight for the peach orchard, followed by Willie and about half the regiment, at the same time that he signaled the others to go the other way, toward the scrim of hardwoods at the other edge of the field, on the flank of the blackjack thicket where the other battery was. Henri started off that way—this direction put him at longer range from the enemy cannon, at least at first.

Matthew was still with him, and Major Strange now—he didn't see Kelley anymore. When they slammed through the tree line he felt a sting as if a snake had bitten his thumb but in a moment he had forgotten that. He could hear Forrest howling, half a mile off, as they fell upon the rear of the battery in the blackjack thicket, scattering the gunners and driving off the horses, some still dragging the caissons behind. A handful of Federal cavalry rode back with their sabers flashing above their heads, and Henri gritted his teeth and ducked his head and spurred straight into them, remembering Forrest always said a six-gun was worth a dozen of them overgrown cheese-slicers—*jest wait till ye're not but one short hair from the point a-tetchen ye and*—Henri fired and the first man went down—again and another empty saddle went by. The next blade scored into the shoulder of his coat but hadn't cut flesh before Henri had shot this Federal cavalier from such near range he saw the powder blast of his pistol stain the blue coat. Empty air before him and he still had three shots left! The fourth Federal, wheeling to return, would have split his skull with a stroke from behind except that Matthew shot him down and rode on through, face buried in the chocolate brown mane of his horse.

Cheatham's infantry was pounding up, shouting out gleefully as the men took charge of the captured cannon. They joined Forrest at the back end of the peach orchard.

"Hit's a hornet nest shore nuff and we done busted it!" he hollered. "Boys, we have got'm on the run." Forrest's chest heaved. A man ran up and caught his saddle skirt.

"Captain," he cried out, "give me a gun. This battle hasn't got no rear!"

When Forrest registered his blue uniform he put his hand on the Federal's shoulder. "You're a prisoner, boy," he said. "I reckon ye done laid down yore arms a'ready. Yore crowd may not have no rear but ourn is thataway."

He laughed out loud when the prisoner had gone, then suddenly went still. "Where's Willie."

No one had an answer to offer him. Forrest turned a semicircle to survey the ground they'd just passed over, where still warm bodies lay anonymous, blue or gray. Snarls of blackjack closed the view in most directions that he looked.

"Ole Miss'll have my hide if—" Forrest seemed to bite his tongue. His face had lost all of its color, only the two small pitted scars glowed red above his eyebrow.

"Henry, Matthew. Go hunt for Willie, y'all. Don't stop till ye find him neither. Rest of us got to keep up the skeer." He turned his horse, a speckled gray. "Come on, let's get after'm."

The battle sweat cooling on Henri's skin had an unpleasant bitter tang. He raised his throbbing thumb to his mouth. During their career through the thickets a thorn had run up under his nail and snapped off where he couldn't reach it. He tried and failed to grasp it with his teeth; the effort sent a jolt of pain to his elbow.

"Be damned to Willie," Matthew was grumbling, as their horses picked through the thicket back the way they had come. Henri stopped himself looking at corpses too closely. He only wanted to find Willie alive.

"You don't wish him dead," he told Matthew.

"I never said that." Matthew twisted in the saddle to stare back at him, eyes ringed with white. "Do you think he'd've sent Willie out of a fight to hunt for *me*?"

Henri didn't much think so, in fact. He was still hesitating when Matthew burst out, "I don't mean to miss this one—not when we're whuppen!" He spurred his horse in the direction Forrest had gone, toward the not very distant crash of artillery.

Henri rode in the other direction, though really he felt concerned for Matthew more than for Willie now. The white son was likable enough, but often reckless, and it was true he took a great many things for granted. Henri came into a clearing where some stragglers from Cheatham's regiment were stripping dead Federals of their tunics. Jerry was trudging diagonally across, gunnysack slung over his shoulder, still damp.

"Seen Willie?" Henri called to him, and Jerry replied without turning his head, "No I ain't."

Henri licked at his transfixed thumbnail. It didn't help. Ahead of him Benjamin sat on the box of the ammunition wagon he drove. His mule had lowered its head to crop at a patch of spring grass and wild garlic that somehow had survived the recent trampling. When Henri asked him after Willie, Benjamin merely shook his head. The mule dragged the wagon a wheel turn forward, pursuing the path of its grazing. Henri bit at the splinter again, and winced.

"Let me see that," Ben said, and reached for the hurt hand. His touch was gentle, warmly soothing. Henri became aware of the breath of his horse between his thighs. Ben's head cocked to one side as he inspected the wound. Henri looked at the scar that crooked out of his close-cropped hair and struck down like a lightning bolt across his temple and down past his ear.

"This'll smart," Ben said, unfolding his razor-sharp whittling knife from his bib pocket and in the same arced motion splitting Henri's thumbnail above the buried thorn.

"Bleu diable," Henri hissed, just managing not to snatch his arm

away. How ashamed he felt to be whimpering over a splinter while other men were getting their limbs blown off by grapeshot, just over the next ridge. Through a rip that opened in his mind he saw General Albert Sidney Johnston climbing through the mist toward the dead tree on the crown of the bare hill, still holding in his right hand the tin cup he'd used to direct the latest Confederate attack.

A long shiver ran from Henri's heels to his head.

"Huh," said Ben, displaying the bloody splinter he had drawn. "You got the sight."

Henri looked at the bubble of blood rising where Ben had cleaved his thumbnail. The new pain was fresher, brighter, somehow less troubling. It occurred to him that if Willie were dead he probably would have seen that too.

"Thank you," he said to Ben. As he spoke he saw Willie coming toward him among a couple of other young Confederate blades, herding a coffle of Federal prisoners, calling orders to them and smiling in the pride of his authority. Henri was too far off to hear what Willie said, but he realized he didn't really need to go closer.

Henri rode north over from one glade, thicket or pasture to the next, toward the hills above the Tennessee River, scanning the shifting horizons for Matthew. No battle lines had been clearly drawn anywhere but there appeared to have been hot fighting everywhere. It was late afternoon, the light beginning to turn amber, when he rode into the remnants of the peach orchard. Half the little trees were shredded by shrapnel and the ground was carpeted with pink blossoms that shifted, rustling, as Henri rode through. A little further on he passed a solitary riding boot standing by itself in a shallow ravine where Isham Harris had poured it empty of General Johnston's blood.

Henri set his teeth and rode toward the rumble of cannon on the ridge. Soon he could make out the gray horse's speckled and bluish hide moving along the slope below the Federal battery. A little nearer to him he saw Matthew sitting his horse and shading his eyes with one hand against the setting sun. When Henri rode up, Matthew lowered his hand and blinked at him.

"Go tell him Willie's all right, if you want," Henri said.

Matthew's face rippled as he thought it over. Then he steered his horse up the hill. Henri watched him claim Forrest's attention, saw

Forrest briefly lay his hand on Matthew's shoulder. When the contact had broken, he rode up to join them.

"Did ye happen to see General Johnston back thar?" Forrest inquired.

Not exactly, Henri thought.

"Polk? Beauregard? Anything at all as looks like a *commander*?" Forest squinted toward where some fifty Federal cannon were fisted tight together on the ridge. "Goddammit! I can smell the river. If somebody would just send me a few more men we could tumble all them bastards over the banks afore dark."

But instead the order came for them to fall back, and Forrest, grumbling bitterly, obeyed it. They camped a short way south near the banks of the river, just out of range of the gunboats that had shelled their retreat from the ridge of Pittsburgh Landing, where Grant's army was making what looked like a last stand. As dusk thickened, those closest to Forrest's bedroll ate crawdads hot and pink from Jerry's skillet, too ravenous to bother picking meat from crunchy shell.

Jerry dressed Henri's hurt thumb with spiderweb. At moonrise, Forrest clothed him and Matthew and Major Strange in blue coats salvaged from the dead during the day, and sent them to reconnoiter up the river. They met one post of Federal pickets who let them pass with scant examination. In the vague moonlight shining on the slow flat surface of the river they could see the brushy southern tip of the oval island opposite Pittsburgh Landing. Henri covered a bullet hole in the captured coat with the ball of his hurt thumb. It felt like all the crawdads he had swallowed had woken up to scrabble around the inside of his gut. Fresh Federal troops were ferrying across the river by the thousand.

"We got to jump'm afore day," Forrest said when he heard the news. "Else they'll do us like they done us at Donelson." He thought for a moment. "Like we done ourselves."

He left the camp alone and was gone for hours. The moon had traveled half the sky when Henri propped up on an elbow to hear Forrest muttering mostly to himself.

"Cain't find nobody to listen to me." Air puffed out of him as he settled on his back. "This battle's our'n to piss away, and we done pissed it."

TWO RAIN-SOGGY DAYS LATER, General William Tecumseh Sherman and his infantry command set out in pursuit of Rebel soldiers retreating down the road from Shiloh toward Corinth—abandoning all of the ground they'd won in the first phase of the battle. The Federals were four miles out of their camp when they came upon a long wide hollow strewn with timber. The trees had been felled in this long swale the year before but never hauled off to the sawmill. Bark flaking from them, covered with a fresh growth of spring vine, the logs lay every which way, crisscrossed just as they'd first fallen.

On the ridge beyond appeared a couple of Rebel horsemen. Sherman raised his glass to his eye. The riders didn't altogether look like white men, and that puzzled him for a moment, but they were Rebels sure enough. He had no way of telling how many cavalry lay on the far side of that ridge, but it hardly mattered. The swale of fallen timbers would make a charge impossible; his foot soldiers would certainly have the advantage there.

"Yankees," Matthew called, trotting his horse down toward Forrest. "Lots of them."

"How many?" Forrest reined his gray around, pulled down the brim.

"Fifteen hundred and maybe more," Henri said. "I don't know. They're still coming out of the trees."

Forrest coughed. "That's five to one on us. I wonder where in Hell they keep coming from." He had a hundred fifty of his own men on hand and two hundred other horsemen Breckenridge had assigned to him for the rearguard actions of the day. He began dismounting these men now and ordering to the cover of trees or boulders along the top of the ridge.

"Yankees can't ride for . . . beans," Matthew piped up. He was still astride his horse and exposed on the open backbone of the hill.

"Git down from thar, and mind out for sharpshooters," Forrest snapped. Then he stopped to look down the hill. "No, wait a minute."

The blue skirmishers below were losing all semblance of a line as they began picking their way across the mossy logs. And the Yankee horses balked at every timber, though they were only going at a walk.

"They cain't ride worth a good goddamn, kin they?" Forrest whispered, grinning at Matthew and Henri. And then in a shout: "Mount up, boys—let's go find'm."

THAT BLASTED CATERWAULING—Sherman couldn't get used to it; much of it as he'd already heard, it still raised the hair on the back of his neck. Or maybe it was the impossible disaster spread before him: two or three hundred Rebel horse flying down the ridge into the swale where his men blundered among the logs, flinging up great gobbets of mud from their hooves and leaping among the fallen timbers as nimbly as giant cats. His skirmish line had already been slashed to pieces; and now his regular infantry was on a stumbling run to the rear, with the Rebel riders hard after them. One of the Rebels, tall in the saddle, pistol in one hand and blade in the other, came riding far out ahead of the rest, guiding his speckled gray horse with his knees as the animal jumped one log after another, gaining speed as he reached open ground and bore down on the infantry battle line Sherman had hastily regrouped two hundred yards behind his skirmishers.

As the speckled gray's pumping shoulders smacked into the troops, a segment of the blue line collapsed and began to boil. Forrest had knocked down four or five Yankees with rounds from his Navy six before it clicked empty. The saber in his left hand whirled around and around like the blade of a windmill, till it snagged on a Yankee collarbone and sprang free with a jolt that numbed his fingers for a second. He drew a foot-long knife from his waistband—better for close quarters anyway. His horse made a tight turn on bunched hindquarters and now Forrest saw that his men had not followed him . . . perhaps because they had better sense. He was alone amid a thousand of the enemy, still cutting relentlessly with his left hand and using his empty pistol as a club.

"Kill that man," Sherman screamed, standing up in his stirrups so abruptly the horse shied under him and he almost fell. Others nearer Forrest were also shouting *kill him kill the Rebel* and then a trooper pressed the muzzle of his carbine against Forrest's side and squeezed. The muffled concussion was blunt as a fist banging into him, but Forrest felt his right leg go numb. That infuriated him more than ever, for what if they'd really done him some serious harm? He dropped the empty pistol into his pocket and used his free hand to snatch the scruff of the man who had fired and drag him up behind his saddle, while the left hand slashed at the fingers of a hand that had grasped at his knee.

"Will no one kill that madman?" Sherman howled. Forrest had now broken into the clear, and Sherman saw that his men were holding their fire in fear of hitting one of their own, whom Forrest had hauled up behind him to use as a shield. When once out of range he threw the little man down, shook his fist at him, spurred up and rode on.

Sherman hurled his hat on the ground. "How did you let him get away?"

One of his troopers raised a hand to explain, waggling stumps of two of his fingers. "That was no mortal man," he said. "That's the Devil."

"Sir, are you hurt?" Kelley called as Forrest cleared the ridge. The gray horse streamed blood from so many wounds it was hard to tell where Forrest himself was bleeding.

"I'll live," Forrest said, through his clenched teeth. "Effen I don't die."

Cowan came toward him. "Will you get down and let me see to your wound?" he said. "That leg's not right."

"*I know it ain't right,*" Forrest snarled. "Let me oncet git to Corinth and then ye can pick at it all ye want."

"Will you not ride in a wagon at least?" Cowan said.

"Damn straight I will not," Forrest said. "That'd hurt a lot more than it already does."

Cowan broke from him and came toward Matthew and Henri.

"How bad is it," Matthew blurted.

Cowan glanced back at the bloody man on the bleeding horse. "By the look of that leg he's been hit in the spine." He paused. "I wish you two would ride ahead and send for Mrs. Forrest to come to Corinth."

"As bad as that?" Henri said.

"Mary Ann's the only one can talk sense into him," Cowan said. "And if not, she'll want to bury him, of course."

ARRIVED AT LAST in the Corinth square, Forrest made to turn his horse back the way he had come.

"What are you doing," Kelley asked.

"I believe that damn Yankee has done me in," Forrest said. "I need to go back yonder and kill him."

Kelley snorted. "You've done all the killing you're going to for one day."

But Forrest was no longer paying attention to him, because his horse was melting underneath him, slowly collapsing to the right. Forrest reached down with his right hand and pulled his right foot clear of the stirrup and rolled away from the dead animal as it hit the ground. Lying on his back, he reached out a hand to touch the horse's blood-stiffened mane. Then he used both arms to turn himself over. The others watched him as if in a trance. All knew he would strike any man who moved to help him. Forrest pushed himself to his knees. Then somehow he was not only standing but limping toward the door of the hotel across the square.

"How in the Sam Hill is he doing that?" Kelley wondered. "That leg wasn't working a minute ago."

Cowan looked at him. "I don't have the least dreaming notion," he said. "But I reckon I better go try and find out."

MANY OF FORREST'S ESCORT spent the remains of the day and the evening lingering on the square between the courthouse and the white hotel. The whole town hummed with General Johnston's death and the fear that the Yankee hosts would next strike there. Few had heard enough of Forrest to feel much alarm about his injuries. Presently Benjamin came with two mules, noosed rope around the gray's hind legs, and hauled the dead horse out of the square, leaving a drag trail smeared with blood in the dust.

Mary Ann Forrest arrived on the night train and hastened into the hotel, greeting the men on the steps with a thin smile, not slowing her quick step. Dr. Cowan had not been seen for hours. Now and then Willie came out the side door of the hotel, all the jolliness drained out of him, furtively taking a few drags at a cigar stump before he hurried back inside. Henri watched Matthew watching Willie's brief appearances, without so much of his usual hostility this time.

In the small hours Forrest sent for Kelley to come and bring a pen and paper. Some speculated on the courthouse steps that Kelley had been called to administer last rites or to take down Forrest's testament or both. But Kelley, if he came out again, came by a different door. The first man out of the hotel at dawn was Ginral Jerry, shambling and shuffling, head bowed down (but then he normally walked so, Henri thought), eyes red and a little rheumy (but didn't he always look so?).

How is he? Will he make it? The men clustered round.

"He still kicken," Jerry said. "Ole Miss wif him now." He slipped through the others and walked toward the wagons where mules stood sleeping still in harness in a side street off the square.

The next man to appear was Cowan, raising a smashed minié ball high in a pair of forceps. The surgeon had washed his hands, Henri saw, but there was a crust of dried blood beneath his nails. The lump of crushed lead passed from hand to hand. "Is he going to live?" somebody said.

"I think so," Cowan said. "Ask me, he's too mean to die."

Cowan went into the hotel to sleep. On the outskirts of Corinth, the roosters were crowing. The first real sunlight was staining the hotel facade when Kelley came up to the courthouse and dropped a bundle of newspapers on the lower step. He raised a hand to quiet the men spluttering questions at him, picked up a paper and folded it open.

"Hear this," he began.

200 Recruits Wanted!

I will receive 200 able-bodied men if they will present themselves at my headquarters by the first of June with good horse and gun. I wish none but those who desire to be actively engaged. My headquarters for the present is at Corinth, Miss. Come on, boys, if you want a heap of fun and to kill some Yankees.

N. B. Forrest
Colonel, Commanding
Forrest's Regiment

When he had finished Kelley smiled faintly and handed the paper to Nath Boone, who stood tracing the words with a fingertip, lips moving slightly. When he got to the end he dropped the paper against his thigh. "Ain't it the truth?" he said to all. "Hit's nobody can tell *us* what fun is."

CHAPTER TWELVE

August 1857

MARY ANN HAD LAIN DOWN through the worst of the late-summer afternoon heat, but could not sleep. Where men perspired, ladies must merely glow, and yet she felt herself to be sweating like a horse through the thin sheets between which she restlessly reclined. It was near four in the afternoon when she began to hear the household coming back to life on the floors below. She sat up and arranged her clothing and went down. On her way to the porch she collected a basket of pecans lately sent to the Forrest family as a compliment from friends in Georgia, and a pie pan to hull the nuts into.

Forrest's sister Fanny was paying them a visit and had already settled herself on the porch with a bucket full of green beans to break. There too Mary Ann found Doctor Cowan, who sat on a rocker rolling an unlit cigar between his slender fingers.

"Too hot to smoke," he said ruefully, glancing up as Mary Ann came out to join them.

"Ain't it the truth," she answered, aware of her just brushed hair already going lank against her forehead. "I can scarce draw a breath."

She settled herself to crack and pick nuts, rocking gently as she worked—all three of them rocked, for the small motion stirred up the ghost of a breeze. Around the borders of the front yard a half-dozen magnolia saplings sagged, their limbs seeming almost too weak to support the glossy dark green leaves. A planting of grass in the yard had died out and the surface was going back to dirt. Too late for a watering to renew it.

Nut meats ticked against the tin. In the slave pens next door a commotion broke out. The sharply raised voice of John Forrest, a thump, a grunt, slap of a strap against something. A moment after these sounds had subsided, the high wooden gate of the pen creaked open and Catharine came out, unperturbed and moving languidly, carrying a twig broom. She came into the Forrests' front yard by the waist-high picket gate and began to sweep dead leaves and dust across the surface of sere yellow grass.

Mary Ann folded her hands over the nuts. "There are times," she remarked, "when I do wish my dear husband might take up some other line of work."

Bite your tongue, she thought at once, forbearing to steal a glance at Fanny. It was the heat that made her feel quarrelsome, she thought.

"I don't know . . ." Doctor Cowan raised a bushy eyebrow toward her. "Well, some of the family have thought so too, I reckon— You know your mother did."

"I know she does still," Mary Ann said, aware of a wry twist in her lips.

Cowan crossed his eyes on the tip of his cigar, then tucked it away in his breast pocket. "I won't deny I felt the same in the beginning," he said. "Everybody despises a slave-trader. It's like he was a man defiled. But then there's nobody in this country that don't depend on slavery—"

"Now that's a leaf right out of his book," Mary Ann said.

Cowan rocked, reflecting. "Well, but leave the slaves a minute. Consider this. You may buy yourself a fine horse. Trained up and schooled to the last inch, till all you practically have to do is think where you want her to go, and there she goes, before you even need to touch her with your hand or heel."

Mary Ann considered her own mare Nelly, whom Bedford Forrest had given her—the quick sensitive grace of all her movements. Animal knowledge. Half-consciously she watched the slave girl move through the yard, her back straight, head slightly inclined, expending the precise bare minimum of effort required to keep the dry broom whisking. Oh, and she was glowing, certainly; her sweat-darkened calico twinned with her hot flesh like sealskin.

"Who knows and cares for that mare the best?" Cowan said. "The one who uses her and rides her? Or the one who broke her and trained her to your service?"

How the Devil should I know? Mary Ann stopped herself from saying. Instead, feeling a cross knot tighten in the center of her forehead, she set aside the tin pan, stood up and dumped an apronful of broken nut shells onto a patch of yard Catharine had just swept.

"Hmmm. Perhaps it's a little too warm, this afternoon, for philosophy." Cowan smacked his palms on the knees of his trousers, then pushed himself out of his chair. "Ladies. I believe I may attempt a stroll."

The picket gate didn't catch, but drifted open slowly once Cowan had gone out. A lean tawny dog paused to look in, eyes dull with the heat and tongue lolling over black gums.

"Git, you." Catharine stepped over to shake her broom at it, and snapped the gate firmly shut as the dog trotted off. Then she returned to sweeping up the nutshells, with the same faintly indolent grace as before, expressionless. There was nothing about her comportment that Mary Ann could have fairly called sullen. The futility of her spite lumped in her throat. Though she might have given the girl some new command, she simply watched as Catharine swept her liquid way toward the magnolias at the far end of the yard.

"Don't you know he loves you?"

"I know it," Mary Ann said, before she thought to ransack her memory for where in the previous conversation this question might spring from—they'd been talking about horses, hadn't they . . . or had Fanny Forrest just read something straight out of her mind. She was Forrest's twin, and looked much like him if you took away the beard, tall and rawboned and with the same strong features thrusting from her face—good-natured but somewhat abrupt in her manner, "plain-spoke" as she'd have put it herself.

"But now sometimes I wonder about it too."

A couple of sparrows had landed in the shade of the magnolias now lengthening toward the porch across the yard. Mary Ann watched the little brown birds pecking in the dirt.

"Well," Fanny said. "*I* know he loves you. More'n anything he's got. More'n me or Mamma, or anybody really."

She rocked, considering; her beans were done. "Except Fan, I reckon. How he loved little Fan . . . Too much, maybe."

"Can a person love too much?"

Fanny didn't respond to that. Mary Ann was watching Catharine, who had tucked up her broom and left the yard, and was moving at her molasses-smooth pace back toward the board gate into the slave pen.

"Suppose he loves her?" Mary Ann blurted.

"Well," Fanny said. "Suppose he doesn't."

"Then he lies with her without loving her," Mary Ann said. "And which way would I rather?"

"Sister," said Fanny. "If it's a thing you cain't know, you might be better off not to think about it."

CHAPTER THIRTEEN

August 1864

THE RAIN HAD SLACKED a little when Henri came back into Oxford with a wagonload of corn foraged from the farmland east of the town. With Ginral Jerry and a handful of others from Forrest's escort he'd spent the better part of the day playing hide and go seek with Federals of A. J. Smith's command who were also scouring the country for supplies, and with better success since they were four times as numerous.

"Rosen-ears!" Lieutenant Dinkins called out brightly, slipping up to the wagon to peel back a green shuck.

"*Git* yo' dirty paws offa that corn," Ginral Jerry told him. Dinkins hunched his shoulders and pretended to slink away. Forrest looked toward them from where he stood with Chalmers on the lowest of the courthouse steps, his boots slathered to the top with tar-black Mississippi mud.

"That ain't no rosen-ears," he said. "That's hoss-corn."

"General," Chalmers called his attention back. "What do you mean for me to do while you are gone?"

"Play like we ain't gone nowhere." Forrest's dark eyes turned toward Henri. "Well, Ornery? Air ye ready to go?"

Go where, Henri thought. He said nothing. He had been riding around the country all day.

Forrest's whole face brightened. He grinned through his beard, then let out a wild cackle that brought every ragged soldier lounging under the eaves around the square to his feet, whether booted or bare.

"Come on, boys," Forrest whooped. "We're a-goen to Memphis!"

THE RAIN PICKED UP as night fell and the column moved west on the road toward Panola, two by two. Henri rode beside the wagon, watching water stream off the brim of his hat, trying not to listen to the growling of his stomach.

"Cornbread," Lieutenant Dinkins said suddenly. "By Godfrey, I smell cornbread."

"Leave your dreaming," Henri said.

"No, Hank, but I swear I do. Hot pone at two o'clock and not three hundred yards forward."

"Hesh up," Ginral Jerry said from the wagon. "You maken me think I smells it too."

But around the next bend of the road they came upon a couple of dozen women of the country standing under a brush arbor by a long trestle table, handing up pieces of cornbread to every man as they passed. Henri got a chunk the size of his fist. It had a drip of molasses on it to boot. The burst of saliva at the back of his mouth was painful when he took the first bite.

"Glory be," Dinkins said, with real reverence, before he stopped his mouth with cornbread. Henri forced himself to eat slowly. He liked riding near Dinkins, who was a cheerful soul. Scarce twenty years old, he still managed to live the war as a frolic. He never seemed to know that his feet were blistered to his iron stirrups, bleeding through the socks that were all he had to cover them. The rain poured down. Henri rode on, content with the bread still warm in his belly.

"When we once get to Memphis," Dinkins said softly, "I mean to have me a buttermilk biscuit."

IT WAS STILL DARK when they reached Panola, but the rain had stopped at last and the birds were starting to tune up in shrubs and trees by the side of the road. They stopped to shed horses and men too weak to continue. Forrest sent back two cannon as well. The two remaining needed double teams to drag them through the mud. They crossed the Tallahatchie River with the rising sun warm on their faces and continued north, a slingshot west of the railroad track. Men who hadn't seen the sun for days cheered up as their clothes began to dry, and started to brag of all they'd do in Memphis.

Above Senatobia, Forrest pulled up his horse and glared at swollen Hickahala Creek. On the far side a flatboat had drifted into a flooded field and snagged on a couple of hackberries in a fence row. Captain Bill reined up beside his brother.

"Where do you reckon Smith is at?" he said.

"Sixty miles back of us by this time," Forrest said. "I ain't worried about Smith. But we cain't set here and wait for this crik to go down." He turned toward the corn wagon. "Henry!"

In an hour's time they'd stripped plank from every gin mill and shack for a mile around and were making a bridge lashed together with grapevine, using the salvaged flatboat for a pontoon. Forrest spent the delay culling out more men and horses that couldn't hold the pace. He sent about fifty more back under command of John Morton, calculating this detachment should serve as a decoy if Smith had scouts alert enough to have spotted his quick movement north. In two more hours they'd trundled across the creek, toting their last pair of cannon by hand.

Seven miles on they struck the same situation at Coldwater River, a ford too flooded for them to cross. This water was wider and it needed more time to makeshift a bridge. A red fox came out of a canebrake along the bank and watched them as they worked. Henri watched back, a little uneasy. A fox was a shy creature normally speaking, and it was the season of hydrophobia. But this fox seemed in perfect possession of itself, sitting down quietly and licking its paws. When it had looked its fill it got up and went calmly back into the cane with the red brush of its tail waving high.

This bridge was longer, and thinner on planks. The horses went fetlock deep, boards bending under them as the men led them cautiously over, and one of the two remaining cannon nearly foundered the whole rig.

"Best leave this wagon," Major Strange said. "I do believe it's too heavy to make it across."

"I'll be *goddamned* if I'll leave this corn," snapped Forrest, who had been pacing the bank like a caged wolf for the last hour. "Horses are all half-starved as it is—they got to have a feed afore we go to Memphis."

"Suit yourself," Major Strange said. "This wagon is apt to sink and the bridge along with it."

"Unload it then." Forrest was already reaching into the bed, wrapping his long arms around near a bushel of corn in the shuck. "Come on, boys. Step lively."

Matthew was quick to grab an armload and follow. Henri did the same and others fell in behind them. Matthew was near as tall as Forrest, and had the same long back and long legs, Henri noticed, as he crept over the bridge behind the two of them.

"Any man drops an ear is swimmen to git it," Forrest announced, without turning his head.

In fifteen minutes the empty wagon had crossed and been reloaded. By dusk that day they were riding into Hernando, where the people came out hallooing to greet them, and not only because it was Forrest's hometown. Smokehouses were opened to them all over the place, and as the cooking began the men fell to shelling corn for the horses. Men cooked bacon wound around sticks, holding hoecakes beneath to catch the dripping.

Legs hanging off the back of the empty wagon, Dinkins chewed happily, jaws glossy with fat. "One thing I like about the Old Man—" He looked around to be sure Forrest wasn't in earshot. "If he eats, we eat too."

They'd come a long way in a large hurry, with twenty-five miles yet to travel to reach Memphis. Forrest gave his men two hours leisure. He rested between his two brothers, stretched on the ground. Captain Bill snored. Colonel Jesse fidgeted with a nickel watch and chain. Forrest himself lay with his shoulders propped on the shaggy bole of a cedar, eyes half-shut, with just the whites showing, though it seemed to Henri, who had stretched in the back of the empty wagon, that somehow Forrest was still seeing whatever was there. Matthew, who still showed childish ways once in a while, was playing mumblety-peg with a couple of Hernando boys by the light of a sliver of moon. Since Willie Forrest had been left behind with Chalmers at Oxford, Matthew had seemed easier in his mind.

When the church bell rang out nine o'clock they set off again, with much gaiety—too much maybe, as Forrest kept having to shush their singing. *Peas, Peas, Peas, Peas, Eating Goober Peas!* No sooner had Matthew been shut up than Dinkins would take it up again, or somebody else further back in the column. But four miles out from Memphis the fog from the river began to roll over them and they marched the rest of the way in strict silence.

All quiet on a Sunday morning, a good two hours before dawn. Forrest called his commanders in: Captain Bill, Colonel Jesse, Colonel Neely. In low harsh whispers the plan was reviewed. With ten men picked from the troop they called the Forty Thieves, Bill Forrest, still wincing at times from the thighbone he'd got broken by a bullet at Sand Mountain, crept further up the Hernando road. When the first picket challenged them, Bill called that he was bringing in Rebel prisoners. With that ruse he was able to get close enough to knock the Federal silently down with the butt of his Navy six. When they reached the second line of pickets, one of them got off a shot, and Forrest's men returned fire. *Yaaaiiiieee!* the Rebel yell went up; it always made Henri's short hairs rise with it. He might scream himself till his throat was raw, yet never hear the sound of his own voice.

Forrest was holding in King Philip, a restless horse said to be as good as two men in pitched battle. He jostled into the bugler Gaus and ordered him to sound the charge. But the horn was almost lost in the yelling and pounding of hooves. They charged right into a muddy slough past the corner of Mississippi and Kerr Street, bogged down for a moment, soon pulled through.

Bill Forrest ran right over a small artillery post and turned his horsemen down Gayoso Street toward the river. Neely swept through an encampment of Federals east of the road, routing sleepy soldiers till after they had run for some distance they rallied at the State Female College and began to shoot back. Dinkins came racing back from that engagement with a huge grin and a pair of new shoes swinging around his neck by their laces, just snatched from a Yankee soldier's tent pole.

Memphis women were cheering the raiders from their windows, throwing up their sashes and leaning out. Some even dashed out onto the street. One leapt up at Dinkins and gave him a buss, then sprang back abashed at her own audacity—a tousled honey-blonde still warm and flushed from her sleep, tittering around the fingers she'd stuck in her mouth. Pink nipples pressed against the damp cotton of her nightgown, looking out like a second pair of eyes. Ginral Jerry, who'd driven the empty wagon into town on the chance he'd find something to fill it with, gave the gaping Dinkins a nudge.

"Go on," he said. "Ax her if she got a biscuit."

Jesse Forrest pounded across Desoto Street to Union to storm the headquarters of General Washburn there. Washburn tumbled out the window in his nightshirt and ran like a rabbit to Fort Pickering, half a mile off on the South Bluffs. Colonel Jesse captured his dress uniform but without any general inside. Captain Bill rode his charger straight into the lobby of the Gayoso Hotel and wheeled, swinging his sword around the chandelier, while his men burst into General Hurlbut's room. But that officer, to his great good fortune, happened to be spending that night elsewhere. Bill's men tore into every room in the building, looking for Hurlbut and rounding up whatever members of his staff they could.

Day should have broken, but fog smothered the sun. It muffled gunfire, shouts and hard riding, to the advantage of the raiders. Forrest overtook Henri and Ginral Jerry and Dinkins at the corner of Beale Street. He was not in that state of possession he usually entered during a battle, Henri noticed. His eyes had not turned that wildcat yellow, though he did seem to be looking for something. Three or four blocks toward the river they could hear men shouting and women shrieking and glass breaking out of the windows of the Gayoso Hotel. But Forrest was looking the other way, at a woman languidly crossing Beale Street, leading two small boys along by the hands. A bigger lad trotted along behind. Henri couldn't make out her face through the mist, but no white woman ever walked like that.

"Tom," she called back in a low husky voice. "Why doan you hold the ginnal's horse?"

The biggest boy caught King Philip's reins just behind the bit. The horse tossed his head once, then subsided. Forrest turned his head to the others.

"You boys go on. I'll be right behind ye."

As they moved off, Matthew sat up in the wagon bed, and stared back at the boy holding the horse. The woman had moved close against Forrest's saddle skirt, and the pair of them were silhouetted in silver by the mist.

"That's curious," Dinkins was saying. "Most of the time he's right out in front of us."

"Well," Ginral Jerry told him. "You best not worry bout it."

"You look right prosperous," Forrest said, gazing down at the smooth dark oval of her face, shaped by the blue dotted kerchief she wore knotted to the top of her forehead. Tongue-tied for a moment, he studied her full cheeks and deep eyes, gone ghostly in the mist. She had pressed herself up against his booted leg so that he could feel the whole warmth of her front working through the leather, but the real heat was in her eyes when she looked up at him.

"An' you, Ginnal Forrest . . . you po' as a snake nigh bout." She gripped his thigh above the knee, and the thrill of that touch shot clean up his backbone. "All skin and bone, Mista Forrest." She smiled. Her voice had the same saucy lilt he remembered. Sound teeth and a sweet breath. He'd remarked that from the very first.

"Hit's still some gristle left on my bones," he joked at her. "A scrap of meat here and there if it should be wanted."

"Seein's believen," she said, reaching for his arm to draw him down. "So climb down off that horse and rest yo laigs a spell."

Forrest unstirruped his right foot and let his seat go slack. He could hear the commotion from the Gayoso Hotel still, and another big disturbance down Union Street. More firing could be heard from the vicinity of Female College, better organized, but it seemed to stay in one place. He swung down to the muddy roadbed.

His legs were a little rubbery under him as he came down, for he'd scarcely been out of the saddle for the two days. In the guise of supporting him she ran a hand over the placket of his trousers. "Aw now, you tellen me the truth!" With her free hand she turned the brass knob on the door, which opened inward, as he knew. He knew the layout of the room but it was black dark inside with the windows shuttered, and she latched the door firmly when they had stepped in. The niggerish smell was like home to him. The bed was real low, he remembered too late, catching an ankle on it and beginning to fall back, rebounding from the sagging hammock of rope that spanned the frame, supporting a pad of old blankets. *Aw now honey* she was murmuring, catching him up a little with her arms as she pressed him further down with the weight of her body pressing into his. Somehow in the dark she had undone her bodice so that her firm chocolatey breasts caressed his cheek, and had unfastened his trouser buttons too, reaching around to grasp the goat tuft of hair at the base of his spine—*thas you aright* she whispered, *thas old Bedford sho nuff.* Bowled over by the warm weight of her, he felt her slide back down his belly, and as he held the long ropy strands of her hair he felt her take him up into her long warm lips as eagerly as a hungry calf seizing on a milk cow's teat. Something Mary Ann could never have conceived. The piercing memory of his wife helped him hold back from going over the edge too soon and she also was measuring his every twitch with her wise tongue's point, withdrawing just before it was too late, cradling him and lifting his balls, mocking him in the same husky tone. *Aint you gone take yo boots off, Ginnal?*

You aint giving me no chance to, Forrest groaned, and that was true. Still holding him where it counted with one hand, she wriggled free of the rest of her clothing and threaded him into her, bucked once and rolled toward him, pressing his back into the sagging web and the blankets. Her heavy lips lowered to cushion his thin ones, the quick tongue darting, while both his spurs went rattling on the floorboards. Now he could hear cannon fire from Fort Pickering, and he thought how vastly his men were outnumbered here, how they'd need to get out right quick once the Yankees got organized, and that thought too helped him to hold on where he was, as her rolling thighs and rasping tongue were rising to the crux. He got purchase with one of his boots on the floor so he could turn the two of them as one and now was driving deep into the sag of the rope bed as both her legs rose up to wrap around his back and bring him tighter in— *Oh Catharine,* he breathed out then, but she only pressed her mouth against his bearded throat, and got her hand on his tail-tuft again to bring him even nearer. He remembered the fox, that afternoon, watching them from out of the cane, its remote composure, a vixen maybe, as if he were now buried to his hilt in her rough red brush, and like a vixen she caught the skin of his shoulder between the points of her teeth and clenched there, stopping her voice, for she never cried out at the very moment, there was only the rush of her breath and the clench and release of her every muscle, as his hot milk burst into her molasses.

Small arms fire came nearer now, circling in several minor skir-
mishes. Forrest heard King Philip snort and whinny and fight the
reins his small minder held. He sat up, fumbling with the fastenings
of his garments. She had one hand on his shoulder still, not to hold
him back but to urge him on. He stood up feeling for his pistols—
one had come loose in the bed and she handed it to him with a sly
smile, grip forward. More children were giggling somewhere, over
the sill of the inner door or maybe just outside. Forrest would have
liked to glimpse them in good light if there was time for it. King
Philip snorted, tried to rear—he needed no rider to go to a battle.
Thomas paid out a length of rein, savvy enough not to let the big
horse break it. Forrest laid a hand on his head as he took the reins
back, the bone warm and solid through the cropped curls, white
eyes looking up at him. Catharine still wore a warm satisfied smile as
she smoothed her kerchief back over her head. She stood embracing the doorpost warmly as he remounted his horse.

"Glad to have you, Ginnal Forrest. Stay longer when you come
next time."

JESSE FORREST came thundering back down from Union Street to
the Gayoso, chivying along a handful of Washburn's staff he had
made prisoner. His men broke into any stable they passed and
brought along whatever horses they could find. Women were still
leaning out the windows in their nightdresses to cheer the raiders,
or coming down to the street to run after them.

"No time to tarry!" Jesse called, squinting back over his shoulder
at the brightening sky. Half an order, half a recommendation. Bill
Forrest was rallying the Forty Thieves in front of the Gayoso. From
the direction of Fort Pickering, a cannon thumped.

"Where's Washburn, Brother," Bill said.

"He run off." Jesse held up the uniform.

"Well, that's purty." Bill turned his head and spat into the muddy
street. "Much good it'll do us."

"You got Hurlbut, I guess."

"I damn well did not. He never even slept here," Bill said.

"Buckland, then?"

"That's him back yonder I reckon," Bill said, jerking his thumb to the north, where, a couple of blocks distant, Federal soldiers were being called to formation to advance on the raiders.

"You don't mean it, Brother Bill," Jesse said. "We didn't get a lick of what we come for."

"I don't know about that," Bill said. "This ought to fetch A. J. Smith back out of Mississippi, if I don't miss my guess."

"We don't mean to wait till he gets here do we?" Jesse said, peering around. The fog was still heavily swirling, but had turned very bright; soon the sun would cut through, and they'd all be exposed.

"No, but where's Bedford?"

Jesse shrugged. "Wasn't he laying back with Neely and them?"

"When was he ever a one to lay back?"

A rhetorical question. Henri opened his mouth to speak, but Dinkins, who'd crossed a leg over the pommel of his saddle to lace on the second shoe he had requisitioned, was ahead of him.

"General Forrest was with us as far as Beale Street."

"Beale Street," Bill Forrest ran a thumb along the bone beneath his beard. "You don't say. . . ."

"We got a passel of horses and prisoners here," Jesse said. "I think we better get a move on, Bedford or not. He's bound to be somewhere."

STUMBLING TOWARD the river and Fort Pickering, General Hurlbut blessed his guiding star that he'd spent the night with a friend, and his lady friends, instead of bunking in the Gayoso, but he cursed the corn whiskey he'd been drinking till late, and which made his head hammer louder than the cannon in the fort, which were blazing at nothing since no raiders were near.

"Will you for Chrissake hold your fire?" Hurlbut yelled, and the guns hushed as he came to the gate. "They aren't coming here! They've got no artillery. You won't fight them off sitting inside this fort!"

Inside the gate he found Washburn, his face purple as a beet, struggling to stuff his nightshirt into a pair of borrowed britches too small for him. An adjutant drew Hurlbut aside to report.

"Well if that doesn't beat . . ." Hurlbut narrowed his eyes at the furious Washburn, and spoke to the adjutant behind his hand.

"They had him relieve me because I couldn't keep Forrest out of West Tennessee, but it looks like he can't keep Forrest out of his own damn bedroom."

FORREST OVERTOOK his brothers at a battery on the edge of town. They'd overrun it on the way in but couldn't spare men to set a guard, and the Federal gunners had returned. Their nerves seemed none too steady, though. Forrest raised a whoop and a holler and rode down on them with a Navy six in one hand and saber in the other, piloting King Philip with his knees alone, as the warhorse stretched out his long neck and spread his yellow teeth to bite. The gunners dropped their matches and scattered without getting off a shot.

"Brother, you look full of piss and vinegar," Bill Forrest said.

"Obliged," Forrest said, panting. A couple of the riders were dismounting now to spike the cannon, while others herded horses and prisoners down the road running south out of town.

"Whar's them three generals," Forrest said.

"Missed'm," said Bill.

"You don't mean it." Forrest holstered his pistol and cocked a hand on his hip.

"Well, maybe you run acrost them somewhere," Bill said, looking at him hard. He was as big a man as his elder brother and some few believed him possibly the tougher of the two. "Wherever you was at."

Bill's face was gray from the pain of his half-healed thigh wound, but Bedford was first to break the gaze.

"Well look yonder, would ye." He gestured with his blade. The Sixth Illinois was just turning the corner, in order of battle and stepping out smartly.

"Aye," Bill said. He swung his horse to face the enemy.

Forrest studied him. "Ye look about blowed," he remarked. "I'm fresher'n you are, I spec. Ye best herd them horses on down the road. We'll give these folks their jollification and be right along— Ornery!" he called.

Henri spurred up, as Bill Forrest, biting his pale lower lip, turned around and rode to the rear. The newly shod Dinkins came along on his right. Henri looked back once, a little wistfully, at Ginral Jerry, who was driving the wagon away down the road, now loaded with sacks of meal and kegs of whiskey. Ahead, the Federals came marching toward them, pale and sweaty, clutching their muskets. Left of their line rode their commander, tall on a big black horse.

"Whar's John Morton," Forrest inquired.

"You sent him back to Oxford," Henri reminded him. And the cannon all the men called the Bull Pups had gone with their commander.

"That I did. Well then . . ." But the gunners had figured it out on their own. The first of their two cannon fired, tearing a hole in the Federal line. As the sun burned through the fog, Henri felt his horse rock forward, following King Philip into the charge. Somewhere behind them, the second cannon coughed. Forrest's double-edged blade whined in the wind. Colonel Starr crashed down from the black horse, wrapping his good arm around a deep gash on his shoulder. A couple of infantrymen came to bear him up. The rest had scattered for cover of the buildings, some flinging down their weapons as they ran.

"Fall back," Forrest called, signaling. The sun gleamed on the whetted edges of his saber, braided now with blood. Henri and Dinkins wheeled their horses and retreated.

Forrest stood in his stirrups, beaming in the sudden sunlight. There was a joyful aspect on him that Henri had not seen in a long time.

"What's got into him, I wonder?" Dinkins said. "He ain't lost a horse all day."

CHAPTER FOURTEEN

September 1863

H E'S HIT." Willie's voice seemed to quaver as he said it, and Cowan, looking where the boy pointed, saw Forrest's long back waver in the saddle. Heat shimmer? It wasn't hot enough for that. Cowan's whole field of vision trembled, then came clear for him to see the blood-slick soaking through Forrest's coat and spreading over the left hindquarter of his horse. Forrest had been gesturing with his sword to troopers he had just dismounted on the slopes of Tunnel Hill, but now as he swayed in the saddle Cowan saw that he might fall. He rode up quickly and put his own shoulder under Forrest's left armpit as the sword arm sagged and Forrest slumped into him.

"Huh," Forrest said, turning his head to look at Cowan from an inch away, the light in his eyes abruptly fading.

"Good Lord," said Cowan. "Help me! Willie, we've got to get him down."

Willie was reaching, ineffectually, for Forrest's shoulder on the other side; meanwhile Matthew had come up from somewhere and caught the reins of Forrest's horse beneath the bit. Anderson appeared, dismounted, and took some of Forrest's weight on his own back as Forrest came down from the saddle. Cowan jumped down from his horse, leaving it for Willie to hold. He turned up the tail of Forrest's coat and pressed the butt of his palm against the blood spurt.

A bullet, awkward as a bumblebee, whined between his head and Forrest's and flumped into a cedar trunk a few steps up the hill. For hours they'd been in a running fight with two divisions under Crittenden, who'd crossed Chickamauga Creek at the Red House bridge . . . thus cutting themselves off from the rest of the Yankee army. Forrest had seen the golden chance to wipe them out altogether but he didn't have a quarter the force required to do it by himself, and no reply had come to his urgent messages to Bragg. Tunnel Hill was the first place terrain favored them to make a stand. Where they'd stopped now, shallow ridges of limestone jutted out among the cedars—pale chips of rock scattering from them as more Yankee bullets buzzed in from down the slope. Cowan jerked his head, aiming the point of his beard to a thicker clump of trees not far above them, and Anderson helped him drag Forrest toward this shelter.

"Look in my saddlebag," Cowan called back to Willie. "There ought to be some—" Willie was running up already with the saddlebags slung over his shoulder. The points of the little black mustache he had recently grown stood out against the sudden pallor of his face.

Cowan was probing the wound for a projectile and not finding one; he groped behind himself into one of the bags and pulled out a wad of clean cotton rag. A flask came out with the rest and clanked against the limestone shelf where Forrest was being supported as Cowan staunched his wound. Matthew's coppery face leaned gravely in, close against Willie's pale one.

"Hand me up that whiskey," Cowan said to the boys. "I think we got the bleeding stopped."

"Never tetched hit," Forrest said blearily. "Never will."

Major Strange ran up, eyes widening as he took in the situation, then dashed back down, calling out, "Hold'm, boys!" Troopers who'd been anxiously peering up to see the condition of their general lowered their heads to the work of fighting once more.

"Don't want no goddamn whiskey no-way," Forrest said.

In the course of the summer Cowan had been obliged to lance a boil on Forrest's backside, which he counted as his most dangerous duty in the war so far. Forcing whiskey on the man might rival it. He spun the cap off the flask with his thumb.

"You've lost a lot of blood," he said. "If you don't—"

Forrest fainted, slumping back into Anderson's arms, and a low cry came from Matthew or Willie, perhaps both of them. Cowan jammed the rim of the flask against Forrest's teeth and tipped it up. Some ran out, spilling over his knuckles, but some had run in for he saw the Adam's apple pump. He handed the flask back to Willie and picked up Forrest's limp left hand, running his fingertips to the inside of the wrist.

Forrest's eyes came open and he coughed and struggled to sit up straighter. "Ye don't need to go holden my hand," he said. "I ain't so bad off as that till yet."

"All right," Cowan said. "What if I'm just hunting a pulse?"

"I'll let ye know I got a damn pulse," Forrest said. "I ain't no baby needs a nursen."

"No," said Cowan. "But comes a day in your life when you need to let somebody take care of you if you don't want to die. And nothing you can do about it."

"I'm obliged to ye," Forrest said, "for that thought."

And never mind stopping another hole in you, Cowan said to himself. Behind them Matthew rose, then offered a hand to help Willie up. It was remarkable how the notorious hostility between the two seemed to have dwindled in the last few months.

Forrest clambered to his feet and reached around to feel the bandage on his back.

"I'll counsel you to let that plug alone," Cowan said. "You don't have a lot of blood left in you."

Forrest grinned at him. There was a bit of whisky-shine in his eyes, for he was truly unaccustomed to it. Matthew handed him his sword, and Forrest closed his hand on the hilt.

"Whar's my horse at?" he said. "Don't tell me I had another horse shot out from under me this mornen."

Willy pointed to where the horse stood snuffling at the stony dirt.

"That much to the good then." Forrest winced slightly as he stooped to gather the reins from the ground. "Ain't I done tolt ye not to let the leathers trail thataway?" he snapped. "Well, never mind. Hit's still a fight on our hands, ain't it."

Cowan watched him as he mounted, then began to repack his saddlebag. He thought of other times when there was nothing Forrest could do about whatever it was. There weren't very many but it hurt to recall them. He took a small dram of whiskey for himself before he put the flask away.

CHAPTER FIFTEEN

April 1863

THE GIRL SWUNG up behind him without missing a beat. In the doorway across the yard her mother dropped her picking basket and raised a hand to the corner of her mouth.

"Emma, what do you mean?" she said. "You cain't just be a-goen off with such a man as that."

"Momma . . .," she began, but Forrest had already swung his horse around in the direction the girl had shown before she mounted. She hung her chin over his right shoulder and pressed her whole long torso snug against his back. In her middle teens, she must have been, and a likely-looking gal, though he had barely looked at her before she jumped on, being more interested in what she had to say.

"Go along the back side of that branch," she told him, her breath teasing the whorls of his ear as she stretched her arm to show him a line of trees that followed a gulley eastward toward Black Creek. The sun was going down behind them, and the lush green of the pasture was washed in a golden light. He squeezed King Philip in the flanks and brought him into a long easy canter. The girl moved smoothly with Forrest's movement, like a vine wrapped into a tree in the wind. He remembered the young horsewoman who had ridden a ways with them toward their first fight in Sacramento a couple of years ago. This one would cut as fine a figure in the saddle, he was sure. But there had been no time to saddle her own horse.

When he reached down to check his pistols he grazed the bare skin of her knee. She must have hitched up most of her skirt when she got astride behind him. But she didn't start at the touch, or giggle as a light-minded woman might have done. She only tightened the whole of herself deeper into him and the horse.

For the last two days his mind had been burning, but now it was calm and clear. Out of the corner of his mind's eye he seemed to see a panther on a fast lope up the round of a hill among the gray boles of winter trees. He shook his head and looked at the real world before him.

"The ford's not far," Emma told him. "We had best get down, General Forrest, for the Yankees may can see us from the other bank."

She dropped down herself and walked out ahead of him, stooping just slightly to keep her head below the snarl of bramble on the west bank of Black Creek. There was plenty of small arms firing a couple of hundred yards downstream, where the Federals led by Streight had burned the bridge once they had crossed, using rails from Emma's family's fences to start the blaze. As the deeper voice of a cannon belled out among the pistols and the muskets, she parted stalks of cane to look out on the water. He pictured her mother stooping to rake the wild greens she'd been gathering back into the basket she had dropped. *Don't be uneasy,* he had told her. *I'll be a-bringen yore gal back safe.*

He drew Emma back by her sleeve and said, "I'm proud to have ye fer a pilot, but I'll not make a breastworks of ye." Indeed a few spent balls had begun to plop among the slender cane leaves where they were hid.

"Right there it is." Emma stood close behind him now, pointing over the creek to a point on the far bank where cane divided around a slope of clay. Black Creek was swollen with spring rain, running fast and deep down by the burning bridge, but here it looked wider and slower too. "There's a sand bar from one side to the other," she breathed to him. "Our cows come across it mornen and night. It's not hardly chest deep on a cow."

"Well, ain't that *fine?*" Forrest said, nodding as he turned back to where he'd hitched his horse to a sapling. He saw his brother Jeffrey riding up, under cover of the trees along the branch where Emma had brought him, the Spanish doubloon on its thong winking at his throat. Behind him, the ball of the setting sun dug into the far fence row. With Brother Jeff came Henri and Matthew and a handful of Bill Forrest's scouts, whom people liked to call the Forty Thieves.

"Ain't ye shown up at jest the right time?" Forrest grinned at them. "Right thar's yore crossen. Run the boys on over and keep up the skeer. I need to take this handsome young lady home, and I'll be with ye."

He mounted and stretched down an arm for Emma, who hardly seemed to need it as she sprang up. Again the old panther loped across a corner of his mind. All his men took off their hats as he rode the girl back the way they'd come.

"Tell me yore name," he said as she slipped down. He could feel eyes on them from the windows of the house, and he felt that she knew he'd heard her name before, knew that he only wanted it to hear it now in her own voice.

"Emma," he said. "There's a good man of mine layen dead thar on yore Momma's stoop. There's bound to be a churchyard round here somewhere and I wish ye'd see he gets a fitten burial."

She nodded, lowering her head a moment before she looked up at him again. The red light of sunset lay across her cheekbone.

"I wish ye would give me a lock of yore hair," he said.

Smiling, she lifted a chestnut strand, then cocked an eyebrow. He leaned from the saddle and cut it with his belt knife and wound the lock around his finger. By the time he figured out that neither of them knew what to do next she had broken away and was running back toward the light of her doorway as a much younger child might have done.

He tucked the lock into his watch pocket and rode back toward the creek bank with a fond smile half-hidden under his beard. It was good dark now and about half of his men still fit to fight had already crossed the ford she'd shown them. He shortened his stirrups to keep his boots dry.

The Federals broke within a few minutes once Forrest's men rode down on them screaming out of the dark. Streight had left no more than a few there anyway, a screen for his rear as he stumbled toward Rome, which was still some fifty miles away, across the state line from Alabama into Georgia. They'd been fighting a running battle for three days now with scarcely a break.

The rush had been hard on Forrest's command too. He'd set out with more than a thousand men but only six hundred had kept up the pace. They'd come more than a hundred miles since they started. Bill Forrest was hurt and captured at Sand Mountain, and of his Forty Thieves some twenty were still standing.

Forrest sent them out now to keep harrying Streight, while he remained on the bank of Black Creek to superintend the crossing of his cannon. The creek was so deep the guns and their carriages were completely submerged and he could only judge where they were by watching the angle of the ropes and obscure swirls on the starlit surface of the water. Someone had broken open a case of wet biscuit that Streight's men had lost in the haste of their crossing. Forrest chewed his square of hardtack slowly, absently brushing crumbs from his beard. In the trees behind him a couple of screech owls carried on their weird throaty whistling. The last of his men on the far bank had gone up to the ford that Emma had showed him, to carry their powder across high and dry. At least it wasn't raining now, as it had been for several days of the chase. He only wished it were raining on Streight.

In the morning they overtook Streight at Gadsden, where Forrest's scouts let him know that the Federals had had no more than thirty minutes to forage and round up fresh mounts. Too hoarse for shouting, Forrest signaled the charge by windmilling his left arm. Cannon brought a bass line up under the rebel yell as they galloped into the town. Streight ordered a few small commissaries set afire before his men made their hasty departure. Some of Forrest's men jumped down to help the townsfolk douse the flames. Unperturbed by fire or smoke, Ginral Jerry emerged from a burning depot with four sides of bacon hanging across his shoulders by the heavy wires that had swung them to the rafters. Two of them were burning at their fatty corners, wreathing Jerry's skinny hips in cheerful yellow flames. Matthew batted at the bacon fire with the remains of his hat.

"Let that alone, son," Jerry grumbled as he swung the bacon up into the wagon and began smothering the fire with straw still wet from the Black Creek crossing. "You want sumpn to do go fetch me that mule yonder . . . This'n here's about give out."

Matthew looked over where Jerry had aimed his jaw. One of the ugliest mules he'd ever seen was tossing his ax head in a corner of two houses. The "U.S." brand on his hindquarter was still raw.

"That thing is wild as a bobcat," Matthew said.

"Sho he is," Jerry said. "You think a Yankee know how to gentle a mule?"

Matthew did have a way of quieting an animal, and he had just got a hand on the mule's forelock when Willie Forrest caught its lip in the loop of a twitch and began dragging it to Jerry's wagon that way.

"You didn't need to do that," Matthew said.

Willie spat on the ground and said without looking back. "You'd of took all day the way you were about it."

The mule reared in the traces as Jerry set about hitching it. "You ain't hardly broke at all, is you?" he said to the animal. Then as he noticed Matthew and Willie glaring at each other, "Whynt y'all go find some Yankees to quarrel with?"

AT BLOUNT PLANTATION, fifteen miles out of Gadsden, Streight stopped again to try to feed his men and stock. They'd barely got their rations out when the rear guard was driven in upon them and Streight was forced to form a battle line.

It was mid-morning when the battle joined, just beginning to get hot. Forrest ordered a charge on the Yankee center, which bowed but a little and finally held. "God*damn* his liver and lights to the *Devil!*" Forrest screamed. "Sonofabitch knows how to fight."

"Amen to that," Kelley responded, and then when Forrest sent him a fishy look, "Well, what do you want me say?"

"We'll turn his right for him," Forrest said. He gave the order, but Streight's right held stubbornly as the center had, and Forrest called a halt, to wait for a few more of his men to arrive on the field. The Federals had him outnumbered by near three to one, though Forrest was pretty sure Streight didn't know it.

By the time they were set to press the attack, Streight had rolled up his line and was withdrawing again, leaving only skirmishers to cover his rear. They'd been skirmishing all the way across from Gadsden, anyway. In a barn lot on Blount Plantation, Forrest skipped down from his horse to inspect a scatter of cartridges fanned out from a box. The damp paper unraveled from the one he picked up.

"He's got his powder wet, God rot him," Forrest said. "Well, *now* we'll see."

Along with skirmishers the woods and pastures they crossed were sprinkled with runaway mules and with packs of the slaves that had been following Streight's camp all the way from East Port, some of them. Forrest told these latter to go home, if they could find the way. "This ain't no time to go see-en the world," he told them.

Presently the road they were following made a dogleg turn through a dense stand of pines. At the second bend the Federals had raised a barricade. Gun barrels glinted amongst the brush and timber. It seemed logical to turn from that situation and cross an open field where an invitingly thin-looking line of skirmishers waited in the knee-high grass just short of a low rise.

"Hold up," Forrest said. "We been bit thataway one time too many." He shaded his eyes with his hand and stared toward the horizon of the field. "Boone!" he called sharply. "I want you to ride a hunnert men through those pines to the left thar. He's filled'm up with sharpshooters, I don't miss my guess. Knock down anything blue and don't leave'm time to draw a bead, d'ye hear me? Mister Kelley, you do the same on the right. And *then* we'll see what's t'other side of that-air rise."

Once gunfire and screaming had taken a good hold in the pines, Forrest slapped his mount with the flat of his sword and led the charge across the field. The skirmishers melted away, firing hardly a shot. The five hundred riflemen lying in wait beyond the grassy crest of the rise were struck from three directions and demolished, their commander killed. Some few survivors ran pell-mell toward Rome, flinging down their guns and ammunition.

At dusk they pulled up by a copse of oaks on the crown of a hill. There they'd stay, Forrest told them, to feed and rest their horses and themselves. He was satisfied Streight had been buffaloed into another all-night march, so best they should be fresh when they jumped back on his trail next morning. Only he would need a few details and scouts to go ahead. Somebody had to be sure to beat

Streight to the bridge across the Coosa River to Rome. And there was a ferry crossing somewhere on the Chattooga River, which still lay between the Yankees and the Coosa.

"I'll go," Matthew said.

"Boy, you don't know this country . . ." Forrest looked at him, considering. "I ain't sending you alone no way."

"I'll go with him." Henri couldn't believe he'd just heard himself say that. In his mind he had already fallen off his mount into a blind ten-hour sleep.

"I'll go," Willie Forrest said then, forcing his voice husky and deep.

"The hell you will," Forrest grunted. "You stay right here by me."

Ginral Jerry gave Henri and Matthew a cup of warm mush each as they set out, tilting the skillet to flavor the cups with grease of the half-cooked bacon. They rode into the thickening dark, licking cornmeal from their fingers.

"*Nom du diable,*" Henri said, as he licked out the cup and shoved it down in a cloth bag strung to his saddle skirt. "How did you talk me into this?"

"I never said a word about you," Matthew pointed out.

"I must have been dreaming," Henri muttered to himself. He thought it over in the midst of a yawn. Like the rest of the men he had not slept more than a snatch in three days. "Maybe I'm dreaming the whole thing still."

Matthew's faint chuckle was interrupted by the scream of a panther well away in the woods to their left. They pulled up their horses and looked toward each other, though no feature of either could be seen in the darkness under the pines. Then Henri clucked softly to his mount and they rode on.

FORREST TOURED his camp as dusk turned to dark, swapping a word or a laugh with anyone he happened to meet. Men were falling asleep with their bacon and biscuit still in their hands. He reminded himself that Streight had been spooked into running all night in no clear direction, that tomorrow his own men would be fresh to hit the Yankees again when they caught them.

By the campfire Ginral Jerry sat with his head thrown back against the bole of pine, snoring, though the whites of his eyes showed a little. Willie lay near him, feigning sleep. Forrest squinted at him for a second, judged the boy would be asleep for real in another two or three minutes or so.

He stretched on the blanket Jerry had unrolled for him, shifting hip and shoulders to loosen the sand underneath. Was there something to think about? No, it would keep.

Forrest twitched and smiled in his sleep. His hard hand thumped the dirt beyond the blanket's edge. Sitting with his knees drawn up, Willie studied him cautiously until he had stilled. A cloud of mosquitoes hovered over Forrest's head, looking for a way in through wild hair and beard. Willie got up and crept barefoot toward the horses, his boots clamped under one elbow and his pistol belt in the other hand.

The panther slipped from tree to tree through Forrest's dream. On some other ridge the dogs were singing, but Forrest was nearer to his prey than the dogs were, and he could see plain as day despite the dark. That was because he was dreaming, of course. While his aunt inspected the dressing of the wounds on his mother's back, Bedford set his mouth in a pale line, lifted the octagon-barreled rifle and the powder horn down from the pegs, and went on the big cat's trail without a word, though his aunt called for him not to go. Sister Fanny knew better than to say anything, and the least ones were busy playing with the chicks on the puncheon floor. His mother said nothing. She was lying facedown with her chin hanging over the edge of the pallet, her eyes big and dark, biting her lower lip against the sting of the turpentine on the red furrows the panther had plowed down her back.

Outside the dogs found sign at once and raced after it bugling, but Bedford scarcely attended to their racket. It seemed to him that there was a clear lucid filament passing through the woods to join his mind to the mind of the panther so that he already knew when and where the animal would be brought to bay and had only to keep walking steadily toward that time and place, his eyes as wide and round as the moon would have been. But it was a moonless night.

·   ·   ·

"HELL AND I wasn't shore it was you!" Willie said when he found Henri and Matthew in a clearing. "It's loose niggers running all over these woods."

Henri picked out Matthew's profile against a patch of starlit sky. The boy's lower jaw stuck out a little from the strain of clenching his teeth.

"Well, it's true," Willie said to their backs.

They rode on through a silence that slowly surrendered its edge. Thirty minutes on, Henri's horse raised its head and flared its nostrils.

"We're not far from the river," Willie said quietly, and Henri guessed he could smell the water too.

It was Willie too who picked up the first flicker of movement by the boulder on the bank, or maybe he heard something, smelled something—of a sudden his whole body lined up behind the barrel of his pistol like a bird dog throws its whole self into its pointing nose. A man stood up slowly from the rock with his empty hands upraised and his head lowered. Against the dim quicksilver sheen of the Chattooga they could all see his body shaking.

"Massa!" The voice trembling too. "We ain't go to do it. It was deh Yankees . . ."

There was the softer speech of the deepest Deep South, somewhat unaccustomed to Henri's ear still. He strained his eyes against the shadow of the rock. There was something else there and Matthew had trained his pistol on it. Henri got down from his horse and struck a light. A woman sat in the shelter of the boulder, cradling a baby in a cloth sling against her breast. She was very young, and the child not three weeks old.

"Put up those pistols," he told the boys, and cupped the flame to shine on his own face. "Stop acting like a slave," he said. "I'm no man's master but my own."

"I *is* a slave," the man said. But he straightened his back and stopped shaking.

Henri nodded to the woman by the rock, and snuffed his light. "Have you been with Colonel Streight?"

"Yassuh," the man said. "Whole lotta folkses gone with him at fust. He say he gone care us to freedom." The man looked out across the water. "He cain't care nobody nowheh now. Half dem hoss sojahs done landed on dey feets. Wo' out till they cain't keep they eyes open no mo'." He laughed softly. "Dem mules dey got too mean to tote'm no way. And don't you know dey jess plum tuckered. I seen one yestiddy walk spang into a tree."

"Where are you from?" Henri asked.

"Peck's plantation. Over to Gadsden." The man shrugged. "We'd go back theh now if we known the way." He looked at Henri, eyes narrowing slightly. "Who y'all with?"

"Bedford Forrest."

"*Bedford Forrest?* He the wust man in all deh state. What dem seh. In all deh South, dey do seh."

Henri smiled in the dark. "I'd rather be with him than against him."

"Dem Yankees do seh Forrest after'm."

"They're right about one thing anyway," Willie said from the saddle.

"Which way's the ferry from here," Henri said, and the man pointed east along the river. Out of the darkness the panther screamed again but the voice was cut off midway by a shot. Henri shuddered.

"Rabbit run ovah yo' grave," the man said, looking at Henri with the same curiosity. If anyone else had heard the sound they gave no sign.

AT LAST HE FOUND the big cat knotted in a high crotch of a leafless oak, just below the crown of the ninth hill he'd climbed since leaving the cabin. He sat cross-legged below the tree, the long rifle sticking straight up from his folded knees, waiting for the light to come. Presently the dogs caught up with him; he calmed them and made them wait quietly as he. At dawn the panther gathered itself, focused its hot yellow eyes. Its smell grew muskier. Bedford stood and leveled the gun as the panther screamed and flung itself at him. The dead weight bowled him over, one claw tearing a gash on his forearm, though he'd hit it square between the eyes and it was just convulsion working now. As the dogs raced a yelping circle around them he cut the cat's throat and, deliciously, washed in the blood.

HENRI HELD the horses on the bank while Matthew and Willy, cooperating smoothly for once in their vexatious lives, poled the ferry midstream. They'd just begun to swim back to shore when Henri thought he heard hoofbeats away in the woods to the west. He scurried along the bank, not daring to call, beckoning furiously, and uselessly since the boys had their heads down and couldn't see him. Sleek as otter they came out of the water and Henri hurried them and the horses into a clump of cedars, seconds before Streight's scouts appeared on the riverbank.

Two hundred yards downriver, the ferryboat struck a snag and began to rotate as it drifted away. The Federal scouts stared after it dolefully. "There's supposed to be a bridge at Gaylesville," one of them said.

AT NINE O'CLOCK the next morning Forrest overtook Streight at Lawrence Plantation, where he'd stopped to try to feed his mounts and men. The Federals were inside twenty miles of Rome but one of Forrest's detachments had beaten them to the bridge there. When Streight ordered his men into a battle line, they lay down on the ground and went to sleep, scarcely disturbed by the balls of Confederate skirmishers buzzing over like low-flying bumblebees.

"He's a hard man to whup," Forrest said, all the same. "Let's see cain't we fox him." The numbers were still running a long way against him, though he knew Brother Bill and others who'd been captured would do all they could to inflate the enemy's idea of his strength.

He looked behind him. What men he had left were drawn up in cover of a fringe of trees on a low ridge. To the left was a space where a gap in the tree line left about fifteen yards of bare hilltop. Forrest turned to Henri with a grin.

"Ornery!" he said. "How many cannon has kept up?"

Henri didn't want to answer. Over his shoulder, Matthew spoke up: "Two."

The shadow of a frown flicked across Forrest's face. "Hit don't matter," he said, and again showed his teeth. "I want ye to bring'm acrost that knob whar the Yankees can see. And I don't mean just the one time neither."

Streight's men, Forrest saw when he went in to parley, were so beat they lay facedown snoring in the mud and the officers kicking them could not get them up. Streight himself looked like he might have some fight in him yet. He was burlier than Forrest, though not as tall, with a thin mustache and a heavy black beard. His hair receded on either side of a high pale forehead, leaving an island in the middle. Maybe his hair had been falling out faster the last few days, Forrest hoped. But there was a set to Streight's blunt features that put him in mind of a snapping turtle.

"I won't surrender unless you show me your force," he said.

"That'll be blood on your head, then," Forrest said. "Yore own boys' blood. I got men enough to whup ye outen yore boots."

He shifted his weight to his heels as he saw Streight was peering over his shoulder. He'd set his back to his own line, so that Streight could see the progress of his supposed artillery, and by now the single pair of cannon must have crossed that gap more than a dozen times. Forrest's officers had amplified the stratagem by marching a few dozen men around the same circuit, till their numbers appeared to mount in the hundreds.

"All right, then," Streight breathed.

"That's the way," Forrest said, and pointed to a tree. "Ye can jest have yore boys stack their guns right thar."

There were not quite four hundred of Forrest's men who had kept up with him still, and when they came forward to take charge of the captured arms, Streight dashed his hat onto the ground. "Give me back my guns and we'll fight it out."

Forrest laughed and tapped him on the shoulder.

"You tricked me," Streight said bitterly. "You lied."

"I'll tell ye what." Forrest's voice hardened. "I never ast ye to come down here no-way. I'm sorry if ye feel ye been hard used."

CHAPTER SIXTEEN

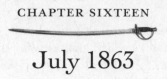

July 1863

Wʜᴇɴ ᴘᴏssɪʙʟᴇ Henri liked to find a rock to sleep on, though of course he often couldn't do it. But there were plenty of limestone shelves all over North Georgia and North Alabama and West Tennessee. If it was dry he didn't mind the hardness of it, and he believed a stone pallet gave him a little advantage over whatever might come crawling while he slept. One dawn he'd opened his eyes on the sight of Nath Boone cautiously pouring a copperhead out of his boot. Another time it was a shout that roused him and there was Willie Forrest, gabbling and shuddering as he flung a foot-long writhing red millipede from his clothes.

If Henri slept well, the slab of stone would turn beneath him, rising and falling like a plank on billows of the ocean, or even sail away into the wind, so that he dreamed the drifting flight of a fringed palm leaf, long enough and plenty for him to stretch out his whole body on the air. There were no such leaves where he slept now, but he knew them well in the country he came from. They had leaves like that in Louisiana too.

Often when he left a dream like that it took more than a moment for him to understand where he had landed in the living world. This morning they were riding hard, but he didn't feel the verve of pursuit. They must not be chasing then. He began to feel sure that they were running. Here was a town of some description. Cowan, Tennessee, in fact—clawed out of not much in the Cumberland foothills about ten years before, called into being by a railroad coming through. Forrest's wife's family had been on this ground for fifty years or so, when there were farms and not much town. Before that it was Indians.

The riders splashed across a fork of Boiling Creek, and soon after clattered over the railroad track. A ways out of Cowan, a tunnel had been blasted through the mountain to let the railroad through, and the last few days there had been talking of blowing it up, so as to stop the Yankees using it to chase Bragg south to Chattanooga. But then the Confederates needed that passway just as much. "Hit's more than a notion to tear that thang down," Forrest said, "and builden it back won't be no easier."

They rode by the log courthouse, not stopping to parley. A clerk in his shirtsleeves popped out the door and stood staring after them, arms akimbo—then turned and raised one hand to shade his eyes as he looked back along the way they had come. Then he darted inside and banged the door. Others in the hamlet were barring shut their houses, reasoning that Yankees must be hard on the heels of such a precipitate Confederate flight.

The last few days they'd been fighting running battles with the forward-most detachments of Rosecrans's Federal cavalry. Fighting and running. Forrest liked running into the thick of the enemy—not away. But Bragg and his whole army had been outmaneuvered and flushed from the East Tennessee Valley; Bragg's command was scuttling south across the Tennessee River to find shelter in the mountains back of Chattanooga. At the evening halt, Forrest would draw Bragg's name in the dirt with the toe of his boot and spit on the word before he slept. "What a sorry ass they done give me to cover." He said that like it was a prayer.

They all slept light, and not for long, so oftentimes Henri couldn't find a rock to suit him and would only stretch in the wormy dirt for a black inky blotting of an hour or two. One-quarter roused by the thumping of boots and saddles, he might ride for a mile or more before he understood just where in the waking world he was. The fringed palm leaf bore him away toward a thing that hadn't happened yet, when they would be fighting a hard battle near the banks of the Tombigbee River, in hot pursuit of Sooy Smith. Just over the bridge, Forrest crossed paths with one of his own privates who'd flung away his gun and gear and was running full-tilt and fear-stricken away from the fight as fast as his frantic legs would carry him. Forrest pounced from his horse and caught the fugitive by the scruff of his neck and threw him down, then broke a green black-berry cane to thrash him with, not caring for the thorns tearing his own palm. When he was satisfied with the switching he yanked the soldier to his feet and shoved him toward the battle again: "Git on, and goddamn ye! Ye'd as well get kilt over thar as here and a lot more comfortable too, I'll warrant." And by then the soldier seemed happy enough to rush back into the fray barehanded.

Another day that was yet to come, Forrest would be reclining on his coat, which he'd spread as a ground cloth, propped up on his elbows and turned on one hip (for his backside was all broken out in boils). He would go thin as a rake that summer, bones thrusting out through the skin of his face, eyes flickering yellow-green like ghost-lights in a swamp.

At dusk he stood up, shrugged into his coat, and in the company of Sam Donelson rode over to scout the Yankees at Verona. Under cover of darkness they rode all through the camp, counting wagons and guns at their leisure and with such a boldness no one thought to challenge them. They'd adopted no disguise but the poor light hid their Rebel gray. The two of them were on their way out when finally a dozen Federal pickets called them to halt. Forrest raised his voice to shout HOW DARE YOU ARREST YOUR COMMANDING OFFI-CER! and in the split second of the pickets' hesitation he and Donel-son laid on the spurs and rode over them, wrapped tight to their horses' necks like a pair of wild Indians and Forrest's tailbone stick-ing up high in the wind as the minié balls showered down all around them. When they were once out of range and had caught their breath, Lieutenant Donelson remarked that the scrape had been a mite close for comfort. Forrest shot him a yellow grin through the dark and said, "If a bullet had jest of bust one of these *godforsaken devilish boils,* I might have got me a little relief."

Today as they cantered through the last outskirts of Cowan they passed a tall rawboned woman standing in her dooryard, pounding shelled corn in a dugout mortar with a pestle half again as long as she was tall. As he drew level with the cabin Forrest's head swiveled around to regard her. She raked a hank of hair from her face and flung out him. "Whynt ye stand and fight like a man, stead of run-nen away like a rascally dog? I wisht Ole Forrest was here, I do. Ole

Forrest'd make ye fight!" They'd gone another half a mile before Anderson cleared dust from his throat to speak. "The cat has got Ole Forrest's tongue, I reckon."

Forrest raised his eyes to the wooded ridge of their horizon and smiled in the tatters of his beard. "Ole Forrest don't want to git whupped with that fence post she's handlen," he said, and they rode on.

CHAPTER SEVENTEEN

June 1854

I T WAS SOMETIME after midnight when Forrest came out of the gambling house, but maybe, he hoped, not very long after. There was not light enough to see his watch, but at least he did still have his watch. He walked over to the riverfront for the stirring of air on the water. Someone hissed at him from the shadow of a low shed.

Hi you! Step over here a minute.

Forrest stopped, searching toward the voice. He stepped into the shadow of a building behind him, to hide his silhouette. One of the men across the way stepped clear of the shed and beckoned. Forrest paid gold coins through the fingers of his right hand in his pocket while with his left he touched the grip of a pistol in his waistband and then settled his grasp on the haft of his long knife—just as deadly and a whole lot quieter. He could see two of them now, just their heads and shoulders visible against the glow of slow-moving river behind them. A pale patch at the throat of one, a cravat maybe. These riverboat agents dressed like dandies oftentimes. They came and went like driftwood on the stream. There might have been a third man in the shadow of the shed. Come on, he thought, raising a heel to the sill behind him, setting himself for the first shock, Come ahead if ye mean to come. He felt keen, alert, the master of himself. He'd quit for once when he was ahead, and it would need more than a swarm of these river rats to rob him of his winnings. But the rats decided to stay where they were, whispering and scrabbling in the dark.

Forrest turned the corner and walked back into town. At the next corner he stopped and looked back once, then released his hold on his knife and went on, turning gold pieces over in his pocket. When he came in view of his house and saw the lamp still burning in the sickroom, his bubble of elation burst. He would have liked to go in the back gate and sit by himself a while maybe, on the edge of the cistern among the nigger pens. Aunt Sarah might come out and bring him water then. But the white folks had already seen him, looking down from his front porch.

The eerie twittering of a screech owl in a tree branch over the porch roof unnerved him rather, though it was only an owl. Resolutely he climbed the steps. His brother John's eyes were shiny with laudanum. Doctor Cowan's looked exhausted but clear.

"No better," Forrest said.

Cowan only shook his head at first. "She's awful weak," he said at last. "I'm sorry."

Forrest went into the house, set his hat on the rack and straightened his jacket. He touched his weapons and his gold, but felt no reassurance from them. He went up the stairs to the second floor, empty hands swinging.

"Don't touch her." Mary Ann's voice was cold as winter stone. "I won't have your black hands on her."

He could see Catharine, standing in the doorway, lamplight soft on the glossy curve of her cheek, her kerchief neat above her brows, eyes empty, mouth expressionless—she was always so when so rebuked.

"Get out," Mary Ann said.

Catharine turned, walked past him, down the stairs. He watched her away, searching for any trace of insolence, a swing of her hip beneath the calico—there was nothing of the kind. Presently he heard the back door close and pictured her walking, straight and slim, past the cistern to the stall where her own healthy child slept calmly.

With an effort he crossed the threshold, into the stink of blood and runny shit. They had just cleaned up little Fan again and were tucking her up in the big bed. His mother came past him, carrying a tin basin out. The stench abated when she had gone.

Mary Ann's eyes passed over him. She did not speak. But I won, Forrest thought to say, and wanted to justify himself still further. I won close on four hunnert dollars. And don't a man have a right to

some relief? I don't drink whiskey nor use tobacco. I don't take laudanum. I don't pray.

Mary Ann lowered her head, and sat stroking the girl's hair and
shoulder as she shifted and murmured in fretful sleep. No word was
spoken until Mariam came back into the room with the basin
washed and dried and empty.

"Mother Forrest," Mary Ann said then, pushing her weight up
from the bedside chair. "I have just got to lie down for a spell."

"Yes, child," Mariam Forrest said. "I know ye do."

"You'll call me if—?"

"Yes. I will."

Mary Ann went out without saying a word to her husband or
looking at him. Slowly Forrest crossed the floor and lowered himself
into the chair at the bedside. Mariam Forrest sat in a ladder-back
chair against the wall.

"That gal has got a right to be weary," she said, with no particular
inflection in her voice. Forrest looked across the bed toward her.
She took up a basket from the floor and went on shelling butter
beans, her eyes bent steady on her work. Forrest felt a little easier in
his mind. Cain't afford to think about it he told himself. He laid a
hand on Fan's forearm. The child had quieted and breathed easily
in sleep.

Butter beans pattered from basket to bowl. The quick nervous
surge of his gambling adventure began to drain away from Forrest.
His eyes were heavy. Poor Fan was breathing with her mouth open, a
light rasp away back in her throat. The ticking of the beans slowed
down and stopped and Forrest looked across at his mother, who was
sleeping in well-disciplined silence, bolt upright in the straight chair
except that her head had rolled to the right and rested against the
wall. A vine of scar wrapped over her left shoulder. Her shoulders
were almost as high and wide as his.

He'd dressed her wounds, that time the panther tore her back. It
shamed him but he'd let no one else undertake it. In fact she'd told
him what to do herself, between clenching her teeth on a rag to control herself at the pain of the liniment. Since then he'd never seen
her bare. He had seen slaves aplenty though, with the weal-grids of
whip scar raised on their backs—lashed there by himself sometimes.

When he must and when there was no other way before him. The screech owl from its post just beyond the open window poured quicksilver gibberish into his ear. He wanted to reach through and wring its feathered neck, but it was thought to be bad luck to kill an owl. He saw himself standing over Catharine, her calico ripped down to her waist, her back still long and smooth and whole though a braided rawhide dripped from his hand and Mary Ann's resentment would make him leave it raw and bloody from a hundred cuts. With a shivering start he came awake. He would go and murder that owl, he thought. But it was due to happen, what he'd dreamed. He didn't want to think on that, but he would have to study it. He could not keep on keeping Catharine so close. In a few years' time, with a little luck and a lot more determination, he'd claw himself out of the slave trade altogether, and be a planter, like the gentry. Or be a planter anyway.

Downstairs in the parlor the mantel clock tolled three times. Mariam's head stirred, crushing her cheek against the plaster wall, but still she slept, a bean pod dangling from her fingers. Fan had shifted in the bed and was reaching for him with both her arms, her dark eyes wide. Her mouth open too though she made no sound. He picked her up and held her against his collarbone. Her face burned against his throat. She didn't have the heft she'd had three days ago or four. She didn't weigh any more than a rabbit, he thought.

As he carried her down the stairs the owl's weird sibilant voice faded. Doctor Cowan and his brother were still sleeping in their chairs. He stood in the night air holding and stroking her back until it seemed she was cooling a little. Then he went inside and settled in a rocking chair before the cold fireplace. When Fan was well she would ride astride of his long shinbone, holding his hands and shrieking with joy with the wild gallop he would give her. Tonight he could only rock her so gently. The faint warmth of her breath on his neck as he slept.

When he came to, daylight had leaked into the room, and his mother stood behind the rocker. Fan's little arm felt hard as a wire across his shoulder.

"Let me have her," Mariam said. "You need to let me have her now."

"I don't want to let her go," he said. "I won't."

Mariam shook her head and set her teeth in her lower lip and then released it. "You have to let her go," she said. "Because, we have got to wash her now, and lay her out on the cooling board."

"The *cooling board*?" Forrest twisted in his chair, feeling how Fan's body moved against him rigid as a plank.

"We air goen to have to bury her, Bedford. Ye cain't hold on to her thisaway."

"Where's Mary Ann?" Forrest said.

"She'll wake to sorrow," his mother told him. "Best let her sleep."

"Fan." Forrest rocked a little. "Fan."

"Bedford." Mariam put her hand on the back of his neck and squeezed. He felt the strength in her hand from all the cows she had milked in her life and was milking still. "Don't you break down."

He couldn't recall how he'd come to surrender the body, but presently he was standing on the porch, empty-handed with his chest and belly cold all the way to the spine. John and Doctor Cowan held their faces sunk in their hands, afraid to look at him, Forrest supposed. The sun was rising in the same place it would have if his dear daughter Fan had not died in the night. He walked down the porch steps and looked up. The screech owl slept now with its eyes squinched shut—a useless cupful of feathers. He no longer wanted to harm it, really. He only wished that enemies would fall upon him now, like the river rats from the night before, surging with the intent to kill, so that he could slash their throats and spill their entrails onto the ground, or tear the limbs from them bare-handed. Yet he knew even this would not relieve his feelings much or for long.

A day later he stood in the burying ground with a shovel hat jammed on his head, choking in a high tight collar, listening to the damned preacher mumbling *ashestoashesdusttodust,* his own thoughts whirling around the same pin Goddammit if there was any goddamn God why would he make a little girl that never did nobody no harm to die of the bloody flux? Answer me that goddamn your eyes. But his mother's eyes were firm upon him and he would not say these things aloud. Son Will was there on his right hand, and Mary Ann, with just a thread of golden hair leaking out of the net of her black veil to catch the summer sun, had tucked all her grief up under his left arm, against the rib cage where his heart beat on.

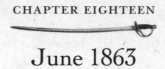

CHAPTER EIGHTEEN

June 1863

Forrest was peeling a little green apple with a penknife when Lieutenant Gould came into the quartermaster's office, carefully moving the smaller of the two blades in a spiral around the knotty fruit, so the apple skin came off all in one curly piece. The nitpicking discussion of supplies and transport had paused as the several other men in the room watched the procedure, waiting to see if Forrest would get the peel off whole. Then Gould swarmed in, with a swirl of the tails of his long white duster, and pressed up against the edge of the table, vibrating.

"General," he said. "The matter of my transfer."

Forrest took a bite of the peeled apple and found it, unsurprisingly, sour. He set it down on the blotter before him.

"All right, Mister Gould," he said. "Let's step out into the hallway where we can speak apart." He pulled the blade through his thumb and forefinger to clean off the apple juice, and snapped the knife shut as he stood up.

"I won't be a minute, boys," he said, and followed Gould out of the room, twirling the folded knife in his right hand.

They paced the corridor of the Masonic Hall, for Gould could not be still. It was a long hallway, and dim; at the east end a little sunshine leaked through a fanlight above the door. In the dusty eaves a handful of little bats hung upside down, asleep. Forrest kept spinning the closed knife in his fingers, kicking it with his thumb to make it turn, looking anywhere but at Gould, and wishing he had never consented to their meeting.

Not long before, Gould had given up a pair of cannon to the

Federals who charged him at Sand Mountain, during the long pursuit of Streight. *I caint keep nobody on that'll let that kind of a thing happen,* Forrest said in his mind, as if explaining it to a third party, John Morton perhaps, *That's all they is to it and they ain't gone be no argument about it.*

Gould's importuning kept breaking into his thoughts. "General, do you not see that this order amounts to an imputation of cowardice?"

"Hush a minute and listen to me," Forrest said, and looked down into the lieutenant's flushed face for the first time. "When you give up them cannon, son, the damnyankees turned them *right* around— they hurt us with'm and hurt us bad and you know that the same as me. They kilt a whole mess of my boys with them guns afore we got'm back. I cain't have no more of that, d'ye foller? Hit ain't nothing to me if ye're a coward or if'n—"

"No man can accuse me of being a coward and both of us live." Gould's face had broken up into pink and white blotches and Forrest was just thinking the words *peaches and cream* when he saw, too late, a pistol-shaped object rising from under the lieutenant's duster— maybe the hammer snagged on the fabric or maybe Gould had intended to fire through the cloth. Forrest caught the hot barrel and twisted it down and away from him. He knew he was hit though he hadn't yet felt pain; the first sensation was the sticky warmth of blood running down the side of his leg. He had opened the penknife with his teeth at the same time as the twisting movement that took Gould's pistol out of the compass of his body brought the two men toe-to-toe and without stopping he drove the longer blade of the knife between Gould's ribs and ripped it sideways. The hallway filled with the sharp bitter smell of a punctured gut. Gould sighed and dropped his pistol. He staggered toward the western door, passing the men who'd flung out of the quartermaster's office at the sound of the shot and now stood with their mouths hanging silently open. The bats, startled by the report, fluttered in and out among the rafters.

Forrest went out the opposite door, unconsciously wiping the knife blade on his pants leg, then dropping the folded knife into his pocket. He was in Columbia, Tennessee, he remembered that, and

there was a doctor across the street. He stepped down into the roadway, wincing. Now he could feel the stitch of pain around his waist-
line.

HENRI WAS STANDING beside Benjamin's wagon when Lieutenant
Gould staggered out of the Masonic Hall, crumpled over the hand
that clutched in his guts. A clear fluid, along with the blood, spilled
through the cracks between his fingers, and the piercing chitterling
smell was all wrong for the warm weather. The men from the quartermaster's office overtook him and supported him by the elbows.
None had gone after Forrest, for none yet realized that Forrest was
hurt. They led Gould into a tailor's shop across the way and set
about making him comfortable, while a couple of other men ran further down the street to look for help.

Henri looked up at Benjamin, who was sitting on the wagon box,
slack reins across his knees. "What do you think happened."

"I ain't know." Benjamin shrugged and looked far off, between
the revolving ears of his mule. "Might be Mist' Forrest cut 'm."

"But there was a shot," Henri said.

"Might be they was," Benjamin said. "Effen Mist' Forrest shot 'm,
he aint gone be walken away."

A bat flicked out the door of the hall and took a crooked trajec-
tory into the leafiest crown of the nearby trees. Henri pushed himself up from the wagon rails and walked up the steps into the hall.
Once his eyes adjusted to the dim he saw Gould's pistol lying cock-
eyed where it had fallen. A blood spoor ran away from it, toward the
door on the other side of the building where he'd first seen Gould
appear. Drawing his own pistol, Henri moved to the eastern door
and peered out around the frame. The blood trail continued across
the street and up the steps to Doctor Yandell's porch.

THE SERVANTS HAD FLED, without a word, when they saw Forrest
stalking toward them, his left trouser leg painting the porch steps
with blood. Paying them no mind, Forrest rang the bell, then
entered without waiting for any response. By the time Doctor Yan-

dell came in, wide-eyed and shading his brow with one hand, Forrest had unfastened his britches and raised up his shirttail to display the wound.

"Well?" he said, with a fierce hook of his black beard.

"General Forrest . . ." Yandell seemed not to know where the sentence should proceed.

Where was Cowan when you wanted him Goddammit, Forrest was thinking just behind his teeth. *Ye cain't hardly trust the first goddamn one of these here other sawbones.* "I need ye to tell me if this here bullet hole is like to cause me airy serious problem."

Doctor Yandell bowed toward the wound. The ball had struck just above Forrest's hip and it seemed to the doctor that it had pierced the external oblique abdominal muscle, whence it would enter the lower abdomen. The wound's dark mouth was fringed with dark shreds of Forrest's woolen trousers and lighter ones from the lieutenant's duster.

"Yes, General," Doctor Yandell gulped. "I must tell you that has the look of a dangerous wound. You must get to the hospital as soon as may be, for in this hot weather it may carry you off. But first if you would stretch out on this divan so that I may—"

"What!" Forrest was already fastening his trousers, though blood spilled over his waistband. "You don't mean to tell me that *yaller dog bastard* has done kilt me. Not by all the fire and brimstone in Hell!"

HIS VOICE CARRIED easily across the street where Henri lurked still in the entryway of the Masonic Hall, raised pistol hidden behind the door frame. Forrest burst out of Yandell's front door and bore down on him like a cyclone. His face was black as a thunderhead. His burning eyes seemed to center on Henri's pistol, even though he surely couldn't see it through the building wall, but as he crossed the threshold Forrest wrenched the weapon from him without even looking to see where it was, then stormed on down the hallway.

From Forrest's hot eyes at that moment, Henri was left with a stream of dots across his own vision, as if he'd stared directly at the sun. Whenever this raging spirit took hold of the general there were only two people on earth who could calm him. Mary Ann his wife might do it, with a word or a touch or a glance. His mother, Mariam, would lay her hands upon his shoulders and hold his burning eyes with hers. When she spoke his name, Bedford Forrest would return to himself and the rage that seized his being would be gone. Henri had been especially struck with this power Mariam Forrest had, to lay on hands as a mambo sometimes might, when a stubborn angry spirit would not give up the human horse that gave him body in the world.

It was soothing too how *Mariam* might almost rhyme with *Mary Ann*. But neither of these women was on hand today. Henri followed Forrest across the street, keeping half a dozen paces back, but still pulled forward by the vortex of the other man's movement. Forrest kicked open the door of the tailor's shop. Lieutenant Gould had been stretched out across a sewing table, and the men from the quartermaster's office were trying to staunch his wound with wads of cotton batting which the tailor had in store. Doctor Wittke had also come to attend him. All scattered when Forrest burst into the room, roaring and drawing back the hammer of Henri's revolver with his thumb, except for Wittke, who only stepped back and said, calmly enough, "General, you have no need to kill him now, for he will surely die of the wound he has already had of you."

When Gould jumped up to run away the blood from his stab wound spurted out in such a jet that Wittke had to step aside so that it would not splash on his clothes. Forrest leveled the pistol and pulled the trigger and the box of the little room filled up with powder fumes. Over the deafening concussion Forrest was howling, "No *damn speckled sonofabitch* can kill me and live!"

Gould had fallen sideways across the back doorstep. All thought him shot dead until he jumped up, ran across the back yard, sprang over the waist-high fence that enclosed it and kept on, flinging his heels up high behind him. Forrest, with as much agility, pursued, letting off a couple more uncharacteristically wild shots as he closed the distance.

Cautiously, Henri stepped down into the back yard of the tailor shop, which was half–grown up in dandelions going to seed. His eye was on the wall of the house across the alley, where Forrest's first stray round had flaked a corner off a brick. Young Sammy Milton sat on his tailbone below, holding his left leg up by the ankle and peering at the underside of his calf, where the ricochet had left a red furrow.

"That's nothing to worry about," Henri remarked. "Only a crease. You're barely even bleeding, Sam."

"That's all right for *you* to say," Milton squeaked. Henri kept going down the alley.

Four houses over from the tailor's, Gould had run out of breath and blood and lay facedown in a patch of bitterweed. Onlookers made a semicircle behind Forrest, who probed the body with the toe of his boot.

"Kin ye credit this *sorry little piece of shit* has put the final end to me?"

"No," said Henri, swinging his leg over another thigh-high fence to come from the alley into the yard where the others were gathered.

Forrest rounded on him. The black hole of the pistol barrel aimed with his eyes. Henri tried to count the shots Forrest had let off during the chase: possible as many as four but certainly less than six. The rage was still on him but it did not burn so brightly as before. And after all Henri already knew that no dark cylinder of Forrest's six held his own death today.

"What's that ye say?"

"No," said Henri. "Nobody has put an end to you yet, General. You are not hurt so bad as you believe."

Forrest's eyes enclosed him then, large and dark as craters on the moon. As if they could pierce and probe out all his secrets, especially those Henri most fervently wished to remain undiscovered. He tried to return the stare with the same penetration, to know even as he was also known. But Forrest was a long puzzle. A hard one. A chanpwel might shed her skin and take the air and shrink herself enough to slip between the atoms building Forrest's skull and discover all the workings there—but what if there should be no workings? No machinery at all, but only intermittent flashes of a thunderous light?

"Ye mean to tell me I won't die today," Forrest had said.

"I do mean that. You won't."

When Forrest finally broke the gaze, Henri breathed deep, then noticed the general was holding his pistol out toward him by the barrel. Henri took it, looked at it briefly, then thrust it back into one of the holsters Forrest had found for him that first day, while they were smuggling guns out of Louisville.

Forrest turned away and left the yard. It was then that someone noticed that Lieutenant Gould was still just barely breathing.

"You *seen* that." As others began to scatter from the scene, Benjamin had slipped up to Henri and stopped with his big handsome head cocked to one side, looking at Henri crossways. "You *seen* the Old Man wa'nt gone die this time."

"He's not hurt bad as he thinks, that's all," Henri said, and looked down at the ground—it was true what he said but Ben was still lofting the question toward him with the crooked angle of his look, for both of them knew Henri hadn't told the part of the truth that Benjamin wanted to hear.

FORREST LIMPED into the house where he'd taken a room, with a couple of doctors cautiously trailing him. Once they'd had the chance to examine him properly, they let him know his wound was not so dangerous as it first seemed. The bullet had not cut into his vitals but lodged instead in the flesh of his hip, whence it could be safely extracted. Then Forrest rose up and drove the doctors off. "Let it alone then, why don't ye?" he shouted. "Hit's nothen but a damn little pistol ball!" But the rage had left him altogether now, and his humor turned darkly inward.

Lieutenant Gould, whose wound did fester in the summer heat, was two or three days about his dying. The doctors kept him mostly quiet with morphine. Sometimes in the night he screamed. John Morton kept him company when he could, for they were friends from boyhood. Leave out the war and they were hardly more than boys now.

"Goddammit!" Forrest erupted, when Morton came to him. "Don't I know what a sorry situation hit is? If he'd shown that much spunk on Sand Mountain we'd not never had no quarrel in the first place."

Morton, whose pale round face was bluish with the small veins underneath the skin, spoke to him again in a low tone. Forrest took off his hat and looked into the crown as if maybe there was a crystal ball up in there.

"All right, John, all right," he said. "I'll go along with ye if that's what ye want."

When Forrest was most uncomfortably seated at the bedside, Lieutenant Gould groped for his hand and held it, and then in his weak dying voice he made a little speech he plainly had stored up in his mind ahead of time, saying he was sorry for what he had done, that the affair was begun in a reckless moment but if it had to end with one of them dead he was happy it should be him and not Forrest to die—it was better for the country that way.

Then Forrest looked Gould in the eye, and said in a voice that didn't quite crack, "I jest wish the whole thing never come about, son—don't ye know they ain't no way on earth I could be glad about doen in one of my own?" Gould didn't say anything more after that, but kept his weak clasp on Forrest's left hand, while Forrest covered his eyes with his right. The other men in the room looked at each other strangely. Forrest never spoke about wishes. He only said what wasn't, or what was.

After a time, young Gould drifted off, and Forrest got up and went out of the sickroom like Morton and the others there were invisible to him. In the night he woke crying, though he didn't know that he was. The saltiness running through his beard into the corners of his mouth only puzzled him. He had dreamed of three women on a brow of a bald hill in the nighttime. His mother, Mariam, leaned forward with her elbows on her knees. Her front was covered with a crumpled cloth but her rawboned arms and her shoulders were bare, her strong square hands turned palm-up to him. Mary Ann had settled behind her, with such a tender and sorrowful expression on her face; she was laving the scars that the panther had left, while behind her, where Mary Ann did not have to see her, Catharine stood holding the basin ready. *Her* face was lost in shadow, but he could see she wore a deep blue cloth tied over her head, with white specks on it shining bright as the stars beyond the hill.

It was him or me, Momma, Forrest said. *It was him or me.*

Oh now Bedford, don't take on. Her eyes deep and dark in the hollows of her head. *I know it was. I know.*

And he knew that she knew just how half-true that was. Awake now, he understood that Gould had died while he was dreaming. He could feel the skin of his cheeks crinkling as the salt dried to the skin, and the itch of the healing wound in his hip. The real trouble was he sometimes thought he would not, could not ever die.

CHAPTER NINETEEN

January 1865

THEY RESTED against each other in the darkness of a borrowed clapboard house, winter wind sawing at the frame of their attic room. An iron grate in the floor released a little heat from the woodstove simmering in the room below.

"Does it still hurt?" Mary Ann said. For a moment she couldn't even remember which one of his many old wounds she had referred to.

Forrest shifted against her, spread his large warm hand across the small of her back. "Right now nothen hurts," he said.

She fingered a lock of his hair in the dark. Right now she didn't feel the cold at all, but she had felt a stab of it when meeting him after months of absence she saw how white his hair had grown.

"I'll never have you all the time," she said, or maybe only thought. "But when I've got you I've got all of you there is."

CHAPTER TWENTY

February 1864

O N HIS HASTY RETURN from rounding up five thousand recruits in West Tennessee, Forrest was quick to send Henri and Matthew out on a scout: Federal General Sooy Smith was leading a couple of thousand cavalry south from Collierville, Tennessee. Bedford kept Willie Forrest back by him, but sent two other men of his escort—Nath Boone, who now had the rank of lieutenant, and a man named Billy Strickland, who would not be killed till the fight around Pulaski at the end of the year.

They set out from Oxford late in the day, heading more or less due east. A good deal earlier, Jeffrey Forrest had been sent, in command of quite a serious force, with the idea of intercepting Smith's advance somewhere south along the Mobile and Ohio Railroad, and the scouts' orders were to find and join him if they could. Bedford Forrest, who knew that Sooy Smith was taking his orders from William Tecumseh Sherman, supposed that once Smith struck the railroad below Corinth he'd keep ripping it up all the way to Meridian and maybe further. Sherman was setting out from Vicksburg to cut his own slash across this Confederate breadbasket, so more than likely he meant to join Smith at Meridian or nearby.

Henri had not ridden so far with his party when they heard a jingle of harness behind. With a couple of hisses exchanged between them, they pulled their horses out of the road and into a clump of cedars to see what might be coming along the road. Benjamin was following, riding the strongest white mule of his wagon bareback, forcing the animal into a reluctant but rapid trot.

Nath Boone and Strickland swarmed into the road, their pistols raised skyward, turning their horses to block the mule's way.

"Boy, state your business," Strickland said.

Ben looked straight at him through the long ears of his mule.

"I come out to jine this scout with y'all."

"Is that right," said Strickland. "Let me see your pass."

"It was Ginral Forrest give me leave," Ben said. "He don't spend time writen out no passes."

Henri and Matthew were watching Boone, who'd been in a changeable humor since his brother Alfred had got killed up in Somerset about two months before. Boone's bushy eyebrows were pushing together like maybe he had a headache coming on.

Strickland was looking at Boone too. "Does it worry you how this boy won't lower his head when he speaks to you? Jest keeps staring right bang in your eyes."

Boone considered, pulling up his horse's head from a patch of half-frozen weed in the ditch. "Hit's Forrest's nigger after all," he said. "I expect he's been whupped for it."

"Been whupped plenty," Ben put in.

"Don't seem to have cured ye," Strickland said.

"Well now," said Nath Boone. "I've noticed he looks the Old Man in the eye that same way too."

"White gemmun," Ben said suddenly. "Here's why I come. You know he caught that buncha white boys trying to sneak off back to Jackson where they was just rounded up last week. You know he made 'm stand by those graves till sunup with the men with the rifles to shoot 'm dead right by there too."

Henri considered. He remembered the same scene queasily himself. The new recruits all had come from West Tennessee, where in the fourth year of the war he was finding men a little less willing to follow the Confederate battle flag than they had been on his previous canvassing trip a year before. A man, a boy, might sooner follow Forrest than most, as Forrest was reputed to win all his fights. They'd taken more than three thousand new men south from Jackson, but scarcely a third of these had a firearm—the lot of them were as green as fresh rawhide and just as happy to run as fight. Henri could picture one such, Briley. How did he come to remember that name? Scarce out of his teens, the boy stood spindly, propped on the shovel at the head of the grave Forrest had ordered all the deserters he'd caught to dig for themselves, eyes rolling white and his lantern jaw trembling.

"Well," said Boone, "he didn't shoot'm finally, did he? Hit's just tryen to skeer'm out of runnen away."

Strickland looked at Ben just as hard as he was looking at him. "It don't seem to have cured *you*."

"I ain't runnen nowhar," Ben said quickly. "I axed for a change of duty is all. Them boys standen in they graves don't sit right by me. I'll take my chance I get shot by the Yankees effen I can ride with you. Best way I can figure to get that other bidness outa my craw."

"Well," said Boone, "that's your plan, you cain't go running around empty-handed."

Benjamin smiled, wrinkling the pale bolt of scar that struck down from his temple onto his cheekbone. A swatch of his tattered blanket wrapped forward from the roll behind his saddle. When he flipped it off (softly so as not to spook the white mule) they could all see one Navy six in his belt and another in his hand—the latter had been trained on Strickland's rib cage throughout the conversation.

After a rather long pause, Boone let out a chuckling sigh. "Put that thing up till we find us some Yankees," he said. "And make yourself welcome to join this party."

THROUGH THE CHILL of that night they rode with the rags of their blankets wrapped around their shoulders. Dark of the moon, so they could barely see each other's horses, except for Ben's white mule, which stood out plainly. The blacks who began to fill the road around them were invisible, some headed east and others west. Some muttered low that the Yankees were coming and others cried deliriously that they were free at last! But none of them seemed to know where they were going. Henri felt his sense of himself as a separate being melting into the milling throng of them all; he was sinking into this dark stream, diffusing into its crosscurrents. He might have slept some in the saddle; if so he was awakened by the crump of cannon in the distance ahead.

The eastern horizon was red with burning. Still a couple of hours to dawn. Boone called a halt and after a quick whispered conference they left the road and picked their way along the bank of the Tallahatchie till they reached the town of New Albany at first light.

There'd been no burning here nor was there any real sign of disorder, though the ways through town were deeply rutted by wagon and gun carriage wheels and trampled by many boots and hooves. Dung from the draft animals lay barely cool. The buildings were all shuttered and barred and no one struck a light within nor ventured out to ask their business.

From New Albany they turned to the south; the Yankees' trail led toward Pontotoc, but they skirted it on a parallel path toward the railroad. In the warmth of the rising sun Henri pulled a nubbin of pone from his pouch, broke it in two to share with Matthew, and put it crumb by crumb in his mouth, holding it there till it softened enough to be swallowed. As they went on they crossed more large parties of wandering blacks and by daylight they could see more plainly that most of these were women and children. They spoke most freely to Benjamin, who had no shred of Confederate gray about him, letting him know that their menfolk had taken horses and mules from their places to ride after the Yankees—going to Okolona, they thought. Henri studied Benjamin as he spoke to one woman or another; there was a natural courtesy to his manner with all of them.

All through the morning a haze had been building on the southern horizon and it grew darker the nearer they approached. By the time they struck the railroad south of Verona, Henri thought he could taste the burning in the back of his throat. They were in Mississippi bottomland now, the black-earth country, where every farmer was required to keep a crib beside the tracks, lipping full of beans and bacon and flour and corn to supply the troops of the Confederacy. With no hesitation, Ben broke the hasp on one with a broken bayonet he carried in his belt, and began to load the white mule with provender.

"Get it while you can, boys," Boone said, following Ben's suit.

"What about the train?" Strickland objected.

"Ain't gone to be no train today."

Strickland shaded his eyes toward the southern horizon. "You think that's Okolona down there?"

"Queen of the Prairie, the Injuns called it," Boone said, turning in the same direction. "That'll be whatever's left of it, if I don't miss my guess."

He turned to the others. "Boys, I believe we better split up. Y'all three go on and have a look at the Yankees. Me'n Billy'll swing around and see if we don't find Jeff Forrest down by West Point."

"Are you serious?" Henri said.

"Why wouldn't I be?" Boone said. "Jest wrap your blanket over your uniform. Ain't nobody gone pay you no mind. Every stray nigger in five counties is down there already, accorden to what we hear. They ain't gone to bother about three more."

Henri looked at him.

"Or come on with us, if you druther," Boone said. "Ben don't mind scouting the Yankees, do you, Ben? You want a change of duty that's just what you got."

"I'm going with Benjamin," Matthew said.

"Fine," said Henri. *"Ainsi soit-il."*

THE THREE OF THEM set out south along the railroad, their blankets wrapped close around them, Indian-style. Even in the afternoon it was frosty enough they could see their breath, and the snorts of the horses made crystal flowers in the chilly air. South of Pontotoc the track had been torn up ahead of them and the rails and ties scattered about like outsize matchsticks—as thorough an uprooting as Forrest himself accomplished whenever he led such operations over ground that the enemy held.

Nearer to Okolona they came upon black men still at the work, lightly supervised by handfuls of Yankee soldiers here and there. The white soldiers made Henri uneasy and he felt perhaps that Matthew was too. Their uniforms were so tattered by now they could scarce be recognized, but their horses were still good, a little too good, maybe, for riders who preferred to pass unnoticed. On the other hand Henri began to take note that many of the black men were just as well mounted, on horses they'd taken from the stables round about. War had not breathed on this region before today, so the land was still fat, the horses sleek and glossy.

All the same they swung east of the track, to steer away from the Federal soldiers, though lines of fire now stood on the horizons all around. The blacks were pulling up track and burning the supply cribs under the direction of the Federal soldiers but they did not limit themselves to that. And what would you call them today? Henri wondered—not slaves, not runaways, not free men. They had passed into a kind of limbo and no one knew in what state they'd emerge beyond it. Today they galloped through tongues of flame and tendrils of smoke with the tails of their confiscated horses streaming out behind them.

A great spirit of destruction soared over this land, and Henri's heart flew up to meet it. He rode with his knees guiding his horse, his palms turned up and arms raised high. At his right hand Matthew's upturned face was bathed in a similar exaltation. *"Koupé têt,"* Henri called to him. *"Boulé kay."* He knew the boy thrilled to the words even though he didn't understand them. They had paused before a grand white-columned house whose brick was cracking under the heat of the fire that swirled between the open front and back doorways of the entrance hall, and rocketed up the helix of the spiral staircase. Soot-streaked blacks kicked their heels through heaps of ash in the yard, singing out a joyous rage. A Yankee officer cantered up to three of them, pale-faced.

"Make it stop," he panted. "This— General Smith never ordered this. We're supposed to destroy railroad and depots and supplies, not burn down the whole state of Mississippi. Even Sherman didn't order this."

Henri looked at him. "No human hand can make this stop."

The Yankee officer gazed blankly at him for a few seconds more, then wheeled his horse and rode away. Presently the three of them prodded their mounts and set off, a bit more slowly, in the same direction the bluecoat had taken. The notion of strategy he had introduced was cutting into Henri's transport of elation. He felt the leaden weight of Sherman, waiting for Smith to meet him at Meridian, wanting to rip the belly out of the whole South like a wild dog eating the viscera of its kill. Forrest knew full well that this was Sherman's dear intention, and Forrest had it in mind to thwart it if he could. It was for that that Sherman hated and feared Forrest and would if possible have him killed.

"Koupé têt," Henri said again in a lower tone; he didn't really feel it now. *"Boulé kay."* It didn't feel the same.

"What's that mean?" Matthew said, and Henri felt that the glow of the moment before had left him too.

"Cut off heads," Henri said. "Burn down houses." He sighed. "I'll tell you later."

As they rode into Okolona he began automatically to calculate numbers of cannon and wagons and men. Either side of them Matthew and Benjamin were doing the same, Henri felt sure. As Nath Boone predicted, bewilderment in the town was so general that the Yankees took no note of their passage.

But at the south edge of Okolona, Henri pulled his horse up sharply.

"Can somebody please tell me why we're going back to Nathan Bedford Forrest right now?"

Benjamin looked at him sidelong. "They's some as would like to ax you the same question."

"I don't doubt that," Henri said. "Right now I'm asking you."

Benjamin touched a fingertip to the source of the scar on his temple. "Them niggers haven a big time now," he said. "Tomorrow they won't know what to do. Fulla fight as they is, they ain't got nobody to lead'm."

"Why not us?" Henri said.

"I ain't taken that up today." Ben faced south along the road. "Get along, mule. Let's us go see can we find Jeff Forrest."

The mule's ears revolved in a backward circle. Henri's and Matthew's mounts fell in on either side.

"Freedom comen," Benjamin said. "One way or t'other. It gone come hard." He met Henri's eyes straight on this time. "I don't know what you hold to in this world. I got my wife down to Coahoma. Nancy, her name—I hope she all right. Yankees come there, they ain't gone take no better care of that place than they done these'ns around here."

"Let it all burn, then," Henri said.

Benjamin smiled into himself. "Time was, my mind was bad like that," he said. "Back when Ole Bedford put this knot upside my head." Again he traced the scar's zigzag with his fingertip. "Oh yes, I seen you looken at it. He flown out and done it before he thought."

"You wouldn't call him 'Ole Bedford' if he was in earshot."

"Reckon I might not." Ben clucked to the mule. "You know, he rough and rageous sometimes, but he don't study meanness like some buckra do. He might have whupped me some more stripes that day, but he ain't done it. No, once he cooled down, he laid back till he known what my trouble come from. Aunt Sarah spoke and told him how I been sold off from my Nancy and she left with folks not treaten her right. He up and bought back my Nancy then and carried her down to Coahoma together with me."

The smoke had cleared where they were riding now, along the banks of a good-sized creek that ran south. The hangover from the burning and riot around Okolona had left Henri feeling heavy and dull. He could no longer backtrack the way through all the cross-roads that brought him to where he was now. When he looked at Matthew across the mule's rump he seemed to see clockwork turn-ing inside the boy's head. If it wasn't for Matthew he might not go back today, he thought. But he wasn't sure why Matthew was going back either.

"I ain't sayen I loves that man," Ben told them. "Ain't nobody love a slave-trader. Even they own people don't. But I seen him give his word to a black man same as he would to a white and I ain't never seen him break it."

A burst of cardinals flew up from a thicket some fifty yards ahead, and then came a snapping sound, like dry sticks breaking. It took Henri longer than it should have to work out that the whine past his head was a bullet. Matthew and Benjamin had already dragged their animals down the creek bank into cover.

Those were graybacks crouched to fire out of the tangle of leaf-less black branches. They must have happened on Jeff Forrest's men. Henri wanted to shout over to them but his horse was crabbing sideways, hooves slipping on the bank of the creek. With one hand he shortened the reins while raising the other empty as if to catch a bullet. A voice he knew sang out of the thicket and then Nath Boone came riding toward him with Jeff Forrest by his side. The youngest of the Forrest brothers, Jeffrey resembled the rest while looking some-how a little milder, with a more delicate turn to his mouth and a gen-tler cast to his eye.

"Henry? Matthew? Is that y'all?" Boone slapped his hat against his thigh. "I'll tell ye what, we like to not known ye—they's too many crazy niggers runnen around these parts."

. . .

FOR MOST of the next day Jeffrey Forrest's brigade skirmished with the Yankee troopers, falling back constantly with the hope of drawing Smith into a soggy pocket formed by Sakatonchee Creek and the Tombigbee River. By mid-afternoon, Bedford Forrest had arrived on the west bank of the creek. Henri and Matthew crossed at Ellis's Bridge to report the strength of Sooy Smith to him: near ten thousand mounted men and more than thirty cannon. Forrest had come across hard and fast from Grenada with no more than twenty-five hundred men—and most of them the green recruits from West Tennessee—to head Smith off from his meeting with Sherman at Meridian.

That night he got word that some of the Yankees had crossed Sakatonchee Creek a few miles north of his camp west of the bridge. With sixty men of his escort he raced upstream to fall upon a small detachment of Smith's men, with a much larger number of their black camp-followers, who were burning a plantation at Siloam. In half an hour he'd made thirty prisoners and scattered the blacks, though the buildings still burned, and the slave quarters too.

"Damn-fool niggers burnen down they own houses," Forrest shouted. "What in the *slobberen blue blazes of Hell* do they think they want to do that for?"

"They want to be free," Matthew said furiously. He'd been boiling over with that, Henri knew, since their ride through Okolona.

Forrest wheeled as if he'd strike the boy. His face was brick-red in the firelight. Matthew stood his ground, unflinching. Henri watched Forrest gradually getting a grip on himself.

"Free," he said. "You call that free?"

Matthew stared back out of eyes deep-set as Forrest's own.

"What is that ye want from me, boy?"

Henri watched Matthew watching Forrest, alert as a fox. The idea of Forrest not being free to do whatever he wanted whenever he wanted to turned over and over behind his eyes.

Matthew turned and walked toward his horse. Forrest stood facing him as he mounted, cocking his two fists on his hips. "The world ain't made accorden to my notions," he said. "I just have to live in it. Fight in it. Die in it. No different from you."

Matthew turned in the saddle. The horse side-stepped and Matthew patted its neck as he looked back.

"Go on, blood," Forrest said. "Make yore ownself free."

FORREST had expected reinforcements from Stephen Lee, but these didn't come. Still, winning with a third of his enemy's force was nothing new to him by now. He wanted to draw Smith further down into the cul-de-sac of the two streams, but Smith was just barely too shy to be drawn. The morning after the raid on Siloam, Smith engaged Jeff Forrest's brigade east of Ellis's Bridge. Forrest reinforced his brother as fast as he could from the west side of the creek and after two hours' fighting Smith was in retreat, meaning to choose his own ground to defend.

"Keep up the skeer!" Forrest cried, one more time, ordering out small squads of his escort to press the receding Yankee rear. Matthew rode in the forefront of these, with Henri barely able to keep up with him and maybe not entirely willing to—*he* felt cold and empty as a washed-out jug since their tour of the riot around Okolona—but Matthew was burning, burning, or it was Forrest's words that burned inside him. *Make yore ownself free.*

What Henri feared was that the boy would find a way to make his ownself dead before the day was done. Whatever fire got a good start in Forrest would burn to the very borders of his being—like the fire that had consumed that manor house outside of Okolona. Today it seemed the same fire burned in Matthew, just as bright. He followed Matthew, but not too close. There was a smell of death in the air, which of course made sense in the midst of pitched battle, but somehow what he sensed today was worse.

Smith's men made a number of small stands as they moved north, all of them rolled up quickly by Forrest's horsemen. They kept up the chase well into the night, and in the darkness and confusion it once occurred that two parties of Forrest's men fired on each other for a minute or so. By great good fortune none were killed. Though Matthew caught a crease on his upper arm he would not even stop to have it dressed, but joined a scout with Henri and Major Strange around two in the morning when the other pursuers finally stopped to rest: they found Smith's men were resting too, a mile or so south of Okolona.

The next morning's first charge drove the Federal rear guard straight through what remained of the town. Smith had drawn up an imposing battle line just the north side of Okolona, but Forrest soon flanked him out of this position and put him on the run again. What at first looked like a total rout settled into an organized retreat. A couple of miles north of the point where Sakatonchee Creek trickled away to nothing, Smith rallied his men into a strong position among the fences and outbuildings on the top of Ivy's Hill.

Jeff Forrest's brigade took over the attack here, relieving Bell's brigade, which had been chasing at a run for a hard nine miles. The bugle blew and the horsemen charged through the pale winter sunlight toward the crest of the ridge where Smith had ranged the first of his two battle lines behind stacked fence rails. Many of Smith's men were armed with the new breech-loading rifles and so could sustain a more rapid fire than before. The Rebel yell ripped back along the charging line, shredded by the wind of forward motion, but Jeff Forrest's cry was stopped short by the bullet that struck him in the throat. He fell backward out of the saddle, arms jerking like the forequarters of a slaughtered hog, dead before he hit the ground.

Bedford Forrest reached him almost before he had landed, tearing the knees out of both pants legs as he skidded to his brother's side, and Doctor Cowan was there too, searching for a pulse in Jeff's left wrist. The death tremor made the left hand flutter in Cowan's grasp like a captured bird. Forrest cradled his brother's head, caressing the pale face as it quickly cooled, stroking the fine silky beard and mustache, while his lap filled up with blood. It looked to Henri like blood might burst out from his eyes. The charge had stopped and the firing had stopped—even the Yankees had stopped firing from the hilltop—and Forrest's men stood mute with their hats in the hands.

Forrest looked at Doctor Cowan and the doctor shook his head. Forrest slipped free the thong of the doubloon Jeffrey wore around his neck and put it over his own head. He covered his brother's face with his hat and stood up. Henri saw his eyes turn yellow, saw his whole body ripple and compress. The bugle sounded. Perhaps Forrest had ordered the sound to occur. He leapt onto his horse without touching the saddle and ran screaming headlong upon the enemy.

Matthew stooped, unfolding a white handkerchief from his pocket. It occurred to Henri to wonder how he had saved it clean and whole through the last months of running and fighting, as if he had preserved it for this doom. He lifted the hat and spread the white cloth over his dead uncle's face and lowered the hat back down. Major Strange was helping Doctor Cowan to his feet saying *We must go after him, Doctor, or he will surely be killed,* and Cowan: *He won't be the only one killed—you know if he only loses a horse he won't stop until he has killed a Yankee bare-handed and young Jeff was his favorite brother.*

There were days when being already dead wasn't much comfort, and today appeared to be one of them. Henri found himself riding with Matthew, Cowan and Major Strange up the hill into the teeth of the enemy, well out in front of McCulloch's brigade, which had just sounded a charge behind them. Though only a handful of the escort had gone with Forrest in his first mad rush, they'd broken clean through the first Federal line, and the point they'd punctured was a melee. Forrest stood with his legs locked straight in the stirrups, his horse trampling corpses of men he'd shot down, and by then his pistols must have been empty for he was slicing one enemy trooper to ribbons with the double-edged sword in his left hand while simply choking another to death with his right. Meanwhile half a dozen of the enemy were reaching to pull him down from the back but just before that could happen the wave of McCulloch's charge washed over them.

Forrest tucked his bloody sword under his elbow like an umbrella and set about reloading his pistols as he charged after the Yankees fleeing through the barns of Ivy's Hill and down the other side of it. They were running pell-mell up the road toward Pontotoc till suddenly they struck a point where the Federals had drawn three lines across a field. Forrest drove into them without a pause, but within the first few seconds of contact his horse was downed by five bullets, the saddle shattered by as many more, and Forrest ran forward on foot firing his pistols with both hands until Benjamin had brought him another mount. No sooner was he well astride than the new horse too was slain in a crossfire and Forrest went down, dead himself maybe, lost anyway to Henri's sight. Henri was trying to get to Matthew, who had got himself into a tangle his father would have been proud of, emptying his pistols into a dozen odd Federal troopers surrounding him, then socking them with his elbows and the shoulders of his quickly turning horse. Sound of screaming just to the rear and King Philip's iron-gray hide broke through the line like the skin of a breaching whale, Jerry not so much bringing him to Forrest as being dragged by him hollering *Whoa goddamn slow down you hellion* while King Philip's neck stretched out straight as a snake's reaching to bite through any blue cloth that he saw. That was what they were all screaming about Henri would have supposed but he paid no mind for he still could not reach Matthew and there was one of Smith's troopers carefully lining up a pistol to shoot him dead and the boy empty-handed facing the hollow of the barrel with that eerie calm of one who knows that death is now inevitable. Dark cylinder turning with scenes of the past and more yet to come. Still Henri could not reach him. He would not. But the Yankee's aim began to waver. Then Henri saw that there was a fountain of blood where the Yankee's head had been and there was Forrest astride King Philip wiping his sword blade clean on the back of the dead man's coat as he swung again toward the second Yankee line. Matthew settled himself in the saddle, plucked the pistol from the dead man's hand just before he fell, and rode on further into the fight.

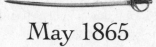

CHAPTER TWENTY-ONE

May 1865

U NDER A THIN SPRING RAIN, Major Anderson rode out with
Forrest from the town of Meridian, Mississippi. They had
nowhere in particular to go and nothing special to do when they got
there. Sometime that day paroles were supposed to be signed for
them and all their men who had a few days before consented to surrender, but neither Anderson nor Forrest could exert any influence
on that event. Their object was to take the air and exercise their
horses, though since the failure of their enterprise to fight off Wilson's fourteen thousand cavalry with less than half that number, the
horses were so played out they could hardly lift their hooves from
the mud, while the men, as Forrest would put it, not excluding himself, were *wore right down to a nubbin.*

They trotted doggedly out into the countryside, halting briefly at
the edge of a blighted farm, its fence rails carried off for bonfires,
livestock scattered or scavenged by soldiers of either or both sides, a
cotton field coming up in hogweed. Forrest clicked his tongue and
rode on. Presently the road ran into the woods. Forrest's head was
lowered under a slouch hat, rainwater running from the front and
back of the brim. Now and then he massaged his upper arm with the
other hand: the half-healed saber cut from the fighting around
Selma the month before. Forrest had killed the Yankee horseman
who'd cut him but it took him longer than usual to get it done.

Sheets of silvery rain poured over him. His long duster, once
bone-white, had evolved into a colorless patchwork that seemed to
be held together by nothing more than grime and dried blood.
When Anderson urged his horse alongside he could see Forrest's
lips working, under the hat brim and inside his beard. He would be

composing something, probably. Though *indisposed to the use of the pen,* as Kelley put it from time to time, Forrest was choosy of the words he wanted in a document and Anderson often had the task of setting them down on paper.

They'd reached a crossroads and Forrest reined up. Anderson waited what seemed a long slow time; he'd never seen Forrest undecided about where he wanted to go.

"Which way, General?"

Forrest hacked out a rough simulacrum of a laugh. "If one goes to Hell and t'other to Mexico, hit don't make me no difference," he said.

Inside his clammy, rain-soaked garments, Anderson's spine got even chillier than before. There were notions abroad of Confederate soldiers haring off to join the Mexican Revolution, but Forrest had seemed to pay them no mind. When invited to carry on the fight west of the Mississippi he turned it down cold. *Nothing but murder* he called that scheme, and any man who entertained it *a fit subject for a lunatic asylum.*

Forrest was still talking, perhaps to himself. "Never yet had to study what to do I just done it." No, he was talking to Anderson after all, flashing him a quick bitter grin. "Anytime I run acrost one of them fellers as fit by note, I whupped him fore he got his tune pitched right. Swallered him whole whilst he set thar a-studyen. But now . . . by damn hit's been too many in that style been worken on our side."

Forrest looked along one fork of the road, then the other. "Cain't afford to think about it," he muttered. "I'm most give out, but I hate to give up. In my life I ain't never give up, not on a thing that mattered. By damn I jest hate the thought of it."

"Then don't give up on your men, General."

Forrest looked at him so sharply Anderson had to harden himself not to flinch.

"I ain't never done no sech of a thing," he said.

"I know it," Anderson said. "Well then, I don't need to tell you, the most of them aren't going off to Mexico. Maybe John Morton and a few of the hotheads, but most won't run off and leave all their folks and they need you to show them—"

"How to lose," Forrest said.

"Just . . . how to *do*." Anderson said. "Like you always have done."

"Well, you're right." Forrest removed his hat to shake off some water, then put it back on. "I reckon I known it all along. I don't mean to leave my folks neither. Men nor women. White nor black. All I own I'll own up to."

"Then what do you say we get out of this rain?"

"All right, Charles." There was a touch of the old warmth now in Forrest's bearded grin. "Let's find us a dry spot and spell out what to say to'm."

CHAPTER TWENTY-TWO

April 1858

Forrest rode down the Memphis waterfront on the black stallion he'd named Satan. Mary Ann didn't care for that name but he'd felt that none other would suit. Between his knees the animal boiled with a dark energy, stepping high and wanting to run. Forrest held the horse in with his left hand, leaving enough give in the reins that Satan wouldn't harden his mouth on the bit, and kept his right hand free for tipping his hat, for once he turned from the river into Beale Street he knew most of the merchants and tradesmen whose establishments lined the western blocks. An acquaintance hailed him with news of a boatload of slaves out of Virginia that had just come downriver, and Forrest raised a finger to signify that he'd look in on his return.

At the corner of Causey Street a blind black man sat on an empty packing case, plucking a long-necked banjo slowly: a short repetitive cycle of notes. The strings were tuned down and the skin head was slack and the hollow slipperiness of the tune connected with an unquiet sensation Forrest had in his entrails. What he might feel at the start of a hunt or the brink of a fight or when he came to a gaming table and felt the first clicking of dice bones in the hollow of his hand.

The banjo faded as he walked the black horse south. In these few blocks of one- and two-room clapboard houses it was quieter than on Beale Street, and he needn't tip his hat, though most of the blacks who peopled this quarter probably knew Mister Forrest by sight. A woman looked up from the wash pots in her swept yard with a flash of frank curiosity in her face, in the instant before she ducked her kerchiefed head away. Forrest felt his stomach settle. Here he came in broad daylight, bang down the middle of the street, riding the finest horse that he owned, head held high and his hat square on top of it.

The house he was bound for was built some stouter than most, with a waist-high stake fence around the yard and a gate with iron hinges and latch. Left of the gate was a hitching post and to the left of that, Jerry sat on the box of his wagon, his big hands lying loose on his knees, eyes hidden in the shade of his cap, still as a lizard soaking in the warmth of the afternoon sun. In the wagon bed behind, the boy sat facing the other way, stiff as a post, a bundle and stick tucked under his heels and his wrists and ankles sticking a little too far from the cuffs of his clothing.

Forrest dismounted and hitched his horse. "Matthew," he said. "Why ain't you gone inside?"

The boy looked past him, his eyes lighting up when they fell upon Satan. When the eyes returned to Forrest they were vacant. Forrest shook his head and turned toward the house, laying his hand on the top rail of the gate. Two railroad tie steps led up to a shallow plank stoop under the overhang of the roof. There on a puncheon stool sat Catharine, nursing the new baby under a light cotton shawl. Her chin was up and her eyes didn't lower. Two proud women, Forrest thought, and wondered again if south of Beale Street would be far south enough. He felt as if the unglazed windows of the several houses behind him were all drilling holes into his back.

"Why, Mist' Forrest," Catharine said, unsmiling. "You welcome to come in."

He thumbed the latch up and went into the yard, pulling the gate shut behind him with a little snap. As he approached Catharine stood up, still holding the baby in her bosom, turned and went into the house, leaving the door open behind her. Forrest glanced back once as he climbed the pair of steps. Matthew and Jerry sat where they were, facing opposite ways in the wagon, immobile as a pair of bronze bookends. The whitewash on the doorjamb was still tacky when he touched it with his thumb. He went inside and shut the door behind him.

The first room smelled piney from the new boards. Catharine sat on a ladder-backed chair, cradling the baby to the breast. She aimed her chin at a stuffed settee. Forrest took off his hat and sat down awk-wardly. Horsehair pricked his back through the ticking. He had bought an item or two of secondhand furniture and had others made at his place on Big Creek. This was the fanciest seat in the house and the least comfortable. Forrest craned his neck this way and that. The back door was open and he could see a few green shoots of something or other coming up from the dirt beyond its open frame.

"Where's Tom and Jimmy," he said.

"Gone over to the river with some other li'l niggers lives round here." She looked up at him, her brown eyes catching a gleam from the front window. Forrest pulled his head back as if he'd been slapped.

"They peepen at them boats what carries po niggers downriver," she said.

Forrest turned his head toward a motion that caught his eye through the back door. A little speckled hen scratched the dirt in the yard.

"Like you ship me downriver to satisfy yo wife," Catharine said.

Forrest's hat fell on the floor as he jumped from his seat. He resisted the urge he had to stomp on it, for a grown man looked foolish stomping on his hat. "Goddammit, Catharine!" he said. "I shipped you a whole ten blocks downriver, into a new-built house with glass in the windows and brass knobs on the doors. Goddammit all to the burning tarpits of *Hell.*"

"Why Mist' Forrest," she said. "You carry on cussen thataway, Ole Devil gone tote you off to that Hell you keeps namen and stick you with a pitchfork."

Forrest stared at her desperately. "Hit's a hard-hearted woman ever which way I look."

Catharine lowered her eyes. He felt that some of the fight had gone out of her. She seemed almost calm, though he knew she wasn't. Her lashes were long and thick, the color of jet. He took a step forward to peer at the infant.

"He looks right stout," he said, though really he was just an old baby with his eyes shut and his mouth busy pulling on the tit; there wasn't a whole lot to see about him. "Favors his brother."

"They favors they daddy." She raised her head, turning her long graceful neck so he saw her in profile. Her hair was pulled up in her kerchief like a crown. She was looking out the front window now. "That'n out there on the wagon do too," she said.

Air whooshed out of Forrest's chest as he dropped back on the horsehair cushion. "His name is Matthew."

"Ain't no matter to me what his name is. That boy is witched if you ax me. Don't speak, don't move, don't hardly breathe. What I want with a half-grown boy round here?"

"Chop wood. Draw water." Forrest took a long breath. "He ain't got nowhar else to go."

"He a nigger, ain't he? He a slave, ain't he? He bound to go where you sends him," Catharine said. "Ain't he?"

"Listen to me." Forrest leaned forward, elbows sliding over his knees. He searched the new planks of the floor for splinters. He felt a surge come over him of the kind he felt in any situation where there was nothing to do but throw down all he had. "His mother is dead. I never did own her. I couldn't buy her. I was liven on my own then, traden in mules. I wasn't with her but the one time. She got sold for a fancy girl down to New Orleans. They wasn't no use in me thinken about it. Then she up and died lately and somebody sent word. I don't know why they bothered. I don't know how they knew who to bother. Two weeks ago I didn't know that boy was on this earth."

Catharine turned toward the front window again. "You looks at him once you knows where he come from."

"That's about the size of it." Forrest sat back. "Well, he done cost me all I could give and then some. He don't seem to want much to do with me and I don't know what to do with him. You can jest picture how Ole Miss would cotton to him at home."

"So you aims to drop him on me."

"I got him schooled to a saddle-maker on Beale Street. Fore you know it he'll be bringen home good money."

Catharine rocked back in her seat and laughed harshly. The baby stirred and she stroked his head with her palm. Black curls were already coming in on the milk-chocolate scalp.

"I'll see your young'ns learn a trade also," Forrest said. "When it oncet comes time."

Catharine gazed back at him evenly. "Will they be free?"

"I'll tell you one thing," Forrest said. "What I'd like to know is will I ever be."

She laughed again but there seemed to be no bitterness in it this time. The baby was sleeping now and she drew him carefully away from the breast. The nipple stood up dark and thick and polished with spit, and she didn't cover it even after she had laid the baby in the box in the corner. She looked at Forrest with her hands on her hips and the one breast pointing at him, her handsome head held high.

"A fancy gal you say. Nawlins."

"They warnt a thing I could do to stop that at the time." Forrest narrowed his vision into her ginger eyes. "I stopped it happenen to you."

"I knows it," Catharine said. "I was right there when you laid down yo money and bought me for yo self."

When she opened the door to the second room there was a flood of light from the windows in the west wall. Through the door-way he could see in the bright pool of sunlight a bed with a quilt made of worn-out work pants with the legs slit and sewn together in Vs. Catharine shrugged her whole upper body and when she turned toward him again she was bare to her navel. Yet what seemed to cap-ture his eye the most was the way the tendon of her neck was cen-tered so perfectly in the cup of her collarbone. It struck him like an arrow to his core.

"Come on, you big ugly mean ole buckra," she said. "Le's see how you claims what you owns."

SOMEONE had cranked the bed ropes good and tight and for the next two hours they needed to be. Forrest was roused from a thick oily sleep by young voices laughing and a splattering sound from the street. He sat up to peer out the window. Outside, Matthew and Thomas tittered and pointed as the black horse Satan hosed down the street with a great foamy piss.

Catharine caught his shoulder and pulled him back. "Lay down," she said. "I don't want'm to see us."

Forrest stretched out on his back, not entirely at ease. He could hear his watch ticking in some pocket of his discarded clothes. A warm hand on his belly. She burrowed against him.

"I wish you belonged to me all the time," she said.

"I know it." Forrest looked into the shadows of the ceiling. "Ain't nobody gets all they wish for."

IN THE GLOAMING he rode north across town toward the home where his white family lived, with an idea forming just below the surface of his mind. Mary Ann was out in the side garden, snipping off buttercups with a small pair of scissors. She straightened and stood willowy as a sapling, holding the yellow flowers in both her hands and looking intently after him as he and the black horse passed. He could feel the look lingering on him after he had gone by, and for a wonder it didn't feel bad. A lot of poison had drained from the space between them since Catharine's departure from the household.

Jerry met him at the stable and took the reins of the black horse as Forrest got down. In the last blue light of the evening, a bat flickered across the stable yard as Jerry led Satan into his stall. Forrest went into the house, where he found Mary Ann arranging her flowers in a little clear vase full of water. From that she turned to light the lamp on the sideboard. For the time being there was no house servant to do such tasks and he felt happy enough that there wasn't. It put him in mind of when they'd lived leaner, in their first dogtrot cabin down at Hernando.

"Miz Forrest," he said. "I got me a notion."

She looked at him coolly, the soft light of the oil flame gilding the down on her left cheek.

"I about had enough of traden in folks," Forrest said. "Got my eye on a piece down to Coahoma. That's cotton country. We could build a brick house with white columns out front and live like the big bugs do."

"All right," she said. Her voice was cool as her regard. But she might have been hiding a smile as she turned from him.

Forrest walked out onto the front stoop and greeted his brother John, who sat within the orb of detachment his evening dose of laudanum provided him. Above the roofs across the way, the stars were beginning to come out, and another bat flicked between the tree-tops, snapping up mosquitoes. Forrest breathed into the darkness gathering before him. He felt like a weight had been lifted from him, maybe not all the way, but some. He knew it wasn't exactly free-dom, but he did feel lighter than before.

CHAPTER TWENTY-THREE

March 1863

FORREST COULDN'T at first understand why his horse was melting underneath him, and this in the midst of a charge at full gallop. They were just now beginning to turn the Yankee flank. But now Roderick stumbled again; Forrest looked down and saw the horse pumping blood from the withers. Well Hell-far he thought, might have shouted or screamed. Over his shoulder he saw Willie overtaking him and waved him to a halt as he slid down.

"Lemme have yore horse, son, I got to—I don't want—" Forrest now took in that Roderick was bleeding not from just one wound but three. "—don't want to lose this one, God-*damn*—" He was up in Willie's saddle almost before the boy had vacated it. "Take him back and see to him." During his last full-on engagement Forrest had had two good horses shot from under him in one day, but he was more partial to Roderick than to either of them. This horse would follow him around the camps, like an overgrown dog as some of the men said, nuzzling his coat collar or nipping at his sleeve, and often as not Forrest would find him a lump of linty sugar or a handful of grain.

Roderick reared, hooves raking the air, wanting to follow as Forrest spurred Willie's horse forward to the fight again. Matthew rode up then and turned his own horse into Roderick's shoulder to bring him back to earth.

"Help me get him back, will you? He's hurt."

Matthew got down and went to Roderick's other side, hooking two fingers through the ring of his bit. The big horse shuddered, calmed a little. Willie looked balefully over his shoulder as they began leading Roderick away.

"Just about to whip'm too," he said.

"I know that," said Matthew. "Looks like we'll both miss it."

They were back among the horse-holders by then, for a good number of Forrest's troopers had dismounted to get themselves in the rear of Coburn's position. The Yankee colonel had struck into them where the road to Columbia passed through Thompson's Station; he had near three thousand men in his command, but now, as the fight went into its fifth hour, Forrest and Van Dorn between them had got him crammed into a corner.

Willie hauled off Roderick's saddle and stood back to look at the three seeping wounds. "Don't look too deep, none of'm," he muttered. "Let your head down, won't you?"

Matthew moved toward Ben, who was coming from his wagon with rags and a blue glass bottle of liniment. Willie had just pulled the bridle loose from Roderick's ears when a surge of battle noise made all three of them turn: a volley, shouts and the brute smack of horses slamming into each other as Forrest's charge found its target. Roderick shook the bit out of his teeth, whinnied and lunged forward.

"Whoa, get him!" Willie shouted.

"I thought you had him!" Matthew caught Roderick's forelock and was dragged off his feet, crooked fingers raking back over the mane—he knotted both hands in tight and managed to pull himself awkwardly up, flopping belly-down across the horse's back at first and then getting a leg over, but his seat was still loose when Roderick went airborne to clear a fence and Matthew almost flipped off over his tail, then when the horse landed buckled forward so hard his nose slammed into Roderick's hot neck. He straightened up, locked one hand in the mane and wiped blood clear of his face with the other.

With no bridle, no halter, not so much as a piece of string, there was nothing he could do to stop the horse or even turn him, and squeezing with his knees only made Roderick run faster—he'd gone into the air again, sailing over a second fence, with a hollow *pock* as the top of his hoof struck a post. They were going back to the fight anyway. In spite of the wind he could feel the hair rising on his forearms and the back of his neck and he knew that Forrest must feel this way when he rode into battle: surrendered to an uncontrollable force that utterly filled him as it flung him forward. He felt that it was Forrest's blood in him that surged.

As Roderick lofted over the third and last fence that separated them from the fight, Matthew caught sight of Captain Montgomery Little, six-shooter upraised, turning his astonished gaze their way. A fissure of silence opened in the roar of battle and Matthew looked through it at Captain Little again; he had lost his pistol now and both his arms worked frantically like the legs of a beetle turned on its back and though still standing he had been shot dead—it was only that he didn't know it yet. With his free hand Matthew groped around his waist for a weapon, exchanging a blurry glance with Henri, who seemed to be muscling his own horse around in a vain effort to intercept them. Roderick, his neck stretched long, had caught sight of Forrest and was rushing to join him where he fought two-handed, hammering a Federal trooper down from the saddle with the butt of his empty pistol in his fist. The noise of battle came back with an explosion, which might just have been the shock as Matthew plowed into the ground. He sat up and saw Roderick lying a little in back of him, dead of a fourth bullet, one foreleg spasmodically lifting and loosening.

The fighting seemed to have ended now, with Yankees laying down their arms, signaling surrender with pocket handkerchiefs; somewhere was a larger truce flag on a stick. Forrest dismounted and stooped to reach for the dead horse, but stopped just short of touching him. Willie pounded up, mouth wide open and face chalk-pale.

"Thought I done tolt ye to carry him back." Forrest sank back on his boot heels, wrapping his arms across his chest. Willie, too winded to make any reply, folded at the waist and braced his hands on his knees.

"It's a shame. D'ye hear me?"

Matthew, feeling himself to be included now, thumbed a last trickle of blood away from his nose, and got up to one knee.

"A *goddamn* shame." Forrest shook his head. "Well. Hit cain't be mended." He turned and stalked off toward the area where the prisoners were being gathered up.

Willie coughed and straightened, gasping. "You hurt?" he said.

Shaking his head, Matthew got to his feet. Willie's chest rose and fell. He tried the black points of his mustache with a fingertip and looked down at Roderick's still body.

"That horse was a better man than either one of us," Willie said.

Without thinking Matthew offered his hand across the carcass. It was like he could see Willie's first thought—*you don't shake hands with a nigger*—and by the time Willie decided to reach for the man inside the skin, Matthew had already turned away, stooping to bloody himself from the dead horse's wounds and make his hand untouchable to anyone.

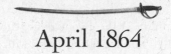

CHAPTER TWENTY-FOUR

April 1864

THEY HAD BEEN FIGHTING around Fort Pillow for hours by the time Forrest himself rode in, grim and weary from more than a day and a night in the saddle—he had ridden over seventy miles since the day before. Henri led him out a fresh horse. Chalmers had launched the first attack on the fort near dawn, and as soon as they swept the pickets from the outer works they had overrun the Federal horse pen and captured the stock. The Federals were just a little more than seven hundred, too few to man the outer works even with the fresh black troops that had just been sent from Memphis, and they had quickly fallen back to the second line of defense, a zigzag breastworks on the top of the hill, with its rear open to the junction of Coal Creek and the Mississippi River.

With a grunt, Forrest swung astride the captured horse. Captain Anderson joined him for a scout of the perimeter. Henri fully intended to stay where he was, but Forrest beckoned him to follow. Henri climbed onto a brown jenny mule that had caught his eye in the Federal stock pen. The outermost works of Fort Pillow encompassed several hilltops and the terrain was cut this way and that by ravines. Henri liked the jenny's sure step over the rough ground and he felt too that she had some particular instinct for self-preservation.

It would have been a pleasant spring morning, bright but cool. Outside the stock pen the hillsides were speckled with tiny white star-shaped flowers and the yolky yellow of new dandelions. Moving in a semicircle southeast from the Mississippi, they passed Ginral Jerry, just out of range of the guns of the fort, going along at a crouch and gathering the bitter greens. Chalmers had posted sharpshooters on the hills inside the outermost works and they were steadily exchanging fire with the Federals in the inner defenses.

Forrest rode halfway up the hillside and turned to face the river again, gathering the reins with one hand and shading his eyes with the other, though the sun was mostly in his back. Behind the zigzag breastworks, atop a bluff at the river's edge, there was a U-shaped inner fort, refurbished with fresh dug earth, with slits for six cannon belching lead in their direction. They were out of cannon range where they were, but a couple of Federal long rifles carried further. Forrest's unfamiliar horse was restless with the whistle of the balls, kept squirming sideways and trying to sit down. Henri stroked his jenny's trembling neck, along the lines of the blue-hair cross that grew across her shoulders.

"Goddammit this oughtent to take *all goddamn day*!" Forrest remarked. "They ain't that many of the scalawags in there nohow. We need to move some more riflemen up to make them sons-abitches put they goddamn heads down."

"Look there," Anderson said, and pointed down the slope. "McCulloch wants you."

Henri could not tell if it was McCulloch or not, but someone was signaling from the zigzag breastworks, which McCulloch's brigade had taken sometime before Forrest arrived. They rode up toward him. Forrest's horse's hooves tore up the grass and lost purchase in the loosened dirt. He arrived at McCulloch's post at a scramble, and dismounted, tossing Henri the reins of his horse.

The horseshoe ring of the inner fort was no more than three hundred yards from the crest of the ridge, but still a few degrees above the point where they stood. The Confederates had reversed the log breastworks to give themselves some cover, and McCulloch's riflemen were keeping up a frequent fire to discourage the Federals from taking clear aim from the top of the earthen parapet opposite. Beyond the fort Henri could see a Federal gunboat steaming along the river toward them.

"General," McCulloch said. "Look yonder if you would." He pointed down to his left, where the ravine behind them curled around the ridge toward the Mississippi. A string of log cabins lined a cove between them and the inner fort.

"I believe a charge would carry that place," McCulloch said. "And from there we can distress their artillerymen a good deal."

"If them cannon don't blow ye to smithereens first," Forrest said.

"Just look at the angle," McCulloch said. "If we once gain the cabins they won't be able to bring those guns to bear."

Forrest squinted down the hill and nodded. It was the sort of move he favored, bold and no more risky than it needed to be.

"Get after'm," he said briefly. He pulled a nickel-backed watch from his pocket and glanced at the face: not quite eleven.

"General," Anderson called. "Mister Nolan would like a word."

The crash of cannon from the fort almost drowned out what they were saying. Henri's jenny shuddered, revolving her long ears. Nolan clambered up the slope at a crouch, then straightened to cup his mouth to Forrest's ear. He wore a buckskin jacket with the hair still on the hide, except for patches where the bristles had worn away from the greasy, sour-smelling leather. Of course the rest of Forrest's men were scarcely in any better trim. Their gray was ragged and many went shoeless now. Their numbers were thin when they started from Georgia and they had been taking up recruits as they could, over three weeks of a crazy looping progress all up and down West Tennessee. They'd swept in Nolan four days before, along with a couple dozen of his riders, raiders, deserters, bushwhackers— nobody knew what they really were and the same went double for Mister Nolan himself. But then it was no time to be choosy, and if Forrest had been as choosy as that he'd have left Henri standing by the Brandenburg road three years before.

They were following Nolan now, continuing the same southeast sweep they'd begun before, on the far side of the zigzag breastworks from the inner fort, across this cheerlessly bare ground, which had all been clear-cut to open fields of fire. Their way was complicated by stumps and logs that still lay where they had been felled. Some undergrowth had begun to return, buck bushes and blackberry bramble, worthless for cover. Anderson's horse stumbled, jumping one of the many shallow gullies. The volume of the cannonade swelled as the Federal gunboat began to lob up shells from the Mississippi.

Forrest seemed oblivious to it. Now and then he reined up his horse to beckon sharpshooters to nearer positions. The Federal riflemen, meanwhile, had corrected their tendency to overshoot and were beginning to bring their rounds much closer to the scouting party. Anderson was just turning to Forrest to say who knew what when a ball crashed through the forehead of Forrest's horse. The animal reared, went into convulsions, and fell over backward, rolling over the rider.

Henri jumped down and sheltered himself beside the shoulder of his jenny, holding her close under the jaw and stroking her velvet nostrils in hope of keeping her calm. He watched Forrest's mount as it kicked itself to death in the ditch where it had fallen, the geyser of blood slowing to a trickle between its eyes. A hullo went up from the Confederate lines to the west and Henri looked over to see Matthew rushing pell-mell toward them astride a fresh horse he was bringing to Forrest. The boy rode well, though he'd not taken time to put his feet in the stirrups. But Forrest had maybe been crushed to death, it appeared. Or no, Anderson was helping him up from the springy clump of buck bushes that had cushioned his fall. Forrest pressed one hand to his side, then straightened.

"For God's sake, General!" Anderson said. "If you must carry on, let's do it on foot."

"I'm as like to get shot afoot as on horseback," Forrest snarled. "And I can see one hell of a whole lot better from the saddle."

And he got up as quickly as Matthew hopped down. The boy looked up at him, panting, his eyes wide and a little glassy. His caramel-color face had paled a shade.

"Git outa here!" Forrest told him out of the side of his mouth. "Git back under cover. Henry, carry him back to the line."

Gladly, Henri thought in a prayerful silence. He sprang onto the jenny and stretched down a hand for Matthew to scramble up behind him. Forrest and Anderson had resumed their course, following Nolan northeast toward Cold Creek. The fire on their party had paused for a moment, thanks to McCulloch's rush on the cabins in the cove. Henri rode gratefully toward cover.

"He never even looked at me," Matthew hissed into his ear.

"Calm down," Henri advised him. "It might just be he doesn't want to see you killed."

AN HOUR LATER Forrest returned, on foot after all (for his second horse had been shot out from under him too), limping from the effects of his first fall, and in a still more prickly humor than before.

"Got holt of yore penstaff?" he asked Anderson. "Good, set this down. *You lowdown bellycrawlen horsethieven niggerstealen passel of murderen rapen renegades have got your sorry ass in a slipknot now! I'd as lief kill ever man in the place, contraband niggers and bushwhackers too, and if ye ain't got the good sense to give up and quit I will damn well do it and do it barehanded for I don't mean to waste no more powder on ye!*"

"Yes sir." Anderson held his paper to the light. "Let me just read that back."

Headquarters, Forrest's Cavalry
Before Fort Pillow, April 12, 1864

Major Booth, Commanding United States Forces, Fort Pillow

Here Anderson paused to clear his throat, while Henri's mouth opened like the mouth of a fish; he had to make a conscious effort to close it. In the course of the morning he had seen Major Booth arrive in the land of the Old Ones, struck in the heart by a long lucky shot, while inspecting the inner fort's batteries.

Major, — the conduct of the officers and men garrisoning Fort Pillow has been such as to entitle them to being treated as prisoners of war. I demand the unconditional surrender of this garrison, promising that you shall be treated as prisoners of war. My men have received a fresh supply of ammunition and from their present position can easily assault and capture the fort. Should my offer be refused, I cannot be responsible for the fate of your command.

N. B. Forrest
Major General Commanding

"Close enough, I reckon," Forrest said as Anderson folded the letter. He reached into his watch pocket but instead of the watch he produced the drilled coin on its leather thong, which he looked at for a moment before raising his eyes to Captain Goodman.

"Well, git ye a white rag and carry that note on over," he said.

Goodman saluted and reached for the paper. Forrest put the coin back into his pocket. "Henry," he said.

Henri, who had just stretched out on the green springy earth, raised up on onto his elbows.

"I want ye to go too," Forrest said.

Why, Henri thought, but there was no telling.

They rode up along the top of the ridge south of the inner fort's horseshoe, bearing a borrowed white shirt raised on a musket barrel. At the sight of the truce flag the guns all fell silent; to fill that vacuum, Henri's ears began to ring. From the height they had reached he could see well enough that Forrest was really not bluffing this time. The ammunition wagons had in fact arrived from Brownsville long before. McCulloch, from the position he'd taken among the cabins of the cove, had completely silenced three cannon of the fort and the others were much troubled by sharpshooters Forrest had moved up from the hills to the east. There was more than one Federal boat on the river, but Anderson was just now marching three companies into trenches dug at the foot of the bluff, to forestall any attempt at a landing. On the north side of the fort, Henri could just make out Nolan's buckskin jacket creeping forward through the ravine beside Coal Creek. A couple of his raiders were visible crawling along after him and all his men were probably there somewhere. It was Nolan who had shown Forrest this weak spot and got his leave to be first to exploit it. Henri couldn't quite fix on what about this situation troubled him so.

With the cease-fire, the heads of black soldiers had begun to pop up above the parapet. Soon enough they got the confidence to show all of themselves, and the parapet was lined with them like birds alit on a rail. They looked very well in their blue uniforms, which mostly had not yet seen hard use. A half-dozen or so stood easily, their arms at parade rest almost, looking at Henri with a calm curiosity. He could feel the force that was latent in them. Where were you in 1859? he thought. Or the year after that. Or the year after that. They were here now, anyway. He thought suddenly that Forrest might have attached him to this party so that he could be seen by these black men. And yet, he merely puzzled them. In Louisiana, New Orleans especially, anyone who looked at Henri would form a notion of what he was, but these men, whose African strain was more pure, hardly knew what to make of him. In these western states he was taken for a half-breed Indian half the time anyway. It would have made more sense to send Jerry, or Ben. If Forrest had even had such a purpose.

Some of the other black men on the parapet had begun to call insults to the Confederate soldiers below—not a good idea, Henri thought. There had been black Federals at Paducah too, two weeks before, and he'd seen the knuckles of Forrest's men go white on the grips of their weapons then. All over West Tennessee there was a dumb rage among white people at the very idea of black Federal troops—astonishment even, as if their own mules and oxen had somehow thought to take up arms against them. A few months earlier General Cleburne had suggested the South muster slaves into its dwindling armies, but no one wanted to hear that, even now.

Not all of the blacks on the parapet were in uniform. Indeed, the loudest among them were not. Runaways had been migrating to this place ever since the Federals had first captured it. There had never been troops enough to man the three-mile-long outer earthworks, but blacks who wandered in from wherever had made themselves at home within this defense. Some carried on trade from up and down-river, dealing whiskey and other contraband. And they were called "contraband" themselves, by whites in the region. The black runaways were not alone there either. The cabins McCulloch had just occupied had over several months filled up with a queer mix of ex-slaves and white renegades of one kind or another: deserters from either army alongside men who'd profited from the unsettled times to turn bandit. Fort Pillow had the name of a vipers' nest, and no doubt some of the tales of rape and robbery were true.

Things had turned ugly in West Tennessee since their last gallop through here in 1863. From the war's beginning the land had been combed over too many times for supplies and recruits. And from one farm to the next it was split between Confederate and Union sympathizers. The confusion opened all kinds of chances to settle scores that had nothing to do with the war. Not three weeks earlier, they'd come across the carcass of their own Lieutenant Dobbs, who'd gone home to Henderson County to raise a few men he knew there, with his face skinned out and his nose cut off and other mutilations too dreadful for Henri's mind to dwell upon. They had to go through his pockets to guess who he was. In Jackson a committee had come to Forrest to claim that Fort Pillow was nothing but a hideout for marauders who did such ugly things as that, and what did he mean to do about it? Fort Pillow had become such a plague on the region that Forrest had trouble keeping his West Tennessee men riding with him, for all wanted to stay home to defend their own families.

Forrest was riding out toward them now, forking his third horse of that day, pulling where the truce flag whipped from the gun barrel at the same time a messenger arrived from the fort: Lieutenant Alexander Hunter, commanding a detachment of the Second U.S. Colored Light Artillery, and with him Captain Young of the Twenty-fourth Missouri Cavalry. Young raised his hat to Forrest, for he had seen him in the field before today. Lieutenant Hunter showed the note that Anderson had written.

"Can you assure me that my Negro soldiers will be treated as prisoners of war?" he said.

"That's jest what it says thar on that paper don't it?" Forrest said shortly. "They'll be prisoners of war if you surrender *right this red-hot minute*. Dawdle, and they're subject to be treated like dead folks."

Lieutenant Hunter looked a young man, his face the color of cold biscuit dough. There was a crack in the corner of his mouth, and a dark furrow in between his eyebrows. "Your Confederate Congress has put it out that Negro soldiers will be sent back to slavery if captured. Their officers executed." He tried a thin smile. "And that would be me."

"Confederate Congress ain't here so they don't git no say," Forrest told him. "Ye'll be treated fair if ye strike yore flag. Don't and ye're like as the next man to get kilt in the fight."

"Major Booth asks for more time," Young told him.

"He damn well caint have it," Forrest snapped. "Pussyfoot around and I won't be responsible. I need me an answer and I need it right quick."

The two Federal officers nodded and rode back to the fort. Why were they dealing in a dead man's name, Henri wondered. But maybe he knew . . . Bradford was a West Tennessean himself but he'd made a bad reputation since he came to Fort Pillow. His orders were to live off the land and he'd followed them to the point of pillage. Old scores of his own to settle, perhaps. And there were insults to women on Bradford's watch, the kind that can only be washed out in blood. Major Booth had arrived at the fort so recently he'd not had the time to make himself hated.

"They hopen to get some he'p out of them gunboats," Forrest muttered, reaching under his coat to finger a bruise where his ribs had slammed a stone in his fall. "Well, we ain't got all goddamn day to set around and let that happen."

Captain Young appeared on the parapet among the black soldiers there. He pointed and said something to one of the more excitable troopers, who capered and kicked out a leg. "Wooo, thas Ole Bedford sho' nuff. We knows him! Yes we *do*." And then the man jumped behind the wall to shelter himself from Forrest's baleful stare. But Forrest didn't look altogether displeased. He'd come out here to be recognized, Henri realized, or at least that would be part of his reason. A little while back Colonel Duckworth had bluffed a garrison in Union City to give itself up with surrender-or-die threats written over Forrest's name—when Forrest himself was on his way to Paducah. Fort Pillow's commanders would be more likely to take those warnings seriously if they knew Forrest really was here in person, and there were apt to be others besides Captain Young who had run up against him somewhere before.

Lieutenant Hunter returned to them, alone this time, his features more drawn than they had been before. He passed Forrest a scrap of paper with the name of Major Booth forged to it, then turned to Goodman and said something to him in a low voice.

"*Your note does not produce the desired effect,*" Forrest spelled out slowly. He looked up at the envoy. "I don't know whoever in there is setten down this horseshit but tell him if the next one ain't wrote in plain English I'll come in there and poke it down his throat with a ramrod."

"I'll do what I can to satisfy you," Hunter said. He nodded to Forrest and returned toward the fort.

"That man smelt of whiskey, I swan," Forrest said. He crumpled the note and threw it down. "Even this goddamn paper stinks of whiskey."

Henri looked again at the walls of the parapet, where some of the capering, catcalling blacks did appear to be a little tipsy. Maybe Bradford would be drinking too, to keep his courage up. Through one of those queer windows in his mind he could see men standing with tin cups and gourds around a keg.

"We will have this place come hell or high water," Forrest said. "If everybody up there has done drunk hisself senseless it's jest gone be too bad."

He rode west along the bluff, peered out at the river, rode back. Rarely had Henri seen him so fidgety. This fort was about as stout as the one at Paducah. There they had sacked the town with no trouble, commandeered a few hundred horses, captured all manner of supplies and destroyed whatever they couldn't carry. They'd had the pleasure of burning a steamboat, and the dock where it was moored. The fort, however, they failed to take. "If I have to storm your works, expect no quarter," Forrest had written when he demanded surrender. The Federal commander called the bluff and when Forrest's men charged they were thrown back, and their leader, A. P. Thompson, killed. Forrest gave up and went away, with his men feeling rightly enough they'd been whipped by niggers, though none of them said anything out loud.

It wasn't going to go like that this time. It would be different, and in the worst way.

Not all of the blacks in the horseshoe fort were drunk. The handful of men who had been studying Henri from the beginning were still sober and serious, and someone had just handed them up a very long rifle with an octagon barrel.

"You ought to go back, General," Captain Goodman said, motioning toward the long rifle. "I think they are marking you out as a target."

"Ain't no man can kill me and live," Forrest said. "Hit's a flag of truce besides."

"Yes, but they claim that we're moving up men through ravines under the truce."

"I ain't moven men through the goddamn ravines any more than they tryen to land men off of their goddamn gunboats—" Forrest broke off. "Yonder he comes."

It wasn't Hunter this time but some other junior officer. The note read, *General, I will not surrender. Very respectfully yours, L. F. Booth . . .*

"It's a plain answer anyway," Forrest said. "Goddamn their eyes! I'm goen up on that hill yonder—and I'll be a-watchen for the first men over that wall. We got Missouri, Mississippi and Tennessee all here. Let's see who can git there first. And git after'm—*keep* after'm, boys, until that flag comes down."

A gust from the river teased out the cloth of the Union flag above the battlement. It seemed that all of them were looking at it for a second. The darkness rising in Henri's mind suddenly took on a definite form.

"General," he said.

Forrest, interrupted, turned on him hotly.

"General—" He saw it plain now, why couldn't he say it? "Mister Nolan is out in advance of Barteau. In the ravine by Coal Creek."

Forrest looked at him like he'd lost his mind. "Why wouldn't he be? Them's local boys thar with him and they know the lay of the land."

They have the local-most grudges too, Henri thought, and they mean to be the first ones in there. He was looking for a safe way to say it when Forrest spoke again.

"All right then. Go see about him. If it's a-worryen ye so." With a grimace Forrest pressed his sore ribs once more, then wheeled his horse toward the rear.

Henri squeezed his heels to the flanks of his jenny and rushed down toward the Coal Creek ravine. Behind him came the high silver tone of Gaus's bugle, then the hair-raising keen of the Rebel yell. The crash of artillery replaced the ringing in his ears. Barteau's men looked up at him as he whipped by, thinking he might be bringing orders as he sometimes did. But Nolan and his followers were already darting up the slope toward the earthworks. Henri jumped down, tied his jenny to a stub of a fallen tree and went after them.

The charging Confederates had thrown themselves into the six-foot ditch at the front of the horseshoe and were climbing all on top of each other in a mad leapfrog to scale the earthen wall. All the defenders' attention was now concentrated there, and though the

angle was too steep for the cannon to be of any use, small arms fire
was doing considerable damage.

Nolan's men meanwhile were making for a point where the
earthwork met the bluff on the north side. There the buckskin jacket
disappeared, over the bluff itself as it looked. Nolan's men went over
after him . . . and more than Nolan had with him when he joined
their force. As many as fifty West Tennessee guerrillas were going
over, and they weren't flinging themselves into the river either, as
Henri saw when he reached the edge. The last of the partisans
stretched back a hand to help him, and by scrabbling and clutching
at a root sticking out of the clay of the cliff he was able to scramble
around the corner of the wall as Nolan and his crowd had done
before—each man beginning to fire as he entered the fort. A keg of
whiskey had indeed been broached, and more than one of Nolan's
men paused there to dip himself a measure.

The Federals might have seen and stopped them easily enough
were they not facing the frontal assault—new riflemen stepping up
onto the catwalk behind the battlement to relieve those who stepped
down to reload, and all in good order until Nolan and his men dis-
rupted it by shooting the defenders in the back. At once the top of
the battlement was covered with a wave of Forrest's men breaking
over it, the wild bone-chilling yell still skirling as they jumped down
into the enclosure, slaying every fish that swirled in the barrel.

"Save your lives!" Bradford shouted, without making any suggestion how his men were to do it.

"Let us fight yet," cried a lieutenant—he was commanding black
artillerymen who still served the cannon—but Bradford howled, "It
is no more use," and threw himself over the bluff toward the river.
One of the black gunners stood up calmly away from his piece, with
no more weapon than his ramrod, which he held at his side like a
staff. Henri remembered his face from the other side of the parapet,
one of the sober, serious ones, and he was still looking at Henri now,
ignoring Nolan, who walked up to him slowly and shot him point-
blank between the eyes. Others were on their knees holding up their
hands for mercy now but they were shot down just the same, by the
partisans who'd entered over the bluff or equally by Forrest's men
coming over the wall. He had seen Forrest blood-maddened often
enough but never had it affected so many; every man who came over

the wall had murder blazing in his eyes. "Kill every last one of the varmints," somebody cried. "That's Forrest's word!" Others were toasting the slaughter from the whiskey keg. The Union flag still snapped on its pole and Henri thought of cutting the lanyard but there was too much fighting there by the flagstaff and it would be better to go and go quickly—

He scrambled back the way he had come, half-falling down the steep slope to the spot where the jenny *grace à Bon Dieu* was still tethered; not bothering with the knot but breaking the dry-rotted reins with a snap of his wrist. He rode, wondering what help to expect. Forrest at least saw the value in a slave. He wouldn't go slaughter so many of them any more than he would the same number of horses or mules. Wasn't that right? Not quite a year back, in May '63, some of Forrest's scouts had captured a handful of black Federals and quietly sold them down the river. They hadn't exactly told the Old Man about that one, but they had lived high for a while on the money. Then again, when they entered the town of Purdy a few weeks ago, Forrest had set a guard from his own escort to protect the wife and family of Colonel Fielding Hurst—not only from Confederate soldiers but from the rage of ordinary citizens all around, for Hurst was a Union man who'd just burned down half his own hometown, and was generally thought responsible for horrors on the order of the torture and murder of Dobbs. Forrest had promised to wipe Hurst off the face of the earth if he could catch him, but he normally shielded even Union sympathizers, so long as they didn't have arms in their hands. The truth of it was, Henri had no notion if Forrest would stop this killing or not but he knew Forrest was the only man who could stop it.

He jumped off the jenny while she was still trotting. Forrest leaned against a tree, twirling the coin on its thong as he looked toward the battle, or sometimes cupping it in his palm to study more closely. That old Spanish doubloon that Jeffrey Forrest had plowed up somewhere in Mississippi and ever after worn around his neck. Forrest had carried it since his brother was killed, and it wasn't an especially good sign when he commenced studying it this way.

"General," Henri gasped. "You must come."

Forrest looked up at him half-unseeing. "Come whar?"

"The fort—" Henri leaned forward, braced hands on his knees

in hope of relieving a stitch in his side. "They're killing, down there—just killing."

Forrest pointed, the coin swinging from the heel of his hand. "Without they strike that goddamn flag they can good goddamn well expect to get kilt."

"They've surrendered!" Henri said. "There's no fight left in them anyhow. There's men being killed with empty hands."

Forrest put the coin away in his pocket, and looked more sharply toward the powder smoke rising from the fort. The cannon were quiet now and no more was heard from the gunboat on the river.

"General." Henri pulled himself straight. *"You are not the man to let this go on."*

They reached the fort in half the time it had taken Henri to get to Forrest's post, Henri lagging a little behind, since his jenny couldn't have kept pace with Forrest's horse even if she'd wanted to. Forrest cantered to the flagpole and cut down the flag with his saber, then jumped from the saddle to the ground.

"Hold your fire, boys," he said. "I never ordered no goddamn massacree! You'll see me settle with any man as says I did—"

What was left of the garrison was going over the bluff like a waterfall to the riverbank below, but the Confederates were still killing stragglers in the enclosure of the fort, strewn now with bodies crossways over each other wherever they'd fallen. Henri got a glimpse of Lieutenant Walker tumbling down among the remnants of his command. Forrest had jumped down from his horse and was going between the Confederates and the Federals, knocking down gun barrels with his saber, his Navy six cocked in his left hand.

From a heap of the dead a black man stood up shakily, catching Henri's elbow for support. One of Nolan's partisans drew a bead on him with his pistol.

"Stop where you are," Forrest told him.

Nolan's man turned to look at him blankly, then renewed his aim on the man who clung to Henri's elbow. He cocked his pistol with his thumb. Most of the blacks who lay dead all around had been shot at about this point-blank range. But the explosion came from Forrest's pistol this time. Nolan's man fell over sideways, his pistol discharging its round into a heap of corpses.

"There's an end to it," Forrest said. With that, the firing stopped in the fort, though at the foot of the bluff it was livelier than ever.

"Lawd," said the man at Henri's side. "Lawd."

Henri could feel his trembling, if it wasn't maybe his own trembling. "What's your name?" he said.

"Green," the man said. "Sam Green. I needs to set down."

Under the splintered catwalk was an ammunition crate where Green could sit without drenching the seat of his trousers in the blood that pooled everywhere in the fort's enclosure. Henri led him there and left him. The blood smell, mixed with fumes of spilled whiskey, was chokingly strong. He went down the bluff, skidding when his boot heels tore out clay from under the thin stubble of weed. He finished the descent sliding on his tailbone.

The *New Era* had steamed away out of range—the Federal gunboat had fired some rounds at the very beginning of the engagement but the sharpshooters with Anderson knew how to strike down the artillerymen by firing into the gun ports, and soon enough she'd been driven back. Anderson and Barteau had converged on the riverbank and caught the fleeing Federals in a crossfire. They were still firing too, mostly into the water now. Henri stood up and picked his way over corpses to the water's edge. He saw Lieutenant Hunter fling himself into the stream, among a pack of his panicked black soldiers, but the lowering sun glared off the water so that he couldn't see what happened to the lieutenant after that.

Some of the Federals were trying to pull themselves up onto a barge that drifted near the bank, but sharpshooters picked most of them off before they could gain cover. The stream was dotted with the dark heads of swimmers picked out hard black against the red reflection on the water, and every few seconds one exploded when a sharpshooter popped a ball into it. Then the body would roll up and float downriver in the sluggish stream. That slaughterhouse smell was thicker than ever in the back of Henri's throat. He raised a hand to shade his eyes and saw that it wasn't only the sun that reddened the river. Thick and viscous as molasses, the Mississippi was running blood as far he could see.

CHAPTER TWENTY-FIVE

I N LIFE Jeffrey Forrest was a gay lighthearted young fellow, and Bedford Forrest loved him better than all save his own son Willie—who was often Jeffrey's companion in frolics and pranks. But Willie and Bedford were not here now, and Jeffrey wandered the crown of the knoll by himself, apart from the others who'd gathered there.

"Did I hear you was fixing real biscuit?" Little said. Jerry, scraping coals over the lid of his iron skillet, answered with no more than a grunt. Rumor was that he had salvaged a sack of white flour from the supplies Smith's Yankees had been toting.

Little and Nath Boone and the Reverend Kelley sat in a row on the gray fallen log, like birds on a rail waiting the right moment to swoop down on a field of ripening corn. Only Jeffrey, as he circled the bare crown of the knoll, seemed to hear the piping of the Old Ones. Presently he shook a leg and commenced to dance. Not all of the Old Ones appeared so old, and soon a couple of the most lively women had joined the Rebel cavalier. Henri saw them in grass skirts and strings of cowries and not much else, but Jeffrey may have perceived his partner in some other guise: a ball gown, say, which his sweetheart might have worn for him in Memphis before he went to war and died.

Ghost fiddlers (when had they been slain?), sawed out the opening notes of "Devil's Dream." Little was staring into the dance, not altogether as if he could see it but more like he was somewhat aware of something from which he desired to be distracted.

"Hey Ornery!" he called, too loud and too rough, so that Henri refused to answer or turn his head that way. He was looking into the cold mists that roiled around the brow of the knoll and there he seemed to see some shapes from Thompson Station.

"Monty," Nath Boone said. "You know he don't answer to that from you."

"Henry, then," Little kept on. "You never did finish telling that story. Where you come from, and niggers rising up to kill white folks and all."

Jerry leaned forward to try the heat of his improvised Dutch oven with his palm. Nodding, he sat back over his heels again, then began to slap a lump of grayish dough flat onto a scrap of board.

"All right," Henri said. "Which did you want me to tell you first?"

Little shot him a suspicious look. "Ain't but one right way to tell a story."

"Fine," Henri said. "I'll tell it backward then."

I'd been to Louisville already the day you crossed me on the road, he said. *I knew the guns were there and meant to have them for my people. I was looking to meet Frank Merriam there, and Osborne Anderson, and Owen Brown. They never showed up. I don't know where they are to this day. I couldn't take those pistols on my own. We didn't have money to buy them you know. I stayed around that town too long, hoping the others were going to come. After four days I crossed Israel Green in the street. What he was doing there I don't know. He didn't make out that he knew me then, but I know he must have for that very night they broke in the door where I was sleeping and the best I could do was jump out the window. I had my shirt and my britches and a knife I kept in the bed with me. No time to get my boots or my gun. They had more men waiting for me down in the street but I climbed up and went over the rooftop and then I ran for the river and floated down.*

"Owen Brown!" Kelley said, eyes widening.

You know that name. The son of old Osawatomie Brown, out of Bloody Kansas. I was with them there at Harpers Ferry. I got away with Owen, and Osborne and Merriam, a few others too. There was supposed to be a thousand slaves rise up to take the guns that we had captured. But it looks like all that came was two.

"Why . . ." Little's eyes widened. "That's the same goddamned murdering abolitionist John Brown the Yankees sings about whilst they march. You ought to been hanged right along with him."

"If you say so," Henri said. "But then I'd have missed being here with you."

"Be quiet, Monty," Nath Boone said. "Let the man tell his story."

But Henri was watching Jerry cut cat-head biscuits with the rim of his dented tin cup. He lifted the lid of his Dutch oven and slicked the iron with a fingerful of lard. The hot smell of molten hog fat made Henri's back teeth hurt.

Nath Boone raised his head to Henri. "Was you to Kansas with the Browns?" he said.

"No," Henri said. "Not Kansas."

"So, then?" Boone said.

"So then before," Henri said. "I'm going backward, am I not? There's always something behind the thing you saw before."

All present then watched reverently as Jerry laid rounds of dough on the floor of his skillet and scraped up coals to cover the lid. All save Jeffrey Forrest, who continued to dance with the shade of his belle.

New Orleans, Henri said. *La Louisiane. I came to Louisville from there and I came from there to Harpers Ferry before that. I meant to raise black men along the way both times. Raise them to fight their way free of slavery. But most of them, they wouldn't be raised.*

"Niggers," Little said. "What do you expect?"

"Mr. Little," Henri said. "There's times I'd like to thread a meat hook through your tongue and hang you from it."

Little stared at him balefully, his jaws clenched tight.

"Don't think it's never happened," Henri said. "I've seen it done to nice little white men very much the same as yourself. You wouldn't believe how much tongue you've got, once it all pulls out. You can't see how it ever fit in your head in the first place."

"Let up, Monty," Nath Boone said. "You don't quit rubben the man the wrong way, he won't never get this story told."

Mister Little has a point. This country did teach me something I'd have never thought before. There is such a thing as nigger after all. Something a little less than a man. Born a slave. Dies a slave. Being a slave is built into him. I'll leave you white gentlemen to consider who it was did that building.

Henri stopped speaking because he could feel Matthew's eyes boring into him, from where the boy sat with his long legs folded like a grasshopper.

I don't mean you. I don't mean me. Nor Denmark Vesey nor Nat Turner nor Gabriel Prosser nor Charles Deslandes. There are black men in this coun-

try who walk with a warrior spirit. But just some is not enough. It needs to be all and so far it's not. Not one time when I went up and down the Mississippi River. They won't rise. Not yet they won't.

"I'd admire to see New Orleans," Nath Boone said. "My uncle went there oncet on a flatboat. 'Course after that he had to walk back."

La Louisiane. It was safe for me there. In a manner of speaking. I speak the languages. Spanish and French and the old tongue too. There's not so much a mystery about what I am in that place. I'll tell you what, Mathieu mon cher, down in La Nouvelle Orléans you'd be a man of color. Up here they count me as a nigger just like you.

Henri stopped, or was stopped, rather, by the bitterness he heard in his own laughter. He'd meant to take a straight line backward, but his story was beginning to slip sideways. Nath Boone called him back.

"You ain't from Loosiana either in the first place, is that right?"

No. I come from Ayiti.

"Well, I never heard of any such a place—" Little began, but it was Kelley who stopped him this time.

"He means Haiti," Kelley said. "The Black Republic."

"What do you mean the Black Republic?" Little said. "That don't make no sense."

"It means the niggers are in charge," Kelley said. "They run the plantations. They run the government. They run the whole country. They speak French too! The bottom rail's on top is what that means."

"I don't understand you," Little said. "What happened to the white folks, then?"

"They died," Henri told him.

"That can't be," Little said. "Niggers running everything. It ain't right. It ain't natural. I don't see how God could allow it."

"I don't see how God allows you," Henri said. "As a matter of fact you've been disallowed already and just don't know it yet."

"But," Kelley said, "why didn't you stay in Haiti? I mean, I don't understand why you would leave there and come over here to fight with Nathan Bedford Forrest for the Confederacy."

"It's a fair question," Henri said. "I'll admit that wasn't exactly my plan."

"Y'all hush," said Nath Boone. "Let the man tell it."

In Haiti is an emperor, a black man named Soulouque. I served in his army, but he took against me. Because of my skin, and the blood underneath it. I saw that if I remained in Ayiti, Soulouque would have me killed.

"So then you came to Louisiana," Kelley prompted.

I'm going backward. His eyes still heavily lidded, Henri rocked slightly from the waist.

"The blood, then," Kelley said. "This blood of yours that scared your black King so."

Ah. Henri rocked in place. His eyes popped open. *Yes. There is always something more behind the thing you see. There is for example Dessalines. Who spilled the blood of every white person he could catch. Hundreds. Thousands. At Jérémie a river of blood five feet across dried up and stayed until the summer rains. The nègres of that zone walked miles out of their way so that they would not have to cross it. But the blood of Dessalines is not my blood. No. I have the blood that made the first rising and sent the white men screaming into the sea. From the man without whom Dessalines would be nothing. Sé fils Toussaint Louvti mwen yé.*

"Toussaint Louverture?" Kelley said. "You're the son of Toussaint Louverture?"

Henri did not appear to hear him.

Et deye sa? Et deye sa? There's always another thing behind the thing you see. Behind Toussaint is Gaou-Ginou, and all the kings in Dahomey since the jaguar spirit made Arada and flew up into the night sky on his burning wings.

"Stop it," Little cried, as if in pain. "Stop all that wild nigger jabber. It's nothing but superstition and savagery anyhow."

Listen, Henri said furiously. *There's something else behind the jaguar too. When God made the first man he was black as the night with no stars in it. You people got that sick color of yours from a sorcerer's curse or some kind of disease. From hiding in caves for five or ten centuries because you don't have the spirit to stand in the sun. I'd like to see you call God's first man a nigger.*

"I don't see that man here," said Little, bristling.

"No you don't." Henri said wearily. "You don't see a damn thing."

Little subsided and raised a placating hand. "Henry," he said. "I don't mean you any offense."

"Dear God," Henri said. "I believe you might be fool enough to actually mean what you just said."

Little opened his mouth but said nothing. He turned his head to spit to the back side of the log where he was sitting, and did not raise his eyes again.

"Let me see if I'm folleren you right," Nath Boone said. "You come here because you want rile up our niggers to kill all the white folks?"

"You could put it that way. It's a shame they won't do it. Things don't always work out like you plan." Henri looked in the fire for a minute, then back to Boone. "On the other hand, you're doing a really nice job of killing each other."

He fell silent. The old language hummed in his head. Going backward had a gravity to it. You fell into that and kept falling. He thought of the giddy surge of black men rising. How it should have been that way for John Brown but was not. Should have been that way for himself but was not. At most of the plantations he had visited the slaves looked at him like he was some dark spirit come to steal their souls. Some did rise to his suggestion, but only a very few—young men, or hotheaded boys really, without attachments or the full knowledge of fear. There were many more willing to run than to fight. The memory of Africa had been bred right out of them.

Still, he was looking across the clearing into Matthew's eyes, which burned yellowish like a cat's in the dark. In the space behind those eyes at least, the flame of Henri's thought found fuel.

Jerry then unveiled his skillet and a warm full baking smell embraced the men. Within the circle of the iron the biscuits, airy and golden, seemed to float.

"Thank God," Kelley said, and surreptitiously wiped saliva from the corner of his mouth. No one said any more of a blessing than that. But when Jerry reached into his poke and drew out a pat of butter wrapped in damp leaves a sigh went round the group. When a honeycomb in a cracked white bowl appeared, that sigh became a moan.

Henri forced himself to eat slowly. So as not to burn his mouth, or choke. To make it last longer too, of course. He thought of the cassava he had used to eat (with luck) during his campaigns with

Soulouque's army. Cassava kept better and one could march longer on a smaller amount of that bread. But these light hot biscuits were very, very good. Henri was near weeping with joy as he ate his portion and he saw the other men were too. Only Jeffrey Forrest, waltzing the woman he held tight in his arms to the thin droning tune the Old Ones sustained, seemed unaware of the feast before them. Even the woman he held had tilted her weight toward Jerry's pan, her soft eyes melting toward a few crumbs that remained there.

"Look here," Little said suddenly. "Something is wrong with this biscuit, Jerry. Look, my jawbone goes right through it."

Jerry wouldn't look at him. Hunkered over the dying fire, he was scouring his iron skillet with white ash. "Listen at the haint fussen bout a biscuit," Jerry said "Haint, you lucky to be getten biscuit at all."

"But . . ." Little's faintly transparent lips were trembling. He put the biscuit into his mouth and bit at it savagely, but the biscuit reappeared whole and unharmed in his palm beneath the point of his jaw.

Nath Boone choked, covered his mouth with his huge calloused hand, and scooted away from Little on the log.

"They ain't nothen wrong with my biscuit," Jerry said. "Sompn wrong with *you*."

AFTER THE MEAL, while the others slept, Henri circled the top of the knoll like a dog following a fence round a yard. The fog that swirled around his knees was yellowish and smelled of burnt gunpowder. It seemed that the bloodstained river wrapped all around this hilltop now, and it also seemed to Henri that the water was rising. Wagons and guns and mules and men were getting sucked down in the bloody stream, where at first there was shouting and crashing and the concussion of gunfire, but as the water rose further it all grew quiet and corpses and wreckage revolved in silence.

By the hollow tree, Kelley hunkered over his heels, gazing intently at a space of packed earth between his knees. His mouth moved silently, Henri could see. He might have been praying. He might have been talking to himself in Chinese. Henri turned back to his view of the river, studying how bundles of blood-thread unraveled in the water without exactly ever dissolving.

"Blood on the moon," Kelley said, bracing his hands to the small of his back and stretching from his long hunker on the ground. "Or to put it more clearly, *the sun became black as a sack of goat hair, and the moon became as blood.*"

Henri looked at him. There was no moon. It was daylight, after a fashion—the damp misty no-time and no-place of this hilltop. Kelley looked at him still, in rather a friendly fashion.

"You know," he said. "I've been thinking about that story you told."

Henri studied him until he understood what he must be talking about.

"That was no story," he said. "That was the truth."

"Ah," Kelley said. From a grubby handkerchief he unfurled a fragile pair of spectacles which he settled fastidiously onto his nose. He looked into the palm of his empty hand as though something were printed there. "I once had read something of your Tuissant le Overture," he said. "It seems to me that he must have died—oh, around the turn of the last century."

Henri watched him. Kelley furled his spectacles back into the cloth and tucked them cautiously into his breast pocket.

"This proposition that you're his son," he said. "Why, you'd have to be sixty-five years old, Henri! At the very least. And I'd scarce take you for forty."

"You people think you know what time is because you invented watches," Henri said.

Kelley put a finger on his lower lip and appeared to be thinking this last remark over. Henri got a grip on himself. "A man may get a child in other ways than with blood and spunk," he said. "A man may have a son of his spirit."

Kelley dropped his hand from his face and looked at Henri with fresh interest.

"A child of God, you may call yourself," Henri said.

"That's from a song you people sing."

Henri looked away from him, shaking his head. Gaps had begun to open in the mist and through them he could see that the bloodstained water was now beginning to recede. On the long shelves of limestone emerging from the flood, there appeared to be etched events from either the past or the future: Fort Pillow, Parker's Crossroads, Chickamauga . . . Was it the future that hadn't happened yet? Or was that the past?

Henri said, "I didn't know *you people* knew about Toussaint."

"Ah well," said Kelley. "We didn't really *want* to know about him, but some of us did. I believe he may have been the most remarkable nigger to have ever lived, as a matter of fact. But it wouldn't do to talk too much about him here—only get *our* niggers all stirred up."

Kelley did not seem much perturbed by the look Henri was burning on him now. "Let's say it's true you were with John Brown," he said. "What would have happened if he had succeeded? Do you suppose a pack of Africans can make a nation? No, they must revert to savagery, and you will have nothing but war and destruction. As you described it under your chieftain—the one who rules Haiti today."

Henri shaded his eyes with one hand, squinting at reflections from the receding water below the knoll. "Pardon me, Mister Kelley," he said, "But what exactly do you think you've got here and now?"

"A judgment on us, possibly," Kelley said. "I have considered that." He regarded Henri with his eyes pale blue behind the speckled lenses. "But what about you?" he said. "Monty has a point, don't he? I mean, the Yankees are fielding black regiments now. Why aren't you leading one of them?"

"Because that's not what happened," Henri said.

A white owl flew in out of the mist and settled on a limb of the dead tree. It preened its yellowish feathers and shrugged. Henri turned away when the owl's large black eyes fell upon him.

"The Romans believed it meant death," Kelley said. "An owl looking at you, I mean."

"That's nothing to me." Henri swallowed a laugh. "Are you sure he's not looking at you?" He knew Kelley would survive the war but more than likely Kelley didn't know that.

"*And the owl, and the nighthawk, and the cuckoo and the hawk after his kind, and the little owl and the cormorant and the great owl, and the swan, and the pelican, and the gyre eagle.* All abominations," Kelley said. "According to Leviticus, eleven sixteen."

"He only meant you're not supposed to eat them," Henri said. When he looked at the owl again its eyes were closed.

"Bedford Forrest is a man I can follow," he said. "I don't know if I can really tell you why that is."

"But maybe I know what you mean," Kelley said. "He takes whoever comes his way one at a time."

"It could be I'm not meant to lead but to follow," Henri said. "That might be why I couldn't get the slaves to rise."

"Or it could be that God's design is for black people to be ruled and governed by white," Kelley said. "Mister Jefferson said so in his book, or rather he *suspected* so. *I advance it therefore as a suspicion only, that the blacks, whether originally a distinct race, or made distinct by time and circumstances, are inferior to the whites in endowments both of body and mind.* A great many others have thought so too."

"Do you really believe all that horseshit?" Henri said.

"I don't know," Kelley said. "I think probably I believed it before I ever thought much about it, but the more I think about it the less sense it makes."

The owl poked up its tail feathers and crapped out a small dry pellet of mouse hair and bone. The pellet made no sound when it struck the dirt beneath the tree.

"And you?" Kelley said. "You think we're all niggers under the skin, didn't you just say so?"

"We're all blood and bone under the skin," Henry said. "And a little gristle. You've seen as much of that these last few years as anyone."

"That notion has been growing in me, though," Kelley said, in no way derailed from the track of his previous thought. "I'm beginning to doubt that a soul has a color, in God's eye."

CHAPTER TWENTY-SIX

September 1863

Under the shade of a great magnolia, Henri stretched on his back in Jerry's wagon bed, his head pillowed on fresh sweet straw. He'd just had a tremendous dinner served to him and Jerry and Matthew in Bellevue's kitchen: fried ham and turnip greens and black-eyed peas and biscuits with cold butter and peach preserves. So now he dozed, full and heavy, opening one eye now and again to watch the pale undersides of the waxy green leaves above him shivering whenever a breeze passed through them. It was twilight and the doves were calling, their liquid voices burbling as they left the ground for the eaves of the mansion or the branches of the four magnolias that framed the white-columned portico.

Matthew sprawled facedown beside him, snoring in the straw. Beside him was a snarl of half-mended harness, a spool of pack thread and an awl. Jerry sat on the wagon box, brushing dried mud from Forrest's riding boots.

"I don't believe he's had theseyear boots off in six months," Jerry said. "Not by the way they smells . . ."

At the sound of tramping in the street, Henri pulled himself up by a wagon rail. A cartridge popped and Matthew shot up like a rocket, clawing a revolver from his belt before his sleep-glazed eyes were well open. Henri pushed the barrel down and away from him.

"It can't be anything," he said. "There's not a Yankee in a hundred miles of here."

But he climbed out of the wagon and peered down the slope from the house to the street. The view was obscured by a high boxwood hedge. Behind him the front door of the house swung open and Doctor Cowan came trotting down the steps, buttoning his coat.

Henri and Matthew straggled after him, to the gate of the spear-point iron fence that enclosed Bellevue's front lawn.

"I heard it but I didn't believe it," Cowan said. "Boys, it's the Nancy Harts."

Down the street came marching some forty women, all ages and sizes but most appearing to be in their twenties, most wearing their everyday dresses and hats but a couple of them got up in hoop skirts. They were armed with a motley of old shotguns and muskets from the previous century, barrels lashed to the stocks with rusting wire. Their leader, a young woman with a flushed face and hair beginning to come loose from the pins under her hat, wore a Revolutionary War sword belted to her slender hips. The scabbard's point dragged a furrow in the dirt behind her.

"Did you ever . . ." Cowan said, and Henri admitted that he never did.

"THE HELL?" Forrest stood in his shirttail, bare toes curling on the board floor, gazing across the portico roof at the end of the queer parade. A threesome of spotted dogs trotted at the heels of the last pair of women in the passing column. He glanced over his shoulder, then looked back toward the street. Mary Ann sat up in the bed, closing her gown at her throat with one hand.

"It's the Nancy Hart Home Guard," she said. "Nancy Morgan and Mary Cade Heard got it up between them."

Forrest shot her a queer look. "How many battles has they fit?"

"Well . . ." Mary Ann slipped her feet to the hearth rug beside the half-tester bed and crossed to the window to join him. She glanced a bit wistfully at the ashes in the black marble fireplace. Her bare feet felt chilly once they'd walked off the rug. It was not quite cold enough for a fire, but she'd ordered one for last night notwithstanding, and she had it in mind to order another. Senator Hill had taken his wife to their place in Athens, leaving the Forrests the run of Bellevue and command of its servants—in honor of Forrest's first leave in eighteen months. Mary Ann had not stopped anywhere quite so fine as this in a very long time and she wanted to try all the mansion's amenities before the whole situation melted away.

"They knocked down a hornets' nest with a stray ball once," she told him. "That engagement was counted a defeat, I believe. And then they killed a neighbor's cow, which one might consider a Pyrrhic victory I suppose. But all that was in the early days, when they were still learning how to shoot."

Forrest looked at her sidelong, suppressing a snort. Though she was not quite touching him he could feel the blowsy warmth of her, fresh from the bedding.

"Mrs. Morgan called this morning, as a matter of fact," Mary Ann said. "With Mrs. Heard. They'd be honored if you would review their troops."

"Review them? Review them? Ain't they no West Pint mollycoddle slinken around as kin review a gang of women soldiers? In all my life I don't know if I ever heard such a goddamn knee-knocken pack of—"

"Stop!" Mary Ann bumped him with her hip; if the gesture was playful, her voice had hardened. "You oughtn't to mock them, Mister Forrest. There's not been an able-bodied man in LaGrange since eighteen sixty-one. Nancy Morgan's husband went off to war before they'd been married more than six months, and her scarce twenty-one years old. And there's Mary Heard running two plantations all on her lonesome and a hundred slaves between them. This militia business keeps their spirits up, if nothing else. And who knows if it won't come in handy before all's said and done?"

"You want me to review'm, Miz Forrest?" He drew her to him, feeling the round heat of breast and belly come willingly against his side through the thin cloth. "All right then— Ladies, stand to arms!"

"What I want you to do is come back to bed." She ran her slim fingers up under his shirttail. "It's been too long and I can't get—."

"It's been fifteen minutes," Forrest muttered, though happy enough to follow where she led. It was an excellent featherbed too—made of the finest, softest down—though already in need of a thorough good beating and airing.

NEXT MORNING FORREST, his boots and uniform well brushed, stood more or less at attention in the square of LaGrange, with Mary Ann beside him in a Sunday dress just slightly shiny at the elbows, watching the Nancy Hart Home Guard drill. Though he had small patience with such exercises even when performed by professional fighting men, he kept a straight face throughout the proceedings. When First Sergeant Adelie Bull demonstrated how she could shoot the pips out of a playing card at thirty paces, Forrest broke into a genuine smile.

"Lieutenant Morgan, Lieutenant Heard—" he said as those ladies presented their arms, "Now by the long scaly tail of the D—"

Mary Ann elbowed him.

"By the beard and the belly of G—"

This time a sharp look was sufficient.

"By all that's *holy* if I may say so, I'd sooner be commanded by the pair of you than that shilly-shallying milksop *Braxton Bragg*."

Though the two young women looked as much pleased as perplexed, Mary Ann piloted him quickly away, through a circle of onlookers around the square. Matthew was there with a couple of his usual companions and it struck Forrest, not for the first time, how his wife could practically walk through the boy without seeming to see hide nor hair of him.

"You've scandalized those poor young ladies," Mary Ann said, once she'd hauled him into the Bellevue parlor. "Or frightened them, even—I worry you have."

"I swan they took it as a compliment," Forrest said. "As for them to be frightened, why we all ought to be."

Mary Ann walked to the rosewood piano, struck a cluster of notes, and revolved back toward him on the embroidered stool. "What do you mean?"

Forrest had said more than he meant to but he saw there was no retreat. Charge then.

"All right," he said. "If what we got now is women for soldiers, I reckon I might as well take counsel with you."

"I reckon you may have had worse counsel," she came back at him. "I've heard of that letter you sent to General Bragg. Captain Anderson says it near scorched his fingers to set down those words."

"You've got no quarrel with Anderson," Forrest said.

"I don't." Mary Ann swung from side to side on the stool, threw back her head of pale hair. "What scares me is you, when you won't rein yourself in."

Forrest paced, boot heels snapping on the floor. "Cain't run on a tight rein all the time. And I've held myself in mighty hard—since Shiloh, or the next thing to it."

Mary Ann parted her lips as if she'd speak and decided not to. Forrest had his head down, tramping heavily around the room.

"I mean to give Bragg a piece of my mind," he said. "He's shouldered me out the road every chance he got—and I don't even know if he does it for meanness or just because he's a *goddamn fool*. Might near ever time I get up a command he makes me turn it over to somebody else. Men I raised myself, and armed and fed and mounted. By God I'd even swaller that if he made good use of'm but he damn well don't."

Forrest stopped and stared out the front window. In the faint reflection from the watery glass she could see him bite into his lip and release it. "Since we got ourselves run out of Vicksburg, I could do us some good on the Mississippi River," he said. "Can I get an order from Bragg to go there? No I cannot."

He raised his head slightly and peered through the glass before him. There seemed to be some kind of interest building in the street below. People were gathering outside the Bellevue gate, though they were not looking up at the mansion. Others were coming out from behind the house, drifting down the lawn to join them. Forrest clucked his tongue and resumed the oval of his pacing. A loose rowel on his left spur clattered as he walked.

"Everbody bet too much on General Lee in the first place," he said. "Like they wasn't any state in the Confederacy but Virginia. Well now Lee has got himself whupped in Pennsylvania and right now hit's the most he can do to keep the Yankees out of Richmond. And d'ye know what that means?"

He had wheeled on her. Mary Ann raised her chin, but he didn't leave her time to answer and she wasn't sure what she'd say anyway.

"What means is that the Army of Tennessee is goen to count and it's a-goen to count for life or death. It's nigh bout the only thing standing in the way of the Yankees eaten our entrails clean across to the ocean. And what has *Bragg* done with that army? Well he let it get flanked out of Middle Tennessee without so much as offeren to fight. He had the Yankees in the palm of his hand at Chickamauga and he damn well let'm walk away."

Forrest closed his own hand and banged his thigh with the fist. "Ain't no such thing as a drawn battle," he said. "Not no more. It's win or lose and by God we look like losen if we don't straighten out and do it damn quick. I know I can beat any pack of Yankees I meet afore air a one of them West Point sonsabitches can get his damn slide rule limbered up. I don't only know it, I've proved it too—"

"I know you have," Mary Ann said, rising from the piano stool. "I'm proud of you for it. We all are. But—"

His eyes shot through her and she paused.

"I don't believe the Yankees can whup us," Forrest said. "I won't believe that. But we look mighty like whuppen our own selves."

"Do you think putting yourself on the wrong side of General Bragg will help that?" Mary Ann said. "You've made me understand he's not fit for his place. But what does it help to pursue a quarrel among ourselves?"

"It'll help me do what I said I would," Forrest said shortly. "I told the man I was comen to see him. Have you known me not to stand behind my word?"

"No," said Mary Ann, exhaling, "and I don't suppose I ever will." Or that I'd have it any other way, she thought.

Forrest's head snapped toward the window. "What's all that hooraw?"

At the bottom of the lawn the street was now fairly lined with people who all shuffled their feet and looked expectantly to the west. A couple of ten-year-old boys were pulling a length of red yarn taut across the thoroughfare, right in front of the Bellevue gate.

"By God it's a horse race." He turned to her, his features flickering with an odd mix of irritation and pleasure, and caught her by the hand. "Come on—let's go see."

They were halfway down the lawn when the rhythm of hoofbeats quieted the rustle and hum of talk among the crowd. Willie, flogging King Philip for all he was worth, appeared neck and neck with young Witherspoon, who was probably riding a superior horse. Mary Ann's breath caught; it was like watching her own heart flying away outside of her body. At the last instant King Philip edged a half length ahead and it was his straining chest that broke the strand of yarn.

A cheer went up. Willie slowed the horse to a canter as he brought him around in the next intersection, then came trotting back, preening his mustache with the thumb of his free hand. Hands reached up to pat his knees. Some people were counting out money to pay their bets. Witherspoon leaned sideways in the saddle to shake hands with Willie. Forrest dropped Mary Ann's hand and strode down the gate. He fixed Willie with a cocked forefinger.

"William! Go and walk that horse till he's good and cool. And I mean do hit yoreself, hear me? Don't ye hand it to nobody else to do for ye."

"Yes sir," Willie said, his triumph now just slightly muted. Forrest had already turned from him and was walking up the slope of the greensward toward Mary Ann, his face the same struggling mix of annoyance and excitement. She took his arm and they stood there a moment more, watching the crowd dissolve.

"Well, he's too big to whup I reckon," Forrest said, a little ruefully. "I'd dock his pay but ain't nobody drawen none!" He shook his head. "That boy cain't think of a thing more fun than a war."

ON THE MORNING of the tenth day of his leave at LaGrange, Forrest woke to a muttering he took at first to be the sound of a light rain. But when he opened his eyes the windows streamed with sunshine. It was a little too warm in the bedroom, from embers of the fire Mary Ann had insisted on lighting the night before. Now she knelt before the window, her bare toes snug on the oval carpet, her knees pressing through the cotton of her gown onto the bare poplar boards beneath the windowsill.

That muttering he'd heard was prayer. For a moment he watched her between the bedposts, the bluish tint of her eyelids shifting as her eyes looked one way or another into the world of the unseen. Sunlight flowed through her yellow hair.

He got up quickly and pulled on trousers and his boots. She did not ordinarily pray where he could hear her and it troubled him to see her do it now.

But now she tied off her amens, he supposed, and rose to face him with a fragile smile. "You don't look like you mean to tarry."

"Time's up," Forrest said, shrugging into his tunic. "I got to git on to see that man I aim to see."

"I know it," she said, lowering her eyes for just a moment before she raised them back to his. "My love goes with you." She tightened a blue ribbon at the throat of her gown. "And my prayers."

Forrest looked away from her, though he was not a man who flinched.

"General Forrest." She took a barefoot step toward him. "Have you never thought to pray?"

"You know the answer," he said shortly. "I ain't never got down on my knees and hung my head to beg nobody for nothen. And I never—" He stopped. "The Lord he'ps those as he'ps themselves," he said. "Momma used to say that sometimes. I reckon it's the only prayer I know. And I say it standing on my own two feet."

He paused and thought for a minute more. "I don't want to be beholden to nobody."

Mary Ann raised her head. "Not even to God."

"To God least of all," Forrest told her.

She nodded. "So be it, then."

He had taken two steps toward the door when he turned back suddenly to catch her in his arms.

"I'm not about to leave you like that," he said. He lifted her chin with the ball of a finger. "I love you with all I got in me, Mary Ann, and I'll come back to you forever, while I live."

She tucked her cheek into his collarbone and they stood so for a moment there. Presently Forrest broke the embrace and left the room without waiting to look into her face again.

THE FIRE in General Forrest's bedroom had burned to ash. Jerry was suffering a touch of arthritis, so Henri and Matthew carried in fresh wood. Matthew tumbled down his load every which way on the hearthstone, but in spite of the clatter Mrs. Forrest didn't seem to look at him.

She stood at the end of the neatly made half-tester bed, in a gown, and plain cotton slippers, and a shawl wrapped tight around her shoulders. It was scarcely cold enough for a fire at all but she held herself as if she were chilled, though without shrinking or stooping. She was straight and supple as a willow, her chin high and her gaze flowing out through the front windows and over the downward flow of the lawn.

As Matthew shoveled ash into a tin scuttle, a few coals came to a dusty red life. Henri pushed them between the andirons with the poker, laid a splinter or two of kindling and three chunks of red oak. He crouched on his hands and knees and blew an orange flame up from the coals. When he sat back on his heels, Matthew was already leaving the room with the scuttle, transparently as a ghost might have done, and Mary Ann Forrest was looking at Henri with a small flicker of interest in her eyes.

Dites-moi, Henri, she said. *Pourquoi est-ce vous qui m'apporte du bois ce matin?*

Henri got to his feet as gracefully as he could manage. *Parce que je voudrais vous servir, Madame.*

The countrified flavor of her French, which she had probably acquired at some finishing school in Nashville, amused him a little. Of course his own would have sounded provincial in Paris. He wanted to hear her again in his tongue, but her next words to him were in English.

"You may be a colored man, Henri, but you are certainly no servant."

"No ma'am. I have never been a servant, nor a slave." He inclined his head. "But I would serve you all the same."

"Then you are gallant." She turned and took a step toward him, and he admired the smoothness of her movement, how her head floated above her shawled shoulders, like a vase delicately balanced there. The women of his own country acquired such grace by carrying water on their heads. Perhaps Mary Ann had circled the parlors of her school in the same manner, balancing a book instead of a jar. Her lips were redder than he remembered, but then her husband had just left her. Henri lowered his head and poked at the fire. It was unwise to look at a white woman directly for too long, most especially the wife of General Forrest.

"Ah." She came nearer to him now, but only to spread her hands above the hearth. "Thank you—it is a grateful warmth."

Henri seemed to feel the glow of her body as much as the heat of the freshening flames. That was no more circumspect than the other thing. He crouched and began to collect the sticks Matthew had scattered and set them into the old ham boiler where they were stored before burning.

"You are distinctly tidier than . . . your companion."

"Matthew?" Henri said. "I didn't know you would acknowledge him, even with your eyes."

That part slipped out. Henri stopped his breath.

"Oh," said Mary Ann, turning more tightly toward the fire. "That one may be better off if I don't see him."

Henri considered how this answer might be both wrong and right. No doubt it was a strictly truthful one, from her perspective. An admirable woman, Henri thought. He began to search his mind for a safe way of getting out of this room.

"Arise," Mary Ann said. The hint of playfulness returned to her tone.

Henri stood up. *"A votre service."*

"Vous êtes sérieux?"

Their eyes met for a moment, before Henri looked down.

"As serious as you," he said. But he had seen she was not really playing.

"Well then." She walked from the fireplace toward the window, dropping her hands and letting them float freely at her sides. "General Forrest is going to call upon General Bragg. To put it more plainly, he is going to pick a dangerous quarrel with him."

"Madame, what would you?"

"I would have someone—" She caught her lower lip in her top teeth, then released it. Henri observed this action in the faint reflection of the sunlit windowpane. She turned toward him.

"Go with him, I suppose."

"I've heard that Doctor Cowan means to go."

"Yes, but Doctor Cowan can't control him."

A harsh, involuntary laugh barked out of Henri's throat. "You know nobody can control him. And I . . . I can't control anything. All I can do is watch."

"Witness." She had found his eyes again.

"Indeed, *Madame,* I have witnessed many things." He looked away and so did she.

"Very well," she told him. "Go witness this one."

IT TURNED OUT that Forrest had not yet departed for his rendezvous with General Bragg. Henry contrived to get himself and Matthew sent to deliver a dispatch to the headquarters at Missionary Ridge. Arriving late, they'd passed the night there, and as nothing particular pressed them to return, they lingered still. The air was clear and the view was fine and they had got a very generous supper among a company of men they knew, whom General Bragg had recently transferred from Forrest's command to General Wheeler's.

Henri was sitting on a broken caisson, resting his back on the bark of a pin oak, dozing with one eye open, when Forrest rode over a crest of the ridge, his dark coat wrapped around him like a storm cloud and his deep-set eyes two holes into the black empty depths of the universe. Doctor Cowan rode to his left, wordless and pale as if he were on his way to a funeral that might be his own.

"I think somebody's going to get killed," Matthew hissed.

Both Henri's eyes were open now, and both he and Matthew had rolled quietly to their feet. Forrest swung down from his dappled gray horse while it was still walking forward and dropped the reins on the ground without looking as he strode toward Braxton Bragg's tent. Cowan dismounted to bring up his rear. Matthew ran to catch up the reins of the dappled gray and Cowan's mount and bring them to a halt.

An aide-de-camp popped out of Bragg's tent, pushing both palms forward as if he meant to block Forrest's approach. Henri saw Forrest's eyes assume their feral yellow glow, saw his body begin its automatic compression and coil. But the aide somehow melted out of his way before anything had touched him. Through the raised tent flap Henri saw Bragg starting up from behind his camp table, mouth open, one hand falling to his hip as Forrest transfixed him with an index finger which looked dark with blood. The same forefinger, Henri thought, that Forrest had used to close the hole in his horse's jugular on the fourth day of Chickamauga.

Cowan followed him in, and the tent flap fell behind them. The walls of the tent shuddered and appeared to glow red, as if everything inside were burning. During one of his crossings of the Central South before the war, Henri had come upon a black bear mauling a coon dog. The sounds that were now coming out of the tent were just the same grumble and crunch and roar of that bear— only he didn't hear the screams of the dog this time.

At last Forrest stalked out of the tent, black in the face and still shaking with rage. Doctor Cowan stood just out of his reach, watching him carefully, as if in case Forrest should fall in an apoplectic seizure, Cowan would nick a vein with a scalpel in time to stop his heart or brain from exploding. But in a few minutes Forrest's face had simmered down to something like its normal shade.

"If you meant to get yourself drummed out of this army," Cowan said quietly, "I expect you might just have done it this time."

Forrest shook his head. "He'll never say a word about it." He took the reins of the dappled gray, just barely registering Matthew with his eyes. Before he swung into the saddle, he spat on the ground. "He'll be the last man to mention it, and mark my word, he'll take no action in the matter. I will ask to be relieved and transferred to a different field and he will not oppose it."

To that Cowan made no reply and no further word was spoken as the two men rode away, the hoofbeats of their horses fading down the ridge toward the river and the lowland.

FORREST HAD GONE on into Mississippi by the time Doctor Cowan rejoined his cousin at LaGrange. He reached the big house at the close of the day, and Mary Ann served him a bourbon and water, with a last green sprig of mint of the season, before she inquired what her husband had said to Bragg.

"Well." Cowan sipped, tilted his glass to capture a ray of sunset, swallowed. "To the best of my recollection . . .

"*I am not here to pass civilities or compliments with you, but on other business. You commenced your cowardly persecution of me soon after the battle of Shiloh, and you have kept it up ever since. You did it because I reported to Richmond facts, while you reported damned lies. You robbed me of my command in Kentucky and gave it to one of your favorites—men that I armed and equipped from the enemies of our country. In a spirit of revenge and spite, because I would not fawn upon you as others did, you drove me into West Tennessee in the winter of 1862 with improper arms and without sufficient ammunition, although I had made repeated applications for the same. You did it to ruin me and my career. When in spite of all this I returned with my command well equipped by captures, you began again your work of spite and persecution and have kept it up, and now this second brigade, organized and equipped without thanks to you or the government, a brigade which has won a reputation for successful fighting second to none in the army, taking advantage of your position as the commanding general in order to humiliate me, you have taken these brave men from me. I have stood your meanness as long as I intend to. You have played the part of a damned scoundrel, and are a coward, and if you were any part of a man I would slap your jaws and force you to resent it. You may as well not issue any more orders to me, for I will not obey them, and I will hold you personally responsible for any further indignities you may endeavor to inflict upon me. You have threatened to arrest me for not obeying your orders promptly. I dare you to do it, and I say to you that if you ever again try to interfere with me or cross my path it will be at the peril of your life."*

By the time he got to the end of his recitation, Mary Ann was laughing softly, in spite of herself. "Did he say it as pretty as that?" she said. "Is that just how he put it?"

"No," Cowan said, and nuzzled his drink. "He didn't put it exactly that way."

CHAPTER TWENTY-SEVEN

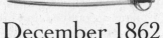

December 1862

"That's Damascus steel," John Morton said helpfully, as Forrest flexed the blade of the sword he'd just picked up from the Federal stores at Trenton. "It's imported, General."

"Is that a fact?" Forrest stroked his calloused palm beneath the blade, studying the intricate whorls of the many-times-folded metal.

Morton beamed back at him, his face as round and friendly as a biscuit. He'd been gamboling around Forrest, glad as a puppy, since Forrest had changed his mind and accepted him, theoretically, as a gunner, which hadn't gone so smoothly at first. Forrest already had a perfectly good captain of artillery in S. L. Freeman, and he didn't care to have that arrangement interfered with. *I'd like to know why in HELL Bragg sent that tallow-faced boy to take charge,* Henri had heard Forrest snarl when Morton first reported. Whereupon Morton rode a hundred-mile round-trip to get his orders confirmed by General Wheeler, and did it in just under twenty-four hours. Forrest stopped backbiting after that, for it was the kind of thing he might have done himself. Just nineteen years old, Morton was tougher than he looked, resilient, jovial, hard to dislike.

Forrest raised his head and glanced around the depot. "Hit's a shame," he remarked. "We'll have to burn up half this stuff."

"What for?" Morton asked him, suddenly crestfallen.

"Don't have men enough to haul it out of here," Forrest said shortly. "If hit ain't one thang hit's another."

"Ain't it the truth," Nath Boone said, exchanging a look with John Freeman, the artillery captain whose barrage had helped induce the Federal surrender earlier that same day. Forrest's men had been going hell for leather all over West Tennessee, since they'd crossed the Tennessee River at Clifton a week or so before, with two thousand men but a terrible shortage of caps for their firearms. Since then Forrest had been scavenging one day at a time, finding caps enough to fight a handful of small fierce engagements, dividing his forces again and again to make them seem to be everywhere in the region at once, ripping up railroad and bridges wherever they went. At night they burned five times as many fires as they needed and Forrest had the wagoneers beat kettledrums deep into the night, to make them seem more numerous than they were. Now here they were embarrassed by these riches.

"I mean to have this sword, anyway," Forrest said. "Christmas is a-comen." His teeth flashed in his beard as he turned toward Morton. "What air ye gapen at thar, son? Ye already done had yore Santy-Claus."

Morton smiled broadly at that thought. A couple of days back, they'd captured a Federal artillery unit at Lexington, made a hundred and fifty prisoners, and claimed a pair of cannon for Morton's use (for Forrest would assign none of Freeman's guns to him).

"Colonel Fry offered you a fine old sword," Morton said. Jacob Fry, a man well up in years, had practically had tears in his eyes when he unbuckled his sword belt to surrender Trenton and its garrison to Forrest. The weapon had been in his family for forty years, he said—he'd carried it in the Black Hawk War on the Illinois frontier in 1832. Then Forrest handed the sword back to him, with the hope he'd not use it on his own people in the future, and what was he thinking, Henri wondered now—did he suppose that Yankees and Rebels were still the same people?

"He won't be cutten nobody with that fer a spell," Forrest remarked. "And I do believe I like this'n better." He settled his grip on the hilt and swung the blade up. "It's light." Damascus steel sang in the close, powder-smelling air of the depot. "And it's limber."

He ran his thumb along the edge and pressed his lips together, thin and tight. The blade had been edged on one side only, as usual for a cavalry sword, and sharpened for no more than six inches back from the point. "We'll see to that shortly," Forrest said, though mostly under his breath.

He walked out holding the blade upright, the scabbard thrust through his wide leather belt, stepping high on the balls of his feet like a big cat. The men followed him out of the depot, into the frosty air of that December evening.

Forrest's camp spread out across the pastures from the edge of the village of Trenton. Campfires burned to the lip of the horizon, as if some enormous host had broken a march there. A dull roll of kettledrumming filled the air. Here Forrest had mustered most of the prisoners he'd taken since crossing into West Tennessee—at Trenton and a few other places.

Benjamin stood up in the back of his wagon, pounding out a dogged beat on a kettledrum as if he were driving railroad spikes. Despite the cold, he had sweated through the yoke of his osnaburg shirt. When Henri climbed into the wagon, Ben stopped thumping, almost gratefully it seemed, and stepped back. Elsewhere the deep rolling beat continued, all across Forrest's thinly spread camps.

Ben offered the sticks with their big round cottony tips to Henri, who shook his head, laying his bare hands on the drum skin, feeling for breath and a spirit inside. Presently he began a petro rhythm, quick, sharp and dry, using palm and fingertips together, cupping the downbeat, catching the deep center note with a roll of his wrist that used the thumb as a striker—Benjamin had drawn the thorn from that thumb, at Shiloh in the spring. He leaned on the rail of the wagon now, watching Henri, beginning to shift his hips a little to the more complicated rhythm, and the white boys passing were hearing it too, looking up curiously into the wagon, some of them maybe a little uneasy. Henri stopped. With a quick smile at Ben he jumped down from the wagon.

A sort of military exercise was under way—the only semiformal drill in which Forrest had ever taken an interest. Leaving their horses hobbled out of sight, about a thousand dismounted men marched by the prisoners in as close an order as they could manage, one detachment after another: left right left, forward march. They passed through the town, out of view of the prisoners, found their horses and left them to graze in some other field, returning to the drill again from this new angle, so it seemed to the prisoners, who would all be paroled the next day (as Forrest had not men enough to hold them), would return to Federal lines in Kentucky to report the Confederates had been reinforced from all directions, all through the night—there was an army at full strength. Already, thanks to such stratagems, rumor had inflated Forrest's numbers from two thousand to five—by tomorrow the guesswork would balloon to twenty thousand. As he passed his circling soldiers now, Forrest stopped to exchange salutes with the officers as smartly as he knew how, then lowered his gloved right hand and passed on, the Damascus sword still riding upright in his left. Most of their wagons were clustered around a livery stable here, and there was a little forge attached to it, idle now, its fire gone cold. Earlier that afternoon Forrest had impressed the blacksmith to trim hooves and shoe the horses that needed it, but the man had gone home to his supper, long since. Ginral Jerry was lingering there; he'd spent the afternoon holding horses for the smith, and soon Ben came to join him.

Forrest passed the forge, the anvil and the bellows, bending his eye on a grindstone, big as a wagon wheel and a hundred times as heavy, riding in a stout wooden carriage under the stable eaves. The pale stone seemed to glow a little in the dusk.

Jerry moved toward the crank handle, automatically, and the great stone round broke its inertia and began to revolve. Its surface was wide as both of Forrest's palms together, and Forrest didn't have small hands.

"I thought you told us a cavalryman was better off with a six-gun," Henri said.

"What if I did?" Forrest set the blade against the spinning stone; a thread of grating sound rose from the contact. "A man's better off with all he kin get."

Morton moved up for a closer look. Whatever Forrest turned a hand to fascinated him. Matthew came up too, rustling at Henri's elbow in the dim. Willie must have gone off somewhere to race the new-shod horses, with other young sports excited by the little victories of the day.

Forrest carried the blade with a slicing motion at a close angle against the turning stone, his grip so firm the metal never bounced or clattered, and the drone of the grinding was steady and smooth. Orville, the young Virginian who'd joined them several months before, kept clearing his throat for some reason. "Hold up," Forrest said to Jerry, who released the crank and let the stone drift to a halt. Forrest pushed back his sleeve and ran the top of his forearm across the freshened edge. A couple of wiry black hairs came away and floated off into the gloaming. "Another thang," Forrest grinned as he raised the blade. "This here don't never run out of ammunition." He turned to Jerry. "Let Ben step up. This part is goen to take a mite longer." A shower of sparks flew up this time when Forrest brought the steel to the turning stone, for he was grinding the blunt top of the blade. Henri exchanged a silent, white-eyed glance with Matthew.

Nath Boone raised a hand to his chin. "He's laid himself out a job of work."

Henri nodded and smiled faintly. He could see now that Forrest meant to file down an eighth-inch of metal on the top side of the blade, to make a second edge where none had been intended by the smith who forged it. He'd end up with a double-edged, razor-sharp sword, and likely it would not be used for shaving.

"General Forrest," Orville piped up.

Rapt in his task, Forrest didn't seem to hear him at first. He seldom paid much attention to Orville, who had been in his first year at West Point when the war began. Young and impetuous as John Morton, he was not half so likable. But he was strong in the saddle, and when he joined their company after Shiloh he'd been riding one racehorse and leading another.

"General?" Orville insisted now. "You're not supposed to sharpen a sword that way." He cleared his throat for the thirtieth time. "It's contrary to the rules of war."

Forrest heard him now, and turned so briskly that every man took one step back, including Ben. The crank kept on revolving with the momentum of the stone.

"The rules of war?" Forrest said.

Henri braced himself for a torrent of cursing.

"War ain't got no goddamn rules." But Forrest's voice hadn't climbed. He said it quietly. Sadly, almost. He let the Damascus blade spin down through his thumb and forefinger till the pommel rested on the ground. He pricked the ball of his finger on the point and showed the fine bead of blood to the men surrounding him. Then he licked it away with the tip of his tongue.

"War means fighting. And fighting means killing." Forrest turned to Ben. "Step up, son, and turn the grindstone."

And the stone's movement drew the other men to it, like a magnet would. Henri expected Orville to slink away, but he remained with the rest of them. The rolling of the kettledrums continued. They seemed to have gathered a shared overtone, a note held deep in a common throat. Henri felt the petro rhythm pulsing in his palms.

"War to the knife," Forrest said, in the same chanting pattern, his hands wreathed in sparks where he held blade to stone. "Knife to the hilt. They say the world itself turns like a grindstone. Over and over. Don't never stop." He looked up, while the metal still sang against the stone, including Morton, Orville, Matthew in his gaze. "Ye may whet yoreself agin it. Or let it grind ye down."

CHAPTER TWENTY-EIGHT

October 1864

HENRI AND MATTHEW RODE abreast through woods a few miles west of Paris Landing, on a trail of a drove of half-wild hogs. A hundred yards back, Ben's wagon lumbered along after them, making a more difficult way through the trees. Forrest had sent them all out requisitioning but it was harder than it used to be around here. Farmers were hiding all they had, from hams and dry corn to their half-grown children, and letting their livestock ramble the woods.

Hogs were crafty, mo' smarter than man, Jerry would say. Did say. Besides which it was hard to draw a bead on a hog with a pistol from the back of a horse cantering over rough ground. But Matthew had wounded a big spotted sow in the hindquarters, and her back leg was dragging a blood spoor over the carpet of oak leaves and acorns on which the hogs fed. At last Henri circled his horse ahead of her, hopped down and planted a bullet between her eyes.

"Bleed her, boy—don't just stand there!" Jerry shouted from the slow-moving wagon. Matthew stood, sword drawn, unsure of what do with it. Jerry skipped down from the wagon and ran toward them, unfolding a clasp knife from his bib pocket. He dropped to his knees beside the sow and in the same motion had slit her throat.

"Now he'p me hang her," he said, producing a length of cord from another pocket. In a moment the sow swung head down from a branch of a white oak. Matthew and Henri both skipped back as Jerry opened the sow's belly with a quick downward pull of the knife blade, and the sharp-smelling huddle of guts spilled out on the blood-soaked leaves. Jerry wiped the knife and looked at Matthew.

"Don't reckon you knows how to clean chitlens?" He snorted. "Done spent too much time hangen round the house."

He turned toward the wagon and called to Ben, who had got down to address his pair of mules. "What you doen? We got us a hog."

"Seen if a mule can eat acorns," Ben said.

"Can they?" Henri called.

"They can but they won't."

A gunshot exploded and Henri crouched and looked for his horse, who had shied away—he crawled two yards forward and caught the trailing reins.

"Hog thieves! Hog thieves!"

At the edge of the trees a starveling boy was reloading an ancient firearm with an octagon barrel twice as long as he was tall. A girl in a ragged skirt assisted him, standing on a stump to ram in the charge.

"Hold up," Ben called from the wagon. "We got money to pay." He waved a fistful of brown Confederate scrip he'd grabbed from a bushel basket of the stuff in the back of the wagon.

"Just as soon have that many dead leaves," the boy called, struggling to steady the long wavering barrel, till the girl stooped and put her shoulder under it. "Ain't worth no different."

The rifle cracked. By hazard the bullet cut the cord and the sow flopped down onto the steaming heap of her innards. A second later the air was as full of flying bullets as if it was a wasps' nest that had been knocked down. Jerry covered himself behind the hog and Henri scrambled onto his horse, following Matthew, who had mounted a beat sooner. The two of them circled behind the wagon, where Ben crouched behind the box, groping for a pistol hidden in a heap of burlap rags. In a moment they had swung out into the open, and Henri found the children again, crawling low and dragging their rifle across a field of corn stubble toward a derelict cabin on the other side. There were three of them, now, two girls and the boy.

With Matthew he cantered back into the trees, now taking the half-dozen horsemen who'd fired on them from the rear. Matthew was screaming like a banshee, firing his Navy six to good effect. Two riderless horses burst out of the woods, galloping toward a line of bluecoats advancing unevenly across another boggy field.

Henri shouted to Matthew, rode back through the trees to the wagon.

"Who's that?" Ben called from behind the box.

"I don't know. Rangers."

"Whose Rangers?"

"How would I know? But there's regular Yankee army in back of them."

Ben sat up, eyes widening. "They ain't supposed to be here."

"We're not supposed to be here. Nobody is." Except maybe those children, Henri thought. They might belong.

"How many Yankees?"

"I don't know. Thirty. Matthew?"

"I didn't stay to count them either," Matthew said. "Too many is all I know."

"We need to get somewhere," Henri said.

"Ain't leaving this meat," Jerry hissed from where he lay embracing the dead sow.

"Wait a minute," Henri said. "If they were coming this way they'd already be here."

As this thought surfaced there was a deep *boom* of a heavy gun, and the rumbling of hooves off to the north. *Yaaiiiiiiyaaaiiiiiih!* came the yell.

"That's ours," Matthew said, and with Henri he rode to the tree line in time to see the charge of Bill Forrest and his Forty Thieves parting around the cabin, then rejoining to bear down on the Yankee line, which had stopped, aghast, halfway across the cornfield. A gunner bent over his touch hole and the cannon boomed once more, but when he raised up he saw the rest of the bluecoats had broken and run and a rider knocked him down with a sword cut before he could get organized to follow them.

As the pursuit faded into the trees, they saw Bedford Forrest himself, outdistancing his brother. In a moment the pair of them came trotting back. Beside the abandoned eight-pounder they halted their horses.

"Purty little thing," Bill said.

"Ain't it the truth?" Forrest grunted. "Let's hope John Morton can get some use outen it."

Not far from the cabin he got down to study the insignia on one of the bluecoats that had fallen there, then squinted up at his brother. "Whar'n hell ye reckon they come from?"

"Dunno." Bill Forrest turned his head to spit on the muddy, hoof-churned ground. "Paducah, maybe."

Henri and Matthew had ridden up beside them to study the corpse. In a moment all four of them became aware that the two girls and the boy were sitting up staring at them like a family of owls caught out in the daylight. They'd sheltered in a shallow hole below a squatty stone chimney that stood on its lonesome a few yards from the cabin's side door.

Forrest rode over and looked down. "What is this?" he said.

The boy stood up shakily. "Hit was another room we had." He wiped his face on remains of a sleeve. "Cannonball knocked it down."

"A cannonball," Forrest said. "Y'all fight a battle here ever day?"

"Don't look like whole lot to fight over," Bill Forrest remarked.

The boy's eyes narrowed. "Air you General Forrest?"

"I am."

"I want to jine up with ye then."

"Price!" snapped the older girl. "Don't you—"

The boy was hefting the long awkward rifle.

"Whar'd ye get that buffalo gun?" Forrest asked him.

"I want to jine. I want to jine!"

"Price, is it," Forrest said. "Well you must be the man I come to see."

Henri looked at the sky, then the ground. Even on their last run into West Tennessee, Forrest wouldn't have accepted a recruit like this. He didn't look any more than twelve, though he might in fact be up in his teens, small for his age from living on slim pickings. In days gone by they'd culled thousands of good grown men from this part of the state, but now there were no more of them left.

"That all the gun ye got right thar?" Forrest said, and the boy nodded.

"Have ye got a pair of shoes?"

"Not right now I don't," Price said.

"Hit don't matter," Forrest said. "Oncet we get to Johnsonville we'll fit ye out proper."

The boy's face brightened and then clouded. "I reckon I cain't jest go off'n leave my sisters here."

Henri looked at the older girl. She had a long jaw, like an ax blade. The boy did too but not yet so pronounced—probably the girl was older. Henry felt like he'd seen that jaw somewhere before.

The boy was thinking. "Y'all could go to the Washburns," he said.

The girl transfixed him with a bony finger. "*You* ain't tellen me whar to go nor what to do when I git thar neither."

"Miss," Forrest took off his hat. "I don't believe you kin really stay here."

"Why not?" The girl held his stare. Forrest fingered his hat brim and studied the cabin. The door had been stove in that very day by an eight-pound shot and the roof tree had caved in at the middle long before.

"Hit—Hit don't look like a good place for young ladies to stay on their lonesome," Forrest said. "Whar's yore Mam and Pap?"

"Mam died," the younger girl said, and shut her mouth on a tight white line.

"Fever," the older one added. "And y'all took Pap a long time ago and he got kilt at Shiloh. Somebody sent us a letter about it. And y'all took Briley, that was not but last winter, and we don't know if he's kilt yet or not—we ain't heard nothen."

Briley. The long jaw. Henri couldn't quite put it together where he'd seen it. "Briley's all right," Forrest was saying. "I believe he's gone to Fort Heiman with Buford."

Was he making this up, Henri wondered, but it was just as likely Forrest might actually know it.

"Tell me about these Washburns."

"Well," Price said. "The men's all gone but hit's a couple of niggers stayen with'm yet. And they still got two milk cows."

"Two milk cows!" Forrest turned to Matthew. "Y'all still got that wagon?"

"Yessir," Matthew said. "Back in the woods."

"Take these young ladies to the Washburns then," Forrest said. "I reckon they can tell ye how to go." He turned to Price. "Young sir, you can come along with me."

"THAT SOW WAS OURN," the elder girl said, as she slung her rag bundle into the wagon beside the carcass, and climbed in after it. Once settled she took a Bible with a dry-rotted black leather cover from under her elbow and centered it in the lap of her grubby skirt.

"Get up, May," she said, but the younger girl had already dragged her own bundle in beside her.

"I expect your brother will get a piece of that pork," Henri said. "And it sounds like you'll find milk at the Washburns."

"Oh, if we *got* to go the Washburns." The girl stretched up toward Ben on the box. "Just go down that road yonder a piece. Hit's in a bend of the river."

Matthew was looking at the girl curiously. "What have you got against these Washburns."

The girl sniffed. "Secesh, fer a start."

"*Secesh!*" Henri blurted. "Your brother just joined the Confederate Army."

"He never ast my leave to do it neither," the girl snapped. "Ain't no good come of it. Jest everbody dead or gone and the ones that's left is starven."

She set her long jaw and stared down the road. Now it came to Henri where he'd seen that bleak regard before: on long-jawed Briley, that was him, standing beside the grave he'd been ordered to dig for himself when he and eighteen more West Tennessee recruits had been caught trying to skip off home last winter. Forrest had reprieved their death sentence at dawn, which meant that he might well remember who Briley was, and know where he was for that matter.

"Rebs ain't brought nothen but trouble," the girl said. "Besides hit ain't right."

Ben turned from the wagon box to look at her. "What ain't right?" he said.

"Holt men in *bondage*." The girl turned almost prim, tapping the crumbly cover the Bible with her nail. "Says it right here."

"What page is that on?" Henri said.

"Jesus said. Hit's on ever page."

"Wait a minute," Henri said, overcome with a strange effervescence of mirth. "This girl's an abolitionist, Benjamin. A black-hearted abolitionist, I tell you."

The girl wriggled all over and ducked her head. Henri thought maybe she almost blushed. He saw she had taken his words as a high compliment, possibly even a flirtatious one. The road now ran between two fields, one blanketed with a host of starlings like a dark snowfall.

"I'll give ye black-hearted." The girl picked up her head and jutted her jaw, like a horse that had got the bit in its teeth. "What y'all done over to Fort Pillow."

"And that was what?"

"Kilt all them harmless niggers as was beggen for mercy."

"Miss," Matthew said. "It wasn't quite like that. They were trying to kill us too."

Harmless, Henri thought, well, not all the time. It was hard to construct a memory of the slaughter under the bluff because it had all been too confusing. It seemed to him though that some of the Yankee soldiers would surrender one minute, then pick up a gun and start firing the next . . .

"That ain't how hit was named to me." The girl looked at Henri. "Ain't you a free nigger?"

Her eyes were almost colorless, like water. He found it oddly difficult to sustain her gaze. "I'll answer to free," he said.

"How bout y'all?" She had turned to the two men on the box. Henri noticed she hadn't asked Matthew and Matthew had turned from the discussion to gaze off over the wagon's tailgate at the receding field full of starlings.

Benjamin passed the reins to Ginral Jerry, who remained silent, facing forward, studying the bristly tails of the mules.

"Don't ye *want* to be free?" the girl asked Ben. He studied her for a moment more, hitched around on the box to face her, one heavy arm hanging down into the wagon bed.

"Here's a thing I been learned," he finally said. "I was out here all by myself I might be free but I wouldn't live long."

"What about your brother?" Henri said, thinking this was how it was now, in this part of the country, where a tumbled-down one-room cabin housed two different kinds of partisan, and no one could tell whose Rangers were whose.

"Hell far." The younger girl startled them with the froggy deep note of her voice. "*He* thinks the same as y'all do I reckon." She snorted and turned to look backward at the starlings. "Rebel to the bone."

CHAPTER TWENTY-NINE

June 1864

WITHIN A GLADE outside the town they buried two deserters in the rain. A third, a boy in his teens, had at the last moment been spared. Forrest, turning his head to one side to spit into the hoof-churned mud, rasped, *Let the young'n live*, and looked as if he might say more, but didn't.

Afterward the boy helped them dig one grave for two. Henri didn't know if he were friend or kin to the two grown men who'd just been shot or if the three of them had ended up in the bottom of the same sack through simple mischance alone. The boy's face was wet as he worked, but maybe only from the downpour. Sticky mud clung to shovel blades and would not be shaken loose. When the grave had at last been filled, Benjamin led the boy away toward the shelter of the wagons. Ben's face looked lined and weary from the digging. He said nothing, but guided the boy with a large hand set between his shoulder blades.

That night Henri lay wakeful under the forked canvas of the shebang, knowing from Matthew's stiffness beside him that Matthew wasn't sleeping either. Moisture beaded on the underside of the sodden cloth, soon enough began to drip. Henri pushed his mind away from the two dead men and the young survivor. He would not learn their names or know their faces. Forrest had been in a savage mood for quite some time. The dismal weather might account for some of it. Braxton Bragg, still nominally his commander in spite of all, kept him annoyed with criticism of his recruiting methods, which were indeed sometimes a bit severe, as the grim events of that day confirmed. Since Fort Pillow, the Yankee papers had been painting him with ill repute. They made him out a *mean vindictive cruel and unscrupulous* man who often whipped his slaves to death and kept a black concubine in his house to quarrel with his wife. There were rumors too that Negro troops at Memphis had sworn blood vengeance against Forrest and all his men. Worst of all, Forrest's plan to attack Sherman's rear as Sherman moved from Nashville south toward Georgia had been thwarted by as many as ten thousand Federal troops who had come out from Memphis, under command of General Samuel Sturgis, to divert him. For the last eight days they had been playing hide and seek with Sturgis in the rain.

Above the pelting on his peaked square of canvas, Henri heard voices calling across the camp, and presently Bill Witherspoon raised a wet corner of his shebang.

"Come on, Hank, let's have some fun!"

The rain was too heavy for Henri to make out Witherspoon's lopsided grin. "What kind of fun," he said.

"Pea-picking, corn-husking. Find out when we get there. We're all going over to Stubbs Farm."

Beside Henri, Matthew sat up, silent, alert, ready. He checked his pistols in the dark.

"It's wet out there," Henri said.

"No more than it is in here," said Witherspoon. "Come on."

Henri crawled out from under the dripping shebang and shook himself like a wet dog. He exchanged a glance with Matthew in the dark. They went to find their horses. In ten minutes they were riding south from Ripley, Mississippi, treetops sagging under the rain in the groves that fell away down the slopes from the ridge where the road ran. Witherspoon took up a song, his pale face raised into the rain.

> Come on boys, let's go find'm
> Come on boys, let's go find'm
> Come on boys, let's go find'm
> Way down yonder in the pawpaw patch.

Finally someone shut him up. Then the rain began to slack. On the western horizon was a glimmer of the quarter-moon and through gaps in the clouds came starlight enough to illuminate their exchanges of fire with the Federals camped around Stubbs Farm. More fun than a pea-shelling, Witherspoon considered, except you couldn't meet the girls. At daylight when they rejoined Forrest up at Boonetown, the weather had cleared completely and promised to be very hot, and they were able to say of a near certainty that the enemy was headed down the railroad line through Guntown toward Tupelo, Okolona and the fields of ripening corn on the black prairie there.

"Let's get after'm," Forrest said briefly. He looked haggard in the thin dawn light, his thin lips buried in tendril of his untrimmed beard. "Catch'm quick and hit'm hard."

"General," Colonel Rucker said. "He's got eight thousand men over there already, and we have scarce got two."

"When did that kind of a thang start to worry ye," Forrest snapped. Then in a more considered tone, "It ain't about how many they is. Never was—won't never be. I'd take one of ourn over ten what they got, any day of the week and twicet on Sunday. Damyankees ain't got thar yet today and they got yet a ways to go. It's comen up hotter'n hell already and oncet they run five miles through that sucken mud they'll be so beat we'll ride right over'm."

Where's *there*, Henri thought, exchanging a glance with Witherspoon, and then he thought that maybe he knew. Forrest's orders were to fall away south and join Stephen Lee, perhaps Chalmers also, to defend Okolona and the fields of unharvested grain. But considering last night's reconnaissance they'd have a good chance to find the enemy at a much nearer point, somewhere between Stubbs Farm and Guntown. Last night he, Matthew, Witherspoon and the rest had returned toward Boonetown across a bridge over Tishomingo Creek, and passed through Brice's Crossroads. There were thickets of blackjack oak all about to cover their approach.

A younger voice piped up. "General Forrest, sir?"

With a shade of impatience Forrest turned his head.

"They say hit's a passel of niggers come out with the Yankees, gone carry you back to Memphis in chains like what you put on them. Say they gone burn you, and skin you alive."

"Boy, that don't make no sense," Forrest replied. "They'll need to skin me afore they burnt me, else they'll not git much of a skin."

No one laughed. Henri, reluctantly, turned his head toward the questioner: the same stripling who'd escaped the firing squad just the day before. His pinched dirty frightened face, like a rat with the plague among them.

"And then they'll need to catch me before they kin carry out any part of that plan," Forrest said.

"They say they gone kill everbody." The lad's voice began to shake. "Say they gone kill us all and take no prisoners."

"They can say what they want to," Forrest said, and made to turn his back.

"But do they mean it?"

Forrest rounded on him then. "How the hell should I know if a body means what he says or not? If I was to say it I'd damn sure mean it. That's all I know. The rest we'll find out when we git thar. And I mean to git thar quick."

"All right," the boy said, stepping back. "All right."

They rode south from Booneville on a track west of the rail bed. Beyond the thickets further west Henri could hear the faint trickling of a stream. It was already very hot, as Forrest had predicted. Now and then a woodpecker tapped at a hollow tree; the staccato drumbeat carried a long way through still air.

"What about us," Matthew said.

Henri looked over his shoulder.

"I mean what do you think they'd do to us."

"They?"

"The black troops with the Yankees. That wear those badges— *Remember Fort Pillow.*"

Henri slowed his horse so that he and Matthew fell a few lengths behind Witherspoon and the other white men of their company. "I doubt many of this bunch were ever at Fort Pillow," he said. "They couldn't have been. You know that." He paused for a moment, recalling the river at sunset, running with blood; at the edges of the great blood slick, threads of blood unraveled in the water, tendrils trying to reach or root in something.

"What is it that they say they remember?" Henri asked. "What really happened or what somebody told them did?"

For a moment Matthew said nothing. He glanced back once at Benjamin, who had left the wagons to Jerry and the other teamsters and was riding in the rear with the arms of a cavalryman in his belt and on his saddlebow. What really had happened at Fort Pillow, Henri was wondering now. Was there still any autonomous fact of that action, or only the story he'd told himself?

"I don't want to fight my own people," Matthew said.

"Matthew," Henri said. "*Mathieu.* You've come to the wrong war."

Directly, Ben clucked his tongue.

"You talk like you know who your own people are," Henri said, stopping himself from a backward glance at Ben. It struck him that maybe he was being more quarrelsome than comforting, as the crackle of rifle fire began to rip through the blackjack thicket ahead of them. Some of the Federals appeared to be armed with the new Spencer repeating carbines, but these were wont to jam in the heat of a fight, while the Navy sixes seldom misfired. And Forrest appeared to be correct that the brushy terrain did everything to conceal how few the Rebels were, at this point, in comparison to the enemy.

Henri could not make out the crossroads or the bridge through the thickets. Indeed there was more than one pair of roads that crossed in these few acres east of Tishomingo Creek. As best he could recall from riding a similar route in darkness the night before, the bridge would be maybe half a mile distant. He circled north, with Matthew and Ben, in the direction of the Baldwin Road. They had got separated from Witherspoon, last seen clubbing a Federal trooper with a jammed repeater he'd snatched from another of the enemy.

The booming of two Federal batteries fell away behind them to the south. They were angling, Henri thought, toward the Federal left flank, though it was almost impossible to locate the lines in this heavily wooded ground. Of three hundred fifty men of the Seventh Tennessee, only seventy-five were still on their feet by this time. They fought dismounted now, struggling with Federals firing from cover of a brush fence at the south side of a trampled pasture. More and more Union flags appeared in the woods behind as the Federals brought reinforcements across Tishomingo Creek. Somehow the fighting had already gone on for most of the morning and the Rebels looked as if they were starting to tire.

Then Forrest came cantering up on a dapple gray horse he

favored. He'd shed his coat and rolled his sleeves; the double-edged saber flashed in his left hand.

"Git round the left," he shouted at the remnants of the Seventh. "Take the damnjobbernowlyankees in the rear there. Git on with ye—if ye're feart to be shot ye best go forward for I'm well and god-dam ready to shoot ye in the back if ye don't."

Henri stared as the dapple gray reared up in the middle of the open field, under a hard rain of shrapnel and minié balls. There seemed no possibility that both horse and rider would not instantly be killed. But no. Forrest leaned forward, the horse's front hooves regained the ground, and with a forward sweep of his blade he cried, "I'll lead ye!" The yell went up, behind, then beside him as what was left of the Seventh rushed past Forrest toward the Federals at the fence. Forrest had turned his horse out of the line to ride back to Bell's brigade, which appeared to be retreating before the Yankee reinforcements constantly arriving on the field.

"Come on I tell ye," Forrest screamed. "I tell ye them sons-abitches is too tired to fight. They was whupped afore they got here. Now *git* over thar and finish'm off." He swatted a man across the shoulders with the flat of his blade. Again the hair-raising yell tore across the field as Bell's brigade charged to join the Seventh. Rebels were jumping the fence now, fighting the Yankees hand-to-hand; Henri glimpsed Witherspoon again for a moment, gleefully trump-ing a Federal saber with his pistol. Further back in the woods, the Yankee line re-formed for a few minutes, attempting a rally, then as ammunition ran low it shattered in confusion.

Henri's ears rang in the weird, muffled silence that followed. Presently he began to hear woodpeckers resuming their work, but as if the sound was wrapped in cotton batting. Matthew was walking on rubbery legs back toward him from the battle line, his face streaked with blood and burnt powder, apparently unhurt. Henri discovered he was holding Matthew's horse.

Forrest was riding toward them now, his sword hand low. His coat was draped across the saddlebow, and his once white shirt was transparent with sweat. Distant firing broke out behind him, a long way off, down in some hollow through the woods toward the creek.

"That'll be Barteau." Forrest grinned. Colonel C. R. Barteau, detached from Bell's brigade, had gone the long way round the Federal left to intercept their line of march from Stubbs Farm.

"Where's John Morton?" Forrest raised his sword point toward Henri. Matthew had just now remounted. Henri turned his horse aside. He remembered seeing Morton, who'd dragged his handful of cannon eighteen miles that morning, the last third of that distance at close to a run, coming to support Bell's charge at the end of the most recent action.

"That way," he said, and he and Matthew fell in behind the dapple gray as Forrest rode in the direction indicated. Shortly they came upon the eight small cannon known to everyone now as Morton's Bull Pups; the battery was still taking fire from the Yankees. John Morton's pleasant moon face popped up from behind a gun carriage.

"General Forrest," Morton said. "You had better go further down the hill, for you are apt to be hit where you are now."

Henri had never seen Forrest meet such advice as that with anything other than furious dismissal. Now he looked irritably about himself, swiping one of his hands through the air as if he could bat down bullets like flies. Then, dropping his hand to his knee, he nodded.

"All right, John. I may rest awhile." He rode down the slope where Morton had pointed, and dismounted beneath an old hickory tree. Matthew caught up the loose reins of the dapple gray horse. Forrest took his coat from the saddlebow, scraped nut hulls aside with the edge of his boot, and spread out his coat between the roots of the tree. He lay down, closed his eyes and appeared to stop breathing.

Henri, Morton and Matthew exchanged a weird glance. Maybe, Henri thought, some missile had pierced Forrest's heart without making any visible wound; maybe he would never rise again. They waited for a sign of his breath and saw none. Morton made to speak and didn't. With a forefinger he pressed his lower lip against his bottom teeth.

Inside of two minutes, Forrest sprang up as if he'd been lying on tongues of blue flame.

"Time's a-wasten," he yelled. "This battle's nigh whupped but we still got to whup it. Got to keep after'm, keep up the skeer! Why ain't that whole line chargen already?"

He yanked Morton to him by the upper part of his sleeve. "John," he said. He was holding Morton almost as close as a lover, while with the other hand he gestured. "I want ye to run yore Bull Pups straight down that road, and keep'm barken right in their faces, hear me? Give'm hell, John."

"Sir," Morton said, "the guns are subject to be captured if I rush forward that way without support."

"Artillery was made to be captured," Forrest snapped. He gave Morton's upper arm a squeeze and added, with his ragged grin, "I'd admire to see anybody capture yourn."

THE DAY WAS WANING. As the sun dropped away to the west, long rays of bloody light came slantwise through the darkening boles of the trees. They were driving a wedge between the Pontotoc and Baldwyn roads. To his left, Henri could hear the Bull Pups cough and roar, spitting grapeshot at the Yankees at point-blank range.

Somehow another two hours passed. Where the two roads met at Brice's Crossroads, the Yankees made another stand. Forrest's men charged them till they broke and scattered back to Tishomingo Creek. Henri and Matthew were both carried along in the rush to pursue. Some distance ahead of them a cry went up.

"*Here's* the damn niggers!"

The black companies they'd all been hearing about had been kept back to guard a cluster of supply wagons drawn up just west of the creek bank. They formed up now in good close order to meet the Rebel rush. The white patches standing out sharp against the blue tunics must be the *Remember Fort Pillow* badges. Excellent target, Henri thought, but his pistols stayed holstered in his belt.

What about us? Matthew had said. The black companies were covering the retreat of the white Federals fleeing from the crossroads of the creek, and doing a determined job of it too. Though the skirl of the Rebel yell filled Henri's ears, the momentum of the charge had been blunted. Matthew, inexplicably, got down from his horse and began walking into the melee, stiff-legged and empty-handed. Henri got down himself, handed the reins of his horse to Benjamin, who had just come up behind, and followed. He was so frightened he wanted to puke. Though their uniforms were so tattered as to be unrecognizable, there could be little doubt about whom they'd rode in with. Yet Matthew seemed to walk robed in his father's untouchability.

Henri followed him through a gap in the line, taking a long step over a corpse still twitching. It was the boy that had asked the question that morning, he thought, who'd been spared the firing squad at the last moment the day before. But he couldn't pause now to look twice and make sure. From a wagon bed someone was sighting one of the new Spencer repeaters on Matthew. Henri's own revolver was cold in his hand. He knew the idea was to take out the rifleman *before* he shot Matthew, but he felt he could not bring himself to do it until afterward. There was something about this enemy's face. Though he did not wear a Fort Pillow badge, he had actually been at Fort Pillow. There he had told Henri his name.

Sam Green.

He must have cried the name out loud, for Green lowered his weapon and beckoned the two of them up into the wagon with him. Matthew, still moving stiffly, like an automaton, climbed up behind the right front wheel. Sam Green stretched out a hand to help him. Henri stuck his gun back into his belt and clambered up after. The wagon was loaded with sides of bacon and dried beans in burlap sacks. Somewhere there was a faint odor of coffee. Ginral Jerry would be overjoyed with such a find.

"How've you been," Henri said. The three of them were stretched out now across the bean sacks, keeping their heads below the wagon rails, for there were more than a few bullets singing over them.

"All right, I guess." Sam Green smoothed a palm over the breech of his Spencer. His palms were gray with callus that looked like limestone furrowed by water. "Just tryen to live." Henri found himself trying to think about all the most extreme efforts he had made to live himself, all at the same time. He looked around for something to stop his thoughts. Matthew had turned from the other two men, his body molded over slabs of bacon. He was watching the fight through a crack between two warping boards.

"Hi bout y'all?" Sam Green said.

How about us, Henri thought. It occurred to him that in the end one might betray everything. So that in the end there was no other constant than betrayal. He raised his head to look out of the wagon and very quickly brought it back down.

"They're fighting like there's no tomorrow."

" 'Cause for us they ain't. Kill or be killed. Not no mercy nowhere. That's what they believes."

Us or them, Henri thought, then asked him, "Do these Yankees treat you right?"

"Don't know bout that." Sam Green flattened further on his back. His eyes, tobacco-brown in the whites, looked up at the swiftly darkening sky. "They says we ain't slaves no mo but they don't treat us like we men. Don't leave us drink outen they dipper. Don't leave us drink outen they wells. We come across the country taken what we finds any ways we can take it."

"And then they give you a bad name for it."

"Tha's jess about exactly what they do." Sam Green chuckled softly. In the fairly near distance, a wounded horse screamed. Green turned sideways to squint through the wagon rails. "Colonel Bouton, now, he ain't so much that way. He act like he count on us, most times. Go on and look at him over there now."

Henri raised his head again. There indeed was Edward Bouton commanding with a sure authority, grim but graceful under a flood of fire. Black troops moved willingly to his order, opening their line to let the fleeing Federals through, then closing again to resist pursuit. They disputed every yard of their retreat.

A man with a Fort Pillow badge rushed up to the wagon looking for cartridges and screamed his frustration when he found only beans. With a butcher's knife drawn he ran back to the fight. Horseholders were struggling to hold mules panicking from the racket of battle. Bouton and his black soldiers were fighting ferociously on the right of their line.

"It's hangen for him if y'all catches him, see?" Sam Green remarked. "Ain't no tomorrow for him neither." His head turned suddenly, as if to some specific sound Henri couldn't pick out from the general barrage. Then he jumped out of the front of the wagon and unstaked the two mules hitched to the tongue. Something on

Bouton's left had broken and a whole white Federal infantry unit was coming back at a panicked run. Sam Green clucked to his mules, tapped them with a length of cane. The wagon turned, jostling with others as they moved toward the bridge, some drivers lashing each other's mules as they tried to advance. Sam Green, horribly exposed on the wagon box, murmured to his animals more calmly.

It was almost too dark to see anything now. Red flashes from the muzzles of the guns. Some black soldiers now had joined the flight, sailing past like bats in the gloaming, some ripping off Fort Pillow badges as they ran. Others fought on desperately. Sam Green patiently maneuvered the wagon onto the first boards of the bridge. Then the tiny movement he'd been so carefully conserving altogether stopped. Ahead of them the bridge was blocked by a wagon jammed crossways.

Sam Green craned his neck to peer ahead of him, then behind. Henri followed the direction of his backward glance. In the darkness by the tree line a muzzle flashed red and he saw the ball lift from the barrel and arc toward them like a meteorite, growing till it blotted out the sky. A kind of astral music accompanied it, ringing, shimmering: the music of the spheres. The bullet moved with a terrible dark lethargy toward them, but Henri could not seem to move any faster. He wanted to snatch Green out of the way, while his arms felt like they were trapped in molasses. He was himself bound to the pace of this world that embraced him in its awful slowness. The bullet lumbered into Sam Green's left temple before Henri could reach him, and he pulled him down among the sacks already dead.

Matthew rolled over and opened Green's collar, feeling around his throat for a pulse. Henri watched blood soaking through the burlap under the dead man's head, trickling down among hard pellets of white beans. Events resumed their previous hectic speed. Some of the routed Federals were pausing to set supply wagons on fire before flinging themselves into Tishomingo Creek. Some of Forrest's units had crossed ahead of them, upstream, and were picking the Yankees off as they tried to come out of the water on the other side.

Then Forrest himself rode clattering onto the bridge, eyes flashing yellow like a wildcat's. "*BytheblackflamenassholeoftheDevilhisselfthese-shitsuckendamnyankees're burnen my wagons,* Goddammit!" he shouted.

Oh, Henri thought, they're your wagons now.

"Git up, son," Forrest said to Matthew. "You can't jest lay thar. That man is dead."

Matthew took his hand from Sam Green's throat and straightened as if waking from a dream. "Where's Willie," he said.

"I don't know," Henri said. "I haven't seen him. I don't think he's here."

Forrest had already passed them, was directing a squad of men to heave the jammed wagon out of its place and tumble it over into the stream. More men of their company flowed over Sam Green's wagon, carrying away the bacon and beans, automatic as a file of ants. Sam Green's body flopped onto a few wisps of straw that still lay on the stripped boards of the wagon bed. Then Benjamin's grave face appeared above the rails. Matthew got out and took the reins of the two horses Benjamin had led back to them. Benjamin pulled Sam Green's ankles to straighten his body, then folded the dead man's hands across his breastbone. Other men were already lifting the wagon clear of the bridge, releasing it above the creek. It fell straight down, the wheels grooving into the surface of the water. Henri was somehow back in his saddle without quite knowing how he had got there. He leaned to see water filling the wagon bed, so that Green's body floated calm and free for a moment, still within the frame of the rails. Then the wagon spiraled away in the current and was gone.

FORREST AND his men pursued in relays, some chasing Federals up the road to Ripley and picking up prisoners from the exhausted enemy falling down by the roadside, while others rested and ate boiled beans and bacon from the captured wagons. Forrest himself was still on the trail of Sturgis's scattered remnants when daylight picked out the party he led. There was not much of the joy of victory on his countenance.

"Why don't you look happy," Anderson asked him. "We've had a big day."

"We ought to had all of'm," Forrest said shortly.

"I'll say we got plenty," Nath Boone said. "And still picken up more."

Forrest's hard eyes were scanning the ground like the eyes of a hunter looking for sign. Others of his men kept dismounting to collect discarded packs and weapons. Now and then on the roadway appeared one of those *Remember Fort Pillow* badges men had torn from their uniforms as they fled.

"I'll say one thing, them ornery ole niggers can *fight*—when they back's to the wall." Forrest shook his head, the point of his beard jerking side to side above the hardpack of the road. "If not for them we'd have et up every last scrap of this army." In his mind already he was contemplating a letter to be sent to the Federal General Washburn at Memphis, a few jagged phrases which Anderson would later compose into more polite language: . . . *all the Negro troops stationed in Memphis took an oath on their knees, in the presence of Major General Hurlbut and other officers of your army, to avenge Fort Pillow, and that they would show my troops no quarter. . . . A large majority of the prisoners we have captured from that command have voluntarily stated that they expected us to murder them. . . . Both sides acted as though neither felt safe in surrendering, even when further resistance was useless.*

While Tecumseh Sherman on the news of Brice's Crossroads would be writing to the U.S. Secretary of War . . . *Forrest is the Devil, and I think he has got some of our troops under cower. I have two officers at Memphis who will fight all the time, A. J. Smith and Mower. . . . I will order them to make up a force and go out to follow Forrest to the death, if it costs ten thousand lives and breaks the Treasury. There will never be peace in Tennessee until Forrest is dead. . . .*

By afternoon of the day after the battle they were riding near the town of Salem when some of the men with Forrest remarked their general had gone to sleep in the saddle. His change of state was just barely noticeable; he still held himself straight, but a bit more limber; his eyes had closed; now and then his head rolled to one side or the other with the movement of the dapple gray horse, then righted itself but without the eyes opening.

"But someone must wake him," Anderson said.

"Go on, then," Nath Boone replied. "Help yoreself! You know he's apt to swop your head off afore he knows right well who you are."

Anderson shook his head and took no further action. They rode on, without saying anything more about Forrest's situation, until the dapple gray horse, who was also sleepwalking, blundered full-on into a tree. Forrest slipped down as slack as if his clothes were empty, rolled to his back, and continued his slumber uninterrupted. Men gathered quietly under the tree and watched him as he slept.

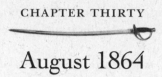

CHAPTER THIRTY

August 1864

Matthew found Forrest at the top of a knoll, beneath an ancient cedar tree. Jerry and Benjamin had stretched a rag of canvas across low branches of the cedar, to block the tepid summer drizzle, and Forrest was there in a reasonably dry spot, sitting on a ladder-back chair with most of the rungs broken out of the back, his wounded foot raised on a powder keg in front of him. He'd been hurt at Harrisburg three weeks before and though he no longer needed to ride in a buggy, he had a bad limp made all the worse by his being too stubborn to carry a cane. When he mounted a horse he could only get one foot in a stirrup, but that didn't seem to hamper him much.

Anderson and Kelley where just leaving the shelter as Matthew came up, and Forrest seemed to have slipped into a brown study. King Philip, tethered on a long lead to the cedar tree, snorted and pulled at the rope when Matthew approached, then when he recognized him, lowered his head.

Matthew stopped outside the dripping edge of canvas. He took off his hat and let the rain soak into the thick curls of his hair. Forrest, head bowed, fidgeting with something inside his collar, did not seem to be aware of him, but after a moment he spoke without looking up.

"Come on, boy, get out the rain."

Matthew ducked inside the shelter. Forrest glanced at a stool by his side.

"D'ye care to set?"

Matthew remained on his feet. Forrest had pulled the rawhide lace from his throat and was turning the drilled doubloon between his thumb and forefinger.

"I'm sorry," Matthew said.

Forrest looked up at him sharply. "What about?"

"You lost your brother," Matthew said. "Jeffrey." My Uncle Jeffrey he didn't say.

"A con*dole*yance call!" Forrest said. "Ye taken yore time getten round to it, son. Hit's nigh on six months since Jeff was kilt."

"I know how you cared for him, the best of all." Matthew swallowed. "Everybody knows it."

"Well that don't mean everbody needs to go chatteren about it," Forrest said. He clasped the doubloon in his palm for a second, then dropped it back down the front his shirt. "How about them thousand men we got kilt back yonder at Harrisburg? You sorry about them too?"

"How would I not be?"

"Huh . . ." But Forrest seemed to have slipped back into his reverie. "I reckon that makes a mess of sorry folks about now. By damn it didn't have to go that way! If—just—if I known as much West Point *horseshit* as what them other officers do, Yankees'd whup me every day I find'm."

Matthew remained standing in silence. A trickle of rainwater dried on his back. Of a sudden Forrest looked up and noticed him again.

"Ye fought a hard fight that day, Matthew," he said. "The day when my brother got kilt. I seen ye and I recollect hit. Ye done right well."

"Thank you sir," Matthew said. "I try to do my best."

Forrest studied him closely now. "Well, was it anything else on yore mind?"

"How's your foot?" Matthew said.

"Hit's a *goddamn* embarrassment is how it is," Forrest snapped. "Hoppen around like a clown in a minstrel show."

"They say Sherman believes you're dead of lockjaw."

"Sherman! He'd dearly love it if I was. I tell ye I hope to let him know hit'll take more to kill me than a hole in the goddamn toe."

Forrest glared at his upraised foot. "Hurts like the devil though, I'll grant ye that. I been hurt twicet as serious and had half the pain." He looked up again. "I'll wager ye didn't come up here about my toe."

Matthew side-stepped to avoid a drip. A swag in the canvas made him hold his head low.

"I seen how ye fought hard that day," Forrest repeated. "What is it that you're fighten for?"

"I want you to recognize me." Matthew pried his jaw open and spoke in a rush.

"Recognize you?"

"Own me. Own up to me, I mean."

"Huh," Forrest said. "Well, hit's a limit. Ole Miss'll only stand for so much. She cain't he'p it. She's made thataway." He turned his head and looked off through the rain. "What is it ye want I got power to give?"

Matthew said nothing. It seemed to him that he couldn't think. In place of thought was the drip of rain on canvas.

"Well, ye come up here of yore own accord," Forrest said. "I never sent for ye."

You sent to bring me out of Louisiana, Matthew thought.

"Own . . ." Forrest said. "Son, I've owned hogs and horses and mules. I've owned land and slaves. Bought'm and sold'm. Et'm or lost'm." He hitched up in the chair, wincing as his foot dragged back across the keg. "I'll tell ye one thing. All that ye really can own is yore actions."

"Your actions," Matthew said.

"Yes," Forrest said. "Because that's the only thing that's truly in yore hand."

The wind blew rain across the canvas, then subsided.

"I seen you and Willie don't fight so much no more."

Not since Roderick died, Matthew thought.

"I won't deny, hit pleases me," Forrest said. "Fer hit warn't never no use in that struggle. Ye cain't stomp yore blood outen him no more than he can stomp it outen you. A thing ye cain't he'p, hit's no use to fight it. Ain't no use think on it neither."

Well, thought Matthew, but how do you stop?

"Ye take what ye're given," Forrest said. "Fer ye ain't got no choice."

"*You* choose," Matthew said.

"Is that what ye think?" Forrest laughed harshly, and drew his foot in, so the heel of it rested on the damp ground. "I reckon I think so myself, most times. But don't ye know hit ain't always that way." He leaned forward, studying through sheets of rain a dozen-odd troopers leading horses round the bottom of the hill, then sat back and passed one hand briefly over his eyes.

"Hit's sometimes," he said. "If I give myself to the doen of a thing I don't know nothen of a minute before nor of what's to come after. All I got is what's right *now.* You got that in ye too, Matthew, I seen it. Hit's biggern both us, it is. Hit don't always come out but it's in there."

Forrest strained to lift his bad foot back to the powder keg again. Matthew moved to help him but Forrest, teeth gritted, waved him away. He settled and waited for the pain to pass before he spoke again.

"You want a free paper?" he said. "I'll write ye one. Only reason I ain't till yet is I got it in mind you're better off, the way it is now, if folks suppose you belong to me. And—it ain't no paper on earth as can make ye a white man. Not in this world we're liven in now."

"You've given free papers to some," Matthew said.

Forrest looked at him directly, a studying look, for the first time in their conversation. "That I have," he said. "But them, they warnt none of my blood, don't ye see?"

Matthew saw no use in saying that he didn't see. He knew it was a compliment, maybe an honor from Forrest's point of view, but he didn't see what use it was to him.

"I reckon I ain't give ye the satisfaction ye come fer," Forrest said. "Tell you one thing I know—you won't never be free of me. No more'n I could be free of you."

Matthew watched him silently, like an animal watching from the dark hollow of a tree. Beyond the shelter, night was falling now, with the rain, and Forrest gazed into the dark.

"I'm tellen ye the truth as I know it," he said.

"And you always know every bit of the truth."

"Only God could know all of it," Forrest said. "If there is a God."

"I thought you didn't believe in God."

"I didn't say that," Forrest said. "I jest don't want God to go messen in my business."

CHAPTER THIRTY-ONE

November 1864

H ENRI DIDN'T QUITE KNOW where he was when he woke on a pile of empty gunny sacks in the back of Ben's wagon—somewhere in Alabama: Florence? Montgomery? He propped up on an elbow, opening his sleep-sticky eyes on the carved wildcats going at each other from either side of Ben's wagon seat. There was a real-life scuffle happening too, between men, not animals, there at the front of the wagon. Somebody from General Hood's quartermaster corps was trying to unhitch one of Ben's mules, and when Ben kept batting his hands off the harness, the white soldier wheeled on him, raising a fist—

"You don't quit foolen with me nigger I swear—"

Ben simply stepped back and pulled a Navy six from under his shirttail. The other man stopped short with his mouth hanging open. Slowly he backed away from the wagon, tripping once before he reached the shade of an overhang where Major Landis, whom Hood had sent to commandeer some of Forrest's mules, was standing and watching the scene.

"He thrown down on me with a gun—that nigger yonder!" He bumped the major's elbow and pointed.

Ben's revolver was no longer in evidence by that time; he stood indifferently as if inspecting the harness of his double-teamed mules. Henri got out of the wagon, flicking shreds of burlap from the rags of his clothes, and stood beside him. Matthew was already there and so were John Morton and Witherspoon.

Before he hove into their sight, they could already hear Forrest in full cry—"By damn if he did I ordered him to do it—by damn that's *my nigger* and I'll answer for him and I won't stand fer nobody messen with him—d'ye hear what I say?"

Witherspoon cupped a hand to Henri's ear and said, "I expect they can hear him clear down to Atlanta." Henri masked a smile.

"Go back to your quarters," Forrest bellowed at Landis, "and don't you come here again or send nobody about no mules neither one. Tell yore *goddamn quartermaster* if he bothers me anymore about any mules I'll come down to his office and tie his long legs in a double bowknot around his neck and *choke him to death with his own scrawny shins* . . ."

Forrest's beard stabbed the air as his lower jaw snapped open and shut. "I whupped the enemy and captured every mule wagon and ambulance in my command, I ain't ast the government for wagons nor stock in the last two years—my teams air a-goen as they are or they ain't goen at all."

There were threads of white in the beard now, Henri noticed, and they hadn't been there when Forrest first overtook him on the Brandenburg road in 1861.

THEY'D COME to Alabama still flush from laying waste to Sherman's depots at Johnsonville, though that triumph didn't make much difference now, since Sherman had taken Atlanta and could take whatever else he wanted from the fat of the Georgia land. Still, Forrest had enjoyed good luck recruiting since he'd come this way.

General Hood had recoiled from Sherman and was marching north with what remained of the Army of Tennessee after the lost engagements around Atlanta (and there was a good deal left of that army still), intending to take Nashville back from the Yankees, then storm on to join Lee in Virginia. Some thought this plan brilliant, others insane. On the side of Hood's good sense, he'd just sent for Forrest to command all of his cavalry—if Forrest didn't get himself cashiered for insubordination.

Not all Hood's existing cavalry was overjoyed by the new commander. One knight grumbled bitterly to his diary, ". . . a man having no pretension to gentility—a negro trader, a gambler—. . .

Forrest may be & no doubt is, the best Cav. officer in the West, but I object to a tyrannical, hotheaded vulgarian's commanding me."

As the blue-tinged smoke of Forrest's oration dissipated, Ben's shoulders sank, and he turned back to his team. He scooped a weak mixture of shriveled corn and lint from a pocket and gave each mule the smallest taste. Henri watched him. Benjamin had showed nothing at all during the altercation over the mules, but now it seemed a shadow lay across his face.

He looked at Henri over a blue cross on a mule's back. "*You* known they wa'nt gone hang me there."

Henri shook his head. "Bedford Forrest wouldn't let that happen."

"Bedford Forrest don't rule the entire world and all what's in it," Ben said.

Henri blew a puff of air. "What's eating you?"

"Got trouble in mind cause I cain't see what's comen. I know sump'n is but I cain't see it. You know what you know 'cause you got the sight."

Henri shook his head again. He wanted to say it wasn't like that but he couldn't think how to say what it was like.

His mind was still worrying over this problem when he found himself walking with Ben and Matthew toward the center of Hood's great camp. Toward the center there was speech-making from the senior officers, with boasts of grand victories soon to come, but on the fringes the tattered soldiers amused themselves as best they might. Those with instruments picked and sang. Someone had set up a shell game on a barrel and men stood around betting for the sheer fun of it with pebbles or with wads of the worthless Confederate scrip—buttons were too valuable to gamble with now.

Henri paused to watch the dry pea disappearing, reappearing, almost always popping back into view where you didn't expect. It's like that, he thought, a little like that. Ben was looking at him, narrowly. Matthew had pushed ahead through the crowd, for General Hood was calling Forrest to the rostrum now.

Henri opened his mouth, closed it. He went through the loopholes in the crowd that Matthew's passage had left half-open. Ben came behind him. Closer to the platform the men thickened in clusters, like butter beginning to clump in a churn, but here in a pocket was a card game going, on the splintered top of an empty caisson. Henri stopped and watched the cards moving under the bitten nails of the dealer's hands. It's a little like that too, he thought of saying, or less like cards dealt with deliberation than the whole pack scattered in a fall, each with some event wriggling on its surface but with no thread to string them all together. He could choose to pick up any card spilled from the pack. He saw that Ben was watching him again and it crossed his mind that Ben himself must have some feel for what people were thinking, or at least for what Henri was thinking, once in a while anyway.

"Come on," he said. "Let's hear what the old man's got to say."

Well, soldiers— Forrest cleared his throat. *I come here to jine ye. I'm gone to show ye the way into Tennessee. My conscripts are goen and I know Hood's veterans can go. I come down here with three hunnert and fifty men. I got thirty-five hunnert conscripts now. Since May I fought in ever county in West Tennessee. . . .*

"You ever see anything ain't gone happen?" Ben said. "Ain't never gone happen?"

"No," Henri said. "I don't think so."

I fought in the streets of Memphis, Forrest was saying, *and the women run out in their nightclothes to see us, and they will do it again in Nashville . . .*

Ben took hold of Henri's forearm and looked into his eyes. Henri could feel Ben's human warmth coming toward him through the palms of his hands, and he realized that he didn't have that vitality in him anymore, and that Ben could probably feel that too.

I have fought a battle ever twenty-five days . . .

"I don't see you dead," Henri said to Ben. "I don't see that. But you don't want to make this run to Nashville."

"All right." Ben let go his arm. "I believe you tellen me the right thing to do. I'll just cut out and go back to Coahoma."

"Best leave your mules."

"Leave the mules and the wagon too." Ben smiled. "Walk till I git thar." He hesitated. "Hope to see you."

You won't, Henri thought. "You'll be all right," he said. "You're headed in the right direction. There's a river of blood to get across before anybody in this crowd makes it to Nashville."

Both of them turned their eyes to Forrest, who was saying, with an air of glee, *I have seen the Mississippi run blood fer two hunnert yards, and I'm gone to see it again . . .*

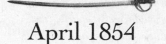

CHAPTER THIRTY-TWO

April 1854

This April evening, close and sweet—in the course of the afternoon it had rained, hard and suddenly, driving the women into their houses, the men into barns and outbuildings, or under trees for shelter if they were caught in the wagons well out on the roads. When the rain had ended it grew much cooler, cool but somehow electrically close. Forrest sat at the end of a horsehair sofa, listening to the low clear voice of Mary Ann spooling poetry out of a book she held in a yellow orb of light from a whale oil lamp.

> *Then let winged Fancy wander*
> *Through the thoughts still spread beyond her*
> *Open wide the mind's cage door.*
> *She'll dart forth, and cloudward soar*
> *O Sweet Fancy! Let her loose:*
> *Summer's joys are spoilt by use*
> *And the enjoying of the Spring*
> *Fades as does its blossoming;*
> *Autumn's red-lipp'd fruitage too,*
> *Blushing through the mist and dew,*
> *Cloys with tasting; What do then?*

The thick blue scent of lilac fumed in the half-open windows. In the short time since Forrest had settled in the Adams Street compound, the women had planted tight rows of lilac and broad trellises of fast-climbing wisteria, with the idea of screening 85 Adams, where the family lived, from 87 Adams, where the slave pens were, and both by sight and by the dense luxurious scent of erect or inverted cones of blue flowers . . .

> *Fancy high-commission'd—send her!*
> *She has vassals to attend her:*
> *She will bring, in spite of frost,*
> *Beauties that the earth has lost;*
> *She will bring thee, all together,*
> *All delights of summer weather;*
> *All the buds and bells of May,*
> *From dewy sward or thorny spray:*
> *All the heaped Autumn's wealth,*
> *With a still mysterious stealth:*
> *She will mix these pleasures up*
> *Like three fit wines in a cup,*
> *And thou shalt quaff it—*

Bedford's brother John appeared entranced, his head rolled back on the high cushion of his armchair, eyes lidded and lips faintly parted, as if the limpid stream of words had eased his pain, or as if the heavy scent of the blue flowers muted it. Doubtless the laudanum also played its part.

> *Thou shalt, at one glance behold,*
> *The daisy and the marigold;*
> *White-plum'd lilies, and the first*
> *Hedge-grown primrose that hath burst*
> *Shaded hyacinth, always*
> *Sapphire queen of the mid-May*
> *And every leaf and every flower*
> *Pearled with the self-same shower.*

Mrs. Montgomery shifted on the opposite end of the horsehair sofa. Biting a thread, she held her embroidery hoop at arm's length and studied it critically. An outline of a bluebird there, a couple of its wings filled in with thread, perched in a cluster of flowers and lurid bright red fruit.

Them berries look pizen, Forrest thought, turning his head

toward the chair where Mary Ann went on reading, the open book obscuring her face, like a fan. The verses ran over him like water, without his picking much sense from them, though he found the rhythms of her voice to be soothing, as though indeed he floated in quiet water.

> *When the hen-bird's wing doth rest*
> *Quiet on her mossy nest;*
> *Then the hurry and alarm*
> *When the bee-hive casts its swarm;*
> *Acorns ripe down-pattering,*
> *While the autumn breezes sing . . .*

Somehow Mary Ann's tone seemed to have become just faintly harsher. With a clatter of pitchers and cups Catharine had come into the room. She wore under her apron a dark gown, of a blue so deep it was almost black, picked out by bright points that might have been either red fruits or red coals. Forrest had issued her this fabric himself, from a store of rolls he'd recently bought to clothe his slaves.

Catharine stood tall, erect as a lion-hunter, the long neck holding her head up high, the weight of the many fine braids of her hair spreading and flowing over her shoulders. Only a slight rattle of the crockery betrayed a trace of nervousness. After a moment's hesitation she moved to serve Mrs. Montgomery first, bending her legs to bring the tray and its contents within this mistress's reach. Mrs. Montgomery served herself delicately from the steaming china pot, added two lumps of sugar, emitted a brittle smile.

Catharine passed the tray then toward Mary Ann Forrest, who waved her off with the back of the book, and went on, a little louder, with her reading.

> *Oh Sweet Fancy! Let her loose.*
> *Everything is spoiled by use:*
> *Where's the cheek that doth not fade*
> *Too much gaz'd at? Where's the maid*
> *Whose lip mature is ever new?*
> *Where's the eye, however blue,*
> *Doth not weary? Where's the face*

One would meet in every place?
Where's the voice, however soft,
One would hear so very oft?

Catharine lowered herself before Forrest now.

"Suh," she murmured, molasses slow. "What will you take, Mist' Fo'est?" Her brown eye caught his for an instant before slipping easily away. Forrest took his coffee black. She'd sewn her bodice firm and tight. A swatch of white muslin tucked in the V still permitted a view of the dark cleft between her breasts. Her nipples pushed red berries up through the cloth.

At a touch sweet Pleasure melteth
Like to bubbles when rain pelteth.

"That'll do me," Forrest said, sitting back on the sofa, careful not to spill his cup, and Catharine caught him again with a sidelong smile as she rose, with a graceful turn away from him, but looking over her shoulder to say to him, "Suh, is that all you want?" As she moved off to serve the men sitting outside on the gallery, it occurred to Forrest that she might be slightly better tolerated by the white women of this household if she could only swing her hips a little less winsomely.

Catharine did not remain long on the gallery. The two Cowan men, Mary Ann's uncle and cousin, had gone outdoors to smoke cigars, perhaps for a discreet taste of whiskey. They did not care for coffee now.

Let, then, sweet Fancy find
Thee a mistress to thy mind:
Dulcet-eyed as Ceres' daughter,
Ere the God of Torment taught her
How to frown and how to chide;
With a waist and with a side
White as Hebe's when her zone
Slipt its golden clasp and down
Fell her kirtle at her feet—

Mary Ann broke off, a little sharply, and without finishing the last few lines of the poem. Again Catharine had appeared in the frame of the doorway. "Missus," she said. "Will they be anything else?"

Mary Ann glanced up without looking at the new housemaid directly. "We'll want no more of you tonight—you can go on to the quarters. But leave the tray with us."

Catharine seemed to smile obscurely as she stooped to settle the tray on a low table. The movement involved an undulation of her long back and brought her derriere in tight relief beneath the fabric.

Mrs. Montgomery had apparently pricked herself with a needle. She sucked a droplet of blood from a fingertip. "Exotic costume for a house servant," she remarked, once Catharine had barely swayed out of the room. "A saucy wench if I make no mistake. I wonder you don't find her stout enough for the field."

Though the remark seemed generally addressed, Forrest rather took it to himself. I wonder if she's stout enough to stand up to your witchery, he thought, but had the good sense not to say it.

Mrs. Montgomery looked at her daughter then, somewhat askance. Mary Ann did no more than to lower her eyes over the verses she had not quite finished reading. Then she closed the book, with a startling slap.

"I believe I'll go up to my room," she said.

"Good night," Forrest said, looking at his wife's heels as they turned. He'd heard her use the phrase "my room" quite seldom, but often enough to know it meant he'd not be warmly received in the bed the two of them normally shared.

He gave her a five-minute lead up the stairs. The floorboards creaked as she moved about. Then stillness. He stood up, stopping himself from yawning or cracking his back, two perfectly natural actions his mother-in-law regarded as unseemly and uncouth.

"Good night, Mother Montgomery," he said.

A loose thread caught in her teeth again, she grimaced at him across the embroidery hoop, signifying her inability to reply. Forrest glanced up the stairs, then stepped out onto the porch. The scent of lilac lay heavy on the moist air, with a wisp of cigar smoke threaded into it. From a hidden perch in a new-leafed maple came the liquid trill of a mockingbird.

"Gentlemen," Forrest said. The two Cowans murmured some answer to this. A draw on his cigar brought a brief orange glow across the face of the young surgeon.

Forrest stepped down into the street, and raised his eyes for a moment to the bedroom window, dark, and for a moment he pictured the volume of poetry carefully placed on a doily by the extinguished lamp, then Mary Ann lying on her side in their bed, her shoulder jutting up through gown and coverlet like the tip of an iceberg.

And I didn't even do anything, he thought. I didn't do anything yet.

The men on the porch would suppose he was going to gamble, he thought, and was irked by thinking it. Ordinarily he acted with no consciousness of another's opinion, not even his own. Tonight he felt his kinsmen on the porch were watching him, considering him, and so were the dark windows upstairs in the house. When he unlocked the gate in the fence enclosing 87 Adams, it seemed to him dozens of eyes turned his way from the pens, though in fact scarcely anyone was about, only Aunt Sarah and a pair of girl-children drying crockery by the pump head in the light of a pine torch.

The chain clanked against the gatepost when he let it drop, and he covered it with one hand to still it. The fence was built so high and tight more to screen the pens from the neighbors than to discourage escape; escape was a discouraging prospect anyway and there were plenty worse places in Memphis than here. Catharine stood in the doorway of the cabin he'd assigned her, gazing calmly across the yard at him, her round-eyed child riding on her hip. She'd put off her apron when she left the big house, and in the blend of torchlight and moonlight the dress sewn from the cloth he'd given her looked painted on. *You can't have her lessen you force her.* The words dropped onto him out of nowhere, as if they'd tumbled out of the poetry book. Once in a brawl someone had managed to strike him between the eyes with a pistol butt, and he had lost consciousness in a flash of white light, though apparently he'd continued to fight until he came to himself somewhat later, many hands dragging him back by his elbows, voices warning him he'd thrashed his assailant half-dead. He could picture himself turning away from the locked gate and going off to Mason's or another gambling house where he could throw his money down and feel the surge of excitement rising. A wave to carry him away. But he did such things without thinking about them; the thought had no appeal. He might simply return to the big house, then, where his son and his daughter had long been asleep.

But Catharine had handed her child to Aunt Sarah and was moving silkily toward the gate, still watching him evenly—her face was turned a little to the side but her eyes were straight on his. A nigger wench might be whipped for the boldness of that gaze. He felt the child's eyes on him too, but then Aunt Sarah clucked and crooked her finger and teased the child's attention to herself.

"It's all right," he said to her, as Catharine stepped out between the gateposts, as if Aunt Sarah might challenge her departure with the master, as if he had to explain to her what he did. The old woman's eyes were lost in the pockets of wrinkle and shadow below the tight band of her head cloth. She swiveled away as he shut the gate, the child's weight pulling her. His hands felt thick and awkward, manipulating chain and lock. His keys fell into his pocket like lead weights.

"What air we doen?" he seemed to have asked her.

"You the mastah," Catharine said.

"I ain't the master of this," he said.

She made some sound, not quite a word, then turned from him and walked into the shadows. Inertia broke and he went after her. She seemed in fact to be leading the way. Or she was walking a pace or two ahead of him to afford him that view she knew he enjoyed, the—— I haven't done anything yet, he thought. Only imagined crowding her into a corner of the dark smoky cabin, exchange of hot breath, flesh straining against the cloth, collapsing to a shuck tick on the floor. Instead he was walking through this cool, flower-scented night, not quite close enough to touch her. A closed carriage passed them; he didn't bother to notice whose. There were lights at some of the windows they passed and surely people sat invisibly in the shadows of their porches too, observing Forrest walking with his slave girl, and let them think what they damn well pleased. They were walking toward the southern edge of town.

Words skittered around the inside of his head like ants, like he'd kicked over an anthill in there. *Fancy* was a word that kept lighting up. From the poem. Forrest had never taken pleasure from reading himself and knew nothing of poetry at all except in some way he seemed to know that Mrs. Montgomery preferred other even duller poets than the one Mary Ann had chosen to read. He hadn't known his mind had captured so many of those words. *Oh sweet fancy let her loose everything is spoilt by use.*

Now they were leaving the ragged southern border of the town, where moonlight splintered through the skeletons of new-framed houses, on streets as yet unnamed. The road they walked tended in the direction of Hernando. He had a mental glimpse of Mary Ann's eyes, flicking at him for a moment over the top of the poetry book *where's the eye however blue* . . . But he could not turn back from the other woman who still walked a pace or two ahead of him, glancing back now over her shoulder, her dark visage calm and serious, perhaps a hint of a smile tucked into her collarbone where he couldn't really see.

The moon a day or so past full, an oblong rather than a circle. A rag of cloud slipped across the lower half of it, hurrying back toward Memphis. She was leading him on, each dip of her step pulling his foot forward as if they were linked by some invisible magnetic shackle. Or it was the force of his intention propelling her forward; how to know? He tried again to think of returning, but could not imagine any sort of future. As near as five minutes from now was a black hole. Deep gravity seemed to be pulling him down, although in fact the road was ascending, climbing to the gateposts of Elmwood Cemetery, which were coming up pale before them in the moonlight.

As they entered he wondered how she knew her way; was it possible she'd come here freely? Certainly she seemed sure of her direction. He overtook her now and walked beside her, on her right, near enough he could have reached for her hand. In the way of such things they'd come to call her Catharine Forrest, he thought, and her children would be called Forrest too, if he didn't sell her or sell them. In time of need or simply for profit he might sell a saddle horse, even a fine one he'd known huge and bold and rippling between his legs . . .

"Ain't you afeart?" he asked her. For a moment he seemed to be asking it of himself. But Bedford Forrest had not been afraid of anything since when he was twelve he got first word that his father was dead. He couldn't remember many times before that either.

"Feart of what?" Her voice low, a hint of laughter in it maybe.

"Haints." By damn, by Satan's horny cloven hooves, he might as well be twelve again and trying to spark some scrawny girl in a gunny sack for a dress.

Catharine's laugh came low and husky. "This buryen ground too young fo' haints." He saw the white of her teeth as she smiled in the dark. "Not no *scary* ones, no way."

It was true—Elmwood had been dedicated just two years before and thus far was most commonly used as a park. Of a Sunday he'd driven the rambles himself, with Mary Ann and the children and sometimes a grandmother. He'd not known of niggers coming here much, though Catharine seemed to know her way.

The air was heavy with crape myrtle aroma, and all the dogwoods were in bloom; white quatrefoil leaves trembling up to the moon. The giddy myrtle scent caught in the back of his gullet. He followed her under a spray of dogwood and stopped beside a waist-high marble slab.

She turned to face him. His fingertips trailed the surface of the stone, dipped into indentations of the letters there.

"You're not afraid," he said.

"Of haints?"

"Of me."

Again the warm syrup of her laughter. "You think I don't know what a man is?" She shook back her hair and stood with her back arched, hands cocked at her waist. "I seen how you looks at me. I knows what you wants."

"But what do you want?" It could not be himself who said these words—asking a black slave wench what she wanted.

She loosed some hidden clasp and all at once the dress fell from her, pooling at her feet. When she stepped out of it, toward him, the warm loamy scent of her seemed to wash over him already.

"What I can git," she told him.

And with a smile, though her almond eyes were not entirely smiling. She looked to him sleek as a seal in the fractured moonlight that fell through the dogwood. Her breasts rose toward him as she breathed. He had not touched her yet, not ever, not even when he'd seen her the first time, chained to a ring on a post of that stall. In a flash before he reached for her he wondered why he would choose this. To be no longer master of anyone, and least of all himself.

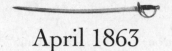

CHAPTER THIRTY-THREE

April 1863

MELEE. A ricochet whine brought Henri to a heightened state of consciousness, focused as if on the rust-red pain of a wasp sting. The horses bunched, Forrest's charger jostling Henri's mount. A string of curses *why that slipslidenfleabittenwormriddeneggsuckenliverblownhorsestealengraverobben son of Satan I'll tie his skinny legs around his neck in a sweet bow knot afore I'm done* . . . It seemed the shooting came from all sides now, three hundred and sixty degrees of a circle closing in. The point of Forrest's double-ground sword stuck up, revolved, as if to cut little crescents from the clouds in the blue sky overhead.

Henri looked at Forrest's magnificent bay war horse and couldn't think of the animal's name, couldn't seem to remember if this was the fifth or the fifteenth horse Forrest would have shot from under him—and was that an event that had already happened, or was it still to come?

From the rear or what had been their rear a cannon coughed up thunder and grapeshot. Henri was shocked to a slightly clearer sense of the occasion and its time and place. It was spring, green grass and the pillowy fresh air told him that much, the fields so lush their horses risked foundering if they overgrazed. Last night Ginral Jerry had come into camp with half a dozen young rabbits slung over his shoulder, so dazed with spring fever, Jerry had claimed, he had only to snatch them up by their ears.

The pitch of the ringing in Henri's ears shifted, and near him he saw a corporal clap a hand around his upper arm. Blood leaked through the cracks between his fingers as the gray cloth stained. To the corporal's woebegone expression Forrest bit off a few words. "Hold yer horse in, son, ye ain't bad hurt till yet."

Smoke to the west—the Yankees had been burning barns and fields. A courier came galloping in amongst them: "Stanley's run over Armstrong's rear! Captured a mess of guns, and Captain Freeman!"

"Is he in Armstrong's rear goddamn him!" But for once Henri had a suspicion that Forrest's battle joy might be just slightly feigned. "By the bloody burning horns of the Devil that's jest whar I been tryen to git him all day! Come on, boys, we'll be in *his* rear terrectly—"

The event assembled itself in Henri's mind. Today they were in Middle Tennessee, south of Franklin on the Lewisburg Pike, riding out from Spring Hill for a reconnaissance coordinated with Van Dorn. In this region the road was embraced by bends of the Harpeth River, one of which the Federal General Stanley had unexpectedly crossed, overrunning Freeman's hastily formed battery before he could get off a shot, then moving into Armstrong's rear. The Confederates would have been set for a rout if Forrest had not rallied his escort to charge back on the attackers—by the first shock of contact most of the riders had persuaded themselves that Stanley really had fallen into a trap set by Forrest, and their wildcat shrieking turned triumphant:

Yyyyyyaaaaaaaiiiiiiiiiiiiiiiiiiiiiiiiieeeeeeeeeeeeeeeeeeee!!!!!!!!!!

They'd overrun Freeman's cannons now, though not the Federals who were rushing back toward the river crossing with their prisoners. Forrest, his bearded face in a genuine battle blaze, leaned toward Henri from his saddle and said, "Ornery, did I git around to tellen ye the time this puts me in mind of—" while on the other side of him Matthew turned his horse in closer, risking a collision to capture the anecdotal pearl—

Harried by their mounted captors, prisoners from Freeman's battery ran or tried to run in a herky-jerky slow motion across the field to the water maples lining the riverbank. Something bad was going to happen or already had. Freeman was heavy, used to riding with his caissons; he could not keep the pace. He sank to one knee, blowing in the sodden grass, a Federal soldier turned back, raised a pistol; the captured surgeon there at Freeman's side threw up one of his hands— Forrest was going to finish his story later, or no, he had already finished it, at Parker's Crossroads in December, about four months before. Was the past the part that had already happened, the future still to come? That battle would be, had been similar to this one, at least in some of its particulars . . .

They'd spent the days around Christmas tearing up railroad track up and down the line between Jackson and Union City, rolling kettledrums and building ghost campfires each night to make their weakness look like strength. Forrest had come into West Tennessee short of two thousand men, and made the Federals believe he had ten times that many. In fact the Federals in the region outnumbered him by five to one and were doing their clumsy best to hem him in against their gunboats on the Tennessee River. Forrest, meanwhile, slipped east toward McKenzie, meaning to hook around and strike the railroad again south of Jackson, if he could avoid a fight till then.

Year-end weather was miserable with icy rain. Crossing the Obion River they had to use captured sacks of coffee and flour to give the wagon wheels traction through the mud—a sacrifice which depressed the quartermasters. But they still had plunder enough to slow them down and when Forrest saw he was on a collision course with the Federals south of McLemoresville, he concluded to give them a whuppen if they wanted one. The Clarksburg and McLemoresville roads crossed in the front yard of the Reverend John Parker's house; Forrest sent his brother Bill with his Forty Thieves to lure the Federals under Dunham toward the crossroads. On the morning of New Year's Eve, he opened fire on Dunham's line, first with a single cannon rushed to a ridge above the Federal position, and then with Freeman's and John Morton's batteries working in close concert. By afternoon the artillery barrage and a couple of charges had separated Dunham from his own cannon and trapped him in a timber lot a little ways south of the Parker house. Forrest sent in a demand for surrender and was resting and waiting for a reply when rifle fire broke in their rear.

A courier rode up with his horse in a lather to announce that fresh Federal troops under Sullivan had broken in among Forrest's horse-holders in the peach orchard on the back side of the Parker house. Dunham must have been stalling for this development; from having his enemy surrounded Forrest was now pinned between two lines of hostile infantry.

"What'll we do, General?" the messenger panted, and Forrest snapped back at him, *"Charge both ways."*

He drew out the double-edged sword he'd taken at Trenton a week or so back, and spurred up his horse to ride to the rear. Henri followed him, with Kelley and Anderson. At their heels ran men who'd dismounted to do battle with Dunham's infantry, now desperate to recover their horses from the Federal surprise, but this movement looked less like a charge than a panic.

In the peach orchard there was a sudden flurry of skirmishing, but Forrest was directing a retreat rather than a real charge, as some of his men did recover their horses; there was still a path open to safety to the east. Sweeping the sword with his left arm, Forrest pointed them the way. As the troops began filtering out of the trees, he steered his horse nearer to Henri's.

"Ornery, did I never tell ye?" he began. "Back when I was naught but a shirttail boy, I had me a little spotted pony we called him Whiskey. Smarter'n a whip and mean as a snake. Did I kill me some snakes back in them days? Seem like Bedford County was all over snakes then, specially in the springtime. Copperheads, rattlers, cottonmouth too we used to see . . . I wouldn't kill a black snake though, account of a black snake keeps down varmints."

Raising his sword, he twisted in the saddle to shout a command to Dibrell, who was forming up men for retreat along the road toward Lexington. Then he returned to Henri with his ordinary speaking tone.

"It warnt all work back in them days, when we still had that farm on Caney Spring Creek, back afore my Daddy died. Work aplenty, but we had good play times too. They was other boys had ponies round that way and we used to ride all over the county. Hit wasn't hardly fenced up then, not like it is now.

"They was one time a pack of dogs took after us. Nigh on a dozen of'm I wouldn't be surprised, and big, ugly too . . . the biggest stood might near tall as our ponies. They got to running us and made our ponies run."

By now almost all their men had cleared the orchard. Forrest drew up his horse before a corpse splayed on its back: the young cavalier who'd objected to his sharpening the back side of the captured blade at Trenton.

There was something unlucky about peach orchards, Henri thought, remembering General Johnston's bloody boot. At this season the branches were wiry and bare; horseshoes had scuffed up a few bony pits. Forrest dismounted and planted his sword in the ground by the dead youth's head.

"Well now, Orville," he said. "How'd ye git yoreself kilt back here? I'd sooner thought to find ye forward, up front with the flags."

Kelley and Anderson exchanged a glance across his empty saddle. Forrest crouched, considered, then turned back the dead man's lapel. A whiff of lavender came with the handkerchief he drew from the inside pocket, as if it might have been a lady's favor. Forrest opened the cloth and covered the dead face. He stood up and shook the dirt from his sword.

"I never did take to a good-looken feller," he said with a frown. "I don't know why that is."

Between the orchard and the Parker house was a small cemetery set about with a hedge. Here they halted for a moment, looking down at the weather-worn humps of limestone. Kelley took off his hat and held it to his breast. His pale lips moved in a cold wind from the west. Forrest's face was still clouded from the meeting with the corpse.

"I tell ye panic oncet gits started good in a pack of what have ye," he said, "hit moves like fire afore the wind. Well I know you seen that yore own self plenty of times since we started in fighten these damyankees. That was a mean pack of dogs, that day I named. We all of us boys known'm. Half-wild. Hell I think some of'm was all the way wild. We known them to pull down cattle sometimes . . ."

A squad of blue cavalry rode out of the orchard, an officer calling for them to surrender. Forrest turned his horse toward them.

"I already have done surrendered," he said. "I'm jest getten my people collected to come in."

The Federal officer hesitated. "If you've surrendered," he said, "then why is your sword unsheathed?"

As if in surprise Forrest glanced down at his left fist gripping the sword hilt. "It's right handy for explainen folks whar to go at." He grinned. "Don't fret—I'll fetch hit to ye fore ye know it."

With that he trotted his horse away around the Parker house toward the crossroads, the other three riders following him. Henri felt a cold spot between his shoulder blades that grew to the size of Jerry's black skillet. He forced himself not to look back.

When they'd once faded into the trees south of the roadway, Forrest wriggled his whole spine like a hound stretching. "Boys," he said, "I thought we was done for, back thar." But he was addressing Henri alone, for Kelley and Anderson had drifted away. "Goddammit!" Forrest said suddenly. "It's scarce half an hour they was a-fixen to surrender to me."

John Morton swung in beside them then, his biscuit-pale face warm with action. He and Forrest saluted each other. Henri recalled how Forrest had sent him away when he first appeared to join their company, not wanting Freeman to be troubled by this whey-faced upstart. How Forrest would come to depend on Morton absolutely once Freeman had been killed. But Freeman would not die till April—

Forrest's horse reared at the crack of a shot that sounded like it had gone off between Henri's ears.

"General," said Morton. "Are you all right?"

Forrest calmed his mount and took off his hat. A minié ball had notched the brim. "By the hardest," he said. "That was mighty damn close."

"Are we not going to charge them both ways, then?" Henri blurted.

"Today?" Forrest laughed shortly. "Today we won't and say we did."

TODAY WAS the spring of 1863 and Captain Freeman could not keep up his lumbering run. He sank to one knee, breathless in the trampled pasture short of the bank of the Harpeth River. Doctor Skelton raised his hand to ward off the shot and the bullet passed through the center of his palm before it smashed into Freeman's face.

When Forrest overtook the scene, Freeman's body lay bulky as a bear's. He got down to raise the dead man's head; the exit wound was so engulfing it bloodied his arm to the elbow. His face twisted.

"That's dirty work by damn," he said. Tears ran from his eye sockets down into his beard. He would not see Forrest weep again, Henri realized. Not for Lieutenant Gould. Not for his brother Jeffrey. Whose deaths were still to come.

"By damn I'll get some for ye," Forrest said as he withdrew his hand from Freeman's head. "Goddamme if I don't." He wiped his forearm on the flank of his horse, remounted and rode toward the riverbank.

HE COULD HARDLY believe the dogs could keep up with the panicked ponies, frightened beyond a gallop into a dead run. But some of the dogs were long-legged, tall enough to snap at Forrest's bare heels. He was riding bareback too, and he could feel himself losing his seat as the pony bucked, kicked at the dogs, landed in still a faster run, leaving Forrest in the empty air behind his whipping tail.

He landed on his back with a slam, half his breath knocked out of him, but curling up his head automatically so it wouldn't strike the ground. The dogs scattered, startled by his landing in their midst like a bombshell. A stone came under one hand and he threw it. A stick under the other; he flailed it, screaming in their jaws. *Keep up the skeer.* The dog pack broke and ran yipping into cover of the thornbushes all around. "Hell," Forrest said, with his rasping laugh. "Them dogs was more afeart than me."

CHAPTER THIRTY-FOUR

November 1864

A CLEAR NIGHT: Orion masterfully striding across the dome of the winter sky. Among the others of Forrest's escort, Henri and Matthew lay wrapped each in the remaining tatters of his blanket, on the same ground their hobbled horses nuzzled for pale shreds of winter grass. Since they crossed into Tennessee they'd had some kind of fight every day, trying to slow the retreat toward Nashville of the Yankee troops under Schofield and scout their movement and intentions for General Hood at the same time. Just as darkness fell that evening they'd laid an ambush that had thrown the Yankees into disarray, and more than likely they'd be moving again before dawn—maybe toward Mount Pleasant where the Yankees were supposed to have a depot, thinly guarded.

So Henri should have been taking these couple of hours to soak up all the sleep he could, yet he lay wakeful, eyes open, expectant of something. Forrest's tent was nearby, its canvas glowing from the orb of a lantern inside, and Henri could hear muttered voices of a conference between Forrest and Majors Anderson and Strange. The tent went quiet when the two officers came out, but Forrest didn't snuff his light.

There was something watching from a line of pale and leafless oaks, flanked by dark cedars, and when Forrest's conference had ended it detached itself and moved softly toward the tent. Man-sized, something familiar in the step. Matthew rolled to a crouch. There'd been rumors for months that Sherman had assassins on Forrest's trail, though now that Atlanta had fallen to the Yankees, Forrest's threat to the railroads that ran south from Nashville mattered less than it did before.

As Matthew darted forward, Henri drew a short knife and went after him. Cold ground shocked the arches of his bare feet. The prowler was beside the tent when he turned quickly, showed his empty hands. The lamp glow through the canvas caught the unscarred side of Benjamin's handsome head.

"You were *gone*," Matthew hissed, and Ben motioned furiously for silence.

Henri beckoned them away from the tent. "It's all right," he said to Ben. "He's not going anywhere."

All three of them returned among the horses. Matthew's mount raised its head to snuffle and blow hot air into the bib of Benjamin's overalls.

"You were *good* gone," Matthew said.

"Halfway home," Ben said. "Ain't it the truth? But I kept feelen that cold down my back. Ain't right to run off without taken no leave. Ain't like I was runnen north noway." He turned sideways, slipping the horse's muzzle from his chest. "Got no sugar for you today," he said. "Ain't got no nothen."

Henri found a chunk of cold cornbread in his sack and handed it to Ben, who bit into it sharply, nodding his thanks.

"He done give free papers to some," Ben said thickly, through his food. "I knows it. Some from Coahoma plantation same as me."

"You came all the way back for a piece of paper?" Henri said. "When you've got as good a chance at a hanging noose or a ball between your eyes?"

"I come back for an understanden," Ben said. "Look the man in the eye one time. Like he do me."

"He never gave me any free paper," Matthew said.

"Huh." Ben looked at him carefully, in the watery light of the winter stars. "You ax for one?"

"Not exactly," Matthew said.

"Come on with me when I goes in there," Ben said.

"What makes you think I have any pull with General Nathan Bedford Forrest," Matthew said. "I'm a thing he owns the same as you."

"I ain't but his slave and he got plenty," Ben said. "You his blood son. You knows it. He knows it. Everbody knows it. They might not say it but they knows it."

Matthew stared at him.

"You ain't obliged to say a mumblen word," Ben told him. "You'll stand there with me, won't you?"

Henri followed them to Forrest's tent. When the other two were admitted he hung back, but he could see plain enough through the open flap. Forrest was studying maps by the light of his lantern; his papers spread on a folding camp table. He looked at Ben.

"Brought ye a whole delegation, I see."

Ben pulled himself straight and caught his lower lip in his teeth.

"Thought you done left me," Forrest said.

"Reckon I started," Ben said. "Next I thought I cain't do that. I needs to ax leave."

"Aint like ye was a sojer," Forrest said. "You're a teamster, more like."

"Hell if a mule deserts you go after him," Ben said. "Never mind a man."

"Notice I ain't come after *you*," Forrest said.

Ben laughed almost inaudibly. "Figured you jest hadn't come *yet*."

"Don't think I didn't notice though," Forrest said, as if he hadn't heard. "Watching you leave was like seeing birds go before a storm. Low to the ground and fast as a bullet. Hit's a sign."

He laced his fingers behind his head, and looked up at the sag of canvas over his head. "We've looked right po'ly for quite a spell, since Atlanta went down, and I know what all Sherman's doen down to Georgia—I might of stopped that bastard if they let me. But right now, I'd still say we got a chance to whup it. We're bout to get the drop on Schofield, and if Hood can take back Nashville after that, why boys, hit's gone be a whole new day."

He looked at Ben inquiringly, out from under the deep shade of his brows.

Ben straightened again. "I come to ax your leave to go home, General Forrest."

"All right." Forrest leaned into his camp table, dug awkwardly at a clean sheet of paper with a pen crabbed painfully in his left hand. He took a long time to finish and sign.

"Benjamin," he said. "I'll give ye this here free paper. No, I won't say that. I'll say ye earned it."

Ben reached for the document. "Thank you, sir."

"Say hidy to Nancy and the chirren when ye git thar," Forrest said.

"I'll be sure and do that," Benjamin said. Forrest still held the paper not quite in his reach.

"If ye'll wait till morning I'll have Major Anderson copy it out fair." Forrest grinned. "Ye know I hadn't got much of a hand fer writen."

"That's all right," Benjamin said. "I'll be more'n happy with what you wrote."

CHAPTER THIRTY-FIVE

THE ASHES of Ginral Jerry's fire had gone cold. He hunkered on his heels, scouring the iron with a handful of sand, without looking at the work his hands were doing. Instead he peered across the dead embers into the hollow of the dead tree there on the hilltop, white-stubbled chin lifted, his watery brown eyes alert.

From the stump on which he sat, Henri followed the direction of Jerry's gaze. The candle that sometimes burned in the hollow had gone out—it looked as if the wick had consumed itself all the way to the end, leaving lacy, wraithlike wings of white wax melted to the wood. Around the wax came a cold boneless movement, muscle pouring itself through a loop inside the hollow of the tree. Henri was startled enough that he froze, and his breath stopped for a moment when he realized it was a snake that wore those colored bands. In these parts he could recognize the copperhead, moccasin and rattler, also the green garter snake and the speckled chicken snake. The serpent in the tree was none of these, and Henri could not find its head, to know if it had the wedge shape of a viper. Then presently the snake's head rose up from a crockery bowl that had been set at the bottom of the hollow place. The head was narrow and its color was duller than the rest, as if it had been dipped in . . . milk. How would Jerry have come by milk in this country?—which between the Rebels and the Yanks had been scraped as dry as that black skillet scoured with sand. The ribbon of black tongue flicked in, out of the scaled mouth slot. The colored body of the snake dripped off the convolutions of the inner wood, until the whole creature had disappeared into a lower crevice of the tree.

"Jerry," Henri said cautiously.

"King snake," Jerry told him. "Ain't pizen. Ain't no harm in'm at all . . ."

The hilltop was contained in a pocket of mist, a pearly gray dimness like a cataract. Henry got up and walked the rim of the hill to the cardinal points. West: through the parting of the mist, he could see the distant figures of Forrest and his escort fighting a rearguard action to cover the retreat of Hood's decimated army, from the bloody disasters at Franklin and Nashville. South, Forrest sat his horse beside Charles Anderson, facing down a darkly wooded trail like a tunnel, debating whether to fly to Texas or Mexico and continue the doomed struggle there. These were not scenes Henri desired to enter.

Through the vapors to the east he saw, down a long brushy slope of the hill, young Matthew sitting on the tailgate of an empty wagon, swinging his long legs just an inch or so short of the ground, his head lowered despondently, rolling a revolver from one hand to the other. Henri nodded to himself and started down the steep slope toward the boy, picking his way through buck bushes and briars. He was halfway down when a fine big rabbit popped up practically at his feet and went bouncing away around the curve of the hill. By the time Henri thought to produce his own pistol the rabbit had lost itself in the ground cover.

He hung the pistol back on his belt and hopped out to the level ground where the wagon was stalled in its ruts. It was Benjamin's wagon, Henri noticed. Ben had carved the back of the box seat with two wildcat heads snarling and spitting to right and to left. Benjamin himself slept in the wagon bed, cushioned by a heap of tattered flour sacks.

Matthew glanced up briefly, looked back at his knees. He was rolling the empty cylinder in and out of the frame of his revolver. It made a sharp metallic click whenever it snapped back in.

"What are you back here brooding for?" Henri said. Back along the road the wagon had come from he could hear an intermittent boom of cannon; smoke rose on the horizon to mingle with dust in the setting sun.

Matthew shrugged. "No cartridges."

"You'll find plenty forward, I'd expect."

This time Matthew held Henri's eyes. "You?"

Henri turned to gaze upward at the Old Ones' bald hill, but it was gone; he seemed instead to have descended a much wider slope, a neglected pasture going to brush and blackberry bramble and the orange-blond sage grass. At the top of the pasture was a partly collapsing rock wall fence and above that the crown of the hill was covered with a tight bristling top knot of trees. By this landscape Henri could tell they were in Tennessee, and by the king snake colors of the leaves he knew it must be fall. "He don't need me for nothing," Matthew said. The cylinder rolled out of the pistol in his palm, clicked back.

"They don't really need me either," Henri said. It was November, he recalled, and Forrest was at Johnsonville, destroying the Federal supply depots there where the railroad met the Tennessee River. The startled Yankees had been spooked into burning their own boats before they scattered, while a thoughtful barrage of Forrest's artillery set fire to the warehouses east of the river. Thus the smoke . . . Forrest himself was passing the time by taking jocular charge of one of Morton's guns, one of the few instruments of war he had no real idea how to manipulate, calling out nonsensical comments and commands: *a rickety-shay! Elevate the breech of that gun lower!* A last merry dance on the brink of ruin. Those burning stores were meant for Sherman, but Sherman had already taken Atlanta. General Hood was already marching the Army of Tennessee north from that defeat toward its ultimate doom in the shallow ditch south of Franklin. There was nothing now, except pillage, between Sherman and the Atlantic Ocean.

"He caught Willie horseracing again," Matthew said. "Punished him hard. Made him tote fence rails with the rest of the boys, until he was ready to drop."

"And so?"

"He didn't do a thing to me."

"And you're complaining about that."

"He didn't even see me," Matthew said. "Like I just wasn't there. I would have won the damn race too, if he hadn't stopped it."

Henri looked up the slope again, wondering how many more rabbits might be hid in the wiry scraggle of buck bushes. His stomach folded in on itself. A gust brought a swirl of rust-colored leaves from the hilltop to settle among the patches of sage grass in the pasture.

"Don't tell me he didn't see you," he told Matthew. "He might not show anything about it but there's not much he doesn't see."

"Here's one thing I can't stand about Willie," Matthew said.

"Just one?" Henri forced a smile.

"Just—every day of the week, every *hour* of the goddamn day, Willie knows who he is, or he thinks he does—no, he doesn't even bother to think about it. That idea never once crosses his mind—"

"And you don't know?"

"How would I know? Am I soldier or a saddle-maker? White man or a nigger? A body can't be both, can they? Not both of those things jumbled up together?"

Henri cocked an eyebrow at him. "You might want to try just being a man, and never mind the rest of it."

Matthew ducked his head. "It's different for you."

Well, that was true, Henri thought. Or maybe it was just half-true.

"I hadn't seen such a lot of Willie lately," he remarked.

"*He's* keeping him back." Matthew raised his pistol sharply, sighted it down the empty road, then lowered it again to his lap. "So he'll be *safe*."

Henri considered. It could be true. Forrest might indeed have grown more solicitous of his only son, since his brother Jeffrey had been killed in the pursuit of A. J. Smith.

"That's his Momma wants him safe," Henri said. "Forrest has got fighting blood. He wants his blood to fight."

"If I'm his blood," Matthew said, "he never has claimed me."

"He has," Henri said. "A time or two. I've heard him."

"If I'm his blood," Matthew said, "then why would he stick me in an old nigger shack at the bottom of Memphis? Where he slips around at night to fuck that nigger wench who plays like she's my momma though she ain't. Fucks the wench like she was a dog."

"Wait a minute." Henri raised a hand to dam the flow of ugly words. Benjamin was motionless on his pallet of sacks; only his eyes darted, beneath closed lids, tracking whatever he saw in his dreams . . . Henri considered the Memphis raid, when Forrest had fallen behind them on Beale Street. In his inward eye he saw the

woman with those little boys, recalled the liquid grace of her movement. *Son.* Dark honey in her voice. *Why don't you hold the ginnal's
hoss?* The thing that hadn't made sense then did now. He could see
the woman and Forrest inclining toward each other like a pair of sil-
houettes cut from black paper.

"Does he do her like she was a dog?" He waited.

"No. I don't guess so." Matthew looked at the ground between
his dangling feet. "It's like he can't get enough of her." He raised his
head to the smoke-stained horizon. "Like she can't get enough of
him."

Henri followed his eyes to the smoke. The dots in the air across
the river must be buzzards.

"They act like they love each other." Matthew spat.

"Well," Henri said. "I suppose that's not much use to you."

"It's not much use to nobody," Matthew said. "You know he'll
never claim the sons he got with her."

Henri looked away up the hill. There was no argument with that,
he knew.

"He claimed you once," he said. "I heard him do it."

Matthew looked at him.

"The day Sam Green got killed."

"Oh, that," Matthew said. "Well, he'll call anybody *Son*. He's
probably called *you* that before."

Henri reached around in his memory. It might be true; he wasn't
sure.

"You ever hear him say a thing he didn't mean?"

Matthew stared at the dirt between his feet. His right hand
clenched the handle of his empty weapon. "But he never *thinks*,"
Matthew said. "He never thinks about how it might be like for me."

"You might be right as far as that goes," Henri admitted. "If he
got all tied up thinking thoughts like that he wouldn't be able to do
like he does."

"Oh yes," Matthew said. "Do and ride on and never look back."

"Listen," Henri said. "He won't claim you like he does Willie.
You're not headed for a bunk in the big house when all this is done.
I know that as well as you. That won't happen in your time, not anywhere in this country. But you're not headed back to slavery time
either."

Matthew looked up at him sharply. "How do *you* know what's going to happen."

Everything has already happened, Henri thought, but he knew it wouldn't help to say that.

"If we're not headed back to slavery," Matthew said, "then what are we fighting for?"

"Oh," Henri said. "You think I don't ask myself that every day?" He had begun to laugh and couldn't stem the tide of it any more than if he had been vomiting. Ben stirred on the sacks but did not quite wake. Matthew did not join in.

"If we're fighting for slavery," Henri said, once he had a partial grip on himself, "we're not going to win."

Matthew clamped one hand on the grip of his pistol and one on the barrel, squeezed as if he meant to bend it. Then his hands loosened and he laid the pistol on the worn boards of the wagon bed beside his thigh.

"I'll never be more than a nigger to him," he said.

"Listen to you," Henri said. "All twisted up about a word. You think he never was called a bad name in his life? A word never meant that much to Bedford Forrest. It's what's inside your skin that counts. Bone and gristle. Blood and heart."

The yellow light of anger faded from Matthew's eyes, replaced by a weariness that was also familiar. Henri felt a little sad that he couldn't stay with him all the way. But Matthew would survive the war.

"Mathieu," he said. "Listen to me. You're trying to pry something out of him that you've already got. You got as strong a dose of him as Willie does. And *he* knows it just as well as you do. Take that. Live your life with that."

"But am I his son or am his slave? And I can't figure out if I love him or hate him."

"That's right," Henri said. "You're right about that. Suppose maybe you're allowed to do both."

Matthew's gaze narrowed. "You talk like a hoodoo man, sometimes," he said. "What *are* you, anyway?"

Zanj, Henri thought, *the spirit that walks with you.* "Just an idea," he said instead, "of what you might become."

· · ·

HE WAS ALREADY GONE when Benjamin sat up, blinking slowly, his eyes coming clear. He dropped off the back of the wagon, took a few steps below the roadway, and pissed on the fading autumn grass. Buttoning his trousers again, he walked back toward Matthew and the wagon.

"We best get on," he said, as he climbed aboard.

Matthew nodded and joined him on the decorated box. Ben clucked to the drowsing mule and the wheels began to turn.

"You oughtent to spend so much time talken to dead folks," Benjamin told him. "They's a whole lot of life ahead of you yet."

CHAPTER THIRTY-SIX

November 1864

Forrest, with his escort about him, sat his horse to the east of the Lewisburg Pike, from a point where he could see Federal sharpshooters on a knoll just across the Harpeth River, picking off men from the van of the Confederate column marching doggedly, upon Hood's order, head on toward Schofield's entrenched works in Franklin.

"Jackson," Forrest hollered, twisting his hat in his hands, "take yore boys across that stream and run them Yankees off that hill." He continued abusing his hat as Jackson and his men obeyed the order. Henri, followed by Major Strange, rode their horses close into Forrest's left side. "That's how it ought to gone all over," Forrest was muttering. "Hood had the sense to listen to me, I'd flushed Schofield out of all his works the same way and we might of whupped'm solid here . . . instead—" Forrest jammed his hat on his head, pulled the brim down to shade his eyes. His fingers had turned blue with the sharp winter cold. "He's set on killen ever last man he's got, chargen'm head-on into them trenches."

The bloodbath was already coming, Henri thought, most certainly it had already begun, away to the left of their position, with heavy constant firing along the Columbia Pike, where Hood had insisted his infantry charge the Federal trenches and abatis across a couple of hundred yards of open, frozen field. Forrest took off his hat again, rolled it tight, then idly reshaped it on the pommel of his saddle. "We had'm in the bag at Spring Hill," he said. "Sent for him once, sent for him twicet. No sir, General is not to be DISTURBED *goddamn his eyes.* Too full of whiskey and opium to raise up his sorry ass outen the bed."

"Sent for you yesterday," Henri said. An expression he'd learned among slaves of the South. "Now here you come today." Such a heart sadness in this handful of words. Forrest did not appear to hear the sound of them, much less capture their sense.

"And today he *damn well* won't hear what'd fix it."

"Well, now," Major Strange said as he stroked his long beard. "He might have been better disposed to you if you hadn't offered to tie his quartermaster's legs around his neck."

"Might have been don't make no matter." Forrest was talking to Major Strange, though Henri had his horse and himself positioned right between them. "We'll need ever last mule we got fore this is over and done with and Hood will too, to get his wreckage hauled away. Hit's his whole damn army getten itself blown to smithereens down there."

"Ain't it the truth," Major Strange said sorrowfully. "Just as well we're not down there with them."

"Ye think so?" Forrest looked sharply at Major Strange, looking right through Henri. "Well . . . ye might say that. Hell ye might say Hood has saved my life by sending me way around to Hell and gone and this far out of the action. Only single question I got— Why he'd have wanted to?"

The winter wind blew in their faces.

To the west, the grumble of gunfire rose and fell. The shallow trench so hurriedly dug by Schofield's men before the Carter house was now beginning to fill with blood. Henri knew this though he couldn't see it from where he sat.

"He might have known he'd need you more another day," he said. But they were running out of days.

Forrest shot an irritable look straight through Henri to Major Strange. "What's that ye say?"

"I didn't say anything," Major Strange replied.

He can't see me, Henri thought. A bolt of cold shot down his spine. And he always sees everybody, for better or worse; he sees every man and knows him.

CHAPTER THIRTY-SEVEN

H IS HEAD ROCKED sharply back, painlessly but very hard. He
lifted his hands to both sides of his head, but was afraid to
touch it. He merely framed it airily with his fingertips. A hollow ran
through his head from front to back with a brown wren flying backward through it, a discreet and modest little bird.

Forrest was riding out ahead of him still, ahead of them all,
standing up straight in the saddle, slashing and screaming defiance
and rage. It appeared to Henri now that the slit in the world's fabric
which Forrest galloped effortlessly through was now this very same
echoing hollow passage through his own head.

His limbs were weakening, the grip of his knees on the plunging
horse began to loosen, to give way. He snatched at the wild-flying
reins and missed, then clutched at the saddlebow. Beginning to fall,
he kicked free of one stirrup, but the other was caught. In terror, he
knew he was sure to be dragged. Then something else surrendered,
a stirrup leather broke; in one flighty instant Henri was airborne.

Then darkness, or rather a pearly mist, and still no pain.

As he came to, he smelled cooking first. Fatback sweating grease
on hot iron. His eyes didn't seem to work right yet, or else he just
somehow couldn't open them. He felt about with the flats of his
hands and seemed to be lying on one of those limestone shelves he
favored whenever he could find them. All over the hills of Tennessee
they were usually easy enough to discover.

Apart from a distant high-pitched ringing, both his ears seemed
to work all right. He could hear the first hectic notes of "Devil's
Dream" on a fiddle nearby. Who was it used to fiddle that tune so?

Henri sat up, tucking his legs up under him, and looked about

the edges of his pallet of stone, for scorpions or centipedes or sting-
ing woolly worms or snakes. He could see now, well enough. Satisfied there were no venomous creepy-crawlies in his range, he
stretched his legs and lowered his bare feet into the dirt beyond the
stone. The dust between his toes was cool, but not unpleasantly so. If
he had not lost his boots in the fall then someone must have
removed them while he was laid out here.

Ginral Jerry tended a small hot, almost smokeless fire, over
which he was cooking coldwater cornbread, a single hoecake that
occupied the whole circumference of the pan. He hunkered, tailbone hanging over his heels, flicking the hoecake now and then
with a clean chip so that it would not stick.

The cornbread had a nubby surface and a faint bluish cast, like
the limestone shelf where Henri had reposed. He knew it would be
not quite as hard as limestone when at last he bit into his piece, and
it would be just fleetingly sweet from the white corn it was made of—
Jerry had not got his hands on sugar, honey, or molasses for weeks.
Henri's mouth began to water, and he swallowed a time or two.

The boy was still fiddling. Faster than before. This was a tune
meant to pick up speed as it advanced. A challenge to see how fast
you could work the bow without dropping a note. Young William
Lipscomb had the fiddle now. Had it always been he who played
"Devil's Dream"? Lipscomb was killed or was to be killed at the age
of eighteen, in the course of a skirmish on a rainy night when Forrest, profiting from the dark and the wet, sprang a surprise attack
with a few of his escort on a much larger Federal cavalry unit under
Cabron. November 1864: Forrest had been on his way to join John
Bell Hood as he marched the Army of Tennessee from Atlanta
toward Nashville, leaving Sherman unhampered to lay waste to
Georgia. Lately Forrest had equipped his escort with the new
Spencer repeating rifles and that and the fact that his men were well
camouflaged in their wet rubber slickers made up for the disadvan-
tage in numbers. The escort routed Cabron's men as they struggled
to raise their tents in the rain, took fifty-odd prisoners and still more
small arms. Riding away with a smaller group yet, Forrest was
accosted by a company of Federals who tried to take him prisoner—
one had touched a gun barrel to Forrest's breastbone, but Major
Strange clipped his arm so the shot went wild. In that whirl of con-

fusion in the rain and dark, young Lipscomb caught the bullet that killed him a day or so later. William Wood was also killed in that brief engagement at Fouché Springs. He sat now on a stump looking up at young Lipscomb, tapping a toe and rattling pebbles in the cup of his hand to mark time.

In the hollow of the dead tree the usual candle burned. But there were far more candles than usual, waxed down all amongst the roots of the tree. Some special service must be owed to the Old Ones today. From the branches dangled small cloth packets, bound up with snatches of red and black string. On the trunk of the tree people had pinned up keys and small rusty padlocks, bills of the worthless Confederate money, burnt cartridge paper, locks of hair, ribbons and love letters from home.

Henri stood up. He was terribly hungry. He felt a hole through his midsection like the hole through his head, but so much bigger that a buzzard could have flown through without grazing a wing tip.

Mist roiled around the bald crown of the hill. The bone flutes and gourd rattles of the Old Ones had joined in the fiddle tune. They had handfuls of teeth in their shakers today. Through a gap in the mist strode R. H. Auman and Jacob Cruse, both killed at Chickamauga on the same day as Henri. They tipped their hats to him as they walked by. Jeffrey Forrest beckoned them to join the dance.

Henri himself did not feel like dancing, though the music tickled and jumped in his head. He looked down at himself, at his bare sunken ribs. He was still poorer than the day Forrest first found him by the roadside in Kentucky. No shoes and no shirt, just a red wanga bundle round his neck on a string. His butternut trousers were rags to the knee. His weapons were nowhere. He was done with the war.

Out of the mist climbed Felix Hicks, a quartermaster slain not long after Brice's Crossroads—he'd asked to ride with Forrest's escort to attack A. J. Smith, just for the adventure of it. Auman handed Hicks a gourd. He drank, and passed it on to Henri. The gourd held cool water with a faint taste of field mint. Where was there mint now, in all this country? The horses had eaten or trampled it all.

He handed the gourd to Tommy Brown, just coming up the hill with Bill Green, both of them killed near Lynchburg in 1864. They'd surrendered already, but when a Union officer ordered them shot on the spot, Green snatched his pistol and killed him with it. In the next few seconds they were both gunned down. Henri walked around the crown of the hill, not quite dancing, though his step grew buoyantly light and his hips just barely began to flow with the music. The Old Ones had tipped up hollow logs and were drumming. Henri raised another gourd of water that had come into his hands, saluting the four directions with a splash. From the east, more of the dead kept arriving: Jim Shoffner, Bobby Reeves, Bill Robinson, Jacob Holt, Alf Boone, Pone Green, who was killed at Tuscaloosa. C. C. McLemore. Sammy Scales and P. S. Dean.

Here came John J. Neal, shot down as he rode with a dispatch from Forrest to Hood. The message said what?—*Don't come. Death is waiting.* More than six thousand men to be felled in one day.

Now, from this now, Henri peered into the mist, knowing that beyond it he might see the Army of Tennessee hurling itself to total destruction against Schofield's fortified line south of Franklin. Blood running in the trenches ten inches deep. Forrest almost biting his own lips off in his frustration that Hood would not order him to flank Schofield out of his hastily dug works, preferring to charge, head-on, to his ruin.

Here came Will Strickland, killed near Pulaski on Christmas Day, 1864, while he helped Forrest cover Hood's wretched retreat from the carnage of Franklin and Nashville—the last shredded remnants of that army slipping across the rivers to the west. Forrest had been fond of Strickland, who'd come without leave from an infantry regiment to join the escort—liked him so well that he sent seven men back to the Twenty-seventh Tennessee to replace him. Green recruits they might have been but still there were seven of them.

There were Union boys coming in now too. Henri did not know their names, though he recognized many of their faces. They had not only met at sword's point. Sometimes they'd find each other in some smokehouse or cornfield, hollow and famished, together in that as they scavenged for food. By the war's end, one in every ten able-bodied men in the Union states would have been, had already been killed in some battle. In the Confederacy, it would be one in four.

Jerry could not possibly feed so many! But Henri had a chunk of warm pone in his fist, and when he looked at the skillet there was some left there. Not a lot, but there was some.

What a faithful service Jerry had made. No matter what had already happened he always managed to feed them something. And the dead were always, endlessly hungry. Henri was grateful. He wanted to weep, but the dead have no tears.

Some of the new arrivals seemed to look at him strangely. Henri scratched his head. There were burrs in his hair. With his bare chest, bare feet, tattered trousers held up with frayed rope, he must look like a contraband, a runaway slave.

His cornbread was finished. Last gravelly crumbs in the back of his craw. He would always be hungry but he wanted to rest. He went back to the limestone shelf and stretched out. Around him the fiddling and drumbeat grew distant.

He covered his face with his forearm to block out the pale light of the sky. But his arm was transparent; he could see right through it. He could see straight through his own eyelids too. The hilltop was empty. Nobody was there. He himself was not there. There was no one but Jerry, serving the dead.

CHAPTER THIRTY-EIGHT

May 1865

J ERRY LOOPED a piece of soft old rope around King Philip's big head for a hackamore. After the war there were not enough ready-made halters to go around. He stroked the velvet of King Philip's nostrils and clucked to him as he tied him to an iron ring in the hall of the barn, then went to clean his stall.

There wasn't such of a whole lot to do because this task was done every day; still Jerry grunted every time he bent to fork up a clump of wet straw and manure. During the war he had often got wet and slept cold and now he had a touch of that arthuritis in both his knees and his right hip. The place on his hip worked around to the back sometimes.

He racked the pitchfork in the barrow and shook out a little lime powder on the damp spots in the stall. Once they had dried, he would scatter fresh straw. But now he got a stiff brush and a metal comb and went to work on King Philip's mane and tail and coat. Being so near the big hot-blooded horse would warm and ease the arthuritis pains that came and went with the morning dew, and it also seemed to soothe and loosen his mind. He had give up his commission same as General Forrest had, so people didn't call him Ginral Jerry no more, but mostly just plain Jerry, though some did call him Mister Forrest, since he didn't have any other last name but Forrest and that was a name that carried respect. He was free too, now that the war was over, and although the state of freedom had not much changed the way he lived, he liked to think about it and did so several times a day.

"Whoa, you," he said, when King Philip shifted a leg or shivered, his low voice scrambled in his mouth. In the course of the war most of his natural teeth had fell out and General Forrest had got him a fresh set of wooden ones, like what George Washington used to have. The wooden teeth were not very comfortable, but Jerry liked to wear them anyway, except when he needed to eat or talk.

When King Philip stirred, Jerry slipped a hand out of the brush's strap to stroke the horse with his bare palm. Nestling against the warm hide of the horse, he muttered at the level of his breath *I'se free now,* and let that whisper shimmer, and then thought *My chirren free. My grandchirren be free.* He combed some burrs and loose hair out of King Philip's mane and thought *My greatgrandchirren gone be free,* and stopped with that. There was something about the freedom of his great-grandchildren that always seemed to trouble him a little; he didn't know why. Maybe it was because he didn't have any great-grandchildren yet, that he knew of. He didn't know what this trouble could be, though it was true that now some people appeared to be worse off free than they had been slave . . . but Forrest's people did all right, except they were poor, but then everybody down South was poor, white or black, since the war. Only Jerry thought Forrest would be rich again soon. He seemed to already be working on that.

In the other stalls horses had begun to nicker and stamp. "Hesh, y'all," Jerry said, slipping his hand back into the strap of the brush. "Be still." He looked about—the boy who should have been dropping a handful of grain in their feed boxes had wandered off somewhere. That was one of his grandsons, Sophus. Through the open barn doors, Jerry caught sight of him up near the fence, shading his eyes from the rising sun to look at something that must be coming down the road.

He made to call Sophus back to the barn, but he couldn't get his voice to carry very far past the wooden teeth, and it was awkward to take them out because he had the brush and comb strapped to his hands. As he considered this problem, he felt King Philip bunch up against him. There was a flash of blue on the road.

King Philip backed up, surged forward, made to rear. With a ripple of his long muscular neck he broke free of the hackamore.

"Whoa, you hoss," Jerry said, shaking off the brush to reach for a hold of forelock or mane. King Philip shook free and charged for daylight.

"Shit far," Jerry said. He had learned this expression from his master.

The barn doorway was secured with a two-by-six plank slid between the doorposts at waist height, but Sophus, going out, had left it barely caught on one side. The plank bent away like a twig as King Philip went through it, then sprang back to catch Jerry in the midsection, knocking him flat and knocking the wind clean out of him. In the split second he lay on the dusty clay floor, he caught sight of an old ax handle waiting there to be set with a new head, and he snatched it as he got up and ran. Scattering fence rails like splinters, King Philip had burst onto the road to attack the little party of Federal curiosity-seekers who'd come out in hope of a glimpse of that devil, Forrest.

They were getting more devilment than they'd counted on now. Like a certain number of other old soldiers, King Philip had not really accepted the notion that the war was now over. Blue cloth and brass buttons sent him clean out of his mind. Forrest didn't ride him off the place anymore, since all North Mississippi was crawling with uniformed Yankees, and Forrest even did business with some of them. This bunch, though, was nothing but a bunch of *featherhead-edlollygagginggoddamngolliwoggawkers* as Forrest would certainly have let them know, if he had been near.

King Philip had laid his ears back and bared his teeth and had his neck stretched so long and straight he looked more like a hydra than a horse. Sophus was yelling for Jerry from the raw bottom of his throat, and Jerry wanted to call back *stay way from dat hoss* but he couldn't have got so much past his mouthful of wood if he'd had breath to holler, and he had none to spare. King Philip had knocked down one of the strange horses already and as the rider rolled clear he reared to attack another one with his front hooves. A third Yankee horse wheeled to kick, nearly throwing his rider in the process. A fourth horseman swung his mount away to make room to draw a pistol.

Jerry jumped over a couple of fence rails and knocked down the gun arm with the ax handle. The pistol fired wild when it struck in the ditch; the report drove King Philip still crazier. Jerry smacked a couple of the Federal horses with the ax handle to drive them back, then turned to put his body between King Philip and the enemy.

The big horse hesitated. The fallen Federal ran up and caught Jerry by the shoulder from behind. Reflexively Jerry batted him away with the iron comb he didn't realize was still attached to his left hand. King Philip charged and the Yankee rolled under the belly of another horse to get away. Jerry dropped the ax handle to snatch at King Philip's mane and came away with a handful of coarse hair.

Forrest, who'd been assisting a blacksmith at the forge, came burning up all soot-streaked, black beard jutting and eyes shooting sparks. As he passed Sophus he grabbed a rope the boy must have had the good sense to fetch from the barn. In a moment he had caught King Philip and brought the horse under some kind of control.

Jerry put his teeth in his bib pocket and took the rope's end. He ran the curry comb lightly over King Philip's spine. The big horse shuddered and subsided.

"Whoa, you," Jerry set. "You jess settle down. War done over. You let these Yankee gemmun alone."

For a moment they all watched each other, breathing. One bluecoat fondled his forearm where the ax handle had bruised it. Another nursed a red row of scratches from the iron teeth of the comb.

Lieutenant Hosea took off his hat.

"General Forrest?" he said.

Forrest folded his arms across his chest.

"Dear Lord," Hosea said. "Your niggers fight for you. Your *horses* fight for you. No wonder you were so hard to whip."

Forrest looked back at him, yellow gleam in his eye, and said, "I ain't been whupped till yet."

CHAPTER THIRTY-NINE

December 1853

A SUNNY MORNING, following a night of rain not quite cold enough to freeze. It was warmer now, though a chill breeze came off and on from the river. Forrest was walking back from the docks on the Memphis riverfront when something thumped into his leg. A little black boy, no more than two years old if that, rebounded from the collision and was gathering himself to run again when Forrest caught him up.

"Well, hello."

The boy was dressed in just a rag of osnaburg, with holes cut in it to make a smock. The cloth was grimy but the child was clean. His hair was cut close against his scalp and his arms and legs were glossy, well fleshed.

"Now who do you belong to?" Forrest said. He ran his thumb over a ringworm circle on the boy's shoulder where it emerged from the smock. The worm was dead and the mark of it looked to be half-healed; there was a faint odor of a coal oil poultice when he lifted his thumb away.

"Somebody been taken care of you, anyhow," Forrest said. He'd noticed too that the neck and arm holes in the smock had been neatly hemmed; never mind the cloth itself was worn to near-transparency.

The boy twisted in his arms and kicked at him with both bare feet.

"Quit that," Forrest said. "Fore ye break yore toe."

The boy squirmed and looked with white eyes toward the river, where a boat horn blew a long low hoot.

"Now where did ye drop from?"

Wordless, the boy gaped at him, revealing a flash of sound-looking teeth, then puckered his lips tight shut.

"Cat got yore tongue, hah?" Forrest said. "Well I reckon ye didn't just fall from the moon."

He looked in the direction the boy was refusing to look, and saw R. J. Willis come huffing around the corner, all in a lather, a rope leash in one hand and a short braided riding crop in the other. Forrest swung the boy to his left hip and set his right leg forward. Willis stopped for a second when he saw them, then came on at a slower pace.

"You don't mean to use all that on a little ole shirttail boy," Forrest said. He was wearing a pistol on his right hip and he touched it briefly through the coat flap beneath which it was hidden.

"Goddamn runaway needs to be tied." Willis halted about three paces away. "Needs to be taught a good lesson too."

"I got him, don't I?" Forrest said. "He ain't goen nowhar."

"That there's my propitty, Forrest," Willis said. "Hand him over."

Forrest looked about himself. Women with their shopping baskets were tucking pale faces away in their bonnets as they discreetly left the street, and the shopkeepers stood well away from their windows. In one of the shops a plank shutter banged closed, though it was well short of the dinner hour. Disputes between slave-traders could turn very salty. Forrest himself had been a witness in the case where Bolton shot poor McMillan, claiming McMillan had sold him a free nigger. He still felt troubled when he thought of that business, for McMillan had been uneasy about going to see Bolton in the first place, and Forrest had advised him to go, and not seen till later he ought to have gone with him. He had traveled with McMillan once in a while, running coffles upriver from New Orleans in the early summer, when the heat made unhealthy to keep too many slaves in the barracoons down there, and he'd been struck by the fact that McMillan never carried a pistol and never seemed to need one to govern the people he was transporting.

Bolton must also have known McMillan generally went unarmed, for he shot him in cold blood and threw down a knife afterward to make a claim he'd been attacked. McMillan had lived long enough to tell this story; they carried him back to Forrest's house to finish his dying. In the back of his mind Forrest had thought Bolton too much a coward to do what he did—a poor risk to misjudge a man that way. Though Forrest and others testified to the murder, Bolton went free. As for the free nigger, it turned that he really was free and could prove it to boot, so he had been turned loose a good while before, and whoever had paid for him lost his money. There was no use thinking about any of it really.

"Did I say he ain't?" Forrest was saying to Willis meanwhile.

"Ain't what?" Willis said.

"Yore propitty," Forrest said. The boy had gone stone quiet on his hip, like a rabbit caught out in an open field, hoping to hide himself in stillness.

"He ain't worth much all by hisself, little bit of a thing like that," Forrest said. "Let's see what you got that goes with him."

Tobacco-stained teeth framed the hole in Willis's heavy jowls. After a moment he snapped his jaw shut, hung the rope's end over one shoulder, and stuck the riding crop in a back pocket. He looked at his empty palms for a second, then raised his eyes to Forrest.

"All right, then," he said. "Come on."

Forrest hitched the boy up on his hip and followed. The riding crop jigged up and down in Willis's back pocket as he walked. The boy hadn't run so far, after all; Willis's establishment was half a block around the corner from where he'd first appeared.

Duffy, hanging around the gateposts, took a long step back when Forrest came in. He'd been with Bolton at the time of that killing, had backed up Bolton's lies with his own, and he'd been a little shy of Forrest since the two of them met in court. Forrest didn't bother to look at him twice.

Willis's pens weren't much different from his own, except not so clean, which was a difference you could smell. The boy stayed quiet on Forrest's hip, only his head searching and turning. They both watched Willis pull a wooden pin out of a hasp on one of the stalls. He turned and nodded to Forrest, almost expressionless as he pulled the door wide.

Inside, a black girl crouched on a shock of straw, holding her head in both her hands. As the door came open, she jumped up with a rattle.

The boy wriggled free of Forrest and ran to her, clutching her leg through her calico skirt. He let out a little sound like a cat would make. Or maybe it was her.

Both their heads turned together to regard him. Her neck was long and she carried her head high. Dust motes, stirred up by her sudden movement, swirled in the air between them, sparking gold when they caught the shafts of sunlight planing in through the cracks in the broad boards of the stall. Or maybe it was those bright spots that sometimes filled his field of vision if he straightened up too quickly, from bending down low. He did feel a little dizzy as a matter of fact, though he couldn't think of a reason why. The brown honey of her eyes and a look that went clean through him.

"What's his name?" Forrest heard himself asking.

"Thomas." The voice seemed to come out of nowhere and when it stopped on those two syllables he couldn't remember the sound of it at all. Had she even opened her mouth to speak? Now he saw her catch her lower lip in her top teeth, then release it.

He turned toward Willis. "What's *her* name?"

"Catharine." Willis was peering at a paper he must have found in his pocket or somewhere. "Two a's."

"Is that right?" Forrest said. "I'd not've took ye for such a keen speller." He wasn't much for spelling himself, if it came to that.

Willis shrugged. "I can read how it's wrote." He glanced back at the paper. "Seventeen years old, born'n'raised in Terror Bone Parish—"

Forrest raised up a finger to stop him, and stepped out of the stall into the bright chilly sunshine of the yard. He needed a minute to get his feet back under him—he knew that much, though he couldn't quite figure what had knocked them out. He felt off-balance, somehow missing the slight weight of her son on his hip. It put him in mind of how he'd sometimes tote his daughter that same way. Though Fan, at five years old, was bigger . . . A picture flashed on him of Mary Ann in her mother's buggy, stuck fast in the ford. The sweet opportunity he'd seen and tasted there. He pushed that image from him, staring at the pointed planks of Willis's gate till his mind was blank, and then he stole another glance at Catharine. The long oval of her face tilted slightly upward, like a dark flower strain-ing for the sun. Fiercely tight braids of her hair hung from beneath the point of her kerchief down between her shoulder blades. He could have her, he thought, with a lurching thrill. He had the money. Business was good.

He might offer a thousand dollars. Throw in a hundred more for the boy. Thomas, she'd said. His mind reached to recapture the sound of her voice. He turned back and spoke through the doorway, searching to find her again in the dim.

"Did you work in the house, where you come from?"

"Yassuh, I did." Her eyes didn't drop when she answered him. Trouble there, maybe. For sure. She held his gaze until, to calculate, he had to look away himself. They did have need of a housemaid at home. He pushed away the thought of Mary Ann's reaction when he presented her with one she hadn't chosen.

Duffy spat tobacco juice over the doorsill. "She worked in the bed where she come from," he said.

His guffaw cut off when Forrest turned his head half-toward him, not so far as to have to really look at Duffy but just enough to mark where he was.

"I want to hear from you I'll ast," Forrest said.

He looked at Catharine again now. Catharine. This time he did not meet her eyes, though he could feel they still lay on him. He looked at the point where the cords of her neck converged in the cupped hollow of her throat. A red button strained on a loose thread there. She was broad and firm through the hips and shoulders, plenty stout enough for field work. Any slave girl could say she had done house work if she thought that was what he wanted to hear, but maybe not this one. A girl with the boldness of her gaze might not be quite so handy with a lie.

Care had been taken with her dress: the calico new, with a pale flowered pattern, and it almost looked to have been made to measure, cut to flatter the full breasts and slender waist. If she'd made it herself, she was a good seamstress. Recalling the neat small stitches that hemmed the boy's smock, he opened his mouth to ask her if she sewed, then shut it without saying anything.

Mary Ann would quiz her on all such points. He squeezed the idea of that interview out of his head with the rest. Hell, he thought, she was young enough—she could learn whatever she didn't know.

From the grace of her stance alone he felt sure this girl would not be clumsy at anything.

He looked at her hands, long-fingered and slim. If she'd worked the fields of Terrebonne Parish, her palms would be scarred with a thousand cuts from cane leaves, but they looked smooth from where he stood. Maybe Duffy was guessing right or even actually knew something. A fancy girl wouldn't normally sell upriver. But this one was mighty black for the New Orleans bordello trade, where there were plenty of women for sale you couldn't tell from white without a keen look at the fingernails and ankles, without a special occult sense for what the Frenchmen called *jenny say quoi*.

Willis took out his riding crop, flicked the loop against the heel of his hand, stooped slightly to raise Catharine's skirt from her calf.

"Let that alone," Forrest said. "I can see all I need to."

Willis shrugged, withdrew the crop.

You ought to at least look in her mouth, Forrest told himself, knowing that he wasn't going to. He'd seen a shackle on her left leg when Willis picked up her hem with his crop, and that offended him because you didn't use more restraint than you needed—start with less and edge up to what you might turn out to really need—and that went for a slave as well as a horse. Only a fool would ruin the mouth of a good horse with yanking a bit on it too hard, too often, and what kind of fool put iron on a leg like that?

As if he were explaining it to someone, he thought, there's some things ye jest cain't explain. He didn't want that skirt to be raised to his eyes till she might be willing to lift it for him herself. But then he realized he couldn't imagine a circumstance when that would ever happen. Cain't afford to think about it, he told himself. That thought crossed his mind from time to time, in the business of buying and selling folks. I'll jest figger it out oncet I've bought her.

"Twelve hundred dollars for her and the boy," he heard himself say.

Now it was Willis's turn to spit tobacco. "Ain't for sale," he said.

"What?"

"Been sold a'ready."

"Who to?"

"Mister Hill," Willis said. "Left me his note and tolt me he'd stop back today with the money."

"Well, Hell," Forrest said. "That's Forrest and Hill, ain't it? That's the same like you already sold her to me."

"If you say so," Willis said. "Must be I lost count of the firms you're involved in."

Forrest searched his face for insulting intent and decided it wasn't worth finding it there. It was easy enough to stare Willis down, much easier than the black girl on his chain. And it wouldn't be the same, not really, he knew that. If he wanted her now he'd have to buy her back out of the partnership, and that would be noticeable, on top of the rest.

"I ain't never said Hill bought the boy," Willis remarked.

Forrest looked at him. He and Hill had an understanding not to bust up families, or at least he thought they had it, though it hadn't been written nor spoke too plain. Breaking up families worried your mind, and it was better business not to, he had learned—everything worked out better if you went on and paid the extra at the start. In this case it made no sense at all to buy the girl separate. Unless Hill meant to sell her for fancy.

"All right," Willis said. "He did buy the boy."

Forrest nodded. "That's fine," he said, and reached into his pocket to bring out a sack of gold coins. "I reckon I'll jest settle with ye now," he said. "Save Mister Hill that extry trip."

Willis looked at him uneasily, stirring the loop of the crop in the palm of his hand.

"You don't mean to say my word ain't good enough," Forrest said. "Here's the money. Let me see that note."

Hill had got the pair for a thousand, some less than Forrest had first meant to offer. Of course he'd probably pay the difference in buying the both of them back from the firm. He watched till Willis had counted out the sum, then turned to Catharine again.

"You're coming with me," he said, and explored her face for some sign of consent, but he couldn't tell anything one way or the other. *What would I do if I were her?* He'd never pictured being a woman, much less a black woman who was a slave.

"Strike off that chain," he said to Willis.

Soon the hammer rang and the shackle jumped free. Forrest's mind went reeling again, as Catharine stepped clear of the sundered iron ring and he raised his eyes once more to meet hers. He couldn't have said what he really wanted, but he knew he was going to take the gamble. He knew he would risk everything, for this.

CHAPTER FORTY

September 1863

RIVER OF BLOOD, somebody said, as they crossed the stream. It might have been Matthew who'd asked the question that *river of blood* was the answer to. That's what Chickamauga meant in Indian, somebody said. Henry, Forrest thought it might have been— Ornery as he preferred to say it—that colored feller that kept company with Matthew, that some thought looked a little like an Indian himself, and who sometimes acted like he knew what Indians used to think.

It was a stretch to call the Chickamauga a river, though it made a right good-sized creek. They'd crossed over Reed's Bridge to the west and been happy to find the bridge was there—defended by a handful of Yankee pickets, who offered some hand-to-hand fighting across the planks, though not enough of them were killed to make the stream run red. Forrest reckoned the Indians must have passed some time killing each other here, back when Indians were numerous in these parts, and strong. Blood in this water would flow more or less north, the threads of it twisting and tangling along the winds and bends of Chickamauga Creek till it dumped in the Tennessee River north of Chattanooga.

Now there was another Indian name, and maybe Henry knew its meaning also. It was a curiosity having an eddicated nigger like that in the company . . . But Forrest's mind was on other matters now. For days now they had been playing hide and go seek with the different Yankee divisions General Rosecrans had scattered, maybe even got lost from him and each other, in the wooded hills and coves between Chickamauga Creek and the high ridges east of Chattanooga. Lost and confused and ripe for a whuppen. But Braxton Bragg, that no-count mollycoddle, could not get his mind made up to go in and start the job and get it finished with. Forrest caught a wisp of beard in the corner of his mouth and began to grind his teeth on it—a sorry habit that seemed to come over him whenever he had to study on General Bragg. It must be in cases like this, he supposed, that a feller might like to chaw tobacco. Bragg had let himself be out-flanked and maneuvered and shoved out of the forage-rich farm-land of Middle Tennessee, as if it were his own shadow that had spooked him clear south to Chattanooga, and then he gave that up too when Rosecrans and his army appeared, yielding the town and its critical nexus of railroads without the ghost of a fight, arguing he would lure the Yankees out into the mountains and beat them there.

And that, Forrest thought, was a plan that could work, had even already started to work, if only Bragg could make up his mind to use the opportunity. But there didn't seem to be one spot on earth where this man was willing to make a fight. These last days he'd done nothing but whine and complain: *It is said to be easy to defend a mountainous country, but mountains hide your foe from you, while they are full of gaps through which he can pounce on you at any time. A mountain is like the wall of a house, full of rat holes. The rat lies hidden in his hole ready to pop out. Who can tell what lies hidden behind that wall?*

Goddammit! Forrest said, aloud without meaning to, loud enough Highlander tossed his spirited head at the sound, and Willie, riding a half-length behind, looked over at him, perturbed. Forrest's head was pounding with the fight bottled up inside of him. By damn I wisht Johnston hadn't got kilt, he thought. That wish had come to him many a time since Shiloh. He spread his hand over Highlander's mane, feeling the heat and the strong pulse of blood through the big horse's neck. A magnificent animal, a gift to him from the citizens of Rome, Georgia, when he'd saved them from Streight's raid, the previous spring. The flow of Highlander's energy under his hand helped him calm himself a little, but not much. His voice sub-merged into his mind. Cain't he see he's spose to be the goddamn cat? he thought.

All day they skirmished through the hills and hollers west of the creek. True enough that it was hard to figure just where your enemy was in this country, but Forrest was getting an unpleasant suspicion that the Yankee units that had been scattered and isolated a few days before were now beginning to cluster and concentrate, like flecks of butter lumping in a churn. At day's end he and his men broke contact and made a buttonhook to the south, to camp not far from Alexander's Bridge, a ways upstream of their crossing earlier in the day. As the darkness grew, the pattering of small arms fire faded away in the distance like the end of a light rain.

"Let's have a few of y'all *desert*," Forrest said with a wink, once their scant rations had been shared out and swallowed.

"I'll go." Matthew was quick on his feet.

"And me." Willie was up on the other side of the cook fire's ashes, narrowing his eyes on Matthew, then looking away.

Forrest nodded to Matthew; to Willie he said, "You stay here."

The party of so-called deserters scattered down the slope and fanned into the woods toward where the Federal camps might be. Forrest spread his duster on the ground beneath a pin oak, and stretched out on his back. He would have closed his eyes a minute, except his strapping son stood over him, fists on his hips behind his holsters.

"Why is it I don't get to go?"

"Why is it I don't want you hung for a spy?"

"Who says I would be?"

"Who says you wouldn't?" Forrest paused, turned onto his hip. Acorns dug into him through the cloth of his coat. "I might jest have a feelen."

"You always say feelings are for women and witches."

Forrest exhaled through his flared nostrils. It was true that he did often say such a thing.

"You let Matthew go," Willie complained.

"They won't worry a nigger. They'll reckon he's contraband and let him alone. They'll not want to have to take care of him neither. He can git in and out of thar easier'n a rabbit." Forrest chuckled. "A lot easier if ye think about it, 'cause won't nobody want to throw him in a skillet."

Willie's posture relaxed a little, his hands swinging loose. But he looked as if he might say something more.

"Git on with ye, now," Forrest said, raising up on an elbow. "There'll be fight aplenty for ye tomorrow. And the day after that, if I don't miss my guess."

When his son had gone off, Forrest peeled back his duster and brushed a handful of acorns from under it. Again he stretched out, looking up at the canopy of oak leaves. From the far side of the tree he could hear the whisk of Jerry's comb on Highlander's coat. His back hurt him some, from the wound he'd taken at Tunnel Hill a few days before. He made himself quit thinking about the pain until it passed. The patchwork of the shifting leaves let through some points of starlight. Now and then a dry leaf drifted down. Forrest did not know he had slept till he woke abruptly and rolled to his feet, with the knowledge that something was coming toward him.

The stand of oak trees was at the head of a little rise, and to the west a couple of acres of cleared ground rolled down to meet a denser tree line at the bottom. There, a couple of human shadows detached themselves from the shadows of trees: ostensible deserters who'd already managed to slip away from the Yankee camps to the west. From the other direction, toward Alexander's Bridge where Bragg's headquarters was, a narrow ray of yellow light came rocking along—an aide carrying a dark lantern to light the way for General John Bell Hood.

"Shut that light," Forrest said as they came up. As the aide closed the metal cover over the lantern's beam, he reached for Hood's right hand and clasped it briefly. Hood was a tall man, fair, with a wide fan of beard and deep-set sorrowful eyes, like a bloodhound. His left arm hung limp in a brown-stained sling.

"Proud to see ye," Forrest said. "Is Longstreet here yet?" Word was that General Longstreet had been dispatched by General Lee from the disaster at Gettysburg, to support Bragg at Chattanooga with the divisions of Hood and McLaws.

"On his way," Hood said, and began to relay Bragg's orders, for he had just come from a conference with the chief of the Army of Tennessee. The plan called for Forrest to lead a flanking attack on the Federal left, the first of a series of movements intended to roll the blue line south along the bank of Chickamauga Creek till it would be crushed into McLemore's Cove.

Forrest listened, but his eyes were on a single shadow approaching him now, up the cleared slope, stepping out over the rows of dried corn stubble, now overgrown with late-summer purslane. "Hold up a minute," he said to Hood, raising one finger. Matthew came up and leaned into him, whispering as his eyes lingered, over Forrest's shoulder, on the unfamiliar face of Hood.

"You done good, boy," Forrest called in a stage whisper as he moved away. Matthew paused a moment, maybe turned his head, but in the floating darkness his expression was illegible; he moved on.

"A fine order of battle," Forrest said, returning to Hood. "If only the damyankees would jest stick whar they was at last week."

"What are you thinking?" Hood said.

"Thar's subject to be a whole lot more of'm up here now on this end of the line than what that d—— what General Bragg is counten on."

"You have intelligence?" Hood said.

"Some," Forrest said. "Come mornen we're apt to git all the intelligence we can swaller." He looked up and down Hood's long body in the starlight. "How about that arm you got thar?"

Hood shrugged, then winced at the pain the movement brought. "It'll either get better or I'll get it sawed off."

Forrest released a short barking laugh. "I'll be glad when Longstreet gits in," he said. "Fer I know he ain't one to dawdle." He looked into the dark woods rising into the ridges to the west. From somewhere out there came a few liquid notes of a whippoorwill.

"Hit's a fine chance we got here, by damn," Forrest said. "What frets me is, have we already done missed it?"

THERE WAS FOG the next morning and Forrest rode through it, north again in the direction of Jay's Sawmill, which was more or less due west of Reed's Bridge, though it was hard to figure just where anything was in the pea-soup atmosphere.

"They can't see us, anyway," Anderson responded to Forrest's cursing of the weather.

"That's a red-eyed fact, and we can't see them neither," Forrest said, and twisted in the saddle to ease his healing wound. Then with a rasping laugh— "Why it's worse than having to fight in the mountains, by damn—and we still got to fight in the mountains too."

Near ten the mist lifted to unveil a mass of Federal infantry maneuvering through the woods.

"Sonsabitches won't stay put, will they?" Forrest said, reining up Highlander. "By damn they're all the way around our right, or they will be, here in a minute. We're supposed to flank them and they're gone to flank us."

Where the mist still lingered, half a mile to the south, the rattle of rifle fire began. Highlander sidestepped and raised his head toward the sound.

"Devil take'm down to the brimstone pit!" Forrest burst out. "They done hit Davidson's brigade afore he got set." He and Anderson had passed Davidson, at the far right of General Pegram's division, scarcely fifteen minutes before, when the fog was so dense the men were finding each other by touch. "Go get us some help and get it right quick," Forrest told Anderson. "Don't and they're about to do us like we meant to do them."

Anderson spurred away, and Forrest rode to find Pegram. Between them they got Davidson's men into some kind of order and held a line till Dibrell's brigade arrived to support them. By the hardest, the right flank had not yet been turned. Forrest could see just that much as the morning mist began to lift from the struggling lines of battle.

"Dibrell—that's all you brung me?" Forrest said to Anderson. "I sent for Armstrong's whole division."

"General Polk cannot send more because General Bragg—"

"Damnfool General Bragg wants to fight 'm where they was yestiddy! Don't he know they're all up here right now?" Forrest, who had turned his customary fired-brick color during the morning's action, tore off his hat and made to fling it. When Highlander bridled, Forrest smoothed his hat brim over the horse's mane. "Hit's more than one division coming in us right here—" He caught sight of John Morton and subsided slightly, put on his hat and rode over to meet him.

"Good thing at least you got here, John. Now get your puppies up to the front and give the damyankees something to think about."

Forrest fought his men dismounted, side by side with the infantry. They knew how to use cover and were marksmen enough to make their shots tell. Pushed to the front, Morton's Bull Pups spat grapeshot to discourage the Federal advance for a time. But the weight of numbers was overbearing. Mistrusting any messenger, Forrest rode for reinforcement himself, and came back shortly with Walker's brigade to throw into the line.

He'd ordered Pegram to hold his position at whatever cost, and while Forrest was off hunting Walker, Pegram had lost fully a quarter of his men. The Federal tide ebbed for a little when Walker's brigade slammed into the position. Then it began to rise again.

"Where in the hell do they keep coming from?" Forrest howled at the smoke-blocked sky. "They're going to run us right into the creek, next thing."

He sent for General Ector's brigade and put it in to fill a gap between a line of his dismounted horsemen and another of regular infantry. The fog had long lifted but was now replaced by swirls of gunpowder smoke and the dust the boots and hooves swirled up. Forrest rode to the left, peering into the murk. One of Ector's aides overtook him as he paused behind John Morton's battery.

"Sir! General Ector sends me to say he is uneasy about his right flank."

"He don't need to worry," Forrest said, without turning. "Go tell him I'll look after it."

The Lafayette road ran parallel to the creek, and Forrest rode up it away to see what chance there might be of turning the Yankee left. All he saw was more and more Federal reserves piling up behind the fighting lines. They kept coming like ants toward a spill of molasses. As he returned to Morton's battery, the same aide rode up to him again.

"General Ector is concerned for his left flank, sir—"

"Go tell General Ector I am by God here and will see to his left and his right flank both," Forrest snapped. As the aide rushed away, he brushed at his duster—white that morning, it was now covered with a silt of burnt powder, blood spray and dust. Automatically he cleaned his palm on the sweating hide of Highlander's shoulder. John Morton was shouting for more ammunition; at that moment Benjamin and Matthew rolled up with a caisson and jumped down to unload it.

Ector's brigade, though it hadn't been flanked on either side so far, was being pushed back step by step. That line could only bend so far before it broke. Then there was a rally, for Liddell's division had just arrived behind Ector, coming in at a run as the Federal line wavered. A break came in the firing from the Yankee side. "By God I think hit's *them* runnen low on powder now," Forrest called to Morton. He swept his sword up to signal a charge.

In the next moment they had overrun a Yankee battery as the gunners fled, and broken out through a last screen of trees, their bark splintered by shrapnel, into a field of corn stubble, snarled with withering pea vine. Liddell's men pursued at a run, as bluecoats scattered in the next clump of woods to the west. Forrest galloped in a curve across the cornfield, swirling his sword to urge them on.

There was a hitch in Highlander's stride. They had been fighting for three hours maybe, but it was too soon for this strong horse to tire. Yet he seemed to be fading, his power shrinking between Forrest's legs, like a blown-up hog bladder with the air rushing out. Highlander was collapsing underneath him, and Forrest swung free, landing hard on his boot heels, as the horse's big shoulder folded into the ground. One of the snapped reins hung from his hand.

Anderson pulled up behind them, eyes bleak with shock. Forrest looked down. Blood was pulsing out of his horse, soaking the bleached leaves of the crumpled corn. He couldn't tell where the blood was coming from. It might as well have been coming from everywhere. He wasn't going to be able to stop it. Highlander might be the finest horse he would ever ride. Rage at the waste of it clouded his mind.

Distantly he registered that concentrated firing had taken up again, not far to the west, where the Yankees must have been reinforced, or re-formed their lines without reinforcement. He could see himself, stark as a scarecrow, his reflection curving over the dim orb of the horse's eye. He had just drawn his pistol to put an end to it, when a movement to the west distracted him. A lone grayback popped out of the trees to the west, weaponless, head down, fleeing the slaughter.

"Whar the damn hell ye think ye're goen?" Forrest turned the pistol on the runaway, bracing his right hand over left wrist. A trace of breeze stirred the tails of his duster. He drew back the hammer with his thumb.

"General Forrest! Think what you're doing—"

Anderson's voice. Forrest wheeled toward him. Cocked pistol

solid in his hand, sighted on Anderson across Highlander's carcass. He needed to satisfy his feelings someway. "Let one start in to run-nen and the rest of 'm will too," he said. "How can you tell me not to shoot him? Son of a bitch is too sorry to live."

"I never told you not to shoot him," Anderson said levelly. "I asked you to think about it, is all."

The barrel of Forrest's pistol sank slowly. The weight of it dragged down his arm like a plumb weight. He noticed the scrap of leather still in his left hand and tossed it away. A couple of bluebottle flies had arrived to whir around the horse's dead eye. With an effort Forrest raised his pistol and settled it back into the holster.

"I know you, General," Anderson said. "I'd not tell you to do any-thing or not do it. If I had, you'd have shot him and me both."

BETWEEN MIDNIGHT and morning Forrest woke with the certainty someone, something, was watching him. A wild bristling scent on the chilly night air. He hadn't slept at all, more like, beyond an episode of very fitful dozing. If it had been all up to him he wouldn't have taken even that much a lie-down, but his men were spent from a hard afternoon fighting dismounted through the thickets west of Chickamauga Creek. And Bragg of course was of no mind to recog-nize the victory others had won for him, much less to pursue it.

About the clearing lay the huddled shapes of other men. Willie, he thought, and Major Anderson. But the watching eyes were else-where—directly behind him, he sensed—he could feel them, bor-ing into the crown of his head.

A horse whickered in the trees nearby, and took a hobbled step, and under cover of those faint sounds Forrest rolled away from his pallet and came up on one knee, his right hand aiming a pistol into the sector of darkness where the watcher must be, left fingertips grazing the hilt of the sword. At first he saw nothing, then the trunks of two cedars, with a shelf of limestone jutting up from the point between them. One of his men was lying there, the one with the queer taste for sleeping on stone, and soundly too, for Forrest could hear the rasp of his snores.

Or maybe it wasn't snoring at all. To the right of the stone shelf there was something, low and dark against the ground, pressed against it, and above and behind this faint black shape, something switched tensely from side to side. Forrest made that out before the rest: the flicking tip of the panther's tail, clear now against a patch of starlight between the thinning trees.

It wasn't snoring, then. It was what a cat that size did instead of purr.

He could see the ears now, just the tips of them, revolving forward. He thought of other cats he had seen stalk. But if he were the thing being stalked, then the panther would certainly have seen him move. Would be thinking it over now, considering its chances.

Come on, Forrest thought. Come ahead and let's see what you're made of.

The panther stood up, shoulders hunched high, the head still low. It looked jet-black, though that was only because of the darkness. Forrest had heard tell of jungle panthers in South America who really were that color.

One of the embers broke in the fire and a little flame shot up, catching the yellow gleam of the panther's eyes. Forrest held the look, for a long moment. Then the panther raised its head and looked away, shrugging almost, like any cat pretending it never really cared for its quarry. Just stretching . . .

Like that it had turned and was going away. Long tail still switching. Forrest caught his gun belt free of his blanket roll as he stood up, and slung it over his left shoulder. The second pistol, in its holster, slapped against his heart. He ran lightfooted to the tree line, stopped. The panther had opened up a long lolloping stride and was well away, high on a slope of trampled pasture, above where Forrest stood staring after it. In the brighter light of the open area, the big cat looked more gray than black, except the black spot he could now make out on the very tip of its tail.

He watched it go, feeling his own edge soften, half-regretting he hadn't shot the panther, half-glad of it. A varmint, troublesome—but there were Yankees aplenty yet to be killed and no need to spend powder and shot on a varmint.

He strapped on his belt and holstered the pistol in his right hand, then yawned and rolled his shoulders. That wound in his back itched him now, but the itch only told him it was healing. The itch that couldn't be scratched was that he'd let Cowan buffalo him into taking a drink of medicinal whiskey, soon after he'd been hit. Well, let that go.

It would be an hour yet until dawn. Forrest turned back to the campfire, concentric rings of sleeping men, lying there quiet as children. A memory of little Fan flashed upon him and he sent it away with a quick sharp hand clap.

The sleeper came up alert from the stone. Willie turned over, coughed, still dreaming.

"Boots and saddles!" Forrest called. He had not taken off his own boots to sleep. And Jerry was already bringing him a fresh horse: a big, stout-looking bay, with a blue-black mane. I won't bother given this'n a name, Forrest thought. The death of Highlander, two days before, still lay heavy on his mind.

He rode with some four hundred men at his back, in varying states of readiness, some already keenly focused on the horizon ahead them, others still rubbing sleep from their eyes, blinking into the predawn darkness. The moon had long since set, and mist on the fields confused the starlight. The Yankees would be running for the pass over Missionary Ridge at Rossville, Forrest thought, trying to calculate what gain they might have made in the dark. With the right will and enough men in the right spot, the rest of the whole Yankee army could still be scattered or destroyed. Git thar fustest with the mostest. Forrest didn't have near enough men for the job, but he'd worry on that when the time came.

They rode fanned out through groves raked all the previous day by minié balls and grapeshot from the cannons. Wood of the torn trunks stood out stark and pale among the dark boles of undamaged trees. Everywhere the scent of wounded wood mingled with the odor of slow-drying blood. Anderson leaned sideways from the saddle to pluck a splinter for a toothpick, made a light remark and laughed as someone hushed him. Overhead the canopy of leaves was fracturing into fine blue lines like cracks in a china teacup, as dawn washed out the weak light of the stars.

Just ahead through a thinning of the trees the downhill slope of another pasture glowed, steeped in dew. At the bottom where there might be a creek, where certainly there were remains of a disintegrating rock-wall fence, enemy horsemen circled, clustered, faced Forrest's party as it began to break into the open.

"I don't make'm many," Forrest said, squinting in the faint light as Anderson and Major Strange pulled up either side of him. "I don't make'm worth slowen down fer." He'd have called the Yankee cavalry at between a hundred and a hundred and fifty, though of course more might be hidden where the thickets began again, halfway up the swell of the next rise.

He glanced back and caught sight of Willie's pale, excited face as he came riding out of the grove behind them. A dark spot on his cheekbone might have been a bruise or a scrape from one of his scuffles with Matthew—and why did those boys seem to need a session of stomp and gouge even after a long day of battle? Or no, they'd given up all that foolishness lately, hadn't they?—so Willie's smudge might just as well be something else, and anyway Matthew was riding well off to the left, so that for the moment Forrest held his horse between them.

"Sir?" Anderson was saying.

"They won't stick. Not where they're at. Not even thinken about it," Forrest said. "Come on and let's give'm a dare."

The yell went up as he dug his heels into the flanks of the unnamed horse. His throat hurt but he couldn't tell what part of the whole wildcat scream was his. It seemed to float above them all, like the lifting, dissipating morning mist.

The Yankee horsemen wheeled, clustered, rode across the damp ditch line beyond the remnants of rock wall, twenty yards or so up the next rise, and then they turned. Would they have a mind to charge to meet him? No. But now they were close enough for him to see their weapons as they raised them. Long guns. Forrest's horsemen were still too far out for their Navy sixes to count for much and so the men were holding their fire.

At the first volley he heard the thump of metal penetrating flesh, and turned for an instant to see that the colored feller he'd picked up by the side of that Kentucky road had been shot dead in the saddle. Henry. Ornery, in his odd French way of pronouncing it. He'd taken the bullet on the bridge of his nose and the shock had rocked his whole upper body back, but now it slumped forward into the horse's mane, where his copper-colored fingers still convulsed on the reins.

Forrest faced front, where the Yankees surprised him with a second volley hard on the first. By damn they must have got holt of some of the brand-new Spencer repeaters—he needed to get some of them for his own folks. Six-guns among his own party were beginning to pop here and there, though the range was still a shade long for them. Forrest, like the better disciplined members of his troop, continued to hold his fire.

His horse leapt over some stones of the wall, more clumsily than it should have done, missing a stride as it came down, then partially recovering. There was in fact a little creek beyond the wall, narrow enough some of the horses jumped it too, but Forrest's mount plunged straight in—it wasn't more than fetlock deep. The bottom was paved with smooth flat stones; when he looked down he thought he even saw a crawdad. There was blood mixed in the spray the hooves splashed up, and in a flash of disbelieving outrage Forrest saw a slim column of blood spurt from the throat of his cantering horse.

He leaned forward and closed the hole with his right index finger. As he did so he seemed to feel another bullet skim down the whole length of his spine. That much was lucky. Be damned if he'd stop to change horses now.

He was near enough to see the faces of the Yankees. The frost of alarm passing over them as they began to grasp that the horse, though certainly shot dead, was not going to stop carrying Forrest with his arms and his rage into their midst. In fact the unnamed horse was moving smoothly now. Through the wound that united them, Forrest could feel the heartbeat of the animal flowing into his own.

Had he lost one of his pistols, when he stooped to stop the blood-gush? No he must have dropped it into a coat pocket, where he could feel it now bouncing against his hip . . . another sore spot there, where Gould had shot him back in June. His right hand was busy but he could still reach the other pistol with his left. He drew the double-edged sword instead and whipped it once around his wrist. The flexible Damascus blade sang as it sliced through the rushing air.

The Yankees could have, should have, got off a few more shots at him, but by now they must have cottoned onto the idea that no number of bullets would be enough to stop this charge. The Yankees turned and whipped their horses away toward Missionary Ridge.

Keep up the skeer—Forrest didn't know if it was him yelling it or Anderson or Strange or any of the many others to whom he'd taught the phrase and concept; maybe he was just hearing it inside his own head. He spurred up the slope. The Yankees were scattering into the thickets. He locked onto one of them, the nearest, who sensed the pursuit, looked back once to see it coming, his mouth a little red ring of fear. The Yankee rider whipped his horse faster, twisting and turning through the briars of the thicket like a rabbit on the run.

Locust thorns clawed at Forrest's coat sleeves. He saw the Yankee break his crop on his horse's backside, then fling the useless handle away. The blue coat billowed, catching air like a sail. Forrest squeezed an ounce more speed from his horse, raised his sword and howled as he struck. The enemy squealed as the coat parted and the sword's tip drew a red groove in the flesh to the right of his spine, all the way down from neck bone to coccyx. A shallow wound, hardly worth holleren over so. Forrest thought of the claw marks on his mother's back, and different niggers he'd had to whup—it was damn awkward to swing a sword out of this crouch and yet he dursn't straighten up for then his finger would come out of the horse's neck and then the horse would bleed out and die.

Swop his damn head off Goddammit right now, Forrest told himself, spurring up to close again. The tail of the Yankee's horse lashed across his face and he spat out a thread of coarse hair as he cut again with the sword, the blade chopping into the other man's shoulder this time, instead of the throat as he'd intended—hard enough to knock the Yankee out of the saddle, though Forrest didn't much think he had killed him.

He rode past, thinking irritably that he'd still have to claim an enemy life for this dead horse he was still flogging forward. They broke out onto the open road, and here the Yankees had picked up speed, the dust of their departure just settling around the next bend. One of the new Spencers lay by the roadside, trigger guard snagged by a twig of a sapling, and Forrest wanted to stop to retrieve it, but there was the same problem about the hole in his horse's throat and anyway somebody coming behind would get it—the Yankees were throwing down so much as they ran it would take all day to get everything picked up.

He could hear some of his own men clattering around the bend and took a quick glance over his shoulder, remembering the last time he'd done so that he'd seen Henry dead in the saddle. That might have been one of my sons kilt, he thought, but no, there was Willie coming on now, with no holes in him to be seen, and Matthew riding one place away now, with one of the younger troopers, Witherspoon maybe, between them. He remembered how Henry used to put himself between Willie and Matthew sometimes. That was a good man he had lost this morning. He had lost, would lose a passel of good men, afore all was said and done.

Matthew, now he thought Matthew might make a good man too if he lived to get good grown—and Forrest had to mash down that idea right quick because they wouldn't let Matthew be what a son of his ought to be, with his qualities. No matter how the war turned out, they wouldn't let him. But who was *they*?

Cain't afford to think about it. He was striking the crest of the ridge right now, pulling his horse up under a patch of tall pines, atop which some Federal forward observers were turning their field glasses this way and that. Some looked out over the road to the west where Forrest's men were coming, while others peered down the eastern slope along the path their own comrades were pounding toward Chattanooga, abandoning the observers there like so many treed raccoons.

Here in a minute, he'd climb up there himself and have a look-see.

Meanwhile, he still needed to kill a Yankee to pay for his lost horse. He sheathed his sword and drew a pistol with his free left hand. But hell it was damn near next to impossible to draw a bead up a damn tree when he had to crouch down across his horse's neck all the time.

By damn, Forrest said to himself, I might jest spend this entire war tryen to hold the whole world together with one finger.

Matthew and Willie and more and more of the others were reining up now, forming a loose circle around where Forrest had halted. A riderless horse broke through the ring, blood on the saddle, mane clotted with blood. Forrest recalled how Henri liked to ride stretched out along his horse's neck, like he thought he was a wild Indian or I don't know what. Like he thought that style would spare him a bullet.

He stuck his pistol in the holster and squinted up at the treetops again.

"Might as well come on down," he called. "Y'all prisoners now. Ye won't be harmed."

He sat up straight and dismounted quickly. The blood spurt from his horse's throat was not half the strength it had been at the start. Forrest's right hand was black with drying blood. His left just speckled from his swordplay a couple of minutes before. He used the left hand to stroke the unnamed horse's forehead. As the horse's legs melted out from under it, Forrest cradled the whole head in his right arm, still stroking rhythmically with his other hand.

His mother had taught him to hate waste—sometimes with reason, sometimes with a strap. Softly as he could he laid the dead horse's head down on the stony surface of the roadway.

"That there's a horse done give everything he's got."

His mounted men faced him, haggard, exhilarated.

"And ye know that's all I ask of the lot of ye—"

One hand pressed to the small of his back, he straightened up and looked across at his people.

"—all ye got. And ye give it too. But boys," he said, and lowered his head to look again at the dead horse, wasted. "Hit's sometimes I wonder, what in the Hell are we doen this for?"

A Chronology of the Life of
Nathan Bedford Forrest

JULY 13, 1821

Bedford Forrest and his twin sister, Fanny, are born in Bedford County, Tennessee, on Caney Spring Creek, fifty miles southeast of Nashville—the eldest children of William and Mariam Beck Forrest.

1833

After losing land in Tennessee, the Forrests move to Tippah County (now Benton), Mississippi, where they lease a farm.

1837

William Forrest dies; Mariam Beck Forrest becomes head of the Forrest household.

1841

Bedford Forrest joins a Mississippi military unit to go to fight for Sam Houston's cause in Texas. He sees no military action there, and spends a period splitting rails to earn money to get home.

1842

With his mother soon to remarry, Forrest leaves home. He has been doing well in trading livestock and his Uncle Jonathan offers him a partnership in Hernando.

1845

March 10: Forrest's Uncle Jonathan is attacked and killed on the street in Hernando by members of the Matlock family. Defending his uncle, Bedford Forrest dispatches two or more Matlocks, using a knife tossed to him by a bystander after his own pistol is emptied. Subsequent to this affair, Forrest is appointed constable in Hernando.

September 25: Forrest marries Mary Ann Montgomery, whom he has met about a month before, thanks to having assisted her and her mother when their carriage was stuck in a ford.

1846
William Forrest is born to Bedford and Mary Ann Forrest.

1847
Frances A. Forrest is born to Bedford and Mary Ann Forrest.

1848
John Forrest, next in age after Bedford, returns as a cripple from the Mexican War.

1852
Bedford and Mary Ann Forrest move to Memphis, Tennessee, where Forrest expands his business as a slave-trader.

1853
From Hill & Forrest, a firm in which he is a partner, Forrest purchases "a Negro woman named Catharine aged seventeen and her Child named Thomas aged four months."

Forrest buys adjacent lots on Adams Street in Memphis: 85 Adams for his personal residence and 87 Adams for his slave pen.

1854
June 26: Forrest's daughter, Frances, dies of dysentery.

1856
Forrest buys some 700 acres in Shelby County.

1857
James McMillan is shot in a dispute with another slave-trader, Isaac Bolton, and dies of his wounds in Forrest's home.

June 26: In the wake of a gambling-related murder, Forrest is elected to a vigilance committee to run gamblers out of Memphis (despite a serious gambling habit of his own).

1858
Forrest is elected alderman in Memphis. He buys 1,900 acres of cotton land in Coahoma County, Mississippi, and 1,346 acres across the river in Phillips County, Arkansas. He adds eighty-five feet of frontage to his Adams Street property between 2nd and 3rd Streets and moves from 85 Adams to another house on the south side of Adams between 3rd and 4th Streets.

1861
January 14: South Carolina, Florida, Alabama, Georgia and Mississippi vote to secede from the United States, followed by Texas and Louisiana.

April 3: Confederates win victory over Union forces at Manassas, Virginia, in the first battle of Bull Run.

May: Forrest buys a forty-two-acre farm seven miles north of Memphis for his mother and stepfather, James H. Luxton.

June 8: Tennessee secedes from the United States.

June 14: Forrest, his youngest brother, Jeffrey, and his son, William, enlist as privates in the Confederate Army at Randolph, Tennessee.

At some point during these early days of the war, Forrest offers freedom at the war's end to those of his slaves who are willing to serve as teamsters in his command. Forty-five men accept this offer.

July 23: Swiftly promoted to lieutenant colonel, Forrest runs a newspaper ad for "Mounted Rangers." He travels to Kentucky to recruit and buy arms for his company.

October: Forrest and his Rangers are ordered to Fort Donelson, in Tennessee.

December 28: In his first Civil War engagement, at Sacramento, Kentucky, Forrest kills two men with a saber.

1862
February 13: Union commander Ulysses S. Grant attacks Fort Donelson. Bedford Forrest fights a five-hour engagement with Union troops on the Fort Henry road.

February 14: As fighting continues around Fort Donelson, the Confederates finally drive the Union troops from the field. Forrest gets fifteen bullet holes in his coat and has two horses shot from under him—one with seven bullet wounds and the second blown up by an artillery shell.

February 15: Refusing to surrender with the other Confederate commanders, Forrest evacuates the men of his command in the direction of Nashville, Tennessee.

February 23: Having broken up mobs of looters with a fire hose and provisioned his men from Nashville stores, Forrest leaves Nashville for Murfreesboro, just in advance of the surrender of Nashville to the oncoming Union Army commanded by General Don Carlos Buell.

March 10: Reinforced by a new company raised by his younger brother Jesse, Forrest is elected colonel of a force now at battalion strength. Ordered to Corinth, Mississippi, Forrest scouts and determines that Grant, moving south from Fort Donelson, is intending a junction with General Buell, moving west from Nashville.

April 6: Supported by Forrest, Confederate General Albert Sidney Johnston attacks Grant at Shiloh, Tennessee, before Grant can be reinforced by Buell. The Confederates win the day—Willie Forrest is briefly lost in the action, then found herding prisoners. That night Forrest, scouting with a party disguised in captured Union coats, finds Buell crossing the Tennessee at Pittsburgh Landing to reinforce Grant. Though he realizes that Confederates must attack before daylight or be overwhelmed, he can't find a general to authorize the attack. Johnston has been killed and replaced by General P. G. T. Beauregard.

April 7: The Confederates are forced to retreat from Shiloh toward Corinth.

April 8: Forrest breaks pursuit by the cavalry command of William Tecumseh Sherman with a charge at the Fallen Timbers. Overshooting his 350 troopers he fights his way out—though shot in the back—using "a rather small Federal trooper" as a shield. Forrest rides to Corinth, where his horse dies of its wounds. Furloughed for sixty days to Memphis to recover from his own gunshot wound, he returns to duty after three weeks, advertising for 200 men who want to "have a heap of fun and kill some Yankees."

June 11: Forrest is detached from his regiment by Beauregard and sent to Chattanooga, Tennessee (with his personal escort of some two dozen men), with the idea he will organize disparate cavalry units in the area to interrupt Buell's movement toward Chattanooga.

July 13: On his birthday, Forrest, with a consolidated force of 1,500 men attacks Union troops at Murfreesboro, Tennessee, at 4:30 a.m., defeats them and frustrates their attempt to burn down a jail full of Confederate prisoners. Through ruses Forrest induces the surrender of other bodies of Union troops posted outside the town. He destroys the railroad at Murfreesboro and retreats to McMinnville with some 1,200 prisoners. Eight days following he is promoted to brigadier general.

July 18: With 700 troopers, Forrest raids within sight of Nashville. Two weeks later he strikes the railroad at Manchester, Tennessee. In this period Union General William Nelson complains that Forrest's men are mounted on racehorses, thus fruitless to pursue with infantry.

August 22: General Braxton Bragg, urged by Forrest to attack Nashville, instead orders Forrest to the Sequatchie Valley.

September 3: Forrest joins Bragg on a maneuver into Kentucky, distracting Buell with diversions at Sparta, Lebanon and Murfreesboro.

September 17: Supporting Leonidas Polk, Forrest helps force a surrender of 4,000 Federals at Munfordville, Kentucky.

September 23: Forrest (injured by a horse that rolled on him) is ordered to turn over his regiment to Joseph Wheeler and return to Middle Tennessee to raise new troops and raid.

Forrest establishes a base in Murfreesboro but then (as Bragg retreats from Kentucky, Robert E. Lee from Maryland, and Earl Van Dorn and Sterling Price are defeated at Corinth) retreats to Tullahoma.

November: Bragg places Forrest under Wheeler's command.

December 3: Forrest writes to Wheeler complaining about John Morton, young son of a Nashville physician, being foisted on him as an artillery commander. Extremely keen to serve under Forrest, Morton makes a 104-mile round-trip from Columbia to Lavergne and back to get updated orders from Wheeler.

December 10: Bragg orders Forrest to West Tennessee.

December 13: Forrest crosses the Tennessee River at Clifton.

December 18: Forrest routs Union troops from Lexington, Tennessee, capturing two cannon for John Morton's use. Through ruses such as beating kettledrums, lighting extra campfires and marching his men in circles, Forrest persuades Union commanders in West Tennessee to inflate their estimate of his strength from an actual 2,000 to 5,000. During the next few days he destroys the railroad north of Jackson and captures a Union garrison at Trenton. From Trenton stores he obtains a sword of Damascus steel and, contrary to military regulations of the time, sharpens both sides of it.

December 21: Through bluffing, Forrest induces surrender of the U.S. garrison at Union City.

December 31: Caught between two Union forces at Parker's Crossroads, Forrest is said to have ordered his troopers to "charge both ways."

1863

January 1: Returning from his West Tennessee expedition, Forrest crosses the Tennessee River. Bragg, meanwhile, has retreated from Stones River to Tullahoma.

February 3: Forrest, Wharton and Wheeler make a concerted attack on Dover, Tennessee. Forrest has a horse shot from under him in a charge. Later a second horse is shot from under him in the failed attack. Forrest (who opposed the Dover attack and lost a lot of men in it) quarrels with Wheeler the night after the battle and refuses to serve under him any longer.

February 25: Forrest is transferred to the command of General Van Dorn.

March 5: At Thompson Station, Tennessee, Forrest assists in the defeat of Union troops under John Coburn and the capture of 1,200 men. His favorite horse Roderick is killed in this battle, as well as Montgomery Little, an early organizer of Forrest's escort.

March 25: Continuing to raid around Middle Tennessee during the month of March, Forrest captures two Union garrisons and arms at Brentwood, about ten miles south of Nashville. General G. C. Smith engages Forrest's force but cannot defeat or destroy it.

April 10: Forrest attacked by General David Stanley near Franklin, about fifteen miles south of Nashville. His artillery commander, Captain S. L. Freeman, is killed. Forrest is reported to have wept at Freeman's funeral the next day.

Late April: Forrest quarrels with General Van Dorn, who challenges him with a sword (over Forrest's having appropriated weapons seized in Brentwood for the use of his own troops). Forrest is ordered to Alabama and Van Dorn is killed by a jealous husband in Tennessee.

April 23: Forrest is ordered to reinforce Colonel P. D. Roddey in Tuscumbia, Alabama.

April 26: As Forrest is skirmishing at Town Creek, Union raiders coming from Nashville, commanded by Colonel Abel Streight, move south of him with 1,500 men—on a mission to cut the railroad from Chattanooga to Georgia.

April 30: Forrest attacks Streight's rear guard and Streight lays an ambush on Sand Mountain. Forrest's brother Bill Forrest, whose scouts led the attack, has a thigh shattered by a bullet and Bedford Forrest loses two cannon commanded by Lieutenant A. W. Gould. After five hours of fighting Streight moves on, then prepares another defense at Hog Mountain, using the captured cannon. When Bedford Forrest attacks this position by moonlight, he has three horses shot out from under him—but recovers his two cannon, although spiked. Streight moves on to lay a third ambush at 2 a.m. Forrest allows his men two hours rest.

May 1: Streight reaches Blountsville at 10 a.m., departs at noon and is soon attacked in the rear by Forrest. After another battle on the shores of the Black Warrior River, Streight completes the crossing of the Black Warrior at 5 p.m. and heads for Gadsden. To rest his outnumbered men, Forrest is pursuing in shifts, and with a force of 600 he overtakes and attacks Streight at a bridge over Black Creek. Streight's men burn the bridge after the crossing, but a local girl, Emma Samson, shows Forrest a nearby ford where his men quickly cross. Streight forces an all-night march, destroys stores at Gadsden and makes for Rome, Georgia, hoping to delay Forrest by burning the bridge over the Oostanaula River there.

On the same day, the Confederate Congress legislates the return of black slaves captured under arms to their owners and the summary execution of white officers and noncoms in these new black Union units.

May 2: Forrest harries Streight's rear, with Streight losing stragglers until he is forced to stand and fight at 4 p.m. With much of his ammunition wet from his rapid river crossings, Streight moves on, sending an advance of 200 men to secure the bridge at Rome. Streight eludes an ambush at Centre, Alabama, moves along the Chattooga River to Gaylesville, where Confederates have destroyed the ferry. Streight then gets his command lost in a logging area, happens on a Confederate ironworks and destroys it, and finally crosses the Chattooga just before dawn.

May 3: Streight halts at Lawrence Plantation, twenty miles short of Rome. Forrest sends in a demand for surrender, reinforced by circling the same pair of cannon over and over within Streight's view. Thanks to this ruse and to circular marching of the troops, Streight surrenders nearly 1,500 men to Forrest's 600 (although, once he understands the trick, Streight asks for his arms back to continue the fight). This pursuit destroys 300 of Forrest's 550 horses but he replaces them with Streight's—while making an effort to return mounts Streight had commandeered to owners in Alabama. A grateful citizen of Rome gives Forrest an excellent horse named Highlander.

May 13: Following a meeting with General Bragg, Forrest is promoted to major general and begins reorganizing his command in Middle Tennessee.

June 13: At the Masonic Hall in Columbia, Tennessee, Forrest is shot by Lieutenant Gould, who lost the two cannon during the pursuit of Colonel Streight, and is disputing his transfer orders. Forrest retaliates by cutting Gould with a clasp knife and then pursues him with a pistol, declaring, "No man can kill me and live."

June 25: Union General William S. Rosecrans advances from Murfreesboro toward Shelbyville, and Bragg falls back toward Chattanooga. After two days of skirmishing in south-central Tennessee, Forrest is retreating through Cowan (his wife's hometown) when an old woman berates him for cowardice, shouting, "Old Forrest'd make ye fight!"

August 9: Forrest requests transfer to his home ground in West Tennessee and North Mississippi, probably hoping to escape the command of Braxton Bragg. Bragg has been flanked out of Middle Tennessee without a battle, and driven back to the Chattanooga area, where Forrest commands the cavalry attached to Bragg's command. Forrest refuses to obey Bragg's order to dismount cavalrymen led by John Hunt Morgan who have returned from an unsuccessful raid through Ohio and Indiana.

September 7: As Union troops close in around him, Bragg evacuates Chattanooga for Lafayette, Georgia, again without a fight.

September 13: Forrest is wounded in the back while opposing the advance of Union troops under Thomas Crittenden on the Georgia-Tennessee border. Though a lifelong teetotaler, Forrest reluctantly obeys the order of his surgeon (his wife's relative, Doctor J. B. Cowan) to take a medicinal drink of whiskey.

September 18: The battle of Chickamauga begins with Forrest skirmishing with Union troops along Chickamauga Creek, west of Chattanooga. His splendid horse Highlander, gift of the citizens of Rome, is shot dead from under him.

September 19: Forrest and his men are heavily engaged in a long day of inconclusive fighting.

September 20: Reinforced by General James Longstreet and his force, the Confederates finally rout the Union soldiers and send them fleeing back toward Chattanooga (except for a section of the line held stubbornly by Union commander George H. Thomas). Despite urging from Forrest and others, Bragg fails to capitalize on the victory and allows the Union Army to retreat and regroup in Chattanooga, more or less unmolested.

September 21: In pursuit of retreating Union forces, Forrest has his horse shot through the neck and closes the wound with his forefinger so that he can continue to ride. He reaches the crest of Missionary Ridge, where he is able to see the confusion of the Union troops in and around Chattanooga. Though Forrest urges a rapid advance, the Confederate leadership does not respond.

September 28: While enjoying a rare ten-day leave and visit with his wife at LaGrange, Georgia, Forrest is ordered by Bragg to turn over his troopers to Wheeler for a raid. Forrest responds with a furious letter denouncing Bragg for dishonesty and cowardice. Soon after, in the company of his surgeon, Doctor Cowan, he rides to Bragg's Missionary Ridge headquarters to denounce him in similar terms to his face. Though duels were fought for less during the Civil War, and Forrest certainly intended his visit as a challenge, Bragg lives up to Forrest's prediction that he will "take no action in the matter."

In the aftermath of Chickamauga, Forrest, losing confidence in the Confederacy's chances of success and suspecting that he himself may soon be killed, frees a number of the forty-five slaves who have enlisted with him as teamsters.

October 13: General Bragg approves Forrest's request for transfer to the Mississippi River region. Forrest goes to Okolona, Mississippi, with his sixty-five-man escort, four cannon, Morton's sixty-seven artillerymen and part of Jeffrey Forrest's regiment, bringing him to a strength of 350. Jeffrey, though reported killed in North Alabama, reappears as an exchanged prisoner.

November 25: As Bragg is driven from Chattanooga by Grant, Forrest goes raiding and recruiting in West Tennessee; ten days later he reports to General Johnston that he has 5,000 recruits and more coming in.

December 13: Forrest writes a letter of complaint to General Stephen Hurlbut, commander of Union-occupied Memphis, about the Union military's mistreatment of Confederate sympathizers in West Tennessee.

December 24: Forrest has to withdraw from Jackson, Tennessee, with his 3,500 raw recruits, only 1,000 of them armed, but receives official word of his promotion to major general. He eludes pursuit and protects his considerable beef on the hoof and bacon supply by sending out many decoy detachments.

1864

January 2: Confederate General Patrick Cleburne proposes that the Confederacy offer to free any slaves willing to serve in its army. This idea is swiftly suppressed by President Jefferson Davis and the Confederate government in Richmond.

January 12: Northern press reports: "Forrest, with less than four thousand men, has moved right through the Sixteenth Army Corps, has passed within nine miles of Memphis, carried off a hundred wagons, two hundred beef cattle, three thousand conscripts, and innumerable stores; torn up railroad tracks, destroyed telegraph wires, burned and sacked towns, ran over pickets with a single derringer pistol, and all in the face of ten thousand men." Union Generals Grant and Sherman begin to take serious alarm at Forrest's ability to carry out such operations behind their lines.

January 13: "Forrest's Cavalry Department" established for North Mississippi and West Tennessee.

January 27: General Sherman writes orders for General William Sooy Smith to organize a two-pronged raid into the Deep South. Sherman intends to raid from Vicksburg to Meridian, Mississippi, while Sooy Smith moves out of Memphis through Okolona to join him at Meridian for a combined maneuver against Selma, Alabama, destroying Confederate communications and foraging and looting as much as possible along the way. This operation is a trial run for Sherman's eventual march through Georgia; Sooy Smith's maneuver is in part intended to divert Forrest from Sherman's movement.

February 12: Forrest threatens to execute nineteen deserters at Oxford, Mississippi (all recent West Tennessee recruits). Forrest reports that Sooy Smith with 1,000 men has passed Holly Springs—he sends Jeffrey Forrest to engage Smith at West Point.

February 19: Smith begins wrecking railroad tracks near Okolona. Some 3,000 freed slaves in his train are burning fields, barns and houses so indiscriminately as to shock Smith himself.

February 20: Jeffrey Forrest, after a forty-five-mile march, interrupts Smith's progress to Meridian at West Point. Smith eludes a trap set by the Forrest brothers and plans his retreat.

February 21: At Sakatonchee Creek, southwest of Okolona, Smith begins a diversionary battle with Jeffrey Forrest's command. Bedford Forrest thrashes a Confederate trooper fleeing from the Sakatonchee bridge and sends him back into the battle with the admonition, "You might as well get killed there as here." Retreating from the bridge, Smith's men make occasional stands till finally they halt at 2 a.m., three miles south of Okolona.

February 22: At daylight, Bedford Forrest and his escort charge Smith's rear guard, chasing the Union troops northwest from Okolona. At Ivey's Hill, Sooy Smith makes another stand and Forrest's brother Jeffrey is killed by a ball in the throat during the action there. Bedford Forrest charges into the thick of the Union force (outrunning his hugely outnumbered escort) to kill three men in hand-to-hand combat, decapitating one Federal cavalryman. Forrest has two horses shot from under him in the course of this day; a third mount, King Philip, survives despite taking a bullet. At the end of the day, Forrest abandons pursuit of Smith, thanks to exhaustion and ammunition shortage.

February 26: Sooy Smith's battered force reaches Memphis, having lost 388 men by the general's report. Because of Smith's failure to join him at Meridian, Sherman returns to Vicksburg, abandoning the advance toward Selma. Forrest quarters his troops in Columbus and Starkville, Mississippi, and prepares for another excursion into West Tennessee.

March 20: Forrest returns to Jackson in West Tennessee—a region now shredded by partisan warfare, full of deserters and preyed upon by scalawags and bushwhackers.

March 24: Colonel W. L. Duckworth bluffs a Union garrison at Union City, Tennessee, to surrender by sending in a note purportedly written by Forrest himself.

March 25: Forrest attacks and briefly occupies Paducah, Kentucky, but cannot reduce a fort there occupied by Union troops, who refuse to be bluffed into surrender by Forrest's warnings and threats. The fighting at Paducah is Forrest's first engagement with a force of freed slaves in Union service: 274 men of the First Kentucky Heavy Artillery.

April 3: Forrest reaches Trenton, Tennessee. James R. Chalmers, commanding some of Forrest's troopers, defeats a force commanded by local Union sympathizer Colonel Fielding Hurst, near Bolivar.

April 4: Forrest writes to request that Morton's artillery be sent to him from Mississippi to aid in attacking boats and the river forts. He begins to consider requests from West Tennessee Confederate loyalists that he reduce the Union garrison at Fort Pillow, at the junction of Coal Creek with the Mississippi River. Commanded for the Union by West Tennessean Major William Bradford, Fort Pillow had become a tinderbox of local partisan antagonism. Bradford's men stood accused of wholesale looting, insult and rape; atrocity crimes, including mutilation, had also occurred. Many of Forrest's own men were West Tennessee natives as well (some very recently recruited) and so took such matters personally. Local Confederates regarded Fort Pillow as a nest of outlaws which harbored a number of runaway slaves. Shortly before Forrest's arrival in the area, the fort had been reinforced by 292 black Union troops sent north from Memphis, under command of Major Lionel Booth.

April 11: Forrest orders Chalmers to advance on Fort Pillow; Chalmers rides thirty-eight miles from Brownsville in the rain to reach the fort for a daybreak attack the next day. Also on April 11, Buford, en route to Paducah, sends a diversion to Columbus with a surrender demand saying "negroes now in arms" will be returned to their masters if they surrender but killed if they resist. White troops will be treated as prisoners in either case. Forrest returns to Jackson to find his brother Aaron dead of pneumonia.

April 12: Forrest reaches Fort Pillow in the mid-morning, following the first wave of the attack, having ridden seventy-two miles in twenty-seven hours. Booth has been killed inside the fort by one of Forrest's sharpshooters, though the Confederate besiegers don't know this. During his first reconnaissance Forrest is rolled on by a horse shot from under him. "They are not many, we must take them," he concludes. Forrest's demand for surrender offers to treat all the men (black Union soldiers implicitly included) as prisoners of war, adding, "Should my demand be refused I cannot be responsible for the fate of your command." With the demand for surrender refused, Forrest's men storm the fort, reportedly slaughtering a great many of the defenders even after they have attempted to surrender. Forrest eventually intervenes in person to stop the killing. By later reports the Mississippi River ran red with blood for 200 yards below the fort.

April 15: Forrest writes to Jefferson Davis requesting that he be sent to Middle Tennessee (the Nashville area and supply lines north and south of that city) to disrupt Sherman's preparation for his campaign against Atlanta and the state of Georgia. Forrest's plan is discredited by his old adversary Braxton Bragg. Forrest is ordered to return to Mississippi, where he begins to refit his troops after the West Tennessee campaign.

April 18: An article entitled "The Butcher Forrest and His Family: All of Them Slave Drivers and Women Whippers" appears in the Northern press. Describing events at Fort Pillow as "the cowardly butchery . . . of blacks and whites alike," the article goes on to claim that Forrest "had two wives—one white, the other colored (Catharine) by each of which he had two children. His 'patriarchal wife,' Catharine, and his white wife had frequent quarrels or domestic jars." A "Remember Fort Pillow" movement begins among black Union troops quartered in Memphis.

April 29: Apprehensive that Forrest may in fact destroy his planning in Middle Tennessee, Sherman replaces the Union commanders at Memphis and writes to them urging that "It is of the utmost importance to keep his forces occupied, and prevent him from forming plans and combinations to cross the Tennessee River and break up the railroad communications in our rear."

April 30: Samuel Sturgis, the new Memphis cavalry commander, sets out in pursuit of Forrest, who withdraws from Jackson to Tupelo, Mississippi.

May 15: Sherman outflanks the Confederate General Joseph E. Johnston by crossing the Oostanaula River. Using delaying tactics and fighting battles with Sherman at three different locations, Johnston is pushed back toward Atlanta. Concerned that Forrest may still break up his lengthening supply lines in Tennessee, Sherman orders Sturgis to lead another expedition against Forrest.

May 17: Though actually on his way from Mississippi to Middle Tennessee, Forrest is ordered back in the direction of Tupelo to deal with the threat from Sturgis. Forrest's idea of aborting Sherman's march through Georgia is thus itself aborted.

June 10: At the battle of Brice's Crossroads, Forrest resoundingly defeats Sturgis's superior force—Forrest's 4,800 men against the Union 8,000.

Stubborn rearguard resistance by black Union troops commanded by Colonel Edward Bouton helped part of Sturgis's command make a safe retreat, although black soldiers, when routed themselves, tear off and throw away the "Remember Fort Pillow" badges they are wearing. In pursuit of the routed Union force, Forrest and his horse both fall asleep, to be awakened only when the horse blunders into a tree.

June 13: Forrest writes a complaint to Union General Cadwallader Washburn at Memphis about useless bloodshed at Brice's Crossroads, brought about because "Both sides acted as though neither felt safe in surrendering, even when further resistance was useless." In this letter he denies he ever had a policy of slaughtering surrendering men.

June 15: In the aftermath of Brice's Crossroads, Sherman writes to U.S. Secretary of War Edwin Stanton terming Forrest the "very devil" and claiming that there "never will be peace in East Tennessee until Forrest is dead." To President Abraham Lincoln he writes that he is sending out generals from Memphis "to pursue and kill Forrest."

June 28: Forrest writes to his immediate superior, Stephen D. Lee, complaining of an attack of boils and asking that he be relieved of command.

July 8: Union General A. J. Smith, leading 14,000 men out of Memphis in pursuit of Forrest, moves through Ripley, Mississippi, leaving a ten-mile-wide swath of destruction.

July 13: Reconnoitering Smith's positions on the Pontotoc–Tupelo Road with Lieutenant Sam Donelson, Forrest narrowly escapes capture.

July 14: Participating, under Lee's command, in a full frontal assault on A. J. Smith at Harrisburg, Forrest is painfully wounded in the foot, but remounts and rides to the front again to reassure his men he has not been killed. At the end of this costly and futile engagement, Forrest is reported to have snapped at Stephen Lee, "If I knew as much about West Point tactics as you, the Yankees would whip hell out of me every day."

August 7: Based on inaccurate reports of the outcome at Harrisburg, Sherman anxiously inquires of General Washburn, "Is Forrest surely dead?"

August 8: A. J. Smith, advancing from Memphis again with another large force, crosses the Tallahatchie River to threaten Oxford, Mississippi.

August 10: Forrest arrives in Oxford.

August 11: Washburn to Sherman—"General Forrest is not dead, but was in Pontotoc four days ago."

August 19: Forrest eludes Smith in Mississippi and races north to raid Memphis.

August 21: Forrest's men storm into Memphis at 4 a.m., occupying the city for just a few hours. Although they fail to capture any of the three Union generals who were targets of the raid, they take 600 prisoners and force General Smith to abandon his second Mississippi invasion and return to his Memphis base.

September 2: Atlanta falls to Sherman; Forrest's planned movement against Sherman's supply lines has been delayed too long. Nevertheless Forrest is ordered back into Tennessee with the object of wrecking the railroads supplying Sherman. Despite reducing a number of small Union forts at railway stations in Middle Tennessee, Forrest is unable to reach the principal Nashville–Chattanooga line.

October 5: Forrest is forced to retreat across the Tennessee River. Again he begins to regroup, but due to recent losses and the attrition of four years of war he now must depend more than ever on recent and comparatively unreliable conscripts, and to deal with persistent shortages of men, horses and munitions. He writes to General Richard Taylor: "I have been constantly in the field since 1861, and have spent half the entire time in the saddle. I have never asked for a furlough for over ten days to rest— and except when wounded and unable to leave my bed have had no respite from duty." Nevertheless he agrees to start another expedition into West Tennessee.

Mid-October: Forrest reestablishes his headquarters in Jackson, Tennessee.

October 26: General Taylor orders Forrest to report to General John Hood in Middle Tennessee as soon as his current mission has been completed. Retreating northward from the loss of Atlanta, Hood now intends to recapture Nashville and make a junction with the army commanded by General Robert E. Lee in Virginia.

October 29: Forrest's men destroy the Federal steamboat *Mazeppa* at Fort Heiman on the Tennessee River.

October 30: Forrest's men capture another federal transport ship on the Tennessee, along with a gunboat, the *Undine,* and use these boats for an assault on the Union depot at Johnsonville.

November 2: After losing an engagement with two Union gunboats, Forrest's men burn the *Undine* and desist from further naval activity.

November 4: Attacking Johnsonville by land, Forrest destroys a vast amount of supplies ultimately destined for Sherman in Georgia.

November 8: Lincoln wins reelection as U.S. president, putting an end to faint Southern hopes that a Democrat president might be inclined to reconcile with the Confederacy.

Mid-November: Forrest joins Hood at Florence, and makes an energetic speech predicting a Confederate success in Nashville.

November 19–24: Moving his cavalry in advance of Hood's main body, Forrest fights daily engagements with 2,800 Union troops commanded by John Schofield, attempting to retreat northward toward their Nashville base.

November 28: Forrest gets one of his divisions across the Duck River near Columbia, maneuvering to the north of Schofield's line of retreat.

November 29: Thanks to miscommunication and some overconfident negligence on the part of General Hood, the Confederates fail to block the Columbia–Franklin Pike, and during the night Schofield slips his men away through Spring Hill toward Franklin.

November 30: Schofield entrenches a line of defense on the south side of Franklin (about twenty miles south of Nashville). Forrest offers to flank Schofield out of this hastily dug position, but Hood refuses, preferring a full-frontal assault across an open field, and orders Forrest to the far right of the line (essentially out of the action). Hood loses over 6,000 men in the ensuing catastrophe, along with twelve of his generals, including Patrick Cleburne.

December 1: Schofield continues his retreat to Nashville and Hood pursues, dispatching Forrest to Murfreesboro.

December 15–16: In the battle of Nashville, Hood's Army of Tennessee is routed by a Union force about twice its number.

December 18–19: Forrest assists the remnants of Hood's army in the crossing of the Duck River at Columbia and encourages Hood to move the men he has left further toward safety.

December 20: Hood continues his retreat, leaving Forrest to mount a rearguard action in Columbia.

December 21: As Union forces cross the Duck River, Forrest begins to retreat.

December 23: Five miles south of Columbia, Forrest's men take advantage of terrain to temporarily halt the Union advance.

December 25: Forrest mounts another counterattack at Anthony's Hill, southwest of Pulaski.

December 26: Forrest lays another ambush to buy time for Hood's remnants to cross the Tennessee River.

December 27: Forrest retreats across the Tennessee and reports to Hood at Tuscumbia.

1865

January 13: With the Army of Tennessee for all intents and purposes destroyed, General Hood is relieved of command. His successor, General

Richard Taylor, puts Forrest in command of all Confederate cavalry in Alabama, Mississippi and East Louisiana. At this stage of the war, the new command consists of no more than 10,000 men scattered across three states; Forrest is forced to resort to firing squads to maintain discipline and discourage desertion.

February 29: Forrest (who in happier times would join in the sport) arrests a party of his men, including his son, Willie, for horseracing past his tent (though he had bet on the races himself before they were concluded).

March 18: The Confederate Congress votes to permit enlistment of slaves in the Confederate Army—though *not* to free them for their service.

March 22: Union General James H. Wilson leads 14,000 cavalrymen across the Tennessee River into northwest Alabama.

March 29: Wilson reaches Elyton, Alabama (today's Birmingham). Forrest, trying to concentrate his troops to defend the Confederate munitions center at Selma, has two alleged deserters shot and displayed to his men on the roadside (a pair of Kentuckians later found to be innocent of the charge).

March 31: After intercepting Forrest's couriers, Wilson is able to outmaneuver him in the race to Selma—mowing down the outnumbered Confederates with Spencer repeating rifles. Forrest and his escort attack Wilson's flank, temporarily separate and scatter his force, take prisoners and then ride hard to the front of his rapid advance, to camp sixteen miles south of Montevallo at 10 p.m.

April 1: Reinforcements fail to reach the Confederates at Ebenezer Church, north of Plantersville. They are routed by the Federals, Forrest fighting furiously hand-to-hand against six Federals slashing at him with sabers and receiving a saber cut on the arm. He is later heard to remark, "If that boy had known enough to give me the point instead of the edge I should not have been here to tell you about it."

April 2: The blood-covered Forrest rides into Selma in time for General Taylor to evacuate by train, leaving Forrest in command in his place. With some 3,000 men Forrest tries unsuccessfully to hold a fort intended for defense by 10,000. Abandoning Selma, his men scatter; Forrest and his escort cut their way out along the same road the Federals attacked by. Near nightfall Forrest kills a thirtieth enemy—the last man he will slay at close quarters during the war.

April 4: Forrest crosses the Cahaba River to Marion to join Chalmers and William H. Jackson, meeting his artillery and wagons just arriving from Mississippi. He and his escort collapse there.

April 8: Lee surrenders at Appomattox. Forrest, arm in a sling from the April 1 saber cut, meets Wilson at Cahaba to discuss prisoner exchange.

April 10: Wilson shoots 500 horses to keep them from carrying Confederates and heads east to Montgomery. Forrest, having re-collected his troops still at large, moves northwest toward Gainesville.

April 15: President Lincoln is assassinated.

The first black soldiers are mustered into the Confederate Army at Richmond shortly before Richmond falls.

April 25: Forrest instructs his troops to disregard rumors of surrender.

April 29: Forrest's commander, General Richard Taylor, meets Union General E. R. S. Canby near Mobile and agrees to surrender.

May 3: Secessionist Tennessee governor Isham Harris and Mississippi governor Charles Clark invite Forrest to go with them to join still resisting Confederates in Texas. Forrest declines, stating "Any man who is in favor of a further prosecution of this war is a fit subject for a lunatic asylum."

May 4: Taylor and Forrest make speeches announcing the surrender to their men assembled at Meridian, Mississippi. "We have made our last fight," Forrest told his troopers. "Men, you have been good soldiers; a man who has been a good soldier can be a good citizen."

May 9: On the day paroles are to be signed, Forrest rides out with his staff member and sometime secretary Charles Anderson, to whom he describes his impulse to go to Mexico, where some nonsurrendering Confederates have ambitions. Anderson persuades Forrest that he has an obligation to stand by his men, whereupon the two together draft a farewell address to the troops. In this speech, Forrest advises his men to purge themselves of "feelings of animosity, hatred and revenge . . . when you return home, a manly straightforward course will secure the respect even of your enemies."

May 15: In conversation with a Northern reporter, Bryan McAlister, Forrest states: "I have lost 29 horses in the war, and have killed a man each time. The other day I was a horse ahead but at Selma they surrounded me, and I killed two, jumped my horse over a one-horse wagon and got away."

May 18: Forrest is erroneously reported killed (following rumors that the family of the Kentuckians he had ordered shot for desertion had sworn vengeance).

End of May: Forrest returns to his Coahoma, Mississippi, plantation. Some of his former slaves return from Georgia, where they had waited out the war, to work for him as freedmen. While pursuing his application to President Andrew Johnson for a pardon, Forrest invites seven Union Army officers into Mississippi and goes into partnership with one, Major B. E. Diffenbacher, in farming concerns. A party of uniformed Union cavalrymen visiting Forrest's premises out of curiosity is attacked by Forrest's reluctantly retired warhorse, King Philip, supported by Forrest's personal servant Jerry.

The black population of Memphis increases from 3,000 to 60,000.

1866
March 31: Forrest exhorts Thomas Edwards, a freedman on his plantation, to stop beating his wife; Edwards attacks him with a knife and wounds him, then Forrest kills Edwards with an ax.

April 6: Forrest begins sharecropping on land he had owned before the war.

May 1–3: During race riots in Memphis, forty-six black people are killed, with ninety-one of their houses, twelve churches and four schools destroyed.

September 25: Having lost much of the property he owned before the war, and plagued by various accusations connected to events at Fort Pillow, Forrest places a notice in a Memphis paper advertising his services as a cotton factor.

December 6: In a letter Forrest describes his involvement in a new project: construction of "the Memphis and Little Rock Railroad."

Sometime during the fall of 1866, Forrest may have accepted an invitation from his former artillery commander John Morton to assume leadership of the Ku Klux Klan. By this time the KKK has evolved from its origins as a loose association of pranksters into a serious and secret terrorist organization intended to defend the interests of former Confederates disenfranchised by the terms of the surrender.

1867
March 2: The United States Congress passes the Reconstruction Act, providing for states of the former Confederacy to be placed under martial law.

May 7: Ads for the Planters Insurance Company of Tennessee, N. B. Forrest, President, run in the Memphis paper.

In a letter to another former Confederate Forrest states that he is "settling up my affairs as rapidly as possible, believing as I do that Every thing under the laws that will be inaugurated by the military authority will result in ruin to our people."

1868
February 5: Planters Insurance Company files for bankruptcy.

Late February: KKK operations, previously confined to relatively nonviolent scare tactics, veer in the direction of whippings and lynchings.

Early March: Forrest visits KKK Grand Dragon John B. Gordon in Atlanta, to discuss a new insurance venture in Memphis and perhaps to confer on Klan matters.

June 10: After much controversy in the course of a meeting in Nashville, Forrest is elected delegate to the National Democratic Convention in New York as the Democrats try to organize opposition to the candidacy of Ulysses S. Grant for the presidency.

July 27: During the Democratic convention in New York, Tennessee's Reconstruction governor William G. Brownlow calls a special legislative session to declare Klan members outlaws punishable by death. Brownlow calls up state militia to take military action against the KKK.

July: During his visit to the New York convention, Forrest obtains a pardon from President Johnson.

August 11: In an address to a large crowd on the steps of the Brownsville courthouse, Forrest denounces Brownlow as a scalawag and a carpetbagger, urges black men in his audience to "stand by the men who raised you," and promises, "If they bring this war upon us, there is one thing I will tell you: that I shall not shoot any negroes so long as I can see a white radical to shoot, for it is the radicals who will be to blame for bringing on this war."

August 28: In a long interview published by the Cincinnati *Appeal* (and later reprinted by the *New York Times*), Forrest affirms the existence of the Ku Klux Klan, estimating 40,000 members in Tennessee and 500,000 more in the rest of the South. Forrest describes the Klan as "a protective, political, military organization . . . sworn to recognize the Government of the United States."

September 6: Following the *New York Times* reprinting of the August *Appeal* interview, Forrest writes a letter retracting many of his August statements about the KKK.

October 28: In a letter published by the *New York Times*, Forrest denounces ex-Union General Judson Kilpatrick as "a blackguard, a liar, a scoundrel, and poltroon." Kilpatrick had accused Forrest of atrocities at Fort Pillow. Forrest's letter amounts to a challenge to a duel, and Forrest's second proposes it might best be fought "mounted and with sabers," as both parties were cavalrymen. Kilpatrick does not respond to the challenge.

November 3: Ulysses S. Grant is elected president of the United States.

December: Members of the Southern aristocracy begin to publish statements to the effect that the increasingly violent KKK has outlived its usefulness. At this point Arkansas, Florida, North Carolina, South Carolina, Louisiana and Alabama have been readmitted to representation in the U.S. Congress.

1869
February 20: Governor Brownlow declares martial law in nine Klan-ridden Tennessee counties.

February 25: Brownlow resigns as Tennessee governor to take a seat in the U.S. Senate. The Tennessee governorship automatically passes to the Speaker of the State Senate, DeWitt Clinton Senter, who runs for a full term as governor on a platform of universal suffrage, including suffrage for the disenfranchised former Confederates.

Summer: Mariam Beck Forrest dies of blood poisoning, having stepped on a rusty nail.

August: Senter is elected to a full term as Tennessee governor, defeating his Radical opponent by a considerable margin.

Ten days after Senter's election, Forrest is rumored to have ordered the KKK to disband permanently, destroying all its records and costumery, during a routine Klan meeting in Nashville.

Fall: Forrest explores partnership with a group of Northern businessmen with the idea of building new railroad lines to carry Alabama coal to Memphis.

1870

March 25: Forrest tells a reporter that he has raised $2 million for a railroad line to connect Selma through Columbus to Memphis, which he expects to be running by January 1, 1871.

December 2: The Memphis *Avalanche* reports that numerous well-known Confederate leaders, including Forrest and others of rumored connection to the Klan, are now supporting the right of Southern blacks to vote.

By the end of this year, the last states of the former Confederacy (Virginia, Mississippi, Texas and Georgia) have been readmitted to the Union. The Reconstruction Ku Klux Klan appears to go out of existence.

1871

March 25: A special referendum votes additional funding for the completion of Forrest's Alabama to Memphis railroad.

June 27: During lengthy, evasive testimony before a U.S. congressional committee investigating the KKK, Forrest denies any direct knowledge of the Klan whatsoever but also states that he "had it broken up and disbanded," perhaps soon after the election of DeWitt Senter as governor of Tennessee (an event in which Forrest professes to have no interest).

1872

With the U.S. economy pushed into recession by the Franco-Prussian War, Forrest's railroad projects are thwarted by difficulties such as the skyrocketing price of iron.

July 11: Forrest approaches the Memphis Chamber of Commerce in an effort to raise more money for the Memphis & Selma railroad.

1873

January: Forrest visits Detroit, seeking new partners for his railroad ventures.

July: A county court inspection committee finds serious discrepancies in the accounting of the Memphis & Selma railroad company.

Toward the end of the year, Forrest writes to Sherman volunteering his services for a war that appeared to be impending between the United

States and Spanish Cuba. Sherman forwards the letter to the War Department with a note describing Forrest as "one of the most extraordinary men developed by our civil war," who "would fight against our national enemies as vehemently as he fought against us."

1874
February 20: Forrest publishes, in the Memphis *Appeal,* an account of the Memphis & Selma company's successes and difficulties.

March 29: Forrest resigns as president of the Memphis & Selma company. With the failure of this enterprise, the Forrest household (then including son Willie's wife and infant daughter) is obliged to leave its rented home. Forrest and his wife move to a dogtrot log cabin on President's Island, four miles downstream from the Memphis waterfront, where Forrest has leased 1,300 acres and arranged to cultivate them with convict labor.

August 28: Responding to a lynching episode in Trenton, Tennessee, Forrest declares in a public meeting in Memphis that if he had "proper authority he would capture and exterminate the white marauders who disgrace their race by this cowardly murder of negroes."

1875
July 5: At a barbecue hosted by the Shelby County black community in the interest of racial reconciliation, Forrest accepts a bouquet of flowers and makes a speech, saying in part, "I came here to the jeers of some white people, who think that I am doing wrong. . . . I came to meet you as friends, and welcome you to the white people. I want you to come nearer to us. When I can serve you, I will do so. We have but one flag, one country; let us stand together."

Summer: Forrest becomes a practicing Christian, something he had promised to do once the war had ended, but delayed considerably in accomplishing.

1877
October 29: Having uttered his last words, "Call my wife," Forrest dies in the Memphis home of his brother Jesse.